# PLEASE, PRETTY LIGHTS

## BY INA ZAJAC

Booktrope Editions
Seattle, WA 2014

Cover Design by Loretta Matson

Edited by Julie Molinari

*This is a work of fiction. Names, characters, places, brands, media, and incidents are either the product of the author's imagination or are used fictitiously. Any resemblance to similarly named places or to persons living or deceased is unintentional.*

PRINT ISBN 978-1-62015-458-8

EPUB ISBN 978-1-62015-468-7

Library of Congress Control Number: 2014912406

# ACKNOWLEDGMENTS

I want to thank the entire Booktrope staff for their dedication and support and for honoring my creative process. To my editorial team: Steven Luna, who served in the all-important role of proofreader; Loretta Matson, who designed the book cover of my dreams; Samantha March, brilliant book manager and supportive source of wisdom and encouragement; and my exceptionally talented, insightful editor, Julie Molinari.

Thanks to Robert Sindelar and the staff at Third Place Books in Lake Forest Park, Washington. I believe neighborhood bookstores are as relevant as ever. They foster community: face-to-face encounters with other human beings. For me, Third Place Books has been a hub full of meaningful real-time conversations, discussions over a cup of coffee where emoticons are never needed because a nod is a nod, a laugh is a laugh, and a smile is a smile.

A million thanks to the musicians who shared their expertise and experience with me—from pet peeves to green room stories: Matt Jorgeson, Zeke Trosper, Jamaica Russo, Kris Kierfulff aka Kris Kobra, Briggs Akers, and Austin Ball. Thanks to the Seattle School of Rock community and Molly Starr Nelson photography.

Thanks to my first writing coach, Caroline Allen of Art of Story Telling, who supported my organic (quirky) process. When I questioned my provocative subject matter, she encouraged me to own my artistic vulnerability. Much love and appreciation goes out to my friend and dedicated editor Corbin Lewars, whose calm confidence and wise counsel steadied me during days of doubt and frustration. I am also thankful for the Pacific Northwest Writers Association and fellow authors who served as early readers: Marni Mann, Conrad Wesselhoeft, Arleen Williams, Ruth Mancini, Dave O'Leary, and especially early, early reader Carla Mead Barokas. I am also grateful for the editorial expertise of fellow author and friend A.C. Fuller. Thanks to my friend Kirsten Bachant, my Vashon Island tour guide. I had no idea research could be so much fun.

Thanks to my best girlfriends, Amy Baisch Campbell and Alexis Puma Keijer. Since our good-old West Seattle days, we've walked a thousand miles together and enjoyed ten thousand cups of coffee. I adore you both.

Love and appreciation goes out to my family in Arizona. I may not see you every day, but I think about you every day. And to my mother, Ingrid Ivy Johnson. Jag alskar dig. Most of all, I want to thank those most affected by my writing whirlwind: my husband, Craig Zajac, and my children, Austin and Alexa. I love you forever.

*This book is dedicated to my late father, James Graham Smith, who dreamed of writing a gritty novel. For my precious family: Craig, Austin, and Alexa. And for anyone who has forgotten their power. It's never too late to remember who you are.*

# CHAPTER 1

SoHo, New York City, December 21, 2004

## VIA

**BACK TO THE WALL,** Via shuffled through the candy cane wilderness, careful not to displace piles of presents or disturb crystal angels. It was so close. Branches prickled against her chin and neck as she stretched into the corner. Needles latched onto her green St. Anne Elementary School sweater. After months of waiting and wondering, there it was—white with a gold bow. She reached out. Her fingertips grazed the paper, the tag. It would have her name on it.

"No peeking," her mother called from the kitchen. "Cookies are almost ready. Come and help."

Guilt settled in and crowded out her naughty curiosity. Mama's feathery voice lingered in the air and mingled with the smell of gingersnaps.

The front door slammed shut. Her body tensed against the wall as it recognized the rumble of her father's approach. Her arm retreated to the safety of her side. The hardwood floor vibrated his location in the foyer. He wasn't supposed to be home from the country yet. He needed his rest.

"Ingrid!" he yelled. "Violetta!"

He called her Violetta when he was angry. When he was happy, he said she was the heartbeat of the universe. Now that she was eleven, she wasn't a little kid anymore, but she still called him Daddy. He made her promise she would always call him Daddy.

His voice was muffled. The floor was still. He must have stopped to check the front bedrooms, but for how long? That tummy pain was back, the one that burned from the inside out; the one Dr. Peyton said fifth graders shouldn't have. Being the daughter of Joseph Antonio Rabbotino wasn't easy. Kids at school called her Rabbit and were never allowed to come over and play.

The floor trembled more and more. He must be standing nearby, maybe next to the piano, she thought. She couldn't see past the tree's festive colors and prayed he couldn't either. She had promised to be a good girl.

Her mother's voice rushed over from the kitchen. It was shrill. "Oh, my God," she said. "Put that down. You're not yourself right now."

Put what down? Via wondered. Sometimes he brought home presents or pets.

"You think I'm crazy?" He let out a harsh laugh she had never heard before. "You think you can drug me and leave me in Connecticut to rot?"

A bell near her elbow began to jingle. Don't be a spaz, she told herself. She had to stop shaking; she just had to. Being invisible meant being silent, so she leaned to the right and smothered it. Her other arm met up with something pointy.

"But, you wanted to go, remember?" Her mother was talking really fast. "Dr. Goldman said you should rest, give the new meds some time."

Daddy had a lot of doctors. Daddy took a lot of pills.

"I know what you think of me," he said. "That the critics are right. That I'll never paint again."

"It's okay. It's all going to be okay," her mother insisted. "But you've been drinking. We've gotten through this before. Remember?"

"Why do you do this to me?" he asked. "Evil little actress. Acting like you love me."

"I do. You know I do."

"Liar."

"Please, put that down. We'll call Dr. Goldman."

"You sent me away. Do you know what it was like there? Knowing you betrayed me? All you had to do was love me, but you've ruined me!"

"No, you wanted to go. You needed to rest. Please remember. Please."

"Where's my Violetta?"

"Still at school."

"She should be home by now—home with us. We should be together now. She hiding under her bed again?" His words turned and trailed back toward the front bedrooms. "Violetta! Come when I call you!"

"Mama?" She called through the branches.

Her mother didn't seem surprised at all to hear her. "Shh," she said, faint but firm. It was not her normal 'shh.' Something was wrong.

Her father's voice was already growing louder again. "Violetta!"

"I'm right here," she tried to say. She decided that she would come out; then he would be angry with her, not her mother. But a strange sound surrounded her, like baby birds and chimes. It seemed to come through the Christmas tree lights. She blinked. They were such pretty lights—colors she had never seen before. Buzzing into a haze around her, they were mesmerizing.

Shh, it's all okay, the lights told her, but not in words.

She felt their meaning in her teeth and bones.

Come and play with us, they urged. Come play pretend.

They flurried about. She tried to speak, but they settled against her tongue like candy-coated snow. They loved her. She watched them spin and shine and gleam and glow. They were everything she needed in that moment, and so she relaxed into the soft aura of Christmas.

Her mother was screaming, "She's not here! She's not here!"

The purest colors were born and danced within reflections of those who had come before. You're not here, they echoed. You're with us. They snuggled in and tucked themselves around her. Be still, they insisted. This isn't real. She knew they were right. Nothing was real. She was everywhere and nowhere at all, safe between worlds. Her mother's golden wall clock started to ding its hourly announcement—once, twice.

"You did this," her father said.

A third ding.

"You made me do this."

Four.

Mama's voice fluttered. "Remember who you are."

A loud noise exploded throughout the apartment. Ornaments rattled and slipped from their homes, and Via with them. Her hands came up to cover her ears, but his voice soon rode the wave of ringing and broke on through.

"Why?" he cried. "Why did you make me do this?"

Another explosion ripped away the space around her. She sank down overcome by the bells ringing around her. Why? Why were the bells so loud? It was a gun, she realized. The sound vibrating through her was gunfire. Her shoulder came to rest against the edge of the big box—white with a gold bow. Air came into her lungs in notches, each tighter than the last. She didn't know what to do. Her trembling hand grasped a branch with a candy cane hanging from it. She began to pull it back.

"Mama?"

*Don't look*, the pretty lights warned her. *It's not real. It's not her.*

But it was too late. She had already peered past the angels—and through to the other side.

"Ma—"

Mouth open, heart lost, she released the branch and it sprang back into place. Its candy cane held strong. The pretty lights spoke no more, but hummed and tingled. The murmur of their adoration grew faint and she began to panic. She curled up into herself, tight and small, desperate to disappear back into their protection.

"Please, pretty lights. Please don't go."

She blinked and the lights were just lights. The floors roared. New voices overtook the fading bells. People were yelling. People were coming. An alarm shrieked overhead. The taste of gingersnap dust burnt through the air.

"Please, pretty lights," she called out again, even though she knew they were gone.

# CHAPTER 2

Seattle, September 12, 2014

## VIA

**VIA TRIED** not to stare at his forehead. So sad, it now occupied another three inches of what used to be blond-hair territory. His once-flat stomach now competed with the table's edge. But his eyes were the same Nordic blue. Just like Mama's. Via zoned out on the Seattle skyline and tried to pretend she was somewhere else, someone else. She had worried the Space Needle's rotating restaurant would make her sick, but its movement was so subtle, she kept forgetting it was happening.

Uncle Erik's East-Coast urgency snipped and snapped all over the waiter. So not cool. It made her want to slink out to the observation deck and jump, but she knew the 605-foot-high needle wore a crown of safety wires.

"I'm so sorry," she said, more to the waiter than her uncle. "Missed the ferry in from Vashon Island, just moved there. I'm kind of a spaz." She settled back against her chair and took in her uncle's annoyance, as obvious as his recent weight gain.

"Where's the fiancé?" he asked. "Still in Africa building churches?"

"And digging wells," she said.

"A heads-up on the proposal from him would have been nice."

It hadn't even occurred to her that Dan should have gotten his blessing first. Her uncle had been little more than her trust fund executor. Now, all of a sudden, he expected father-figure treatment?

"I'm sure he's a good guy," he said. "But you're way too young. Just because you got your degree early doesn't mean you have to get married. It's ridiculous. You should wait until you're twenty-five, at least. Thirty would be better."

She returned her attention out the window and admired the evolving evening light. "You'd like Vashon," she said. "It's just like Manhattan." She craned her neck and pointed behind him. "See, you can kind of see it over there, just past West Seattle." In truth, Vashon was nothing like Manhattan. There were no bridges, and only 14,000 residents, unless you counted deer, raccoons, and the occasional passing pod of orca whales. It's where Dan grew up, where his church was, and so now it would be her home, too.

Her uncle didn't bother to turn and look. She faked a no-worries smile and focused on Mount Rainier to the southeast. The hostess had said it took the restaurant forty-seven minutes to make one 360-degree rotation. Her uncle would probably bail for the airport before Lake Union to the northeast even came into view. She sighed.

The waiter returned with an elaborate cocktail. "Happy twenty-first birthday, miss," he said. "The SkyCity Millionaire Martini, with Remy Martin Louis XIII, Grand Marnier, sweet & sour, and fresh lime. Topped with Nicolas Feuillatte champagne." Gold shavings glinted and awed. Another server set down a fresh drink for her uncle. Clear with an olive, no gold or sparkles.

"Yours was actually just under two hundred dollars," he reassured her. "It wasn't a full million, of course, but happy birthday."

She wrapped her fingers around the fragile stem, but hesitated. She knew it wouldn't actually taste like blood, but still. Money was a paradoxical bitch. While it brought her loads of guilt and little pleasure, the idea of living without it terrified her. Her uncle handled the details for her; he had paid cash for her Honda. She had a couple credit cards, but hated shopping. She never checked her accounts. There would be enough to last twenty lifetimes, so what else was there to know? Dan said the money could work miracles for the poor in Africa. She watched the thin top layer of bubbles burst through the surface, fun and free. She took a sip. She imagined it was what sugar-laced lighter fluid would taste like. The next sip was so much better—borderline magical going down.

The waiter hovered. "How are they tasting?" he asked her uncle.

"I think the birthday girl is happy," he said. "But I've got a flight to catch, so let's order another round now. Something fast. Two gin and tonics."

She took another drink. Dan wouldn't approve. It had been three years since she'd gotten wasted and fallen off that totem pole in the quad. He had carried her to the student health building and prayed over her broken arm. She had been his prayer-in-progress ever since.

"He'll just *have* to sign a pre-nup," Uncle Erik said. "And, you'll have to come back to New York. That meeting is January 4th. We've got to discuss the collection."

Oh hell. Since the shooting, the ten-work Rabbotino collection had been held in a secure location, hidden away from public scrutiny. They were all oil on forty-eight-by-sixty-inch Belgian linen, awash in browns, blacks and blues—interwoven into nightmares. Even before her father's death, critics had praised his "soul scratchers" for their sinister subtext. They were the beloved children of his tortured mind. Both of her parents had been trust fund babies, so there had never been a need to sell them. Now they were hers. She thought about how much more the collection would fetch at auction if the crazy orphan died beforehand. She had been fighting dark thoughts all day. Today was not only her twenty-first birthday, but also one hundred days away from the tenth anniversary of her parents' death day.

"You've really grown up," he said, interrupting her introspection. "You're so much like her now—just like a dark-haired Ingrid."

The sound of her mother's name made her swallow hard. Mama would hate her thinking this way. After everything she had done for her. God, she had to stop thinking this way. She would find some way to be happy—right now. She looked out the window down to the Seattle Center below them. Some sort of concert was going on outside the Experimental Music Project Museum. There were several hundred people down there, probably having the time of their lives. A tiny light from the stage, like a beacon, caught her eye.

"Sorry I can't stay much longer, but I'm sure you've got some girlfriends to go out with tonight."

"Sure," she lied. "Going out dancing."

"There are still some things we need to talk about," he said as he checked the time on his phone. He took out his wallet, put his credit card on the edge of the table, and pulled out a small, white velvet box. "Your father's former students want a retrospective, a show in the spring. They want you to be involved with the planning, and to say a few words."

She closed her eyes and tried to shake away the image. There would be hors d'oeuvres. There would be critics—skinny women with harsh eyes. They would size her up and wonder if she was psycho too. There would be photographers. They would expect her to cry.

Beams of sunlight demanded her attention. She took a sideways glance toward the sun disappearing behind the Olympic Mountains. Copper brilliance cast off Puget Sound. It was the Seattle tourist money shot. She took another drink, and another, until her glass was empty, except for few holdout gold flakes at the bottom. He watched. He wanted an answer.

"You really want me to host a show? Talk to people about him? I can't." She turned back to face him, but her field of vision was muddled with iridescent blotches. "I can't talk to people… about him."

"You'll be great," he said. "You can share your story, raise awareness—about domestic violence, about mental health issues."

His suggestion disgusted her. Mortification bore into her forehead and nested into the space where her brain had been. She'd used her mother's maiden name, Sorenson, since the shooting for a reason. It was unbearable, the thought that she would be recast as that pathetic little girl who had shivered and listened to her parents die. The girl who'd lurked in the shadow of Christmas.

The waiter had come back with the drinks. Her uncle was speaking to him, his tone mellow. "Yes, and add a chocolate mousse for her. Anything she wants."

The taste of her gin and tonic made her gag a little, so she squeezed the lime on the rim, tossed it in, and stirred it with the little black straw. Curious, she wondered what was in the velvet box. She wanted to reach for it, but didn't dare.

"I see you aren't wearing an engagement ring yet," he said. She hadn't been in a big hurry; it could wait until January, or whenever. "I guess I should give this to Dan to give to you, but he's not here. So, happy engagement." His enthusiasm fell flat as he leaned over and brought her hand in his. He lowered his voice. "It was your mother's."

He popped back the lid. Of course it was. He took it out and put it on her left ring finger. It was a tad snug, not bad. "Maybe it can be a nice, long engagement," he said with a hopeful smile. "And if you change your mind, you can always wear it on your other hand."

Applause startled her, yanking her back into the world. Why were people clapping? Didn't they realize her heart was breaking? A woman at the next table offered her congratulations.

Her uncle shook his head and stood up. "This is my niece, for Christ's sake," he scolded the woman. The word "niece" brought a collective gasp from those around them.

He leaned over and gave her an awkward hug. "I hate to leave you like this, but I'll call when I get back from Taiwan." He kissed her on the top of her head. "I love you, you know that."

Did she? His hasty exit seemed to activate a dark energy field around her, powered perhaps by her own sense of unworthiness. She kept her head down so her long hair shielded her from the curious eyes she sensed. Dan would be home by New Year's, she reminded herself. He would have been here now if the travel dates had been up to him.

She took another sip of her drink and admired her mother's ring. It was a glorious marquise, wide at the center with tapered points at the top and bottom. Mama used to fiddle with it when she was upset. Via had no idea what its carat weight was; it was probably a bit showy. But it had rested against her mother's skin for sixteen years, and that made it priceless. She wiggled her finger and got lost in a million mirrors of divine complexity. They'd taken it from her dead body, she realized. The death day countdown was on. How was she ever going to find the strength to make it through the holidays? Did she even want to? Stop it, she told herself. She had to stop thinking this way.

The view had shifted again, east toward the snarled traffic of I-5. She had missed Lake Union entirely. A new server came with chocolate mousse.

"Another drink, miss?" he asked.

She looked back out the window, down at the world going on below. The sun was setting on her twenty-first birthday.

"Sure, why not?"

# Chapter 3

## Matt

**MATT ADJUSTED** his bass strap so the smiley faces were right-side up. He ran his hand though his hair just above his right ear, then again until it was close enough to perfect. Time for one more song; the first seven were toast. How had another set gotten away from him? The best ones always did. It didn't matter that they weren't getting paid or that their set had been cut to just half an hour. Gigging in the shadow of the Space Needle made him feel alive.

"We're Obliviot," he said into his mic. He used his mellow-cool stage voice. Serious enough for the guys, but with a tinge of sexy he hoped the girls would appreciate. He gave them a moment to settle down. "Thanks, thanks. We'll be playing Nectar next Saturday—come check us out."

"And the Showbox!" Nick yelled from behind the drum kit.

"Oh, that's right," Matt conceded. "We're playing the Showbox December 21st to raise money for Seattle Kidz Rock. All of your holiday favorites."

"No favorites!" Nick yelled down. "No requests, no regrets!"

Matt shot his best friend a shut-your-face glare, then turned back toward the crowd. It was a good mix of teenagers, rockers, hipsters and hippies. Matt squinted and averted his eyes from the intensity of the setting sun reflected off the purple-mirrored side of the EMP Museum. "We have time for one more." He glanced back to make sure the guys were ready. A garbled chorus of requests rose up to the stage, but he waved them off, laughing as he looked back out over the sea of faces. "You all *think* you want to hear 'Smells Like Teen Spirit.' I hear you back there," he said. A hard whistle came from the back. "But, what you're going to get is 'Breed' and you're going to love it."

Josh stepped forward and unleashed the lesser-known Nirvana guitar riff. Feedback-heavy and distorted, it met Nick's beat, fast and fierce. Matt and Jeremy joined in, let the noise build, then broke it loose all over the crowd. The mosh kids surged forward. They launched their bodies into each other, hard and hyper. Security hadn't wanted anything rowdy, but hey, it was their last song. The next act was reggae, so people would mellow out soon enough.

Matt teased the crowd with a smug, drawn-out, "You're wel—come," then focused on his favorite four-string bass, a green Mike Lull-custom he called Envy. He had a lot of gear, but she felt so comfortable against his stomach, so easy on his fingers. At times, he could swear she was the one playing him.

Jeremy screamed into the mic. His attempt at the Cobain rasp made Matt shudder, but the crowd didn't seem to mind. They were all about the beat. It was always about the beat. Nick sounded right on time, steady, in the pocket as always.

All was well…but then it wasn't. The sunset reflected against the EMP's now fuchsia-mirrored side blazed into his eyes. He squinted and looked back to the drum kit. Nick's disco ball hat wasn't helping the situation. It was from his crazy cap collection, giving him a look that landed somewhere between Slash from Guns N' Roses and Abe Lincoln at a rave. They locked eyes, and Nick gave him the "do it, do it," head flick.

Matt's nerves flared when he remembered their bet. He stared down and contemplated leaving the safety of the silver tape flanking him on both sides. Thankfully, he knew Nirvana basslines about as well as Krist Novoselic himself. Though his fingers autopiloted their way through the groove, his feet were unresponsive. He swallowed down the taste of dread. A three-hundred-dollar bet was a three-hundred-dollar bet, he reminded himself. He willed himself closer to the edge, but his boots seemed to fuse to the stage.

He preferred a dark club where he could only make out faces in the first couple of rows. Cute girls wearing white always stood out, their faces brightened by the stage lights. Tonight, he saw them all, rows and rows of people, all wanting something from him. Maybe something meaningful, something they could take away and keep forever. It was just too bright. He didn't want to start thinking about it. *Overthinking* about it. But, it was too late. His mind was already off and running toward that place called crazy. It was all so stupid, and that's what made it so paralyzing. At the sight of those hands outstretched toward him, he stepped back behind his protective tape marks.

He and Nick had been playing together since junior high, giggling in bars long before they could drink in them. Before Obliviot, they had been Salt-A-Slug, Weed Trinket, and Ear Slop. They found Josh and Jeremy a few years back and became Obliviot. The name captured what they were, nineties covers—no apologies.

Standing in his tapped off square, he felt Nick's lava-hot glare searing into the back of his head.

Over the years the two of them had developed an extensive array of glances and nods. He doubted people watching their shows ever noticed their frequent facial banter. But, when they were in tight sync, they laid a platform for the rest of the band. Matt raised an eyebrow when a solo was going long, gave a wide-eyed bob when Josh was a bit off, and a dozen more. Nick had a particular grimace when Jeremy had his amp up too high. Matt would answer back with a frown that meant, "I know, he needs to get over himself. I can barely hear my own monitor." There were also a variety of head tilts to convey the location of the choicest girls in the crowd.

He turned back. The look Nick was communicating was clear, "Do it now. Don't be a little bitch."

He tossed back an irritated nod that said, "Fine, fine."

Their face lingo also translated into their off-stage world navigating the shark-infested waters of West-Coast cocaine trafficking. Their boss, Carlos, was a reef shark with a Jaws complex, who cruised the waters between Portland and Seattle. They secretly called him The Skeeze. He would go off if they were too late for their eight p.m. shift tonight at the club. Hotties was only five blocks away; they could still make it. Carlos wasn't a fan of rock-and-roll time, which was standard time plus twenty minutes.

Warm air breezed against his face, smelling like chronic, funnel cakes, and beer. He stepped out between his monitor and a wedge. God, he didn't want to have a heart attack in front of all of these people.

If he passed out this close to the edge, he would fall. No doubt. What if they didn't catch him? He would break his neck for sure. They would make him go to the hospital, no matter what he said. His imagination began to explode blood and guts everywhere.

He felt Nick's support nudge him toward the edge. Just a few more inches. Push yourself. Just for a minute he told himself, then he would go back behind to the safety of his silver-tape pen. Down in front was a gaggle of cuties, he guessed sorority girls. They probably all looked amazing naked. Just like Kaytlyn. He inched closer toward the edge, just shy of their frantic fingers. He tried to focus on his own hands, on the song, but their energy terrified him. Sharp, sparkled fingernails reached up for him. They could grab at his boots, his jeans—that was okay. But they were getting dangerously close to the green sweetheart slung from his chest.

He focused on Envy's rosewood neck. He looked down the fretboard; from the first to the twelfth to the twenty-first. "I'm good, I'm good," he mumbled as he continued down to her pickups. He smiled when he reached the high-shine glory of her swamp ash body. It's all about distraction, he reminded himself. Fear dies without attention.

He felt Nick's approval slap him on the back. "That's good, man. That's good." Relieved, he pulled back just in time. Something like a laser beam shot past him. He looked back. Ah, just the sunset reflecting off Nick's disco ball hat. Idiot was going to blind somebody.

Back between his tape marks, he began to settle down. He fought to catch his breath. And it was over, just like that. The song was dust. The day was dust. While the cheers that welled up around him were sweet, he didn't have time to take it all in. He leaned over and unplugged from his amp, then made his way off stage with the guys. He came down the metal stairs and into the makeshift backstage area, which wasn't much more than a few tarps slung over half-assed fencing. He was surprised when he recognized the orange-painted path under his feet: the Seattle Center Labyrinth. They had gone on from the other side, so he hadn't noticed that the stage had been set up on top of it. Cool, he had been standing over it that whole time. Maybe it was lucky. He wondered if it meant something amazing was about to happen.

"Matt, Matt," a cute blonde shouted as he passed. She didn't look familiar so he gave her a courtesy wave and kept walking. He needed a break from blondes. No more Kaytlyns. A low-drama brunette would be good. Maybe a mellow girl with soulful brown eyes.

He found his gig bag and got Envy situated.

Nick was in his face. His perma-grin would have been obnoxious on anyone else. Performing had that effect on him. He wasn't high on anything other than being balls-to-the-wall awesome. Mr. Dedication would never get lit before a show. Nick had serious chops, and was the only person Matt knew who was determined enough to actually make it big someday. "Today it's outside the EMP," he said. "But someday it'll be inside—the Sky Church, in front of that big-ass screen."

They had a long-standing list of must-play Seattle venues. They still hadn't played the Central or the Crocodile and they probably never would without an original set list. Someday.

"Where's my three hundred bucks?"

"I'll take it off your rent," Nick said. "Let's go. Josh and Jeremy said they'd get the gear when they're done with goodies." Obliviot was known for random, borderline inappropriate, giveaways. Tonight they had bacon-flavored bubble gum and zombie finger puppets. It was an all-ages show so they would save the glow-in-the-dark condoms for El Corazón and the Tractor Tavern.

Nick looked down at his phone. "We've only got ten minutes. The Skeeze will go off if we're late again."

"Maybe he'll fire us," Matt said, looking toward the rising moon. How cool would that be, not having to worry about waking up in some nasty jail cell. "I'm good, good," he told himself. It was going to be a long-ass night.

# CHAPTER 4

## VIA

**VIA LEANED AGAINST** the side of the 7-Eleven and pounded her third mini bottle of chardonnay. After leaving the Space Needle, she had walked around the same block three times—past that same Pink Elephant Car Wash, three times. She couldn't find her car to save her life, which was proof she had no business behind the wheel anyway. She had called a cab company, but they could only take her as far as the West Seattle ferry terminal. If she were to walk onto the ferry, she would have to go to the upper deck and just knew she would run into people from church. And she didn't want to go home anyway. Her chest felt toasty warm.

She scarfed down her last mini powdered donut and threw away the wrapper. It was a sign, an actual, literal sign. In the next parking lot over, the Hotties marquee changed colors for the two-hundredth time—hot pink to purple to white, and then red, red, red, and then hot pink to purple to white. The letters flashed, "Gallery Night. She's a Masterpiece. Amateur Night. Win $750."

She had nowhere else to be. Screw it. Why not? Before she'd started dating Dan, she and her college roommates had often gone dancing at the Blue Tonic, a bar just over the Canadian border where the drinking age was just nineteen. Its big dance floor had two dancing platforms, each surrounded by a gilded cage awash in spotlights. Toward the end of the night, the bouncers invited a few girls to go inside and dance a song or two. Ceremoniously opening the side doors, the bouncers escorted the chosen ones inside. There was no lock. The bars were wide enough that the girls could climb out at any time. Via had gone in often and never gotten out early—not once. Drinks could wait, her bladder could wait, flirting could wait. A fire alarm could wait, because her time there had felt precious and fleeting, and her soul had wanted to stay and dance forever. Rarely making eye contact with the men watching her, she'd felt their lustful stares. She had fed on their energy and lit up from the inside out.

This is how it is supposed to be, she had realized, lost in the lights. Her opera-obsessed parents had chosen this life for her the day they had chosen the name Violetta over Brunhilde. The day they had chosen Verde over Wagner. They could have named her after a Norse warrior woman who rode a flying horse and kicked ass, but instead they'd chosen an Italian slut who coughed blood into a hanky. She could have gone by Hilde or Hil. Maybe she could have been brave. A badass.

The Hotties sign drew her in even more. The flashing neon began to morph, then hum and buzz. She blinked. Wait, she realized. Wait, she knew those lights. Their unadulterated love blazed toward her. They danced and shimmered just for her. They vibrated their epiphany. *Pretend, pretend,* they urged. *Don't you remember?* The recollection teased her, but retreated before she could fully recognize it. Instead she softened her focus, and let them blur and beam and snap her into a new state of being.

She tucked her last mini bottle into her purse for later. While crossing over into the Hotties parking lot she tripped, but caught herself. She just laughed it off, too wasted to care. Should she take her mother's ring off? she wondered. No, it would be safest right where it was. She rubbed her thumb back and forth over it for luck, for courage. She didn't let herself pause at the tinted double doors for fear she would change her mind. Just one night dancing. Lost under the lights. She couldn't stand being alone with herself, so she would just be somebody else. Just for the night.

\* \* \*

# VIA

INSIDE, THE LOBBY felt like the entrance to a Denny's restaurant, except everything was bright white. Everything from the white patent-leathery couches lining the white walls to the glazed white glass light fixtures hanging overhead. The matching high-shine tile floor completed the look. A tall guy about her age stood at a white podium. It was heaven's waiting room and he was a super sexy St. Peter. The fly of his black pants was open wide and he was doing something weird with his hands. She stopped in her tracks.

"Sorry," he said as he shot her the guiltiest little-boy face. Like one of her church youth group kids caught stealing an extra juice box, except more sincere.

Pink flushed up his neck and cheeks, into his semi-scruffy light brown hair. She realized he was just tucking in his dress shirt, so she smiled and waited for him to zip himself back into place. He was built like a football player and looked like he could really mow down a quarterback.

"I'm not some creeper, I promise," he said. "Just had a show. I'm a drummer." He looked at her like that should mean something. He raised his eyebrows and looked her up and down. He didn't seem impressed. "First time here, huh?"

"Here?" She looked around. She had almost forgotten. What was she doing? Dance music thumped in from the other room. This was crazy. She turned to leave.

"When a guy thinks it's your first time at a strip club, that's a compliment," he said. His tone was flirty and full of warmth. It made her turn back around.

"But, I'll need to see your ID."

She found it and handed it over. She imagined he would make an excellent junior high school teacher. He would be the popular one— cool but tough.

He inspected it for a moment. "Happy birthday, sweetie," he said. "I'll buy you a Red Bull later."

"Red Bull?"

"Or soda or espresso in a can," he said. "No liquor on site—it's the law."

"Oh," she said, afraid he may search her purse.

"You here to dance?" he asked. "You here alone? On your birthday?"

She felt her own cheeks growing warm. "Is that okay?" she asked, knowing she was the biggest dork in the world.

"Of course," he said, but she couldn't help but notice his worried glance into a back hallway behind him. He leaned forward over the podium, lowered his voice and asked. "You know Carlos?"

"Who?"

"That's cool," he said. "I'm Nick. I'll keep an eye on you."

What a sweet guy, she thought. He led her into the main lounge. It looked so much like a crime-show set, like CSI, that she got the giggles. Was this place for real? Everything was black and the lights were low. Built-in couches lined the sides and back of the room. The couches in the very back were like deep-set booths. Each had its own black curtain. Two of the booths had their curtains closed and a bored-looking guy even bigger than Nick stood between them.

The music pumped through her body and she couldn't help but move from a walk to a borderline strut. Out of the corner of her eye, she spotted the source of her inspiration: a deejay stood inside a booth on a raised platform outlined with spinning lights. The stage spanned the entire room and jutted out into runways to the right, left, and center. On it were three golden poles reaching up into the ceiling. The center runway bulged out into a semicircle. Several small round tables with chairs snuggled against it.

"See, that's Alicia, aka Autumn," he said as he smiled toward a tan blonde woman who circled the gleaming pole on the right. Her breasts were held captive by a bright pink bra. She wore ultra-tight soccer shorts with thigh-high socks and what looked to be cleats with five-inch heels. Several men watched, engrossed, but they seemed mellow. They weren't throwing money in the air or stuffing bills into her short-shorts. She reached up high on the pole and propelled herself until she was upside down. She lifted herself higher, pulled her legs wide, and then spun around the pole, again and again.

"She's pushing forty, but the college guys love her—she's cash. Everybody wants to bag a cougar or a MILF these days."

Via was stricken by insecurity. More wine would be good. She slipped her hand into her purse and pet her last mini bottle.

A tall brunette in a white cheerleader outfit walked toward them, adjusting her pigtail ribbons. "Hey, Legs," Nick said. "Via, this is the queen of MILF-topia, Willow. She'll show you where to get ready."

Willow did a quick spin for him. "Hey Nick-o-lust," she said, her voice low and sultry. Her cheer panties were silver. "She can call me Whitney—unless she's interested in a lap dance, that is," she said and flashed an I'm-up-for-anything smile. Via had never been sexually attracted to women, but this girl was so insanely hot, she couldn't stop looking at her. Her eyes were bright light green, like a cat's, and she smelled like Hawaii.

Nick gave a little bow. "I leave you in good hands," he said. "Later, tater."

"Tot," Via shot back. She regretted it immediately. It was something her church kids said. He just shook his head and walked back to his station.

Whitney led her toward a black, floor-to-ceiling curtain and turned around. "There are only a few other girls so far. You look like you need some help with your hair and makeup." She grabbed the edge of the curtain and swooshed it over to the side, revealing a bright pink hallway. Via hesitated, wondering if she was drunk enough.

"Don't worry," Whitney added. "We'll help you."

Yes, she thought. Help. She needed serious help.

# CHAPTER 5

## MATT

**MATT SAT ASTRIDE** a long wooden bench in the middle of the locker room facing a cute topless girl named Jasmine. Overall, her body was decent, but her areolas were bugging the hell out of him. With his second smallest brush, he blended a cool shade of mystic blue body paint outward, making her silver incision lines disappear. He was a wizard with scars, but there wasn't much he could do about poorly placed, over-muscle implants. He had already spent ten minutes transforming her tan lines into stems for her hanging buds and he still had another girl to do before he could take off for Portland. That uncomfortable uneasiness began to creep up his spine. It'll be a good trip, he told himself. "Safe trip, safe trip," he said under his breath.

"I was out dancing in Belltown," she said. "And Carlos came up to me and gave me his card, and—"

"I'm good. I'm good," he mumbled.

"What'd you say?"

"Nah," he said. "Just humming a song."

"That's cool. So, you sure you can't help me score some blow?"

"Sorry." He never sold without going through the proper channels—referrals only—and The Skeeze hadn't mentioned this chick at all. He pulled his head back a foot and evaluated his heaving canvas. It killed him to give up, but he knew he wouldn't be able to make her floral arrangement look any perkier. "All done. Knock em' dead." He told all of them that because it sounded better than, "Break a leg." He reserved that for Nick before they went onstage. It seemed better suited for rock and roll than girls in high heels.

"Knock, knock." Nick stood near the doorway, leaning against the wall next to a rack of clear stripper heels. "You're up," he told Jasmine as he held the door for her. He waited until she had squeezed past him. "So, there is one more Bambi coming in and she's going to singe the hair off your brushes."

"Good, she'll be fast then," Matt said as he stretched. He misted his brush with disinfectant and wiped it two times against the microfiber cloth on his lap—one, two.

Nick screwed up his face. "Only you could make painting tits seem like hard work. We can trade. You can deal with the frat boys."

Matt was used to getting slammed about his duties. He painted the girls because he had wanted to be an artist at one time, but he took little pleasure in it. Decorating an already hot girl's body with glitter glue was like Auto-Tuning a soulfully imperfect song or slapping trendy paint on a classic car. Carlos agreed with him, but reminded him that guests came in for the fantasy. Most Hotties patrons probably had decent-looking wives or girlfriends waiting at home.

"So, I met her up front and we need to keep her away from The Skeeze—"

Matt glared and flicked his head toward the pervert closet behind him.

Nick just kept talking. "It's cool," he said. "He's not back there." He smiled into the double-sided mirror and fixed his hair. "In his office. Swapping party favors for sexual favors with Bianca. So, this girl is clueless and drunk, and bro, he's gonna love her look—like a young Sonia."

"Can't help with your damsel. Bailing as soon as I can, got that Portland run," Matt said. "Back in the morning." Safe trip, he thought. One, two.

Nick was halfway out the door, but turned around to taunt him. "Oh, and Josh called. He tried to get your bass, but some nasty ape with hepatitis snagged it. He found your happy face strap, but it's been slimed."

Matt growled and shook away the image. His friend never tired of messing with him. "*You're* a nasty ape," he yelled after him.

"Are you Matt?" Her voice was small, tentative. She hovered in the doorway like a kid late on the first day of school. Nick was crazy. Sonia, on her very best day, could never look as good as this girl. They had already done her makeup, which disappointed him. Her hair was nice though. It was the color of dark chocolate and fell into full, glossy waves. He wanted to feel it between his fingers and maybe pull it up into a ponytail. He loved to see long hair pulled back, leaving the neck vulnerable. When a woman let him kiss her neck it meant she trusted him, and that felt good.

He realized he hadn't said anything yet. How long had he been spacing out on her hair? Too embarrassed to apologize, he stood up, went over to her, and reached out for her hand. He didn't usually shake hands. Girls would normally come in and plop down in front of him, but she'd just stood there with her hand out.

"I'm Via. Nice to meet you."

"You too. Come sit."

"They said I only have a few minutes." She clutched her white terrycloth robe against her body and rubbed her lips together.

"I'll do something simple," he told her. "It's no big deal. I see boobs all the time."

She laughed and he smelled the wine on her breath. No surprise. Most of the girls had booze stashed in their bags and lockers. "You're nervous? Did you lose a bet or something?" He hoped to distract her, so she would open that robe.

Hotties was upscale compared to the competition. Their cover was steep. Their ATM fees were brutal. But their girls were smoking hot, so it all worked out. They had Gallery Night twice a month. It had been Carlos's idea. He'd described it as a way to bring in new talent, girls who may be intimidated to go naked right off the bat. They kept their thongs on and Matt's nipple flourishes helped them not feel completely naked when they took off their bras, bustiers, or bikini tops. The Skeeze said that from there he was just a hop, skip, and a jump away from couch dances and hand jobs.

"I can do this," she said, more to herself than to him. She was like a kid not quite ready to jump off the diving board. He wanted to hug her. "I can do this," she said again. Yanking her arms through the sleeves, she let the robe fall off her shoulders and onto the bench behind her. Girls usually just pulled it back off their shoulders. This one was just sitting there in a thong. Technically, she was also wearing one of the black pleather bikini tops from the wardrobe closet, but it had been pulled down around her waist. She was as good as naked. "I'm keeping my eyes closed," she said. He was relieved because then she wouldn't see the way he was gaping at her.

He was usually an abstract kind of artist, but he wanted to paint her—really paint her. He dipped his widest brush in his lightest shade of gold, tapped three times, and started below her collarbones; he had a thing for collarbones. Her bone structure was delicate and her skin had a warm undertone, which was why he had chosen gold. She didn't have any tan lines or obvious scars. No ink he could see. Her skin was light contrasted against her hair. Her eyes were closed, but she was so fair he assumed they were blue.

"You can't keep your eyes closed when you dance though," he said. "You could fall off the stage."

"Thanks, I hadn't even thought to worry about that."

He liked her, a smart ass. But still, there was something odd about her, sad maybe. As he skimmed his brush along her skin, he kept looking up at her face. Her cheekbones were high, but sparkled in blush that was too dark for her. She just sat there with her eyes closed and slid her slick lips back and forth against each other. He wished girls would all get together and agree not to wear lipstick, ever. It tasted funky, felt waxy, and stained.

She laughed when he got to her left nipple. "That tickles."

He pulled back his brush and waited. She kept her eyes shut. He quickly finished and moved to the other, also ticklish. He used his thinnest brush to add three bronze swirls around the tops of both sides. They curved around her nipples and fanned out. He added a few muted lavender and pink accents below her collarbones. He stopped to take a look at his progress. She was soft and natural.

"You know, you can open your eyes," he told her. "I'm almost done. It won't get any worse." He found his buff brush and swished it over her entire chest with iridescent finishing powder.

"I'm just so nervous," she said. "I just wanted to see what it was like, to be on stage. But, what if I'm terrible?"

He realized she must be married. He looked down and saw the diamond ring occupying her left ring finger. Damn. He should have known. Any woman this beautiful, so starved for approval, must be married. The fantasy developing in his head flickered and died.

"You here for some attention?"

She blushed through her blush.

"Well, yes, I guess."

"Need somebody to tell you that you're pretty. Is that it?"

She opened her eyes. They were deep brown.

"You're pretty," he said. "There, now you can go home."

She kept looking at him. On closer inspection, her inner irises were honey-colored. She rewarded him with a smile. Pretty wasn't a word he used often. He knew a ton of girls who were cute, and many who were doable or even hot, but there were few he would call pretty. Pretty involved a certain sense of modesty.

He was finished, but they just sat there, and after a moment he thought maybe she was changing her mind. He heard one of the girls yelling from down the hall.

"Via, come on! Whitney's going on!"

She jumped and went over to the mirror. "Wow, I love it," she said. She turned back around and tucked herself back into her bikini top, careful not to disturb his flourishes. "It looks like a shield, like protection," she said. "So I don't fall."

"Sure. You're lucky now." He stood up, grabbed her robe from the bench, and held it out while she slipped it back on. He took the liberty of freeing her hair, trapped into the back. Too much hairspray, he thought. But he imagined it was probably silky-soft when clean.

"Thanks so much," she said on her way to the door. He realized he hadn't wished her good luck. Instead of yelling, "Knock em' dead," he yelled, "You're pretty!" He started gathering his supplies together so he could bail. She had improved his mood and made him less anxious about Portland. He knew he definitely did not want to see her dance, though, and he hoped Carlos wouldn't see her either.

*   *   *

# NICK

**NICK COULDN'T BELIEVE** The Skeeze had caught him in the hallway. Now he had to squeeze himself into the pervert closet with his shady boss and scout the very same girl he was trying to protect. The Skeeze was disheveled and said he didn't want to be seen on the main floor.

Nick slid the door latch closed and turned his nose toward the corner in an attempt to evade the smell of whiskey and ass. It was a secret viewing station, the same size and vibe as a rock festival port-a-potty. There wasn't a sound system, which Carlos said was fine because he found his girls most attractive when he didn't have to listen to them.

"Her tits look real," Carlos said. "What do you think, about a 34C? Maybe just a B." His boss prided himself on being a good "breastimator."

Nick kept his opinions to himself. It was hard acting like what they were doing wasn't sketchy. The Skeeze was already blabbering on anyway, so he just kept quiet.

"Why does she have her eyes closed? Chicks usually love Mattais, don't they?"

"I guess," Nick conceded. Matt did okay, but he did much better. Girls almost always preferred drummers to bass players. Of course, there were always plenty of admirers to go around. Obliviot gigged a couple times a month and had a rowdy fan base. They didn't use the term "cult following," but some of the Seattle entertainment reporters did.

The Skeeze rubbed his nose and then started scratching the side of his head. Nick assumed he'd been up all night doing blow again. There was a time when his boss never sampled the product. There was a time when he wasn't sloppy. But divorce changes men. Every couple of weeks, they moved four keys of the purest product up from Portland. Some stayed, was cut and distributed. The rest made its way to Canada. They called it "side work." He and Matt had helped with side work for several years. They also hooked up special clients. At eighteen, bouncing, working bachelor parties, and running drugs had been exciting. At twenty-four, it wasn't so cool. He had been sure their music would have made them rich and famous by now.

"Not too skinny...good hair," Carlos was saying.

Nick thought she'd looked better in the lobby before the girls had gotten ahold of her. He couldn't see Matt's face, but she started smiling pretty damned hard all of a sudden. What had he just said to make her light up like that? Probably just told her he was a rock star and that their next show was at Nectar. That he would put her on the guest list.

"She looks like my bitch wife," Carlos said in a snarled voice. "I'm gonna fuck her."

Charming, Nick thought.

The Skeeze's mind games had grown hardcore since Sonia had bailed with their kids last spring. He spread the hurt around, showing no hint of remorse. He didn't seem to have a specific type and claimed to be an equal opportunity womanizer. Kaytlyn had been his latest project. He used fat lines of blow like bacon-flavored dog treats and kept her high enough to put up with the insults he hurled at her. It was hard to listen to, but she never wanted rescuing anyway, so he just kept his mouth shut.

"I want to see her ass," Carlos said.

"I didn't get a good look in the lobby, sorry." He was queasy, sick of sharing oxygen, rank and ripe, with this hyper-perv.

"How am I supposed to imagine her bent over my desk?" He didn't laugh, just let out a ragged breath, like a wheeze. "I want a better look."

And as if on command, Via stood up and glided over to the mirror to admire herself. She hadn't been wearing only a thong and heels in the lobby. Damn, Nick realized. In spite of his noble intentions, a crispy sensation raced through his body, culminating in and around his junk. His own womanizing was healthy, he told himself. He loved them, as long as they didn't get too serious. He followed the path of least resistance. He didn't put up with their tests or drama because he didn't have to.

She turned around to say something to Matt and The Skeeze finally got the view he'd been waiting for. "And there you go," he said like he had just won a hand of poker. "Get that on the menu."

She pulled up her bra, a black pleather one, while Matt held out her robe like a total gentleman. Even helped with her hair. Nice move.

"She's gonna make me good money," Carlos said. "She could do the farmer's daughter thing or the exotic freak or—" He stopped. "We still have that Salome seven veils shit?"

"Sonia's old costume? I'll check." Of course, the twisted troll would want to dress her up in Sonia's old clothes. He told himself it was none of his business. He was relieved Whitney and Alicia were both too smart for his bullshit stories.

They watched her rush out of the room. "Her name is Via, by the way," Nick said, but The Skeeze was already talking again.

"When she wins, I'm calling her personally," he said. "I'll get her to come back, and she'll be...Vixen."

Vixen, really? Nick shook his head but said, "I'll go tell Leon." He needed to escape the foul air—of the pervert closet, the club, the business. It made him dizzy when he thought about all the time he had wasted in the Skeeze's world. Playing the hell out of the drums was all he cared about.

"I'm getting out," he said. "I'm gonna puke." He opened the door and took a deep breath as his eyes adjusted to the pink hallway. "I'm getting out."

*   *   *

# VIA

VIA STOOD BACKSTAGE and watched Whitney blur around the pole, an inverted, half-naked display of centrifugal force. Her white cheer skirt fanned out, reminiscent of an Olympic figure skater in a spiral.

I can't do this, she thought, and turned back to the trashcan she had been leaning over. She chugged the last few swigs of warm wine, careful not to spill on the white half-halter Brittney had fastened around her. Looking around, she didn't see a recycling bin, so she tossed the bottle in the trash. She wiped her mouth and turned around to see the club manager, Ben, on the other side of the stage. He shook his head and pointed to her mark. She wasn't sure whether he was disappointed in the drinking or the not recycling. She loved AC/DC, but never realized how long "She Shook Me" was. The air backstage felt oppressive. Perspiration trailed down her back. Her over-sprayed hair weighed her down like a sweaty shag carpet. She guided her shaky hands back against her scalp, gathered up some hair, and piled it on top of her head.

She caught sight of herself in the full-length mirror hanging against the wall. A smile spread across the face of the goddess in the glass. Could it be she was that sexy bitch looking back? Her legs were freshly spray tanned and oiled up courtesy of Brittney and Bianca. The six-inch clear stripper pumps Whitney had given her to wear made her legs look long and lean. Under the tiny plaid skirt Brittney had Velcroed around her, she wore a rhinestone thong—so uncomfortable, but it sparkled in the bar light and was hers to keep.

Was that Metallica? She listened and heard the call of that guitar riff she loved. Whitney was done already? She turned her attention to the now empty stage, bringing her hands to rest against her hips. She heard the "Enter Sandman" riff again. The one she had listened to a thousand times in her room at Bethany Christian. This was the song she couldn't *not* dance to, but now, as she heard it building dramatically, she panicked.

And a deep deejay voice said, "We have a real stunner for you tonight. It's her first time ever on stage, so let's help her feel welcome—Vixen."

Vixen? Yes, she would leave Via cowering in the wings. For all she cared, Via could just sneak out the side door, and catch the next ferry home. She glanced back at the hot bitch in the mirror. Yes, she deserved to be Vixen, at least for one night. The music was honing in on her, charging her up. She felt turned on, in control, and ready to go. This is what she came for. The deejay had told her to take her time. She had forty-five seconds to hit center stage. At fifty-five seconds, it would drop wide open. She would go and claim something, exactly what, she couldn't name.

She walked out and found herself in the spotlight, squinted and lowered her gaze. The rubber on the soles of her shoes gripped the high-gloss floor. Strutting toward center stage, she felt the magic of the intensifying drumbeat. It wouldn't let her fail. Her lucky, painted chest shield would ensure she wouldn't fall. She couldn't bear to look out into the audience yet, focusing instead on the song, her call. The riff repeated again and again, and in eight or ten seconds it would reach orgasmic proportions.

And there it was, slick and shiny and wrought with peril. Any fear of the audience she'd had dissolved as soon as she touched the golden pole, which seemed the center of the known universe. She reached out, grazed the cool metal, and brought it into her shaky grasp. Whitney's words of wisdom echoed in her head, "The pole is your friend." She relaxed her expression. It was like someone else was moving her body. Like she was somebody else. Yes, exactly, she was Vixen.

She looked down and saw several men grinning approvingly. They didn't seem to mind her trembling hands. She moved toward them, slow and seductive, and was surprised to see just how close they were. More Whitney advice fell back into her mind. "Make eye contact, and hold it. Make each man think he is the one you want." She looked out toward the crowd. Her heart plunged into her stomach and flew back up into her throat. What if they were laughing at her?

Lights flashed behind her, played beside her. She wanted to close her eyes, but she heard the boob painter's sexy voice, "You could fall off the stage."

She brought her head up and made her way down the runway. A group of guys in their early twenties, all with super short hair, sat at the far end. At first, she was afraid to look at them. Instead, she focused on the gleaming black floor. She hadn't even made it halfway before she heard them calling for her. They leaned forward in their seats and smiled, but she couldn't hear what they were saying. Whitney told her to tease, build tension. Build their desire. And so she slowly circled her hips in a subdued hula style, and then cut back like she thought a belly dancer would. She paused and made eye contact with one and then another. Their excitement was her validation. This is what she'd needed all along. She wasn't some insecure, boring little Sunday school teacher. Not tonight.

She eased her right hand down and paused on her breast before she gave her halter top a dramatic tug. The pleather bra-thingy almost came with it, so she had to turn toward the back of the stage to rearrange herself. Spaz. There were several "awws" of disappointment from the crowd, so she gave her ass a good shake. She turned back still wearing the pleather bra, sub-micro-miniskirt, and her lucky booby paint. She held out the halter and almost tossed it into the crowd. But then she remembered that was a big no-no. Ben had said clients who wanted a souvenir could buy a hat or t-shirt in the lobby.

A girlie hair shake would be fun, she thought. Cheering reached up around her and held on. She tilted her left hip and started to grind into a loose, lazy figure-eight motion. She had lost track of where she was in the song and was surprised to hear "Now I lay me down to sleep."

Their rapt attention told her they wanted more. She reached up and felt her sweaty fingers slide against the metal. The song's odd interlude grew more intense, "I pray the lord my soul to keep." Whitney had assured her nobody would be expecting pole work from a first timer, but suggested she at least use it as a prop. Via looked out and saw she had the full attention of every face she met. They wanted her. She brought her fingers to the side of her skirt. And ripped it off, tossing it over her shoulder. Some clapped, others just looked to be daydreaming.

She focused her attention on the military guy on the end who looked especially earnest, almost desperate for her. Her eyes met his and dared him to hold on. She tilted her head, strode around the pole, and found him waiting. Her hand traveled from her hip, along her waist, up toward her bikini strap. She grasped it. Held it taut. His mouth fell open. He was in love with her. In that moment at least, she knew he was. She smiled and brought her hand softly against her neck. She opened her mouth slightly and pouted. And, in that moment, she had never felt such power.

"And if I die before I wake." She skimmed her fingers along the string, ready to pull, but realized her hair was in the way. Whitney told her to make sure the crowd saw her grasp the end of the string. Her guy was leaning over the stage going crazy; they all were. She basked in the heat of the lights, the perfection of the moment. A sharp whistle came from the back of the room as she tousled her hair up and over to the other side of her face. She touched the string, looked out, and saw them tugging away at it with their eyes. She had drawn in the breath of the room and relished it as though it were infused with opium.

"I pray the lord my soul to take." She arched her back and slowly pulled the string.

# CHAPTER 6

## VIA

**THE SMELL OF** maple bacon nestled in around her. She sat upright in a bed she knew was not hers and blinked away at her dry eyes. She was revolted by the feel of her own tongue, somehow slimy and crusty at the same time. Her face felt oily and gross, like she had slept in clown makeup. Her memory rebooted and some details returned. She'd gone to that strip club. She was mortified by the thought that she had gotten booed or thrown up on somebody, but then she remembered the cheering. A smile broke out across her face, but she retracted it because it made her head hurt. A handsome face came to her. He was from Fort Lewis-McChord, and he was in love with her.

She stretched and looked around the room, relieved it didn't look anything like an army barracks. One wall was dedicated to one huge poster. It was a side angle of a young, frizzy-haired drummer playing before an ocean of faces. At the top it read: Michael Shrieve—Santana Woodstock 1969. Underneath someone had handwritten "Best Drum Solo of All Time!" The wall in front of her was awash in old posters of drummers. None of their faces were familiar, but she did recognize Stewart Copeland from The Police. She loved the Police and thought Sting was kind of hot for an old guy. Next to the door, set apart from the others, was a black-and-white photo that had been matted and framed. It was of Dave Grohl from The Foo Fighters, but he wasn't behind the drum set; he was playing a guitar.

That's right…it was coming back to her. Nick the bouncer had said she could crash with him. He'd told her Dave Grohl's birthday should be a national holiday. The knock at the door made her stomach drop.

She looked down to see she was wearing a black Green Day t-shirt over the pleather bra and rhinestone thong she had danced in the night before. Her skin was tacky underneath, so she assumed her chest shield had survived the night.

"Come in," she called out, too loud for her head to handle.

The door opened with a drawn-out creak. Nick stepped in and leaned against the doorframe. He was too tall for the doorway. His size didn't intimidate her, though. It came with an easy expression turned up into a smile. He held a big plastic bottle of bright blue Gatorade.

"Hey, Violetta. How are you feeling this fine morning? I come bearing hydration."

Her stomach burned. Her ulcer, she realized. While she tried to keep her demeanor casual, she was terrified that she had opened up and told him something the night before.

He frowned. "Did I get it wrong? I thought you said it was Vee-o-letta?"

She looked down at her hands. "No, you're right, but Via is good," she said, thankful she was still wearing her mother's ring. Her fingernails had been painted teal. "And please forget anything crazy I may have said."

"Well, you did spill your twisted daddy issues," he said, looking right through her. "Your story is full-on hard-core. And I know a dozen strippers, so that's saying a lot."

Her brain was going to bust right out of her head. Where were her clothes? The room was becoming smaller; dozens of legendary drummers were closing in around her.

His laughing startled her. "Nah," he said. "Just screwing with you."

Though she shot him look of annoyance, she was grateful. Thank you Jesus—thanks at least, for that little crumb.

"You just said you're Italian. Violetta is the lead chick in your dad's favorite opera. *La Mañana*."

She wasn't sure if he was butchering the name, *La Traviata* by accident, but she didn't care as long as she hadn't shared any more than that.

He twisted the Gatorade cap and handed her the bottle. She went to town on it. She wished it came in a bag with a needle and an IV. She'd probably need five more units.

"And no Veee-a, we did not get it on last night." He turned around and slapped his own ass. "If you had gotten a piece of this, I promise, you would have remembered."

Whoa...she hadn't even considered that. She came up for air, wiped the blue from the sides of her mouth, and scolded him. "Please don't make me laugh, or I'll choke."

"I swapped out your dress for that t-shirt, which you may not steal by the way. Shirt stealing is an under-reported but serious crime, and Green Day is one of my faves."

"Okay, Tré Cool."

"You know he's their drummer? Nice." She soaked in the admiration he was shining her way. She'd gone through a Green Day phase while at Bethany Christian. She'd practically lived in her headphones back then.

"Damn, had I known you knew your drummers, I would have green-lighted you," he said matter of factly. "Maybe even added you to the rotation."

His straight face and flat tone were disarming. He seemed to like her, but she didn't have enough experience with men to know for sure. She didn't want to come off as a total church geek, so she tried to sound casual. "You must get a lot of action."

"I'm a drummer and work at a strip club, so I do okay." He didn't blush. Not a bit. "You tore it up on stage last night, by the way."

"Did I win?"

"Duh."

Struck with a sense of sex appeal, her mind was a mess. Who was she anyway? She had been feeling like a sixty-year-old living in a twenty-one-year-old's body. This guy was looking at her like she was beautiful, like she wasn't broken.

She wanted to burp, but was afraid she would spray him with a spout of blue puke.

"I have your tip money downstairs," he said. "Clients are usually generous with first-timers, but more than two hundred bucks is rare. Didn't hurt that you were telling every guy in the place how wasted you were."

"No," she said, suddenly too interested in the Gatorade label to meet his gaze.

"I'm so drunk and it's my birthday!" he mimicked. "I'm twenty-one today. I'm so drunk!"

She just shook her head and vowed never to drink again.

"Don't worry about it. Got you here without getting into a brawl, so that's cool. There's a fifty in there, from one of the Fort Lewis guys."

His name escaped her, but she'd sat with him after her dance. He had bought her four twelve-dollar Diet Cokes. "I didn't lap dance or make out with anybody, did I?"

"You don't remember?"

Her stomach lurched. She put her hand over her mouth. "Tell me. What?"

"Nah, nothing," he said. "So, the breakfast burritos are getting cold. I'd make you a Bloody Mary, but last night you kept saying you had to drive somewhere this morning."

"Oh crap," she said. "What time is it?"

He pulled his phone out of his back jeans pocket. "Seven twenty-two."

"I have to get to church youth group," she said.

"On Saturday?"

"Yeah, where's my dress?"

"There, on the back of the chair."

"And my car? Is it here?"

His laugh was punctuated with a snort. "Damn, church girl, you shouldn't drink," he said. "I drove us here in it. It took us an hour to find it. You said I was your knight in shining armor."

She got out of bed, pulling his shirt down until it hovered just above her knees.

He headed back downstairs. "I'll nuke you a burrito. You can take it with you."

She slipped into her dress as fast as she could. Wait, this wasn't even her dress. It was similar, but much shorter. Had she left hers at the club? She didn't have time to worry about it. Dan's mother would be there waiting. Worried.

Crap, she hadn't memorized the bible verse for the week, and would have to learn it during the ferry crossing. Where was she anyway? She threw on her trench coat. Wait, not her coat. She hadn't even worn a coat the night before. Did this guy have some fetish with women's clothes? It was longer than the dress, and her thighs needed covering, so she would take it and worry about it later. She picked up her purse and heels—somebody's heels. Somebody's clear six-inch stripper heels. She made her way down the stairs barefoot.

Nick rushed over holding a napkin-wrapped burrito in one hand and her car keys in the other. "Careful. It's super hot."

"How do I get to the Fauntleroy terminal?"

"Left three blocks then right on California Ave.," he said, forcing her breakfast and keys into her hands. She had to hold her shoes in her armpit. "You'll pass the junction, go another mile, and take a right at Zeek's Pizza."

"Got it."

"Wait, your tips." He slipped a stack of bills, folded it in half, into her hand with her keys.

She stepped out onto the front porch, which ran the length of the front of an old white Craftsman. It must be a hundred years old, she thought. Just gorgeous. She was awestruck by the beauty of the rust-toned trees lining the yard. This was not some crack house in the hood.

"Thanks, Sir Lancelot," she yelled back to him while she rushed down the stairs. She turned back around and—slam—ran into some guy. The lava-hot breakfast burrito squished between them. Eggs, potatoes, and sauce smeared the lower half of his white t-shirt. Money flew everywhere. Her purse slid off her shoulder and onto the path, along with her keys and stripper shoes.

She jumped up and down, reaching into her bra, somebody's bra, trying to free the scalding potatoes from her cleavage. "Ouch, ow, ow!"

His two hands joined hers inside her bra and she pulled back. She looked up. It was the boob painter from the night before, Matt. His black hair stuck up and he needed a shave, but she remembered his kind brown eyes.

He pulled his hands away. "I'm sorry, didn't see you," he gushed. "Checking my phone. Are you okay?"

She wanted to play it off and tell him it didn't hurt, but he was right in her face. She couldn't lie. He was too close. So she pulled away. "I gotta go," she said. Where were her keys? Be cool, she told herself, though she knew it was too late for that. "Sorry about your shirt."

He looked over her shoulder, smirked up toward the porch, and shook his head. "Nick kept you safe from Carlos last night, huh?" He wiped his phone against his jeans and stuck out his bottom lip.

His tone struck her as snarky, but she didn't have time to worry about it. She had to get out of there. Dan's mom would be worried sick.

She had to get the donut table set up. It was the most important job of all. The kids would be so disappointed. She found the shoes that weren't even hers and made a break for her car. She just left him standing there, an island in a sea of cash.

Nick yelled at him from the porch. "You gonna help get her money or just stand there like a dumbass?"

* * *

# NICK

**HE HOPED** she hadn't just spilled that burrito on Kaytlyn's coat because he hadn't actually asked if he could borrow it the night before. He watched Via make her way to her car. It was such an awkward getaway, very entertaining. She had the coat belted tight, like she could be naked underneath. He thought it was a hot look, but it would have been even better if she had put the heels back on. It was a shame girls never wore their heels in the morning. She got into the car and screeched off.

Matt yelled after her, "You're pretty!"

Nick shook his head, and wished to God he hadn't witnessed such a pathetic personal display. Girls seemed to dig his best friend's awkward vibe. They fell all over themselves trying to understand him. They said he was complicated and quirky. Grandma Daney called him eccentric. Standing there in the yard, oblivious to the money blowing around his feet, he looked full-on psych-ward crazy.

"Hey, nimrod—you can't just leave money in the yard," he said. "Mrs. Jensen will see it, and she still talks to my grandma."

Matt ignored him and walked up the path, looking like ass boiled over. What a sorry-looking son of a bitch. The burrito stain screamed against his otherwise bright white t-shirt. His hair splayed out into an anime-kid crest. His forehead was wrinkled up like he was pissed off. He schlepped up the stairs and grumbled, "Please tell me you haven't nailed her yet."

"Who, the Bambi?" Nick called most women Bambi until he could think of a fitting nickname—a 'Nick name.' "I didn't know dibs were called, my bad. I think I'll call her Short Skirt, Long Jacket."

Matt had no comeback, just squinty eyes and an exposed lower lip. It was the same pout he'd used since grade school, except now it sunk into cheeks in need of a shave. He had grown up on the next block over; they had been friends since the fifth grade. Neither had any siblings, just each other.

When his grandma moved into Wesley Gardens a year ago, Nick had promised to take good care of the place. He would be the man of the house, so to speak, though he had been training for the position since his mother had dumped him off there when he was ten. She'd been living in Margaritaville with some scuba bum ever since.

The unmistakable sound of skateboard wheels against pavement made him look up to see Tucker and Toby from across the street—good kids who terrorized the neighborhood in small doses. They didn't have a thing for illegal fireworks like he and Matt had.

"Hey, you guys busy?" he asked. They stopped, spotted the money in the yard, and exchanged matching grins. Twelve-year-old twins made the best neighbors because they were always up for making money, and their affinity for Mountain Dew and Sour Gummies made them mega productive.

"If you pick it all up for me, you can each keep twenty bucks."

One of them yelled, "Sweetness!" Nick couldn't tell if it was Tucker or Toby. Didn't matter.

Matt reached his arms wide and groaned as he stretched. "When I painted her, she was nervous. How was she?"

"Obviously inexperienced, but sweet."

Matt smiled and ran his fingers through his hair.

"Wait," Nick added. "Did you mean dancing on stage or banging against my headboard?"

The punch slammed into his gut so fast it startled him. He wanted to laugh, but had to cough first. Damn, he thought, he must really like her.

"Kidding," he said. Matt should have known he wasn't serious. It was a super douche move to pounce on a defenseless wasted chick. Every guy knew that. "Tucked her into my bed and crashed in the studio."

There were two couches in the studio, which was just what they called the basement, and two more couches in the living room. He collected wayward women like stray cats, except instead of milk they wanted cocaine and a place to shower. It was like a messed up bed-

and-breakfast. They usually had at least one drunk girl or bandmate passed out somewhere. Never in his grandmother's bed though. He kept her room just as she left it. He never went in, but allowed Matt the pleasure of going in to dust from time to time. Matt's bedroom, his safe haven of cleanliness, was always off limits.

Nick sat on one of the faded, forest green Adirondack chairs. They needed painting.

He couldn't wait to hear about Matt's night. "So, how'd it go, bro?"

"I'm here, aren't I?"

"Truth." Nick glanced over to check on the twins, who were making good progress, though some of the money had drifted into the street. "Watch out for cars, please," he yelled down to them. What a terrible way for a kid to die—picking up stripper money from a muddy gutter. "Tell me about the new crash house."

"Same shit, different neighborhood." Matt ran his hand through his hair. It was going to start falling out if he didn't stop touching it so much.

"I pulled into the garage, and they installed this overhead panel," Matt said. "It fits into the gap in between the headliner and the moon roof."

"So, the moon roof still works?"

"Yep."

"So, if a cop pushes the button, it rolls back and—"

"It just disappears." He made a half-assed magician's *voilà* motion. "It's all good. As long as they don't bring dogs."

Nick tried to visualize two kilos of cocaine fitting in such a flat space.

"It's like a pan of G-Dane's cookie squares, just half the height and twice as wide," Matt added.

The thought of warm, gooey chocolate chip squares filled Nick's mind. His tongue arched up into the roof of his mouth in phantom enjoyment. Maybe he would try to bake some and sneak them to his grandmother the next time he went to see her. They wouldn't be as good as hers, but he could try.

He realized he hadn't checked for baked treats. He leaned forward in his chair and scanned the porch. Nothing. No sign of his Betty Crocker Stalker, a fan who liked to drop off drug-laced baked goodies. It was safer not to eat them, and they didn't want any raccoons to either.

"Haven't seen our little friends lately." Some of raccoons had taken up residence in the chimney last June, and Matt was dead set on never using it again for fear of inadvertently roasting one.

Nick felt his drum kit calling to him from the basement, but he should aerate the lawn, and fertilize it, and fill in the bald spots, and rake leaves too. Caring for his grandma's place was physically and financially draining. Something was always breaking. It was a big house, and drafty. The oil bill alone could get up to twelve hundred dollars a month during the winter. The fireplace had been retrofitted, so they could use it, but only on days when the city didn't have a burn ban. Seattle was full of noble planet lovers who would rather freeze than pollute. And then, of course, there were their nesting furry friends to consider.

"Tour of Homes is coming up. I should work in the yard today," he said, hoping Matt would tell him not to bother.

"You should, but you won't."

Nick nodded. Instead, he would grab a cup of coffee, go downstairs, and disappear into his drum kit. Hours would go by and it would feel like five minutes. "Don't forget practice tonight."

Matt brought his fingers together at his temple and gave him a mini-salute.

"Nick, Nick!" Toby ran up to him with a fist full of money. Maybe it was Tucker.

He counted out two hundred twenty-two dollars, nodded, and gave them each a twenty. "Thanks, guys." One day they would probably get the balls to rip him off. He figured that was going to hurt.

"She got two hundred twenty-two bucks in tips?" Matt asked, his voice pitchy. "Two hundred twenty-two bucks?" A hot pot of compulsion seemed to be brewing behind his friend's eyes. "I'll get that to her. You get her number?"

Yes he did, and he had earned it, too. Maybe she didn't remember walking around that damned Pink Elephant Car Wash five times, but he did. He remembered everything. The way she had grabbed his hand was sweet. She had asked him about his dreams.

Nick couldn't help but scowl. "You just want an excuse to see her again." He felt a sense of déjà vu encircle him as he continued. "She could be more trouble than she's worth."

"I'm bored. I need a distraction."

What the hell? Now he was getting pissed. Lately he'd found Matt's lack of motivation irritating. "You could—I don't know—write some new songs."

"Maybe she'll be my muse," Matt said, bringing his fingers up to press the bridge of his nose before closing his eyes; he looked so old.

"I thought you said you were done with dancers, not that she was much of a dancer. And, you didn't hear her drunk rambling last night. She seems like she needs a lot of attention."

"I can definitely help her out with that. What else did she say? Anything about her husband?"

"Not husband. Fiancé, gone 'til January," Nick said. "Heard all about him last night. He's like her first and only boyfriend. Sounds like a tool."

Matt looked as happy as a little girl. "I can work with that."

"Dude, she was saying her engagement ring is like magic, like something from some opera. A ring of power—about how if she had been named Brunhilde she'd be brave."

"Sounds like Lord of the Rings to me."

"Whatever, don't care. Just saying."

"Are you going to issue a warning, like a snarly old wise man?" Matt asked. He widened his eyes, waved his hands Jedi style, then over-enunciated his words into a dramatic whisper, "Young master, this is not the girl you're looking for."

# Chapter 7

## Via

**VIA CAME DOWN** from the ferry's upper deck and scanned the rows of cars, but couldn't remember where she had parked. Thank God she hadn't seen anyone from church. She would have preferred to spend the crossing in her car, but the Gatorade in her bladder hadn't let her. And her stomach had gurgled for tea. She had also tried to wipe off the booby art. No easy task considering her burrito burn. It hadn't helped that the restroom had been abuzz with women coming and going. Staring.

A gust of wind blew through the belly of the Klahowya and whipped strands of her hair against her cheeks. She jerked to a stop and nearly dropped her paper cup of scalding hot tea. In her other hand she held tight to her phone. The spiked heel of her right shoe had wedged itself into the metal grating. "Crap, seriously?" Wobbling her ankle back and forth was useless. It wouldn't budge.

A passing seagull called out, sharp and insistent, "Haw-haw-haw."

She would have bent over and set down her tea, but the dress, somebody's dress, was too short, as was the jacket. I can't flash my thong, she thought. Not on a ferry in broad daylight. Her stomach flipped then spun. Her brain was pulsing and swelling, too big for her skull. All she wanted in the entire world was to go home and crawl into bed for a week. She would never drink again.

A man down a row was getting into his car, but she was too embarrassed to call to him. She turned and looked over her shoulder. Three cars back, two teenaged boys sat laughing at her. One of them pulled out his phone. "No way," she called in their direction. She was not going to become some online joke.

The story about the rock climber trapped under a boulder popped into her mind. He had cut off his own arm to save himself. Voices drifted down the creaky metal stairwell. People were coming. How humiliating. "Just leave the stripper shoes, and go," she muttered.

She stepped out of the right shoe, then kicked off the left. Hobbling barefoot down the row, looking for her car, she found it almost funny. Who was going to come across her cast-off footwear, and what would they think? Relieved, she spotted her car and got in. She stretched and breathed in the sharp, briny breeze coming through the open car window. Now she needed to figure out how she was going to get through the next few hours without people realizing she had been out all night. She looked over her shoulder and found her tan canvas beach bag. Inside were the grimy bejeweled flip-flops she should have thrown away months ago. She reached back, scooped them up, and put them on her feet. The right one was ripped, the toe strap was about to snap. Hopefully, they would last the morning.

She had preordered the donuts from Bob's Bakery, so those would be ready, but there was no time to go home and change clothes. She pulled down the rearview mirror and looked at her chest, which looked even worse than it had in the dim-green florescent lighting of the ferry's restroom. It was red but not blistered from the burrito.

The Klahowya slowed and drifted into position past the guidepost dolphins jutting out from the water. The captain eased the three-hundred-foot ferry in against the timber wing walls attached to the Vashon Island dock. It carried less than ninety cars, but upstairs there was plenty of seating, restrooms, and a cafeteria, and that was all she usually cared about. This morning she could have gone for a Nordstrom and a burn unit.

She would need to Project Runway herself into a church-worthy outfit. She found an earth-toned paisley scarf in the glove box and tied it loosely around her neck. It covered the burrito stain nicely. She couldn't just wear the jacket though; it wasn't much longer than the slut dress.

The slamming of car doors echoed back and forth all around her as people got back into their vehicles, which reminded her head to ache. She knew she needed to eat something, but she wasn't even confident about the tea and Gatorade staying down. She leaned over and picked up her travel bible from the passenger seat and unzipped it. Tucked inside was the youth group topic schedule. This week's bible verse was Ephesians 6:10-18. Amen. She had a plan.

The orange-vested ferry workers unhooked the thick cable netting and gave the passengers the go ahead to disembark. The distinct double thud sounds began as the cars in front of her rolled out of the ferry, over the metal apron, and onto the dock. She glanced down to her bible and began memorizing Ephesians 6:10-18. "Therefore put on the full armor of God, so that when the day of evil comes, you may be able to stand your ground against the schemes of the devil."

\* \* \*

# VIA

**IT SUCKED** that she didn't know the Burton Community Church floor plan better because she could barely see past her sunglasses, wide-brimmed straw hat, and the stack of donut boxes in her arms. Finally, she made her way in through the back doors near the kitchen.

The kids were sitting cross-legged on the floor in clusters of six or seven. All of the groups had an adult group leader except for the one in the front right corner next to the American flag—hers.

Greg, the youth pastor, was on stage running through announcements. "And so thoughts and prayers go out to Jessie Dalton," he said. "The cast should be off in time for skiing season."

She put the boxes of donuts on the table, just to have the pastor's wife, Sarah, pick them back up again. "I'm taking these back to the kitchen," she said, her tone significantly snotty. "So the children don't see them."

Via kept her straw hat on, but took her sunglasses off. "I called Beth," she said, just above a whisper. "I told her I was still bringing them."

The pastor's wife pulled in her thin lips, looked over the top of her glasses, and tweaked up her face. Her return whisper had an edge. "That's all fine and good, but we needed them an hour ago. What are you wearing?"

Beth joined them, sporting a t-shirt that read, "J is for Jesus—Just be nice." She had her curly caramel-colored hair pulled back with a thin headband. Beth was Dan's mother, a supermom who volunteered like seventy hours a week. Her smile could melt ice. She eyed Via's bag-lady ensemble.

"I get it, full armor of God. Cute, Via. You can go ahead and join your circle."

"I'm so sorry," she said. Please don't ask me where I was last night, she thought. She had followed Dan back home to Vashon after they graduated in June. His parents were letting them use one of their three rentals, above KVI Beach in Tramp Harbor. The house was nothing special, but the view was stunning: the beach, the water, and on a clear day, Mount Rainer. And, of course, the KVI radio tower. Her car had been gone all night, which could be a problem. Dan must have told the entire church to check on her often because not a week had gone by without somebody popping in with a pie.

"No worries, love," Beth assured. "Just go sit down. We'll put them in the kitchen. The kids can take one on the way out."

The pastor's wife pursed her lips. "I don't think that's a good idea. Sticky fingers on car upholstery."

Helpless, Via let them decide the fate of the five-dozen glazed donuts and made her way toward her group. Each time she flipped or flopped, her sandals emitted a soft squeak, but she just went with it. If she could dance practically naked in front of strangers, she could certainly look like an idiot in front of fifty or so fourth, fifth, and sixth graders. She was making herself sick thinking about those damned donuts. Those kids had depended on her. She would try to override her guilt by teaching the word of God to these innocent little ones. But just as she thought she was home free, the announcements took an unfortunate turn.

"And Miss Via looks lovely this morning, doesn't she?"

The kids turned and started clapping for her. She did a little spin and was beyond woozy. "Miss Via, won't you come up on stage?"

She just could not catch a break. The kids in her group looked especially excited. She had intended to use her unfortunate look as a teaching tool just for them, not all fifty kids. She joined Greg on stage, giving him a tense smile.

"Before breaking up into our small groups and reciting Ephesians 6:10-18, I think Miss Via wants to go first."

This is so not good, she thought, now shaking and sweating. It wasn't uncommon for the group leaders to dress up and do skits for the kids, but she wasn't sure if she had the verse down.

"Maybe the kids can just come up and cover me with toilet paper?"

The kids clapped and cheered. Several of them raised their hands to volunteer, but nobody seemed to have any toilet paper. Damn. Greg put the microphone back in its silver stand and left her there in front of dozens of kids who sat staring back at her. It wouldn't be right to imagine them all naked. Some of them were already laughing, which was just what she was going for. She understood why comedians have water on stage because she was parched. Her tongue felt huge, and it was hard to breathe.

"Therefore put on the full armor of God, so that when the day of evil comes, you may be able to stand your ground against the schemes of the devil," she said. The room was so quiet she feared they could all hear her stomach gurgling. "Stand firm then, with the belt of truth buckled around your waist." She grasped the end of the orange bungee cord she'd found in the trunk of her car. It was so long she had wrapped it around her waist five times and hooked it onto itself. More kids laughed. "With the breastplate of righteousness in place." She couldn't show them the booby shield Matt had created. Instead, she pointed to the scarf around her neck. More laughs, and some clapping.

She tasted chunky Gatorade at the back of her throat, but powered through. "And with your feet fitted with the readiness that comes from the gospel of peace." She pointed a foot out to the side and—wham— felt herself back on stage at Hotties. But she had to keep going. There would be no gyrating. She had no pole, only a microphone stand. "In addition to all this, take up the shield of faith." She was going to be sick. "With which you can extinguish all the flaming arrows of the evil one." She looked out at her kids and saw Beth and the pastor's bitchy wife. Oh no, she was going to hurl. Dizzy, she tried to brace her wobbling knees.

What was the next line? "I pray the Lord my soul to—"

The kids morphed into whispering fuzz balls. A vortex of voices came at her. She reached for the microphone stand as she fell.

# CHAPTER 8

## CARLOS

**CARLOS THREW** the spent condom in the trash behind the bar and went back to his desk. Back to business as usual. Kaytlyn bent over to re-hook her black garters. He took the opportunity to admire the way her tan thighs peeked out between the tops of her stockings and the bottom of her panties. Ah, he thought, the joys of old-school lingerie. She found her red sequined can-can skirt on the floor, stepped into it, and pulled it up.

"What do you think you're doing, Miss Kandy?" he asked, his tone purposely ambiguous.

She just looked at him, topless and perplexed. All she could manage was a ditzy-blonde, "Huh?"

"Don't put your clothes back on yet," he said. "I'm gonna fuck you again before you leave."

While he had a good time with her body, he found screwing with her head much more satisfying.

She offered up an insecure smile, but held it as she let the skirt fall to the floor.

Amazing, he thought. She actually found that acceptable. She had somehow found some humor, some warmth, where none had been intended. "Keep the stockings on though," he told her. "Go ahead, do another line."

Blow got him super horny and he was usually able to get the job done. He felt sorry for guys who couldn't get it up after too much coke. Such a tragic waste of a stripper.

Kaytlyn was gorgeous, unless she was talking. Could have been a playboy bunny. Could have snagged herself a multimillionaire.

Fortunately, she didn't seem to know that, so she wasn't going anywhere anytime soon. She still thought she could change him. He knew he should probably be a bit nicer. He had snaked her from Mattais a few months back. He was uncomfortably high, so he finished off his scotch and soda. "Baby, make me another drink while I make a quick call."

She was a champ, willing to do whatever. It's why she couldn't pull off the black dominatrix gear that the other girls worked so well. Any girl could be a sex toy, but not every girl was sexy. Confident girls could always play dumb or submissive, but it didn't work the other way around.

He found the phone number Ben had given him. No last name, just Via. There was something exciting about calling a woman for the first time. Like a new adventure.

He started dialing, but stopped when he caught sight of Kaytlyn in the mirror above the bar.

"I said a line—not two. Watch it."

She began to apologize, but he issued a glare that silenced her. "And you need to get your roots done."

While he dialed the number, his mind took a rake to the possibilities. He felt an expansive rush overtake the bitter taste of coke making its way down the back of his throat. This new chick was especially intriguing. It had been almost a week and she still hadn't called about her prize money. He hadn't seen her dance, but she'd brought in three hundred dollars in beverage sales, and as far as he knew, nobody had even told her to hustle. This girl could sell pallets of soda and bottled water. She looked clean. He would keep her top shelf for now, just in case he decided to keep her for himself. If he was wrong about her, she could always work the floor...or if she turned out to be more of a Kandy, behind the velvet curtains.

"Here, babe," Kandy said as she handed him his drink.

Babe? He couldn't help but smile. "That's fine for private time," he told her. "But if you ever call me that in front of someone, I'll throttle you."

She smiled.

"That's good shit, huh?" he asked her. The girl was so high he could say anything and she would just smile. He reminded himself to be nice. Why was it so hard to be nice to her? There would always be other opportunities to make her cry. She was so cute when she cried. "Shush now," he said. "It's ringing. Go sit."

He loved that this new girl looked so much like Sonia. It occurred to him that if he knocked her up, the kid would probably look like Sam or Maya. How furious would Sonia be then? If she wanted to take his kids, he'd just make new ones. Easy. Of course, new babies could never replace *his* babies. He wasn't getting anyone pregnant any time soon. Not again. Girls could always say they were on birth control, but girls were evil liars. He wasn't taking any chances.

He tried not to stare too long at the school pictures on the corner of his desk. Last year's school pictures. The whore still hadn't sent new ones. He doubted she'd even signed Sam up for football. Was her new man even into football? He had to think about something else.

This new girl.

And then she answered.

"Hello?" Her voice was delicate and sexy. Damn, he thought.

He busted out his flirty voice. "Hello, Via," he said. "Carlos Menes, owner of Hotties Gentlemen's Club. Did I catch you at a good time?"

He took in the moment. Taking this one down was going to be fun. He could feel it.

# Chapter 9

## Matt

**MATT WAITED** while Whitney's daughter Bella fished around in her pink backpack just like a woman digging through her purse. She passed over a granola bar, a box of crayons, and a yellow plastic pony.

He picked the pony up. "Oh hey, Fluttershy," he said, holding it up so Nick could see it.

Nick shot him a shut-your-face look.

"What?" he laughed. "You don't want Bella to know we're secretly Bronies?"

They were cartoon connoisseurs. *My Little Ponies: Friendship is Magic* was one of their favorites, especially when they were blazed, which was often.

Bella lit up when she found the book she had been searching for. "Read, Matt, please?"

Hotties didn't open for another hour so the lobby was empty, except for Nick. How convenient, he had papers to shuffle at the welcome podium. Whitney said she just needed a few minutes to talk to Ben before taking Bella to a doctor's appointment. Something about vaccinations. Bella didn't seem nervous, so he didn't mention it.

She scooted across the couch making a squeaky noise. "That's a funny sound." She bounced up and down a few times, giggled, then settled in against his side.

"That's because it's pleather and not real leather or fabric," he said. "It's much easier to clean." She looked up and gave him a baffled look. He felt super creepy for mentioning the merits of easy-clean strip club furniture to a six-year-old girl. Move on, he told himself. Just move on.

"Okay then," he said and opened her book. He saw the tag inside was labeled Gatewood Elementary School. He swallowed hard. The thought of all of the snotty little hands and unchecked sneezes that had touched the pages made him want to hurl. He reminded himself that his go-to hand sanitizer was in his front jeans pocket; he tried to mellow into acceptance of the situation, but couldn't. He focused. I'm good. I'm good. I'm good, he reminded himself.

He put the book next to her and pulled out his sanitizer boasting 70 percent ethanol, none of that weak organic crap. He put a dab of clear gel into her hand, and then gave himself a big-boy dollop. She watched him rub his hands together and did the same.

He sang the alphabet song as he rubbed his hands together. He had hoped she would join in, but she just giggled at him.

He heard Nick laugh, too. "That sounds tight, bro. Let's get that on the set list."

Matt didn't find it funny, but Bella was too cute to ever frown at. "I sing the alphabet song in my head when I wash my hands. You know why?"

She shook her head and sat back on the couch as though she expected a riddle.

"Because that song is twenty to twenty-five seconds long, and that's how long it takes to kill germs."

"Read now?" she asked. Her expression was soft yet convincing. She looked like her mother. Everyone liked Whitney, who wrapped her model-perfect legs around the pole better than anyone. Nick was especially fond of her, but said he liked her way too much to ever hook up with her. To Matt, she seemed that kind of mellow girl who'd be a total catch for a guy in his thirties. A gym hound who rarely partied, she wasn't a typical stripper. It was clear to everyone she was all about the money. Her regulars were funding her education. She said every lap dance brought her a little closer to her nursing degree, and a good life for Bella.

"Wouldn't you rather play a game on my phone?" he asked her. "Look, Pesky Parrots." He held out his phone for her inspection. He could feel panic pooling in his gut. One, two, three, he thought. I have sanitizer. I'm good. I'm good.

She shook her head so decisively that her piggy tails swung back and forth in a clear, "no way" pattern. "Read," she said and pointed to the picture of the princess staring out of the tall castle window.

His heart fell like a brick when he saw her captivated by the perfect pastel picture. He wanted to warn her not to wait for a handsome prince because they usually turned out to be posers or losers. He wanted to tell her that in the real world, princes were rarely in the position to rescue anybody. Most couldn't even afford a decent horse much less a castle or a kingdom. But who was he to ruin a little girl's fairytale. Still, he could put some new-school spin on it.

"Why would a princess want to wait inside her castle when it looks like such a pretty day outside?" He pointed to the bright yellow sun smiling in the corner of the page.

She rolled her baby-doll eyes and yelled over to Nick. "Will you read? Matt's not being a good listener."

Nick looked over from his paperwork and gave his friend a you-are-ultra-lame look. "One minute, okay?" he said with a smile. "Just need the boss to sign this and I'll take over."

Matt felt a mix of relief and embarrassment. "Geez, princess, you are making me look so bad," he said.

She laughed, "You're silly."

"No doubt," he said. "Hey, how about if I make up a story for you?"

"Yes, yes," she said and clapped her hands.

He put the book down, leaned over, and craned his head around the lobby wall to see Whitney and Ben next to the deejay booth. She looked annoyed. The dancers often complained about the deejay and house fees they were required to pay, but he tried not to get involved. Ben was the manager and Carlos had his back.

"Okay, here we go. Once there was this little girl," he began.

"You mean 'Once upon a time, there was a princess,'" she said, looking up at him with anticipation.

"Fine, she's a princess, and she's beautiful. Okay, so the princess decided to go outside and enjoy the day with her friends." He looked down at her to check her level of engagement. She eased into his side, attentive. "And so the princess got on her horse and—"

"Can it be a unicorn?"

"It can be anything you want it to be."

"It's a white unicorn with a pink mane," she said. "And its horn is sparkly."

"Got it. Sparkly," he said. "So she galloped down to the village on her beautiful unicorn. Its name was Sparkles," he said. He looked down and was relieved to see her contentment, so he continued. "She and Sparkles found a big green meadow where there were lots of other happy little princesses playing soccer. And so she gave Sparkles an apple to eat, and then went to play soccer too."

"No, ballet."

"Ballet?"

"They were ballet dancing. In sparkly tutus."

"Okay, Bella, it's your story, you finish." Her cuteness was undeniable. He had to admit that some kids, with the proper adult supervision and unlimited hand sanitizer, had the potential to be pretty cool.

"The princesses danced and twirled," she said. "And she was the prettiest one, and then a prince came to see her dance." His smile faded fast as he realized where her story was going. "And then he took her back to his castle and they got married. And then they all lived happily ever after. The end." She offered up a smile so wide he could see she had lost another tooth.

"Well, if it isn't Princess Short Skirt, Long Jacket," Nick said as he returned to the podium.

Matt turned around to see Via there. Gorgeous. "How long have you been standing there?" he asked, not meaning to come off so interested.

Bella stood up and held out her hand in a way that would have made Whitney proud. "Hi," she said. "I'm Bella. I'm in the first grade now."

Via knelt down. More than leaned down—actually knelt down—into Bella's line of sight, shins against the floor, like she was praying. He didn't know what to think. His first instinct was to grimace, but somehow, she seemed safe and secure. Above it all.

"I'm Via," she said. "It's so nice to meet you, Bella. Are you having fun in the first grade?"

As the two exchanged pleasantries, he was overcome with the realization that the sight of her on the floor didn't make him uncomfortable after all. In fact, he felt amazing. This Via girl was like the ultimate reset button. It was fine. It was all fine.

"You here to see Carlos?" Nick asked. "He didn't mention—"

He was interrupted by the buzzer and the boss man's gruff voice. "Nick, I have someone coming in. Bring her back."

Not Carlos, Matt thought. The floor was one thing, but The Skeeze was another. He held out his hand and helped her up. "I'll take you in."

She stood up and waved goodbye to Bella.

"But first," he told her. "I have to tell you something."

She looked surprised, but intrigued. "Tell me something?" She leaned into him, so he could whisper in her ear.

Her hair smelled so good his words stalled. "Um." Talk idiot, he thought. Use your words. "Um."

\* \* \*

# VIA

**THEY STEPPED INTO** a dim, wood-paneled office. Carlos smiled and directed her to sit down on the couch next to him.

"So nice to finally meet you," he said.

She shook his hand. It felt just like meeting new people at Dan's church except for what looked like cocaine lined up on the coffee table. And, the blonde hanging from the stripper pole in the corner. Craziness, she thought, but tried to act casual. As long as she didn't puke and fall on her ass again, like the other day at youth group, she should be fine. Brittney was there too, kicked back smoking a cigarette. She had a sort of slutty punk-rock look going on—fierce black eyeliner and light brown hair with magenta streaks.

Matt sat on the other end of the couch and acted as though he hadn't just issued her an impassioned request on the way in: "When I leave, come with me. And also, you're pretty." It wasn't really a question, so she hadn't answered. He was much taller than she had realized before. And, she loved the way he smelled, like fabric softener. He was downright handsome. Why hadn't she noticed that the other night? He had been only three inches away, stroking gold paint onto her nipples. Maybe she'd been too drunk. Or too busy contemplating her sanity and worrying about the slick stage. And the morning after, she had been in too much pain to notice anything other than her nuclear burrito burn.

"Brit, get Via a drink," Carlos said as he leaned in and tapped her knee with his index finger. "Rum and coke?" He was Latino and looked to be in his late thirties. Maybe early thirties, she thought. The hint of white hair framing his face made him look distinguished. "Or, you more of a vodka girl?"

Jeez, it wasn't even lunchtime, she thought, but didn't say so. She wanted to come off mature, cool. "Vodka is fine." Her own voice sounded strange to her.

"Here, before I forget—your winnings—seven hundred fifty." Carlos handed her a thin white envelope. She would put it in the offering basket at church.

"Thanks so much," she managed, unsure of proper stripper-winnings etiquette.

"And that's just the beginning," he added. He smiled in a relaxed, familiar manner that seemed almost proud. He wasn't bad looking either. He wore jeans and a plain button-up shirt, but looked at her like he ran the whole damned world. Like the old guy in the beer commercials, always flanked by a couple of hot girls.

"Hey, Mattais," the stripper on the pole yelled over. "Do a line. It's really good shit." Her platinum hair hung down and touched the floor of a mini stage. Mattais? They obviously knew each other well. He probably had a thing for sassy blondes. She sat up straight, not that her average body could ever measure up to a girl so close to perfect.

Carlos's smooth smile dropped into a deep scowl. "Kandy, you're getting mouthy," he said, stressing the word mouthy. "You'll want to check yourself."

The stripper started to apologize, but he raised his arm in a dismissive backhanded motion.

"Via, this is Kaytlyn, aka Kandy," Carlos said as he leaned toward the coke. He looked uncomfortable, his long legs pressed against the glass coffee table. All the guys here seemed big. She had never felt so short before.

Her eyes fell upon the rows of white powder; they seemed the focal point of the room. She had tried cocaine a couple of times during her party days, before she'd started dating Dan. She remembered she had liked it, a lot.

"Mattais, do a line," he said. "It is, indeed, really good shit," he said.

"No, I'm good, thanks."

"Consider it quality assurance."

"Okay, but just a small one or I won't be able to sleep."

On the coffee table sat a white marbled box trimmed in gold, like an exquisite shoebox. Carlos opened it and pulled out what looked like a regular drinking straw. She wondered what else he had in there.

"Kandy, get my scissors from that cup on my desk." While he waited for her to untangle herself from the pole, Carlos asked, "Via-Vixen, would you like one?"

Would she? Her fingertips tingled.

Matt leaned over the glass coffee table and swept half of the end line over to the side, then reshaped it back into a shorter, thinner line. He added the other half to the others, making them all equal. She watched, mesmerized by the precise, fluid motion—skim, skim. It reminded her of one of those white sand Zen gardens. Though, instead of a rake, he used a gold Visa card.

Carlos leaned in closer. "It's okay, you're among friends."

Maybe she should have been scared to death, but she was too excited. Brittney set down a drink in front of her, then sat down and lit a cigarette. No, Via realized, it was a joint.

Brit smiled. "Don't stress, girl. I'll share."

"Oh, no thanks," she told her trying not to stare at the blue butterfly tattoo on the side of this freaky looking girl's neck. "Weed makes me sleepy."

Carlos' s laugh was as sweet as the smoke permeating the air. He pointed to the table where those bright lines of blow stood high against the mirrored table. "*That* will not make you sleepy. Go ahead." He handed her a freshly cut straw.

Her brain sorted through the thousands of excuses she had for saying yes. She was lonely and needed a distraction from her death day countdown, for starters. Her heartbeat ramped up in anticipation. "Why not?" she asked while she tucked her hair behind her ears. She leaned over and brought the straw down and snorted it up, hard and fast. It was terrible, torturous magic. She brought her head up, pressed her thumb against the side of her nose and sniffed hard. Whoa, she realized—awesome. And she was off and running. It was on. "So, is it Matt or Mattais?" She sniffed hard again, attempting to suck the lovely bitterness deeper into her head.

"Matt, please," he said without hesitation.

Carlos jumped in. "Only two people call him Mattais," he said. "Me, because I've been his boss since before he had his driver's license, and Kaytlyn because she's obnoxious. She doesn't seem to understand that he has no interest in her."

"And my mother, when she's annoyed with me," Matt said. "And Nick's grandmother."

Carlos smiled. "How are your folks? Still down in Arizona?"

"Yeah, my dad's parents are there," Matt said. "The weather is finally cooling down, so they're golfing again."

"Good for them."

Why were they talking? She wanted to talk.

"Nick's grandmother, she still crazy as shit?" Carlos asked.

"Nah, she's just a hippie."

"Just doesn't give a fuck, huh?" Carlos shook his head, but kept smiling. "Fucking old people are hilarious."

His swearing excited her Christian ears.

Kaytlyn hovered over the table. "Cute jacket," she said to Via, who wasn't sure how to react. It wasn't even hers, but the one Nick had given her the morning after Amateur Night.

"Should I call you Kaytlyn or Kandy?" she asked with her friendliest smile.

"Doesn't matter," she answered and then sighed dramatically. She looked down at the coke on the table, but didn't say anything more. She had a desperate vibe about her, like the snarky prostitute character on every episode of CSI—the one who gave up too much information. The one who always ended up zipped into a body bag.

Carlos leaned over for another line and motioned for her and Matt to do the same. He seemed to get off on giving orders and everyone seemed vested in following them.

"Word is the Molly you picked up in Portland is exceptional," Carlos said. "We should take these ladies out dancing."

Kaytlyn squealed. "Finally," she said, grinning like a kid with an ice cream cone. "I've been wanting to roll with you guys forever."

Via had no idea what they were talking about, but was afraid to ask. Matt held out his hand toward Kaytlyn and shook his head. "Calm down—no can do. Practice later today." Then he redirected his attention to Carlos. "Yeah, they say it's the best they've ever seen. I can bring some in for you tomorrow. I might save some for after the Halloween show, if that's cool." Carlos just nodded, already refocused on the blow on the table.

"So, Kaytlyn," Carlos said, and then with a dramatic motion, pushed one line toward her side of the table. "You interested in earning a nice, fat rail?"

She nodded, grabbed Matt's straw out of his hand and snorted it up.

"Well, I'm out," Matt said. "I've got to get home. We've got that gig coming up. We're doing some new stuff. Need some more practice."

That was cool, she thought as she imagined him on stage, wild and sweaty. While at Bethany Christian she had spent countless hours listening to the college radio station out of Bellingham. A diverse mix of music and raunchy romance novels had distracted her from the reality of her empty life.

"Wait. Kaytlyn, grab that chair," Carlos said. "We want Via to learn how to give a proper lap dance. Mattais, we just need you as a prop, really. I know you won't mind."

Matt looked in Via's direction and gave an awkward smile.

"Carlos, I can't." she said. "I just can't." She was mortified by the idea of lap dancing at all, much less this very minute with no private practice first. What if they wanted her to strip? She needed a new coat of deodorant. Her legs were stubbly. Her panties didn't even match her bra.

Carlos looked at her and shook his head. "No, not you. I wouldn't put you on the spot. Just want you to see how it's done." He looked over to Kaytlyn. "You're up."

The picture of blonde perfection smiled and brought a chair over to where Matt was standing.

"Fine, just for a minute though. I've got to go," Matt said. He walked over to the chair and sat down.

Via started to snicker, maybe to mask her nervousness. Maybe it was the reefer madness Brittney had been blowing in her face. Matt looked like he was waiting in the principal's office. He whispered something to Kaytlyn, Kandy, whatever her name was. There must be some history between them.

"Via, watch this," Kaytlyn said. "I'll show you how to get a guy crazy-hot."

Carlos found a thin silver remote on the table. "Mattais, I have something you'll like. It's old school." The room filled with electro-hip-hop.

Matt laughed out loud. "You think she can dance to the Beasties? Really?"

"The girl can dance to anything," Carlos assured him. "She's got the 'Skills to Pay the Bills' and then some."

Via sipped her vodka and sat back. Kandy's confidence mixed with the kill-me-now look on Matt's face was hysterical. Kaytlyn leaned in and pulled off her bra with such zest that her double Ds came close to slapping him in the face.

Carlos leaned in and started providing commentary. "See how he's keeping his hands to himself. No touching, no grabbing. The bouncers would be all over him if he touched her. We take very good care of our girls. We have some Velcro bras in the back, but some girls don't like to share," he said. "Now, in the main room you can only be nude in certain zones."

Via wanted to listen, but couldn't stop looking at Kaytlyn's gigantic boobs. She tried to suppress her laughter. Don't laugh, Via, she told herself. Don't laugh. But these people weren't making it easy.

Brittney started rhythmically chanting, "Bring—it—girl. Bring—it—girl."

"That's enough, Brit," Carlos said. His tone was commanding, but not cruel, as it had been with Kaytlyn. Brittney seemed to be much higher in the pecking order.

"Now, you can make a lot of money couch dancing—that's the term we use," Carlos continued. "It's interchangeable with lap dancing. We feel couches provide for a richer clientele experience, more like home."

There was something so odd about him. His vocabulary was a hodgepodge of pretension and ghettoism. His breath was hot against the side of her neck and reeked of whiskey and power. "I'm sorry I haven't seen you dance yet. I'm sure you look amazing under bar light. We'll talk about it next week. You'll make good money." While she had no need for money, his attention was a form of currency she found irresistible. He leaned in even closer, his mouth almost touching her ear, and whispered. "With your cash is my private number. Not just anyone gets that number." He was not subtle. His bold interest made her feel alive.

Matt shot her a concerned look and she remembered his request that she leave with him. "I thought it would just be that one time," she whispered back. "And, I have a lot on my plate right now." In truth, other than volunteering at church, she had nothing. The sick taste of cocaine slid down her throat. She sniffed, swallowed, and reached for her cocktail.

"We'll talk about it next week," he said. "You'll come to see me. We'll talk."

She smiled, but pulled away as she took in more vodka. It comforted her tongue and eased the bitterness in her throat. She looked back toward the show, but sensed Carlos's heavy gaze upon her. An odd sensation settled in around her. It was as though she already knew him.

These people may be crazy, she thought, but they made her feel almost normal. With them she could be brave, bitchy, and strong. They didn't know her at all, so she could be anybody. She could laugh and dance her way through the holidays. She could just pretend.

A cozy bowl of mellow buzzed in her stomach while her chest grew tight with excitement. She felt so high and free. It occurred to her that the next few months could actually be fun. As long as she got to church youth group on time, who was to say she didn't deserve occasional field trips over town? She thought of the pastor's wife Sarah, and the condescending way she kept correcting Via. "Islanders call Seattle over town, not downtown."

Matt was looking at her, and through her. He smiled. He mouthed something to her, but she wasn't sure what he was trying to say. She watched his lips again. They seemed to form the words, "Come to me."

# CHAPTER 10

## MATT

**MATT SAT IN** his favorite spot at the end of the brown leather sectional, across from Nick and Via. Sitting there usually made him comfortable. He could look to the right and see the front door, straight ahead and see both the TV and the bottom of the staircase, and to the left to see into the dining room. But today he wished he could sit between them. She was sitting with her body pivoted toward Nick like she was enamored. His friend needed to go away.

Matt knew Nick to be a dedicated drummer and loyal friend, not to mention one of the biggest man sluts in King County. He was straight up about his quest for variety, which just seemed to encourage wannabe girlfriends. Matt's advice to them was simple: when a guy tells you he's a player, it's not a challenge, but a promise. Once a girl accepts those terms and decides she'll be the one to change him, it's too late. She's already given her power away. She's already given him a free pass to Dickland, and there's no expiration date. All he has to do is remind her that he warned her in the first place. In Matt's opinion, women needed to be better negotiators.

He couldn't stop looking at her. Taking in her energy. Maybe he should be concerned about being the one to get burned. There was some other guy, after all. Still, he loved her attitude. Not bitchy, just unaffected and cool with herself.

She wore very little makeup and exuded a soft, sultry vibe. He was usually lazy in love, but he wondered if maybe it was time to put in some effort. He wasn't sure why, but this girl made him want to jump through a few hoops. Her hair was down, but what he could see of her neck was naked. She wasn't wearing any jewelry except for the engagement ring. It was a bummer, but he didn't know the guy. She was hot, and she was here, and that made her fair game.

Nick was wrapping up his explanation, "Seattle's weather sucks for sports, but is perfect for music—kids stay dry in their basements, learn to play guitar, bass, drums, and write songs, or whatever—angst is environmental."

She reached for the cup of tea Nick had prepared for her. They hadn't offered her blow, because she hadn't asked. That was good sign. Though Matt wanted to roll with her.

"We should test out that Molly," he told her, as though Nick weren't even in the room.

"You don't mean now," Nick said. He shook his head. "You can't drop now. We've got to rehearse. Guys are coming in an hour."

Nick could be such a buzzkill. She hadn't looked all that enthused anyway.

"Can I get a rain check?"

"Sure." He would save it. Good thing she said no. It was a dumb idea, anyway, he realized. He needed a woman to say no, to shut him down. He felt like a thirteen-year-old driving a car without a license.

"So, do you sing?" Her question was as predictable as the recycling truck.

"I sing a few, but it's tough singing the melody and focusing on rhythm at the same time. At least for me."

Nick piped up, "Though Sting does, Gene Simmons, Paul McCartney, Geddy Lee."

He beamed him a shut-the-fuck-up-this-instant look. His obnoxious friend just smiled back.

"That's cool," she said as she leaned forward. Her interest level seemed solid. "So, why do bass players stand in the back? Don't you want to bask in the spotlight?"

This chick was adorable. The pecking order tended to go: lead vocalist, lead guitarist, drummer, bassist, and then maybe the guy on keyboards would get a few crumbs. "The bass player stands back because that's where the drummer is," he explained. "They're the rhythm section. The drummer is the heartbeat of the band, and the bass player is the spine." His analogy seemed to be working because she gave him a dreamy sort of look. It gave him courage.

"Wanna see my favorite bass? It's in my room." He ignored the oh-no-you-didn't look from Nick. Asking a girl up into his room was meaningful. If he just wanted to nail her, he would have asked her down to the studio. It was their go-to for quick-n-dirty encounters. The basement even had a condom machine on the back wall next to the pinball table. When Nick installed it back in the day, it had been an ironic addition. But it didn't require any coins and they kept it stocked, so it had worked out. Sex didn't inflame any of Matt's quirks as long as he was safe and could jump into a hot shower within an hour or two. He wasn't so much of a germaphobe as long as he knew he could reset, re-sanitize himself. There were methods to his madness that seemed random to anyone else. Reading that germ-laden book to Bella would have been tricky, but knowing he had his hand sanitizer in his pocket made it manageable. He would never go into Hotties without hand sanitizer. But his bedroom was always clean and safe, his retreat from the chaotic world outside. She stood up and followed him and his anxiety level increased at the thought of her touching his things, but hopefully not to the point that she would notice.

\* \* \*

# VIA

**VIA FOLLOWED HIM** up the dark wood staircase. The house's interior was so lovely, adorned with deep glossy wood. Intricate paneling anchored the bottom half of many of the walls; bookcases flanked both sides of the fireplace. She looked above and admired the exposed timber beams. "Tell me about this house," she asked him. "Those half walls with the columns are gorgeous."

He slowed his pace up the stairs, which were fitted with a blue and beige carpet runner. "Those are colonnades," he said. "You'll see tapered columns all over this place. They're a signature of the Craftsman style."

She heard Nick yell up from the living room. "It's my Grandma Daney's house," he said. "My great-great grandfather built it in 1916." She turned to see him making his way over toward the bottom of the staircase. "It's on the West Seattle Tour of Homes every year," he added.

She smiled and started to turn around to face him, but Matt grabbed onto her hand and guided her upstairs. "We'll tell you about the house next time. Promise."

Nick yelled up after him, "Tour is coming up, bro. Saturday the 4th," he said. "Don't forget, ten to four. Don't make any plans. You're in charge of snacks." Without turning around, Matt yelled over her, "I know, I know, dumbass!" Matt's tone seemed light, and Nick didn't seem offended, so she assumed it must be their typical banter.

Once they reached the landing, she noticed a bright orange painting hung high on the wall. It gripped her and pulled her attention in toward its deep purple center. As she got closer she realized the center shade was more of an indigo, wrapped in dozens of orange oval rings. Each nested into the next, like an oval solar vortex. His grip on her hand was determined, so she didn't have a chance to investigate it properly. He was a fast walker.

She followed him into his bedroom, amazed by how clean it was. Had he straightened it up for her? He must have just vacuumed because the aligned grooves in the carpet were fresh. The furniture all matched and was black with minimal accents. The bed was made. The desk was bare except for a tablet, some hand sanitizer, and a wire basket full of sheet music. Even the carpet under the desk chair had been vacuumed. For a moment she thought about lifting the bed skirt to check the carpet under the bed, but decided against it.

The soft white walls were bare with the exception of a painting above the black headboard. It was colorful, but muted. It looked to be thirty-six by sixty inches, not as tall as her father's.

"You paint this?"

He nodded. "It's nothing."

She knew he was wrong. Art was always something. Perhaps being in the bedroom of a painter should have made her anxious, but this painting was nothing like her father's work. It offered toasty shades of yellow, orange, and red, counterbalanced with cool violet. The violet was minimal, but drew her in the most. She stepped closer and leaned in. Across the top of the canvas, several layers of multicolored drips cascaded down. Overlaid together, they offered up a subtle shimmer that she hadn't noticed from a distance. She wondered what her father would have thought of it. He probably would have approved of the concept, and looked past its technical failings. It seemed perfect, but she knew artistic perfection was a myth. It had driven her father crazy. She looked to the corner, squinted her eyes and read aloud, "Mattais Smith Romero." His handwriting was poised, not frantic or brutal.

"Smith is my mom's maiden name. She's a Euro-mutt, but my dad is Mexican," he said. "I don't speak Spanish, and get a lot of shit for it, so please don't—"

"No, no." She shook her head. "I wasn't even going to ask about your name, just about the painting." She wondered why he had said, "but my dad is Mexican." Like Mexican was a bad thing. Like she would disapprove somehow. It worked for her. Explained his dark eyes, his thick hair.

"Where did they meet?"

"In Arizona. He was born and raised there. He's a US citizen. It's not like he was undocumented or anything."

He seemed sensitive, though she didn't know why. Her own father had been born in northern Italy and hadn't moved to the US until he was a teenager. She didn't even know his family. He hadn't talked about them. Her uncle Erik popped into her head. He had called from Taiwan the night before to talk about her father's collection, but she had lied to him and said she couldn't hear him. That the cell reception was bad.

Matt had moved over to a corner next to a long closet, which was closed. In the other corner was a bathroom, which from her vantage point, also looked immaculate. Could they have a maid?

"Really, it's nothing," he said, trying to redirect her attention away from the painting. "I don't paint much anymore."

"And the one we passed coming up the stairs?"

"That's the only one I kind of like," he said. "Honestly, none of them really please me." His words felt like punches and pushed her far away for a moment. She regained herself and hoped he hadn't noticed that she had just been thousands of miles away, revisiting her childhood home.

"These two are my favorites," she heard him say. "I have a few more down in the studio that I thrash on."

Her eyes hated to say goodbye to the happy little drips slipping down the canvas.

"Via," Matt said. She turned toward him, loving the way her name sounded through his voice. "This one is my acoustic," he said once he'd reclaimed her attention. He picked it up from a stand on the floor and held it out for her. It was shaped like a traditional guitar and was a piney color with darker wood inlaid around the hole. She took a few steps toward him and tentatively reached out to touch the heavy wire strings. He briefly pulled it back. "Be super gentle, okay?"

She nodded, but wondered at his nervousness. "It's beautiful."

"This is a four string," he said. He took her hand, and led her fingers against the copper-colored strings. "And, these are the frets." He guided her down past several horizontal lines intersecting the strings. "And down here, these are the pickups. Even though it's acoustic, it still has pickups." He had lost her. It was hard to keep track because her tour guide was getting her hot and bothered.

She could not stop smiling to save her life. Don't be a spaz, she told herself. He was grinning back at her though, so it felt okay after all. Any doubt she'd had before, about whether he liked her or not, disappeared. She relished his sexy stare. She couldn't remember the last time she had been so attracted to someone or felt so attractive. God, she wanted him to put down that bass and just kiss her. But instead he let go of her hand, put the bass back on its stand and then picked up the other.

"This is my Mike Lull, four-string custom," he said. "Do you know who he is?"

She had no clue, but could tell he was about to remedy that.

"He's a local manufacturer who's worked with Jeff Ament from Pearl Jam, Nick Harmer from Death Cab for Cutie, Ann and Nancy Wilson from Heart—basically everybody awesome," he explained. "Not only Seattle artists—he's worked with Branden Campbell from Neon Trees and that American Idol judge, Randy Jackson. Did you know he played bass?" He didn't really wait for her to answer. "And Bryan Beller, who's a fucking genius." He just kept talking. He just looked so excited. Music was obviously important to him. "Mike Lull is the coolest. Gave me a smokin' deal cause he knew I couldn't afford her."

This bass was a glossy shade of forest green. Her pulse sped up as she watched him run his fingers down the length of the thickest string. He sat on the edge of his bed with it. Smaller and thinner than the first, its smooth body curved at the bottom and there were two arm-like edges reaching out from its sides. As soon as he placed it on his lap, she understood its shape was not only cool, but also ergonomic. The bottom arm was shorter and fit against his thighs. The upper stretched out further, but not so far as to impede his left arm.

"And, she has a name. Can you guess?" he asked her.

She had to think about it for a moment. It screamed of green. Then it hit her. "Envy," she said. "That's what I would name it."

"Right on," he said. He squinted at her for a moment, then gave her a slight nod. "Keeper."

She turned away. What was happening here? What did she want to happen here? She went over and sat in the chair in front of the desk. She stayed clear of the bed. "Play me a song?"

"Maybe someday," he said, putting Envy back on its stand. He sat back down on the edge of his bed, but she stayed by the desk. He took an awkward pause and then got back into music-professor mode. "You want a little melody or something," he began, "but that's not my part. Nick sets the beat, I help lay down the rhythm. Then the rest of the guys build the melody on that. I do sing sometimes, but it kind of stresses me out."

Duh, she realized. He had already explained that. Her brain was a frazzled mess.

"No worries," he said. "If I didn't like you, I wouldn't bother telling you all this. You get that, right?"

Was he really talking to her like this? His tone was so patient, playful.

"If you hear me practicing, you probably won't even recognize the songs." He came over to the desk and she stood up so he could sit down. But he just leaned over the desk and swiped his finger across the tablet on the desk. Standing next to him, she felt pretty shrimpy. The side of her face met his shoulder. His shirt still smelled like fabric softener. "But when you come hear us—the whole band—then you'll hear me. The baselines will pop."

He felt so familiar. "You should be a teacher," she told him.

"I teach at Seattle Kidz Rock, but just a couple of hours a week," he said. "I want you to hear a song."

In one fluid move, he sat down in the desk chair, reached over, hooked his right arm around her waist, and brought her down onto his lap. It was sweet yet confident.

"A lot of people don't give the bass a second thought, but in reggae the bassist and guitar player switch roles," he continued. "The bass is more prominent. A good example is 'Stir it Up.' Listen."

God, he felt good, and she was content to just sit there while he found his song. He nuzzled into her side, and she felt little kisses just behind her earlobe. Something shifted within her. Like he had correctly entered some secret code she didn't even know she had. She heard the sound of the Wailers start in, and then Bob Marley's distinctive voice.

She relaxed into him. He was her sexy beanbag chair. "Do you hear it?" he asked.

"Hear what?" she wanted to say. How was she supposed to concentrate while his lips worked down the side of her neck? Their warmth made her want to turn her face to meet them.

"Do you hear it?"

Of course, it surrounded them. Deep, rich sound waves came through speakers she hadn't noticed before. "I love it," she finally said. Reggae would never be the same. It was all so easy. He brought his hand up and pulled back the strands of her hair, which had been in his way, then got back to kissing her neck. He had cracked her combination all right.

She wanted to give into it, but resisted and let in her rational thoughts. Still not able to pull away from him entirely, she heard herself say, "Wait." He said nothing, but paused and rested his chin on her shoulder as though awaiting further instruction.

This guy felt so right, but she couldn't believe this was even happening. She was so into him that it made her queasy. Maybe it was the two lines of blow she'd done earlier. The whole point of going to Hotties in the first place was to escape her real life. How much was she going to tell this guy, and when? She didn't want to hurt him. But why hadn't she been afraid of hurting Dan? Why was he just now coming to mind?

Matt hummed in her ear. His soft breath distracted her from her internal quandary.

"I'm engaged," she finally managed to say. Was he going to be pissed off?

He didn't move an inch. He stopped humming long enough to say, "I know that."

Excitement trailed along the path his hand took as he ran it down her side; he was playing her like that damned bass. He put his left hand on top of hers and ran his pointer finger along her ring finger, which was occupied by her mother's ring.

She couldn't help but chuckle. "Oh, right," she said. "I forgot about that." She had forgotten a lot in the past week, which was exactly what she had been going for. She wanted to forget being that pathetic, parentless little mouse. She had already gone off the reservation. Maybe it was time to go and screw around in the desert for a while.

"You probably think I'm a terrible person." She dreaded the thought that Matt wouldn't respect her. Though she didn't know why, she desperately wanted him to like her. She didn't want this drug-dealing bass player to think she was skanky.

"You're way too young," he said. "You going to go through with it?" She was astonished at the way he honed in on the very question that had haunted her for weeks, probably months. She had absolutely no idea.

"I'm afraid I don't love him," she said. She felt liberated. It was true, but she had never verbalized it. It wasn't the kind of thing she could bring up at her ladies' bible study. They would tell her to pray about it. They would assure her that commitment is difficult for everyone, and that it takes work, commitment, and faith.

He continued to hold her close and began swiveling the chair to the left and right. "I know that, too," he said. "You wouldn't be here if you did."

"He's in Africa for a few months," she said. She expected him to ask a few follow-up questions—like what was in Africa, for starters.

"Then I won't ask about it," he said. "I mean, we're just having fun, right?" It hadn't occurred to her that she was being presumptuous in assuming it would bother him. Caring would imply he cared about her, and he didn't even know her. He let go of her hand and ran his hand up her side again.

She pulled away and sat straight up, then got up off his lap. Only then did she notice she had gotten him hard. Make a beeline straight for the door, she told herself, but she was crippled with awkwardness. She couldn't stand the thought of him thinking she was a tease. Leaving a guy in that condition was kind of mean, wasn't it? Seems it would be painful or at least uncomfortable. If only she were a racy sex kitten. If only she knew just what to do, and say. What would Vixen do? The solution became obvious and made her feel both naughty and nervous.

She looked at Matt and tried to put on a self-assured smile. Whitney had given her some "how to be sexy on stage" tips, but this would be different. It was one thing to look sexy and quite another to *be* sexy. He looked at her, eyebrows raised and drawn close together. I can do this, she told herself while she swiveled the chair around so he faced her. There was something about him that made her feel delicious. She knelt down in front of him and offered up her most seductive look. First he seemed confused, then he busted out laughing.

Humiliation would melt her into a mortified puddle, unless she got out of there before he stopped laughing. Maybe he wouldn't even try to stop. Maybe he would laugh until he grew too old to laugh anymore.

"No, wait." He knelt down with her on the floor. He offered a wide-eyed sorry-I-fucked-up face. "I'm sorry," he said. "But, I mean—I haven't even kissed you yet."

"I'm such a spaz, so not cool," she said, her hands plastered against her hot face. "I have no idea what I'm doing."

He leaned in closer, pried her hands away from her face, and held them. His grip was soft, but his hands felt rough. It took all of her strength just to look at him.

"Please don't try to be that girl," he said, his words slow and deliberate. "It's so cool that you're not that girl." He hesitated, like he had a secret to share. "Do you know how many women have cornered me in the men's room, wanting to give me a back-stall hummer?"

"How many?"

"Never mind." He shook his head. "I'm a jackass for mentioning it. Let's just say a lot."

"And so you turned them all down?" She kept her gaze locked on his.

His half-smile became stiff. He edged in even closer as he whispered, "That's not my point."

She whispered back, "What is your point?"

He moved his hands to her waist and leaned her back against the well-groomed carpet. Some of her hair got caught behind her back, but she didn't want to readjust. She preferred the uncomfortable pull to additional awkwardness. She closed her eyes, and let him breathe her in.

This is what she had needed all along. It was all so sweet at first, and then it intensified and morphed into the most fantastic kiss. Shimmering spots played against the insides of her eyelids. Time turned itself inside out. She relaxed into his hand and felt it glide down the side of her face.

Oh, my God, she thought. He owns me now. I'm going to fall in love with this guy. He's going to tear me apart. But she didn't stop him because she figured it was the kind of heartbreak she ultimately deserved.

Time straightened itself out again. When she opened her eyes, he was staring at her, intense and a little smug. He gave her some space and rested on his side. Yes, she thought, a little distance would be good, so she sat up and scooted back a couple of feet. He put his elbow against the now matted carpet. He brushed it back into position with his fingers then rested his chin in his hand, using his elbow and arm as a base. She held her hand down at her side, away from his black-stubbled cheek. She wanted to pepper his jawline with kisses, but knew that should never happen.

"I've got to go," she said as she pulled herself up like a surfer on a board.

He stood up too, seeming so tall and so close. Now he was the one looking embarrassed. "What? I thought—"

She didn't wait for him to finish. "No, it was perfect."

He softened his stance, leaned in, and put his arms around her waist. "Good, I thought it was damn good. You feel good." The last thing in the world she wanted to do was unwrap herself from his arms, but she did it.

"It was two thumbs up, awesome," she said. "It's just, I've got a ferry to catch."

He tilted his head and pulled his lips in tight, like he wasn't buying it.

"Um, it was so nice meeting you," she added. She couldn't believe the words coming out of her own mouth. He'd kissed her stupid.

She made her escape down the stairs and slid into her shoes. She pulled her coat from the rack. On TV, a narrator with a British accent was explaining the likelihood of the multiverse where infinite galaxies certainly existed. Nick was sitting on the end of the couch with a bong on the table. The room was infused with the smell of ganja. He was twisting his hands around something in his lap and she thought she heard squeaking.

He whirled his face around toward her, startled. "I'm not jerking off, I swear," he said. "I'm making balloon animals." He held up a pale blue dog-like creation. "I made it for you." He got up and walked toward her, looking so serious, so romantic. "Via, will you accept this balloon animal?"

She opened her mouth, but no words came out. He broke out into wild laughter. He could totally be on *The Bachelor*. Seemed like he already was.

Matt stared at them from the bottom of the stairs, but didn't look impressed. Nick turned around, and smirked at him as if to say, "Nee-ner-nee-ner-nee-ner."

Via snatched the balloon away, picked up her purse from the foyer table, and opened the front door. She wanted to say, "I'm sorry, I can't do this. See you never." She was supposed to marry Dan. She shouldn't be dancing or drugging or kissing hot guys. She shouldn't even be accepting balloon animals from hot guys.

Matt tapped on the square post that punctuated the bottom end of the staircase. He looked dejected and she didn't want to hurt his feelings.

She looked to him, over to Nick, and back to him again. "Matt, you have the biggest dick I have ever seen. Thank you for sharing it with me."

She stepped out onto the porch, and as she closed the door behind her she heard Nick let out an extended, "Duude."

She was afraid she had overshot the mark. It wasn't likely Matt appreciated her awkward attempt at humor. That would be for the best anyway, she thought. She wasn't ever coming back. Was she? No. But then why did she feel she was closing the door on something special? Kissing Matt made her feel a resurgence of something lost, something fundamental. She waited a moment on the porch and listened, heard Matt's muffled laughter, then beamed all the way to her car.

# CHAPTER 11

## VIA

**VIA STOOD AGAINST** the rail overlooking the stern of the Tullikum. She would need new gloves, she thought. Like sunglasses, she never paid a lot for them because she had a habit of losing them. Her hands found the lining of her coat pockets, and a bulk of cash. Nick must have put it there while she was upstairs with Matt. It felt good to smile. She looked down at the frothy water pulsating below her. It churned, spreading out into a triangular wake before dissipating into the past. It reminded her of the bubbles in her champagne on her birthday. She would need to start returning her uncle's calls, but the thought of talking about that meeting in New York made her want to jump over the rail. Maybe she was coming down from that line of cocaine she had snorted earlier. That had been stupid. Perhaps she was coming down from that kiss. That had been stupid, too. She looked out into the distance and appreciated the rocky beaches and greenery of Lincoln Park while she could. They were already growing faint as the steel workhorse roared across Puget Sound.

Going home to Vashon didn't feel good to her heart because she just wasn't ready to step back into her uncomfortable world. She wasn't ready to face the approaching holidays. It was Day 89, she realized.

The trees in the distance weren't individual anymore, but a long panel of green draped down toward the shoreline. There had been a time when she'd hated trees. When she had been twelve, new to the Northwest, the sick smell of pine seemed to infiltrate every aspect of her life. What had been left of her life.

Her chest was heavy, and she was reminded of Bethany Christian. Those first few years had been horrendous. As she'd grown up, she had learned to tuck her feelings away because every admission of fear or grief would bring about a prayer circle. "Dear God, we pray for Via as she struggles to understand your plan for her." Poor, poor little Via.

That's where she and Dan met, though he had been two years ahead of her. His attention had been flattering and consistent, so when he headed to Western Washington University in Bellingham, just half an hour away, they decided to keep in contact. When she graduated from high school a year early, she had gone there too, but not for him.

Bellingham had a well-earned reputation as a haven for hippies, progressives, vegan astrologers, and hemp-loving atheists. After six years stuck at Bethany Christian, Via had hoped it would be exactly what she needed. But freshman year had ended up being scary for her. The weight and scope of her father's legacy had become more real. She had known her monthly allowance had come from a trust fund, and had never had any interest in knowing anything more. But after she turned eighteen, her uncle seemed to expect more of her. He wanted her back in New York, but she always managed to weasel out of it. Still, he insisted on explaining the estate. She had gone from knowing it was a multimillion-dollar estate, to understanding it was in the neighborhood of forty million, not including her father's collection, which Uncle Erik was advising her to sell. She learned there were complicated tax issues. She had the loft in SoHo to consider. Her uncle hadn't sold it. He said it would be undignified.

Sophomore year, she had broken her arm, and Dan's innate dependability had become more and more important to her. He had grown up the son of a pastor, having already visited or lived in eighteen different countries. Her trauma had been nothing compared to the stories he told her about children walking five miles for clean well water. Beth, dream mother-in-law, had been the clincher. When Dan proposed, Via knew his kind, supportive family would be part of the package. While Via never asked him outright, she knew Dan had proposed before her college graduation because of his family, his church. He'd wanted to move her back to Vashon and share a house without raising too many eyebrows. More than once she had heard him assuring some church member that they had separate bedrooms. Whatever, he was no angel. He had gotten lost in the middle of the night on his way to the bathroom more than once. Though that was back in June when the wind off the Sound was refreshing. It wasn't even October, yet she could already feel its growing cruelty. The holidays were coming.

She heard the announcement telling passengers to return to their vehicles come over the ferry sound system. West Seattle seemed so far away, already. It was cloaked in mist. Focusing her attention there would be a mistake. She left the rail, pulled her coat tight, and made her way back down to the car deck. She got back into her car and watched as the dock came gliding into view. Vashon was undeniably gorgeous. It had its share of fun-loving hippie progressives. She should make an effort to develop some interests outside of Dan's church. Her eyes locked onto the fast-approaching trees at the end of the dock. Just as green on this side of the water. Don't think about him, she reminded herself. He's not the one for you, Dan is.

# CHAPTER 12

## MATT

**MATT'S FOOTSTEPS** caused a cascade of creaking as he made his way down the wooden basement stairs. He paused at the landing and felt the familiar rounded triangular shape of heavy plastic in his front jeans pocket. He continued down and over toward the old leather couch where Nick, Alicia, and Kaytlyn sat getting stoned. It was four-tongue o'clock, according to the Gene Simmons KISS clock that hung on the back wall next to the washer and dryer. Their guitarist, Josh, and lead vocalist, Jeremy, were late as usual.

Nick loaded another bowl into his Mrs. Butterworth's bong. Though he had several store-bought pipes and bongs, as well as a vaporizer, he also crafted his own stoner paraphernalia. Mrs. Butterworth's Syrup bottles were his specialty. He gave them out at Christmastime the way some people gave out fruitcake. They were precious now that it was hard to find glass bottles.

Matt watched as his friend jumped onto the two-foot-high stage, which ran the length of the room. They had insulated the walls with foam, so their sets sounded pretty tight. Nick sat on his drum throne and the girls perked up, no surprise. Women seemed to smell future fame. "Hey man," he yelled down. "I want to talk balloon animals." His tone was serious though he wore a stoner's grin.

The girls exchanged quizzical glances, but said nothing. They sat, seemingly mesmerized by Nick's warm up stretches, which were the very same every time. Matt was an obsessive-compulsive, which made him an expert in noticing the repetitive rituals of others. Before playing, Nick always bent his neck to the right and then turned his head to the right, same on the other side. Next, he moved on to his wrist and finger stretches.

"Imagine if you will," Nick explained from his perch. "I'll create a balloon animal in seven seconds or less while Mike Dirnt here plays his 'Welcome to Paradise' bass solo." He leaned over and grabbed drumsticks from the bag next to his floor tom.

"Which one is he again?" Kaytlyn asked. As usual, her voice creaked like she was a Kardashian cousin. "The Nirvana drummer you're in love with?"

Nick held his sticks just above the snare and released them into a subtle roll. His eyebrows hunched in and highlighted his annoyance. "No, that would be Dave Grohl," he said. He enunciated each syllable like he was talking to a Special Ed class.

Kaytlyn looked confused, like she didn't even know who Dave Grohl was. Matt took this as evidence she was the president of his Girls I Wish I'd Never Fucked club. He didn't expect her to know every Foo Fighters song by heart, but Nick talked about Dave Grohl all the time.

"You guys act so old," she said. "You never listen to anything new."

Matt just shook his head and awaited the incoming burn. Kaytlyn would need more than a sharp mouth and two-inch eyelashes to stand her ground in this arena.

"We're in a nineties cover band, and so, duh on your part, Kandy Cane," Nick called down. He stopped to tighten the bolt on his hi-hat. "You lose ten groupie points."

Matt found Kaytlyn's stripper name fitting. When he had first met her, she had seemed a tasty treat, but the rush was short-lived. Now she just made him sick. He picked up his backup bass from the stand next to the couch and put the strap over his neck. It was an old caramel-colored Squier in decent shape; it would need to be restrung soon. He used a microfiber cloth to rub away the pre-dust he feared would form on the neck and listened to his music-snob friend's snarkfest.

"Too bad Cobain was the only musical genius to ever come out of our little corner of the country," Nick began. The girls both jumped when he hit the base drum pedal, powered through the toms, and hit the crash symbol twice. Crash! Crash! "Oh, wait," he added. "There was that Jimi Hendersen guy. He was alright."

Alicia caught on. "Jimi Hendrix," she yelled out like a game show contestant. Nick gave her a nod, and then hit a double-snare-cymbal rim shot in her honor—da-dant-ching.

"Thanks, little lady. We also would have accepted The Melvins, Mud Honey, Death Cab for Cutie, Alice in Chains, Sound Garden, and then there's..." Nick paused to give them a literal drum roll. "Pearl Jam. Technically, Nirvana wasn't a Seattle band," he said, coming off like the Seattle-sound snob that he was. "Aberdeen gets credit there, and DC."

Matt frowned. "To infinity, okay? You'll never name every Seattle-area band." He swallowed hard. Son of a bitch. That old familiar feeling sprang from his stomach, into his throat. He needed to refocus on something else before his compulsive madness could take hold.

"You forgot to mention Macklemore and Ryan Lewis," Alicia said. "And Sir-Mix-A-Lot."

"Please don't encourage him," Matt told her. He tried to keep his voice kind and calm. Nick was in a cougar phase, so Alicia was high on his wish list at the moment—he'd been calling her Alley Cat and fetching her lattes. They saved their best behavior for chicks they hadn't nailed yet. That's when women held the most power.

"I'm good," Matt mumbled, trying to inconspicuously soothe his nerves. "I'm good. I'm good," he told himself. Intellectually, he knew it was stupid. But what if they forget to mention a band and then something horrific happened to any of its members? He would have to live with himself.

But Nick wouldn't shut up. "Alley Cat, you remember the Screaming Trees, out of Ellensburg? I can totally see you as a grunge girl."

Don't panic, Matt told himself. Nick was branching out to Eastern Washington now. That meant the whole state was now in play. What about all of the Olympia bands, all of the riot grrrl bands?

"Sleater-Kinney," Matt screamed up to Nick, who responded with a what's-your-damage head tilt. Matt just kept going. "And Bikini Kill." His throat began to itch, and his cheeks and his neck. "Shit, who else?" And then it hit him. "Ah hell, and Kenny G."

Nick brought his sticks down and shot back a look of concerned recognition, like he could feel Matt's desperation flooding the stage. "Hey, it's cool," he assured him. "We'll do it later today—name them all. Later though, okay?"

"And Mother Love Bone." His brain was flaming out. "Candlebox. Mad Season. Unnatural Helpers. Who else? Modest Mouse. The Presidents of the United States of America." And he couldn't forget their quirky favorites. "Yuni in Taxco," he added. "Pickwick."

"Dude, stop it," Nick was saying.

But he couldn't just stop. What about the dozens of local bands Obliviot had opened for? He swiped the back of his hand across his sweaty forehead. God, he realized. "Obliviot!"

"That's enough," Nick said. He was leaning forward on his stool now. "We'll google that shit later. Promise. Be cool, alright, Matty?"

Nick called him Matty when he was seriously worried. Nobody else was ever allowed to call him that. It worked though, like a slap in the face. Time to chill. He took in a slow breath. "Cool," he said, just under his breath. "Cool, cool." That feeling faded in defeat, crawling back down into his stomach. And, just like that, it was gone.

Nick got back to business and made his way down the toms, then to the crash, then back again. A dirty grin sprang to his face as he leaned forward, reached out his hand, and stilled the crash. "So, dude," he said. "The other morning, Short Skirt, Long Jacket, called me Tré Cool." He twisted his face and stuck out his tongue. "I'm thinkin' she has a thing for drummers." He punctuated his point with some "Blister in the Sun" snare—da-dant, da-dant!

Alicia started humming the classic Violent Femmes song.

"See?" Nick asked him. "See, that part makes that whole song." His sticks issued another da-dant, da-dant against the snare. "How could Short Skirt not be vibin' me?"

Kaytlyn interrupted, "Who are you talking about?"

Before Matt could decide how to answer, Nick tossed down a save. "Think drummer, think Green Day."

"I mean Short Skirt."

Matt joined in. "Short Skirt, Long Jacket. You know, like the Cake song."

Nick yelled down, "Ooh, Kandy Cane, I have another one. Who played bass for Guns N' Roses?"

She shrugged and glared back at him, but said nothing.

"Come on...guess," Nick taunted her. He began humming the Jeopardy time-is-almost-out song. "He's from Sea-aaa-ttle!"

Matt could see they had pushed her too far, so he shot Nick a stop-being-an-assclown glare.

Nick stopped humming and yelled down, "Buzzz. I'm sorry, but you're out of time. The question we were looking for was 'Who is Duff McKagen?'" He hit the bass drum twice for effect. "Part of Seattle's punk scene before it was cool, then on to Guns N' Roses, Jane's Addiction, Velvet Revolver—"

"Shut the *hell* up already!" Matt yelled.

Nick scowled, then offered an obnoxious cock of his head. "And Walking Papers," he added. "Okay, now back to balloon animals."

Alicia laughed, but Kaytlyn just flipped her hair back, and whined, "You guys are so old."

Nick ignored her and zeroed in on Alicia. "So, Autumn-Alley Cat, you should come back after work tonight." His sticks hovered above the snare. He released enough tension so they fell and rebounded, slow at first. "We can go up to my room and make balloon animals." He brought them to a fast, firm roll, then hit the hi-hat. Then back around the toms.

Alicia's smile could not have been any wider. Matt looked on, jealous. Women seemed to love his friend's corny sense of humor. Nick wore I-don't-give-a-fuck like cologne. It pulled Alicia up onto the stage. She was asking him about the ink on his right arm—Animal from the Muppets. She went around the drum kit and he leaned toward her so she could examine it. Nick lowered his voice. Matt had to laugh—so typical. Nick was probably reeling her in, telling her he had more body art, under his shirt. Matt smiled and shot his friend a tip-of-the-hat look. But then he sensed Kaytlyn.

Matt looked over to see her hips swaying in his direction and was caught in her wide-eyed seduction. He couldn't help but appreciate the way her boobs were heaving out of her pink bra, which was peeking out through her delicate black blouse. A few months back they had hooked up for a while. While she had been fun, the whole thing seemed way too convenient. Even the hottest girls lost their appeal when they tried too hard. He hadn't touched her since he heard she was one of Carlos's back-office sex toys, which made her ineligible to maintain her friends-with-benefits status. He wasn't naïve enough to think girls were virgins, but he didn't want to have a visual. He also loathed that yeah-I-fucked-her-too look that passed from man to man.

She took another step closer. "Your strap is crooked. Let me fix it."

He tensed. It wasn't crooked. He would know. He shifted his weight away from her. "I don't like people touching my stuff," he said, using a tone much harsher than he'd intended.

"You used to like me touching," she gazed up and whispered, "your stuff."

No doubt, the girl had some skills, and she knew it. Black eyeliner made its way across her lids and leapt out toward her temples. She rested her hand on his ass. He wished he could vanish out of the situation and go anywhere else in the world. He would rather clean the couches in the Hotties champagne room after a bachelor party than have to reject a girl right to her face.

Josh was coming in through the side door, and Matt saw his escape. "Hey, man, nice of you to join us," he said as he got up on stage.

Kaytlyn returned to the couch as though she had been scolded for trying to steal a cookie. Maybe he was a jackass, but Matt didn't bother to console her. Mixed messages would be bad. Instead, he turned his attention to the guys. Within a few minutes, just as he had hoped, the girls left without any drama. Nick and Josh walked them out to Alicia's car while Matt remained on stage, muttered, "Bye ladies," and admired his bass as if it was the most fascinating thing in the world. Sometimes he was obsessive, but more often than not, he just didn't want to deal with people.

He positioned a folding chair in his usual spot. It was just upstage and to the right of the drum set. The stage was painted black, but there were three parallel indentations where his bass stand rested. He liked to be halfway between those marks and the drum set. He began tuning his bass, gently resting his pointer finger on the E string and his ring finger on the A string. Growing up, he had dreamed about being on stage playing his bass in front of a sea of enthused fans. He had *not* dreamed about driving keys of cocaine across state lines. Looking back, it was one of those minor decisions he'd made with little consideration.

She came to him again, the way she had smiled. Why was he thinking about this girl so much? She's engaged. Engaged wasn't married, he told himself. She felt lucky somehow. Fuzzy lyrics made their way into his mind.

He wanted to figure out a way to get to know her outside of the club, in broad daylight where he could make out who she really was.

The home tour...

He would call and ask her to help, maybe bring some food. He felt a hopeful smile lift his cheeks. Every year since he could remember, strangers had trounced through G-Dane's house and "oohed" and "ahhed" over the woodwork. Everyone said the staircase was a treasure. This would be the first year that Nick's grandmother would be coming as a guest. Of course, it would always be her house, but he and Nick, and hopefully Via, would act as hosts for the day. She didn't know yet that he and Nick were both decent cooks, that they were perfectly able to entertain the tourists. Just a little white lie. What could it hurt?

# Chapter 13

## Via

**VIA PARKED** across the street, not sure how many cars would be coming and going throughout the day. She was twenty minutes late, for no particular reason other than she had changed her clothes four times. She would blame the ferry.

Her hands were clammy. Her tongue burned from the mint in her mouth. Why was she so nervous?

Day 78, she realized.

Don't think about it, she scolded herself as she opened the trunk and grabbed the mini quiches and baby lemon pies, two trays of each. Should she take two trips? Probably. But the morning air was cold. She had forgotten her gloves.

The house looked so dramatic draped in morning fog. The yard was beyond impressive, though those rust-colored trees she had admired before were now just skeletons. The guys must have had a grand old time raking them all.

She started down the walkway and remembered how she had run right into Matt that first morning. At the time, she'd never thought she'd see him again, yet here she was. She couldn't tell him no when he called. He needed her help. She could never resist the "H word."

She was startled by hissing behind her. What the—? Something was nipping at her ankles. Dogs? She shrieked and ran up the porch steps. They were right on her heels, relentless. Her foot caught on the top step. She bit it, fell to her knees, and watched her goody trays tumble out over the porch. More hissing. Afraid to look, she screamed.

The front door opened and Matt looked out through the screen door, his brows furrowed together in confusion. "What the fuck?"

He opened the screen door enough for her to squeeze through then closed it. She slid up next to him. He put his arm around her. From the safe side of the screen door they watched two raccoons tear apart quiches and pies. Lemon pudding covered their claws and whiskers. A third paced back and forth. Crazed. It bobbed its head from side to side. A fourth hunkered down under a porch chair, licking a cake pan.

"I can't believe this," he said, pulling her hands into his. "Did they bite you?"

She had to think about it. "No," she said. Embarrassment seeped through her whole body. Had she really screamed like that? Were they rabid? Her knee hurt from the fall, but she was too embarrassed to mention it. Her mind was a whirl.

"Wild raccoons in West Seattle?" she asked him.

Nick was there. "What the fuck?" They gave him room to look out through the screen door. The hissing got louder again. One of the raccoons was zooming back and forth from one end of the porch to the other.

Matt shot Nick a look.

"No. You think?" Nick asked.

"Has to be. Special treats from your Betty Crocker Stalker."

Matt let out a little laugh, which led to another. Nick shoved him so hard he let go of Via.

"It's not funny," Nick scolded him. "Stop laughing, chucklehead."

"I don't get it," she said.

Matt spoke right over her. "G-Dane will be here any minute. What should we do? A broom?"

"No."

"Should I get my acoustic?" Matt asked, still snickering. "Play them some Eagles?"

"No, wait. I know." Nick ran upstairs.

"This girl, she creeps on Nick—hard. She's always leaving brownies and cookies on the porch," Matt explained. "We just toss them. God knows what's in them—roofies, PCP."

"The raccoons are high?"

"Hope it's just weed."

Nick came back with a big firecracker and a lighter. "Get back."

"M-80?" Matt asked. "You can't, you can't, they'll go deaf!"

Nick opened the door, lit the fuse, tossed it out onto the porch, and closed the door again. "No way I'm letting tweaker raccoons bite my grandma!"

Matt pulled Via back, deeper into the living room. Nick joined them and they watched through the front window. Boom! Raccoons bolted and scattered in all directions.

"One, two," Nick counted, "three, four. They all seem okay."

Matt scrunched up his face. "That's so messed up. They are freaking out, high as fuck. Where they off to now? Did you even think about that?"

"As long as they stay gone 'til four," Nick said.

"Bro, I told you to talk to that girl."

"Oh no," Via realized. "The food."

Matt opened the front door. They all peeked out onto the porch.

Slivers of aluminum foil were scattered about among splotches of whipped cream and lemon. She could only see three of the pans.

A white minivan was pulling up. The lettering on its side read "Wesley Gardens."

"Ah, fuck me all to hell," Nick grumbled as he sprinted down the walkway.

"I'll grab a mop," Matt told her. "My favorite is in the basement." She wondered how many mops he owned while she collected pans and ran them into the kitchen. By the time she got back to the porch, Nick was coming up the walkway with a one-hundred-pound, white-haired old lady in his arms. Gently, he set her down at the front door.

"Oh my Goddess! What on earth?" she asked when she saw the mess on the porch.

"Raccoons," Nick told her. "Jumped Via here. Scarfed down the food she brought."

The old woman let out a chuckle, which calmed Via's nerves.

"Hi, G-Dane." It was Matt, there with a quick hug. His voice was bright. "I want you to meet Via."

"Via? What a lovely name," she said, her wrinkled pink lips curled up into a kind smile. The little woman shuffled into the house, her face crinkled in adorable determination. She seemed far too young to be using a walker. Her bold turquoise necklace popped against her ivory sweater. Her pants and shoes were basic black. "Sorry, dear, those little buggers have been a pain ever since the neighbor boys threw away their science experiment. Didn't close the garbage lid down tight."

Nick directed them all into the living room. Grandma Daney and a dark-haired woman, whom Nick introduced as Nurse Amy, sat on the couch next to the fireplace.

Curious, Via had to ask. "Science experiment?"

"A three-foot-high volcano made out of Oreo cookies, and it didn't make it through the night. I hope they didn't nip you. They could have rabies."

"No, not a scratch."

"People are going to be here any minute," Nick said. "Dude, will you make the cider? I'll make a Thriftway run?"

"Done," Matt assured him. "I'm sure the ladies will have a good time getting to know each other." On his way through the dining room, he turned and told Via, "She's ultra-granola, thoroughly groovy."

"The house looks lovely," Grandma Daney said as she took in the room. "It feels so good to be home. The energy is so beautiful here."

Via just smiled, sensing Grandma Daney had more to say.

"My grandfather built this house for my mother," she said, looking toward the staircase. "There is love in every colonnade, every beam. He attended to every little detail." She closed her eyes, inhaled, and held it. Then she smiled and exhaled, calm and sure. "I'm ready," she said. She opened her eyes again and smiled in Via's direction. "People can come now."

Looking back into Grandma Daney's thoughtful, pale eyes, Via instantly adored her. The old woman sat with her hands together in her lap. When Via saw the way they trembled she wanted to hold them, ground them in her own. God, if only she could have known her own grandmothers.

"I'm beaming love in your direction," Grandma Daney said. "Can you feel it?"

She could.

Before anyone could say another word, there was a solid knock at the door.

\* \* \*

# VIA

IT HAD BEEN a long day, but even after three-dozen tourists, Nick's grandmother didn't seem the least bit tired. Nick said she was seventy-one and healthy, except for the Parkinson's, which is why her hands shook so terribly. Nurse Amy seemed to be there every hour with another pill. Nick said the medication she took for the shaking made her nauseous and the medication for the nausea made her drowsy. Apparently not today. Her cheeks were rosy, her laughter, frequent.

The porch stairs were a problem, but it seemed like they could easily build a ramp. She would ask Matt about that later. For now, she was happy to stand back and listen to Grandma Daney talk about the house her grandfather had built back in 1916. The latest visitor was a plump middle-aged woman, nice enough.

"Yes, it's true some of the current wall paint is not in keeping with the Craftsman style, perhaps it's a bit bright, but I'm not a fan of mustard yellow, and after all, the Craftsman movement itself was about artistic freedom."

The middle-aged woman smiled. "The ceiling beams and built-ins are gorgeous. The window seats are lovely. But it's a shame you've remodeled the kitchen. The island, and all."

Grandma Daney laughed in the woman's face. "That remodel got me a dishwasher. That's progress. Now please, help yourself to some apple cider. It was so nice meeting you. Namaste." She led Via over to the couch where Nurse Amy sat hunched over, hyper-focused on her phone. "Namaste is what I tell people when I want them to go away," she said. "Now, we finally have a moment to ourselves. Let's sit and chat. Did the boys tell you I can see auras?"

"No. Can you?"

"Auras, orbs, lights—everyone can. We can see anything—anything we are open to, that is. I can see you are a seeker, an Indigo Child, perhaps."

"A what?"

"Special spirits," she said. "Born wise beyond their years—curious, empathetic, creative, intuitive. Mattais is one, for sure. It makes sense he would attract another into his experience."

Intrigued, she turned and looked toward the kitchen, but she couldn't see either of the guys. She turned back. "Special spirit? You can tell that, just by looking at me?"

"I can feel your soul force. It's delightful." Grandma Daney smiled. "You have an energy blockage though. Fourth chakra—that's your heart."

She brought her hand up to her heart. "And?" she asked. "Is there a cure?"

"Oh, of course," Grandma Daney said. "People block off their life's energy, their inner power, all the time." She leaned forward.

Via did too, her hand still against her heart.

"Dear, I'm guessing you tend to be hard on yourself. This life isn't everything, you know. Don't take it all so seriously. Have fun."

"This life?"

"Yes, we are all spiritual beings, having human experiences. Remember, you are eternal. This is just a life you're having."

"You believe in reincarnation?" Wouldn't that be wonderful? Another shot at a happy childhood. Maybe in her next lifetime.

"I prefer the concept of nonlinear time," Grandma Daney said, eyes shimmering. "The power of now. Countless lifetimes, all happening right now."

"Mrs. Daney, please," Nurse Amy said, putting her phone away. "You'll scare her. She's not used to your new age, law of attraction, great awakening rantings."

"She's not scared, and she must be very special to have Mattais doting on her."

True, he had been in to refill her cider, more than once. She loved the way he looked at her. Like he didn't care what other people thought. Dan wouldn't even hold her hand in public.

"He's a sweetheart," Grandma Daney added. "Brilliant, actually, but—"

"But?" Via's chest felt heavy. "But what?"

"I'm afraid he was born to parents who don't understand him. He's a nonconformist. Creative types always are."

"His parents?" she asked. "I don't know anything about them."

"They're wonderful. Live in Phoenix now. They didn't know how to handle his sensitive nature. Poetry and painting soothed him; they wanted football. He didn't go to college and that was challenging for them to accept. Though, life is our ultimate classroom."

"That's enough," Nurse Amy said. "Please stop it. I'm embarrassed for him."

"Sorry, I don't mean to gush, but I am so fond of Mattais," Grandma Daney said warmly. "So, tell me, how did you two meet? I bet it's a cute story."

# CHAPTER 14

## VIA

**BURTON COMMUNITY CHURCH** didn't look much like a church from the road. It had no steeple. It lacked a prominent cross. Its windows were clear and offered no inspiring stained glass portrayals of Jesus Christ in all his glory. Dan had promised her BCC was becoming more and more progressive, but she wasn't so sure. Its board of elders was made up of a bunch of old, white men. While there was a rainbow banner hanging outside, she couldn't help but feel some holier-than-thou resistance, especially from the older parishioners. Dan said it would be a process and to be patient. He encouraged her to focus on the next generation, which she did. She strived to preach tolerance while they were still young enough to grasp it.

The lobby was quiet, thank God. Pastor King was still on announcements, the weekly laundry list of the ails of the congregation, so everyone knew who to pray for and why. Via's youth group puking-fainting incident three weeks earlier had landed her on that damned list. She had claimed a wicked stomach flu, though she had heard the pastor's bitchy wife Sarah had been fanning rumors of an unwed pregnancy.

She opened the church nursery door with care so the jingle bell wouldn't wake up any sleeping babies.

"Thanks so much for coming in," Beth said, relief evident in her voice. Beth was her kind of Christian—upbeat, but not too chipper.

She felt herself snap into Church Via mode—responsible, respectable. Lies, lies, lies, she thought. She was at church, after all, the place where little white lies popped out of her mouth by the dozen. Yes, this raspberry torte is delicious; it's impressive you know the book of John by heart; my, your daughter is lovely. Being nice all the time was exhausting.

Beth handed her a baby named Sophia with pink splotchy cheeks and a mess of brown curls. Via had very little experience with babies. In fact, they made her nervous. What if she dropped one? She pulled the baby in and nestled her, taking in the scent of her sweet skin. Her little tendrils smelled like baby shampoo, until she began to smell a new aroma, sweet yet foul.

"I think she may need a change," Beth added, apologetically.

Crap, literally. She had never actually changed a poopy diaper; she'd dodged the issue a couple weeks back using the same handoff maneuver Beth had just pulled on her. But this time there was no way around it, short of pulling the fire alarm. Her future mother-in-law was going to see firsthand that she sucked at caring for babies. Maybe it won't be so bad, she prayed to the painting of gentle Jesus on the wall. It was her favorite Jesus: the one surrounded by little children.

She put the baby down and pulled out the changing supplies. Dan's mother was already talking about something, Dan maybe. She slipped off Sophia's little shoes and tights and reached over for the plastic tub of baby wipes. The baby crinkled her eyes for a moment and then frowned, thrusting out her arms and legs. It was like she could tell her baby business wasn't in good hands.

Via smiled down, but the baby wasn't having any of it. Her spastic legs were making the wiping-of-the-poop process impossible.

"Why do parents insist on dressing baby girls in full-on Easter dresses and tights every single Sunday?" she asked Beth. "These ruffles are a nightmare." Sophia kicked again and poop smeared inside her frilly tights. "I can't do this. Help!" Via confessed, her horrendous mothering skills on full display, right in front of Dan's mother.

Beth looked horrified, rushed up, and placed the other baby in Via's arms while nudging her out of the way. "Gosh, let me get her for you."

The new baby's face was round, red, and concerned.

"Please don't cry," Via whispered. "I'll sit and rock with you, okay?"

The baby relaxed against her and grabbed onto some of her hair. Go ahead, Via thought. As long as you don't cry.

She couldn't change a diaper, but at least she could change the subject. "Beth, do you ever wonder if maybe babies are the enlightened ones?"

"What do you mean?"

It was something Grandma Daney had mentioned the day before, that life was just an instinctual dumbing-down process. Life on earth was a timeout from eternal enlightenment. It made sense to Via because she felt like the older she got the less she seemed to know. Maybe death was just the remembering of what people knew before they were born. She sure hoped that was the case because then the details of her life wouldn't be so disastrous. Dying for her would be like waking up from a nightmare.

"Like, what if babies know the meaning of life, but forget it as they get older. So when we think we are teaching them, we are actually distracting them."

Grandma Daney had said it was the reason children were better at living in the moment. They hadn't forgotten how to play yet. What a cool woman.

Beth didn't say anything, just put the tights into a Ziplock bag. She wiped down the baby and set her in one of the lullaby swings. Still silent, she pulled the sheet off of the changing table, put that into another bag, and then rubbed her hands with sanitizer.

It was quiet except for the creaking of Via's chair.

"I'm sorry, Beth. Did that sound crazy?"

"Don't worry about that," Beth said. "I've been meaning to talk to you about something much more important."

Via felt relief fall upon her until Beth came over and sat down in the rocking chair next to hers. "Sweetheart, I am so sorry about your parents. Such a tragedy."

The word "tragedy" scared away that sense of relief before it could take hold. Now, she was desperate to disappear, to be raptured up to heaven in a white pillar of smoke. No. He didn't, she told herself. He wouldn't. Had he really outed her? He had promised never to tell a soul, not until she was ready.

"Dan called in this morning and prayed with the Elders about you. He said the holidays are hard for you. Gosh, we can all see why."

The elders knew? The Pastor and his bitchy wife Sarah knew?

"He wants us to keep you company, keep you busy," Beth went on.

He had promised not to tell. Vashon was supposed to be a fresh start, a place where nobody would know about her past. She bit the inside of her lip until she tasted blood. She would keep her church face on, sit and half-listen. She took in the gurgling miracle in her lap. Was she really going to marry Dan, have his babies?

She needed to venture off somewhere else, in her mind. She imagined being high out of her skull. She thought about Matt and the drug Molly he mentioned. Thinking about him, the way he looked at her, made her feel safe and uneasy at the same time. He had given her a rain check. He hadn't mentioned it at the home tour; they hadn't had any alone time. But still, she assumed it was a standing offer. Ecstasy, what a great name for a drug.

Beth kept talking. The baby on Via's lap had fallen asleep while grasping a handful of her hair. Though she wanted to tell her well-meaning future mother-in-law to shut her trap, it was impossible. She gave a subtle smile, looked just over Beth's head, and felt her eyes soften into the rainbow that spanned the wall behind her. G-Dane said the way to see auras was to soften your gaze. They hadn't had time to talk about orbs and lights. Her pretty lights, she was desperate for them. Where were they now?

It was Day 77. How was she ever going to make it?

Matt. She would think about him. He had texted that morning. He wanted to see her again. That knowledge felt amazing.

The repetitive creaking of their chairs punctuated Beth's pity. Via heard wind chimes from somewhere outside. Her body continued to rock, her arms continued to hold, but her throat tightened. She braced herself for that damned expression. If Beth says it, it's a sign, she told herself. If she says those words, it's God's permission to go back and take him up on his offer. Say it. Say it, she thought. Her heart rate sped up.

And then those tired, trite words popped out of Beth's well-meaning mouth.

"We have all been praying for you."

# CHAPTER 15

## VIA

**SHE SAT AT** the dining room table and admired the teacups on display in the dark lacquered hutch in the corner. Each sat upon its saucer. Some were edged in gold, others had flower designs. No doubt they were Grandma Daney's, safe and sound behind the cabinet's thin glass door.

Her stomach was iffy. Mind over matter, she told herself. She wanted to be a bad girl. She wanted to play Vixen again. She needed to psych herself up. Had she really just called him like that? She was back in the house that was beginning to feel like home. Just that easy. Well, not that easy, exactly. Nick had pulled him into the kitchen. She could hear their discussion.

"Dude, you are not thinking this through," Nick was saying. "Rolling with a girl you're already super into."

"Why would I want to waste Molly on a girl I *wasn't* into? Listen to yourself."

"She's engaged."

"She's not married yet, and she's too young anyway."

Nick laughed hard. "You're doing her a favor then?"

"Maybe."

Maybe, she thought. She couldn't wait to find out. Fate was in motion. She would blame fate. Like the real Violetta, it wasn't her fault. It was the role her parents had chosen for her. In *La Traviata* they used the word courtesan, but it didn't matter. Whatever—courtesan, bad girl, party girl, whore—whatever.

"She's gonna burn you," Nick said. "Do *not* tell her you love her."

"Got it," Matt said, in a snotty little kid voice. "Can I tell her I like her?"

"Fine, bro, laugh it off. Just remember I warned you."

"She's waiting. Can I go now?"

"Does she know what she's in for? She said she's never dropped before."

"What's up, Nick? You crushin' on her?"

"Nah, whatever. Just concerned."

"Why do you get so goddamned moral when your dick isn't involved?"

Finally, she spoke up. "Guys, I can kind of hear you." She was dying to ask Nick what he had meant when he'd said 'balance of power,' but decided against it when she saw them come back into the living room. Neither looked happy.

Matt came over and handed her an icy glass of water. "I want to explain this all to you, what it will be like, and then you can decide."

She took a sip. "Okay, I want to." She had already decided.

"No wait," Matt said. "We'll be high for five or six hours, but you shouldn't drive for eight, just in case. You should stay the night."

"Okay." She didn't have anywhere to be.

"Doing Ecstasy or acid or anything like that is serious." He had taken on the tone of a high school principal. "Never, ever, roll with somebody you don't know or trust. You have to make sure you are in a safe environment. No walking around in parks."

"Roll?" She just wanted to get on with it before she changed her mind.

"They call it rolling because the high comes in waves," Nick said. "It's cool that way. You'll think it's mellowing out and then another peak will hit."

"Great."

"This is super pure so there won't be any side effects other than maybe a slight headache, again, I would never do tabs," Matt continued. "They can be sketchy."

"Tabs?"

"Tablets," Nick said. "When most people do E, they take a pill. Some are strong, bound to jack you up, some are okay, but most are cut with a bunch of shit. That's what makes people feel like ass when they come down."

"You swear a lot," she told him in an attempt to mellow his hard expression, but if anything, he looked more annoyed.

"Then there's Molly," Matt said. "It's pure MDMA powder. Now, a lot of people will claim they have Molly, but it's just ground up tabs. Crap included."

"Fine. And?"

"I have unadulterated MDMA," Matt said, beaming. "It's the shit. You'll just dip your pinkie in it and take the slightest bit onto your tongue, then wait half an hour. The guys in Portland said it's the best they've seen in a long time."

"I feel honored."

"You should," Matt said. "But you have to trust me."

She noticed Nick was trying to get Matt's attention. "And?" Nick asked.

Matt shot him a dirty look. "And," Matt said. "We're probably going to have sex."

"Probably a lot," Nick added.

She let out a nervous laugh.

"I'm just saying. If you aren't up for that, tell me now," Matt said. "It would kind of suck to drop and then have to restrain myself, but I totally will. I've done it before. Usually, people do Molly in groups— blow bubbles, go dancing, discuss life. It's a bonding thing for sure."

"Maybe I'm up for sex with you." Saying the words revived her resolve.

"Really?" The guys asked at the same time. She drank down half of her water and wondered why projecting brazen craziness should feel so good. Maybe it was because they didn't know her. They didn't know they should feel sorry for her. She could be anyone now. Matt was looking at her, his eyebrows raised like he wasn't quite sure. If he only knew about the erotic episodes that had been playing inside her head since that kiss. She could still taste him.

Nick got up. "I'm gone," he said and made his way for the door. "Before things here get freaky." He grabbed his coat from the rack and his keys from the skinny table at the bottom of the staircase.

"Love to G-Dane," Matt said. "Make sure it's a nice, long visit."

Nick smiled and gave a little-girl curtsy, but then stopped and looked quite serious. "Dude, make sure she drinks a lot of water, and

Via, stay away from my drum set." He shook his head as he took the blue beanie from his coat pocket and put in on, pulling it down over his ears. "Later."

"Tater," she shot back, hopefully.

He was supposed to say, "tot," but he just left.

"Cool," Matt said before the door had even closed. "I'm going to go get it." He ran up the stairs, but stopped just before reaching the landing.

"And don't worry," he yelled down over the banister. "This won't just be sex. It's about bonding, sharing secrets."

"Secrets?"

*  *  *

# VIA

"I'LL NEVER TELL YOU," she said. "Never, never."

"Tell me," he said. "What perfume do you wear?"

"I'll never tell you," she said. "You'll figure it out someday."

They sat together on the living room floor, swimming in a sea of record albums. Alice in Chains blasted through the speakers.

"How about the Beastie Boys?" she asked.

He frowned. "Sorry, they're outstanding, but I don't have them on vinyl, and we have the Beatles or maybe...." He was holding up a B-52s album in one hand and a B.B. King album in the other.

"Okay, it all sounds amazing to me," she said. "Are we going all the way to ZZ Top?"

"Zappa," he said. "All the way to Zappa."

Overcome with appreciation, she watched him switch out Alice in Chains for the Beatles. What were the odds? That Hotties sign had pointed her right to him. It had to have been for a reason.

"I'm so happy you're here with me," she said.

"Truth, except, you are here with me," he said. "This is my reality. But then again, I guess that in your reality, I am there with you."

Her cheeks hurt because she had been smiling so hard for so long. It was okay though. Everything was absolutely okay.

He came back and sat in front of her. He leaned in close. "Reality is in the eye of the beholder," he told her, their faces a foot apart. His pupils were expansive. "Did you know LSD was once used in couples counseling?" he asked. "Back in the day, before the government cracked down. It helps people access their feelings. It's not like alcohol or weed — we won't forget this, how we feel right now. We'll always remember this."

She swore she could smell his pheromones.

"Now is always now," she said. "It's bizarre when you think about it. Now is all we have because it's always now."

"Forever is now," he said.

"Yes, exactly."

"I know what you're thinking," he said. "Why did I meet this random guy?"

Astounded, she wondered how he knew.

"I'm exactly who you need right now," he said.

Wow, she thought as she took in his words. He spoke the language of her soul. She leaned back and admired the precise geometric shapes etched into the living room's wood paneling. The same paneling continued through the dining room, but fell short of the kitchen.

"I'll write songs about you," he said.

"What if we're like Tristan and Isolde and we fall in love today?"

"Tristan and Isoldey who?"

Opera, she thought. She wanted to share with him what it used to mean to her — and to her parents, how they reveled in its emotion. She wanted to tell him how it had suited her father's flair for the fantastic — his critics called him grandiose — and how her mother had sympathized with the crest-fallen divas.

"It's an opera," Via said. "Wagner. It's complicated."

"Give me a ten-word rundown."

She doubled over with laughter until her stomach hurt. "You want me to explain Wagner in ten words?"

"Come on. It'll be fun," he said. "Try."

She thought about it and said, "Girl accidentally takes love potion with fiancé's nephew. Heartbreak ensues."

His eyes darted up toward the ceiling for a moment, calculating. "That was eleven unless heartbreak is one word," he said. "Eleven is a good number. Two ones, I like repeating numbers."

"Crazy you say that, because I don't like the number four," she said.

"Yes, I'm crazy," he said, his voice sure. "We'll need to talk about that, but first let's start with *your* craziness. Four is considered unlucky in China," he said. "Nick and I watched a show on the Discovery Channel. It sounds a lot like the Chinese word for death."

No doubt, that was the truth. The shooting had been four days before Christmas. And that clock, her mother's antique Swedish clock, had chimed four just before the gunfire. She had forgotten all about that old clock. Why was she thinking of it now? It was so odd. Some details were so clear, while others were cast in shadows a million miles away.

And another memory befell her, right into her lap. She was outside her father's studio door—sitting on the floor, back against the wall, her feet pulled into her chest. The Verdi was loud. She was just waiting, wondering if Daddy was ever going to paint her picture. He used to say, "Violetta, you are growing up so fast, I must paint your portrait before you grow up." Those were the happy days when he listened to Verdi or Mozart or Vivaldi. When he made promises.

How had the universe prodded her ahead, past the number four, and looped back around to opera again? Back to her parents, and their last year. Lately it seemed everything brought her back to her parents. Her mother was so beautiful. She wanted to be beautiful.

"Hey, Isoldey," he was saying. "Where did you go? You just full-on zoned out on me."

"I'm so sorry," she said. Her sincerity was absolute. Being in the past was hard work, and she wanted to play instead.

"We understand each other," he said. "You're not crazy to me and I don't feel so crazy when you're around."

"Like we cancel out each other's insanity," she said. "Can two negatives make a positive?"

"We can make whatever we want," he said. "Forever is now, so let's just remember how we feel right now and we'll always be good, okay, Isoldey? I'll love you in a free way."

"You want to love me on a freeway?" He had thrown a bucket of happiness in her face, and she was drenched. She closed her eyes and laughed for what felt like an hour. Time kept speeding up and slowing down. Her eyes were watering.

He was changing the music again. "Did I miss the Clash?"

"No, this is the happiest song in the world—ever," he said. "Jimmy Cliff."

"I Can See Clearly Now" floated through the speakers and ruffled the air around them.

She climbed up into his lap and straddled him. "You really like old music, huh?"

He nodded and closed his eyes while she brought her hands up to his cheeks and investigated the dark stubble on his face. It was sharp against her fingertips. He was leaning in toward her touch like a pet. She started running her hands through his hair.

He opened his eyes, and squinted at her. "I see purple wavy lines behind your head. No wait, more like indigo," he said. "I see the same color sometimes when I'm meditating."

"You meditate?"

He nodded. "G-Dane suggested it, for stress. It works." He leaned in and grinned, like he had anticipated the little kisses she began to bestow upon him, just below his jaw line. She felt little prickles jumping out at her lips. She just wanted to stay like this forever. He pulled her close and she snuggled in against his chest.

His voice was warm against her. "Tell me more about you. Tell me something."

Of course, she had something. She had once confided in Dan. Matt was not Dan, she told herself. Dan always felt too good for her somehow—too healthy and too entrenched in his faith to understand.

"I won't laugh," he said. "Even though you laughed at me." He moved his hand through her hair again. The motion felt supernatural.

She felt safe enough to venture out of her emotional den and sniff the air. "A few times I've seen pretty colors," she said. "Pretty lights."

"Tell me about them," he said. "Like stage lights? When I'm on stage, under the lights, it feels amazing."

"They're bright, in colors so rich they're unreal," she hesitated. He waited. "I first saw them when I was eleven, when my parents died. They talked to me. They know me." She hadn't meant to say that, but at the same time, she didn't regret telling him. He understood her in a way nobody else ever had.

"I didn't know," he said. "I'm so sorry."

"Please don't feel sorry for me," she said. "People have always felt sorry for me. Being an orphan is embarrassing. I hate it." She couldn't believe she had uttered the word orphan. She had never said that word aloud.

"Okay, I promise," he said.

She felt him pull her in even more. "So, these lights," he said. "Are they angels? Spirit guides?"

"I think they're a place," she said. "Like another reality or a kind of peace. I don't know." She was high as a kite; the wind was free, and there was no string to ground her. He seemed to be trying to grasp her inner being, so she couldn't reveal much more. She was having second thoughts. He felt perfect, but he couldn't possibly *be* perfect. He could hurt her. He was a man, after all. If he never learned her truth then he could never beat her with it.

She sat up and crawled onto the leather couch, which felt cold against her skin. "Leather is weird when you think about it," she said. "It's skin from dead animals."

He looked right into her. "Tell me. Trust me."

"What?"

"I know it's something big. Was he abusive? I mean—" He paused and continued to look into her eyes for what felt like a thousand fairy tale years. "I mean, we don't have to get into it all right now, Isoldey. Just give me a ten-word rundown."

"I only need two," she confessed. And she just let them escape, "Murder, suicide."

He bit into his lower lip, holding his breath before letting it out, slowly. Maybe it was a meditation thing. He didn't look away. When he put his hand on top of hers, he projected so much acceptance onto her that she shivered. She felt caught up with him, in a loop of time back to that first night, when he had painted her. When she had opened her eyes and found him waiting.

"I'll never tell," he said. "But...."

Her heart caught. "But?"

"But, we can talk about it anytime you feel like it. Anytime. I mean it, anytime."

Relief sprang out from every corner of the room and pounced on her like a pack of fluffy puppies. He hadn't laughed or run away. He still sat there. He was still there. He wasn't going anywhere. "And also," he added. "Have I told you today?"

Her smile was irrepressible.

"You're pretty."

Calm, and only slightly embarrassed, she looked for her glass of water. "Let's talk about something else. Anything else." She grabbed her glass and sat with him again. Sex would be good, she thought. He could tell her what he wanted to do to her. That would work. She felt so close to him now, so hot for him.

At first, he was quiet, then a wide smile sprang across his face and he jumped up. "I know exactly what we should do—get up, Isoldey!" And so she did, so excited. He bent over. "Jump on my back." She thought about the story of The Gingerbread Man that her mother used to read to her.

"I don't know. Are you a fox? A wolf maybe?"

"Not a big, bad one," he said. "Just moderately sized, and cool."

"Okay, but no biting," she said.

She thought she was hilarious, but all he said was, "Spaz."

She loved the way he said "spaz," like it wasn't a bad thing. Like her awkwardness was acceptable, endearing even.

He gave her a piggyback ride over to the bottom of the staircase, paused, and readjusted her. He made his way upstairs; the paisley carpet pattern swirled under his feet like magic. She leaned forward like a jockey. "This could be a really awkward emergency room story," she said.

"Trust," he said. "I've got you."

She smiled and thought, he's going to ravish me. She had been thinking about it for hours, maybe days. She had spent countless rainy afternoons tucked away in her room at Bethany Christian reading about torrid sexcapades. Now she was finally going to have one of her own. Neither Thomas Seldern nor John Parrish counted because they'd been high school boys. That had been awkward, guilt-ridden Christian high school sex. This would be different. This wouldn't be like Dan, who tasted like toothpaste. This would be awesome Buddhist sex with someone who knew what he was doing, and she couldn't wait to learn what that felt like.

Matt made it to the landing and she smiled at the sight of that happy orange painting. He readjusted her again, and then started back up the second set of stairs.

"Where are you taking me?" Her stomach was tingling, and her cheeks were stuck in a smile.

"I want to wash your hair."

"My hair?"

"It will feel better to you than anything I could ever do with my dick," he said. She began laughing uncontrollably. She couldn't wait to find out, to compare and contrast.

He carried her down the hallway and stopped just short of Nick's bedroom.

"Wait," she said. "Let's look at Nick's posters."

"Do we have to?" he asked. "I hate thinking about you in his bed." He put her down and she turned to face him.

"Nothing happened between you two that night, right?"

Oh God. She didn't know what to say.

# Chapter 16

## Nick

**NICK WALKED UP** the stairs and pushed his dirty hair back off of his face. No more thinking about Matt and Short Skirt, he promised himself. It was none of his business. But he had never seen Matt look at a girl like that before. He didn't want some engaged chick to Courtney Love his best friend.

"Nicholas is here." Mrs. McGinnis's announcement was followed by the hellos of several of the residents who sat playing cards in the front visiting room. Every time he walked through the doors at Wesley Gardens he went through an emotional reboot. The blush-colored walls and soft classical music brought down his stress level and elevated his overall mood. He felt like an actor walking on set and slipping into character, Nicholas the Great. His role provided him the chance to feel like a good citizen for a couple of hours. He had come twice a week since she was admitted the year before.

He smiled and gave them all a wave, taking a moment to adjust his eyes to the sour sting of ammonia. His old boots squeaked as he made his way across the linoleum. He passed by the official front desk, which was never staffed by anything other than the latest quilting project. He was happy to see the administrator's office was dark because rent was due and he wouldn't have enough money to cover it until they unloaded another ounce of blow. His grandmother's house was paid for, as was the bulk of her Wesley Gardens rent. But there were extras, and he wanted her to have them. He could not imagine having to transfer her to some crappy place. Carlos had already fronted him thirty-four hundred bucks, and he didn't want to ask for more. He hated being Carlos's bitch boy.

He made his way toward the nursing station. Behind the long white desk, Nurse Amy was typing something into one of their ancient computers. The nursing staff at Wesley Gardens always seemed to be on their feet.

Nurse Amy was wearing baggy blue pants tied at the waist, a top printed with kittens, and a sweet smile. He liked to tease the nursing staff that the real reason they got into healthcare was so they could wear children's pajamas to work every day without looking lazy or insane.

"Cute kitties," he said. His tone was intentionally perverted. "It was nice to see you at the home tour, wearing street clothes. You clean up nice." He loved to watch her blush, but knew he was pushing it. He brought his hands up in front of his face to defend himself from the imaginary slap she was inflicting with her eyes. "I'm sorry, I'll stop," he said on his way back toward room 218.

He hugged his grandma, took in the comforting smell of lavender, and then sat in his usual spot on the sofa next to the window. On a clear day, her view extended down the wooded hillside to Puget Sound, across the water, and out to the southern tip of Vashon Island. She seemed to enjoy her view, which was good considering units like hers, on the west side of the building, were an extra eight hundred dollars a month. He wished the view fee could be based on number of clear days per month. The past month had only been worth about two hundred bucks.

She seemed to read his mind, which was something she had been doing ever since he could remember. "The rain is beautiful."

The weather, he thought. Is she really talking about the weather already? It was never about the rain or the wind or the sunbreaks. Nature's talents were just launching off points into something deeper for her, pools of hippie love and forgiveness. He knew he should want to soak in her profound insights, like Matt did. He knew his time with her was precious. There were no guarantees. He could get a call any day. Still, at the same time, appreciating her wisdom was draining.

He braced himself for the metaphysical mumbo jumbo.

"Via was such a nice young lady," she said.

The name caught him off guard. He sat up and readjusted the floral pillow behind his back. His grandmother's couch had entirely too many pillows.

"I sense she's a free spirit. She had to go in such a hurry, but it sounds like Matt met her at an art gallery. He said something about a painting."

Nick chomped down on his lower lip so she wouldn't detect his amusement. He couldn't exactly clarify. G-Dane was progressive, but had no idea they worked at a strip club or the extent of their job responsibilities.

"She's just a sweetheart," she added.

Yes, he thought. Sure. Not to mention a drunk, an exotic dancer, and already engaged to somebody else.

"So, what else is going on?" he asked. "You been avoiding that bingo night drama?"

She acted like she hadn't even heard him, just leaned in and searched his eyes. "We can talk about something else."

Her eyes were still bright, but she did that thing she did with her smile. It was subtle, but he caught the way her lips flexed into the creases of her cheeks. He felt her energy downshift and sputter. Oh God, he realized, she's going to die someday, and I'm going to hate myself for shit like this. He thought fast.

"The music is good though," he offered. "Making progress on that new material."

She sat back. Her it's-fine-dear smile relaxed into a real one, which made his real, too.

"Have you decided what to do, about that other band? You said they invited you to do a jam with them."

It felt good to laugh. It had been a decade since she had turned her basement over to a bunch of boys and their rock-n-roll toys, but she still couldn't get the lingo right.

"What was their name again?" she asked. "Animal Sunshine?"

"Yep, Animal Sunshine." That's what he had told her because he couldn't be honest about their real name. He would die before saying the words "Anal Sunshine" to his grandmother.

"I've been too busy to jam with them." His fingers found a frayed edge on the pillow at his side. He started messing with a loose string. He regretted having told her about that. "I've been working on some stuff, but some lyrics would be good. Matt's been distracted."

"I see," she smiled. "You know…" She looked out the window.

"What?" he asked, not sure he wanted her to drop any wisdom bombs.

"It's your journey, it's your decision, but it seems to me that you should talk to Matt. Maybe you two aren't on the same page anymore. And, that would be alright, right?"

"If he gave up on the band?" Another loose string demanded his attention.

"I know he would be happy for you, if you pursued this other opportunity."

"Obliviot just needs its own material. We can record then, and get bigger venues. We've got that holiday show at the Showbox, you know." The room was feeling smaller. He was past ready to wrap up the convo. He looked at the clock on her desk, next to the picture of him and his mother. He looked away, and waited for that familiar zing to dissipate from his chest.

"You've always been so sure, so focused," she was saying. "You know what you want and I adore that about you. But I hope you'll accept Mattais's dreams too."

"He doesn't have any," he said. His cheeks were getting splotchy; he could feel their heat. "He just wants to screw around, be happy."

Her husky laugh made him shut his mouth. "Isn't that enough?" she asked. "Isn't that what life is all about, being happy?"

He made himself let go of the pillow. "I get you. I'll tell him about the offer, okay?" He felt guilty because he was pretty sure it was a lie.

Her gentle slate blue eyes beamed to him the same unconditional love she'd showered on him as a kid. The older he became—the older she became—the more meaning that look carried.

"Oh dear, you are so good for my soul," she said.

He wanted to be there for her, always. She didn't seem to understand that his hesitation about the new band, about leaving town to tour, wasn't really about leaving Matt behind.

# Chapter 17

## Via

**VIA JUST WASN'T SURE.** She didn't remember much about that first night, other than a generalized feeling that she had made a fool of herself. Had she hit on Nick? She didn't have a clue, but it didn't matter. Matt mattered.

"Why are you so worried about Nick?" she asked.

"Everybody loves Nick," he said. "He's great, but..."

"What?"

"He's just crazy-talented. He's getting impatient with me, with the guys, with Obliviot. He is so ready to get on the road, to get on a festival tour, to see the world. But I've been slacking, I guess. I'm what's holding him here. Never mind. Forget I mentioned it. Please."

He was already headed into the hall bathroom. She followed him, thrilled to just drop the subject. He pulled back the clear plastic shower curtain, leaned over the claw-footed tub, and began running the water.

"It's an old house," he said. "If the tub were bigger I would get in with you, but we'll make it work. My bathroom just has a shower."

She went over and felt the water pouring out of the silver spout. It's warmth beckoned, and she couldn't wait to slip into it. He came back in carrying a stool. He put it at one end of the tub and then started looking at the array of plastic bottles on the high window sill.

"I'm getting undressed," she announced, and pulled off her shirt. She was surprised when he didn't immediately turn around to take in her naked body.

"I'm sorry but we don't have fancy stuff here," he said. "I hope you aren't super picky about brands."

She took off her pants, then her bra, and then her panties. Still, he was fumbling around with the hair products. Disappointed by his lack of attention, she stepped into the tub, closed her eyes and entered a healing hot spring of renewal. She dipped her head back until her ears went under. There was a dull pop in her ears, and then new sounds— *wurzes* and *gurgles* and *slurges*. Tranquility surrounded her and she gave in to the energy radiating throughout her body. Her fingertips tingled and pulsated in their own time.

He stood over her with a silly smile on his face and reminded her of a boy from the playground back home; the one who used to chase her. He had been nice. He had never called her Rabbit like the other boys. She pulled her head back out of the water and heard her ears pop again. Hearing what sounded like Weezer's "Island in the Sun" wafting in from Matt's bedroom heightened her already awesome mood.

"We can't possibly be on W already," she said.

"You've made me forget about the A to Z thing," he said. "You're pretty," he added as he placed a folded towel between her neck and the hard edge of the tub.

"You said that when we first met," she said. "You knew I needed to hear it."

"And you wouldn't come over to me," he said. "You stood there in the doorway and made me come over to you." He sighed. "Why wouldn't you come to me?"

"I was nervous." It was hard to look at him, though she didn't know why.

"You were training me, like a dog."

She rolled her eyes, but he didn't seem to notice. Geez, he was adorable.

"Sorry if I've used too much," he said as he began massaging shampoo into her hair. "I've never washed a girl's hair, ever."

"Really? I figured it was a fetish."

He had used a lot. She could feel the lather developing from the circular motion of his hands. His fingers rhythmically pressed and swirled into her hair and she could hear microbubbles popping in excitement. She tried not to think about the bubbles dying. She was in love with the moment. She let her head fall back into his hands. This was better than any sex she had ever had. He brought his thumbs to the back of her head and pressed them down along the muscles of her neck. A hot rush of pure pleasure sprang from his thumbs and ran the length of her body. Her toes curled in thanks. Before she could recover he started working his way back up, and she heard herself moan, "Oh my God. Don't stop."

"I won't." He laughed. "Just remember how you feel right now, and that I like really you."

He really was like that boy from the playground.

"I wish I wasn't marrying Dan," she said.

She felt him withdraw his hands and stand up.

"Why did you have to mention him?" His voice was dark and fractured. "Damn, I can't even look at you now."

He walked out. No, she thought. Don't leave. She ducked back down into the water trying her best to get the shampoo out. She got out of the tub and put on the white terry cloth robe draped over the countertop. It looked exactly like the one she had worn at Hotties when he had painted her. She wrapped her head in a towel, which also looked like it had come from the Hotties locker room. There wasn't time to look in the mirror. And, if he loved her, it wouldn't matter anyway.

"I can go fix this. I can go fix this," she told herself as she pulled the robe tight against her damp body. A million thoughts spun within her skull, but only one mattered. The man downstairs was the one she wanted. He made her want to be herself, to figure out what that meant. She made her way toward the stairs and tried to think of what to say. When she looked down and saw him at the bottom of the stairs, it was like she hadn't seen him in a year. They couldn't waste any more time.

He didn't look the slightest bit mad. "I bet you're cold," he said. "Let's get into my bed. That's a big step for me."

"You're not mad anymore?" And then she realized it must be the Molly. That's why his mood had turned so hard. She felt it too. Like her high was wavering, petering out.

"Nah, I'm sorry. I'll just write a song about it."

"You'll write a song—about us?"

She studied his expression, trying to figure out his mood. She had done that with her father so many times, but his angst had never been this subtle. This was dramatic, but it felt safe. They were high, but she knew it was real. They would never forget this. The look they shared felt like magic, like it had already happened someplace else. Maybe where the pretty lights danced.

"Come to me," he said.

Recognition rolled through her. She knew this moment. It was exactly where she was supposed to be. "But, your bedroom is up here," she said. She could feel another euphoric wave. He took a few steps up, so she took a few steps down. He took a few more steps and so did she. They met at the landing.

He unwrapped the towel, tossed it aside, and tousled her damp hair. He moved his hand to the back of her neck and leaned in. She felt the presence of the orange painting above them. It seemed to be smiling down on them, giving its blessing. It evoked in her the comfort of eternity. She knew it was his painting; it felt like him. Before she could ask, his fingers were skimming down the front of her robe. His eyes looked black and urgent, like he'd had an epiphany.

"Kiss me," he said.

He grabbed her by the belt, reeled her in, and kissed her. His mouth activated every cell in her body. It seemed they were meeting and merging at a molecular level. She fanned her arms out and let him untie her robe. "Right here, " she said. "Your bedroom is a million miles away."

He pushed the robe back off her shoulders and cast it out onto the carpeted landing. He leaned her back, kissing her neck as he guided her down. He wasn't far behind. With her eyes closed, it felt like they were falling backwards in slow motion. His kisses made their way down and paused just below her collarbone. And then she felt the fluffy robe again, against her back. She pulled him in, and held him close.

A sense of hope warmed her. It connected them. Just like a love potion, she realized. She found it fitting that what he had first done with his brush he was now doing with his lips. Except this time she wasn't ticklish. He didn't ravish her as she had hoped. It felt more like worship, and that was okay too. She needed to feel him; she helped him out of his clothes. Finally, she felt his skin against hers. Finally, she felt a rush of relief. Space swirled around them, while time slowed to a stop just for them. More kissing, for hours maybe.

All time was now. Countless lives were now. Now was all anyone ever had, all they ever needed. There was no need for forever. His voice broke into her awareness. "Are you okay?" His whisper tickled her ear.

She nodded and tried to say, "Forever is now," but couldn't speak, too caught up in the moment. He cradled the back of her head in his hand. He rocked her so slow, so close. They belonged to each other now, and he felt so good she couldn't stand it. She nuzzled her face against side of his neck so she could breathe him in. More and more, she needed more of him. Bringing her arms back down around him, she held on tight. She was never going to be the same. When she wasn't lost in him she was transfixed by the orange sky above them.

# Chapter 18

## Via

**VIA WAS GETTING** orange paint all over her arms and wrists. It felt cold and tacky against her skin.

"Look, Miss Via. Look," Nate said. "Cool, right?"

She couldn't miss the autumn leaf art he was thrusting into her face. "Very cool," she said. "Now go and wash your hands. The others have already gone on to the chapel. You don't want to miss the message today. It's on Jonah and the whale."

She tried to push the hair away from her face with her own shoulder, but it wasn't working out.

Suddenly, Beth's clean, dry fingers pushed the offending strands back behind Via's ear. She was grateful Matt had refused to give her a hickey three days earlier. She'd never had one and had been curious, but he had told her that she needed to respect his boundaries. She felt a warm smile rise up onto her cheeks.

"You seem happy today," Beth said. "Did you get call from Dan?"

"No," came through her lips, hard and fast.

Matt hadn't called or texted either, but she was trying not to think about it.

"He says you've been playing phone tag," she said. "And I guess phone service is bad. I think they're in Kenya, now, right?"

That was the kind of information she should know, but she hadn't talked to Dan in more than a week. It was hard lying to Beth, so she just looked down and pretended to wipe something off the table.

"I think I told you, I've got that new volunteer thing starting tonight."

"At the domestic violence shelter, right?" she asked, but didn't wait for an answer. "Such a wonderful way to keep yourself busy.

I'm sure they are happy to have someone willing to work over night. But, should I be worrying about you?"

Oh no. What was she going to do? What if she knew about Hotties, about Matt?

"I know shelter locations are supposed to be secure," Beth said. "You'll be safe there, right?"

Oh, she thought as she took a deep breath. "No, it's fine. It's safe. That's why I can't tell anyone where it is, for security." The lie just slithered across her tongue. It tasted foul.

"It's wonderful you are serving women in need. I bet your mother would have been so proud."

Via reeled back. Why would Beth throw that in her face? Especially now. Shame soaked her to the bone. Why had she decided to use an overnight shelter as an alibi for the future Matt adventures she hoped to be having? Had she, at some level, been thinking that was where she really should be?

Beth looked concerned and pulled Via in for a hug. "I didn't mean to upset you," she said. "But I want us to be close. I want you to know I'm here for you."

Via accepted Beth's hug though she knew she didn't deserve such kindness. She closed her eyes. She wanted it to be enough. She wanted Beth's love to be enough.

"Thank you," she said. "It's just hard for me to talk about. It's embarrassing."

"Embarrassing?" Beth held her a little too tight. "Whatever for?" She pulled away just enough to look Via in the eye. Via looked down, but felt Beth's questioning eyes.

Without looking up she told her the truth. "I was just a kid. I didn't know what it all meant. I just wanted to be left alone. That's why my uncle sent me here to Washington, to Bethany Christian, so people would leave me alone. So people would forget about me."

"I'm so sorry."

Via pulled away. "No, that's exactly what I mean, Beth. People pitied me. They wanted me to cry and talk about it. Be some kind of poster child. I was supposed to discover God's plan for me, inspire the world."

Beth's took a step back, but gave a reassuring smile. Her voice was soft, but steady. "I need to ask you something, from a place of love," she said. "Did you ever have counseling? Real counseling? More than just prayer circles?"

Via realized she had already said too much. She had to put some distance between Beth's love and her own hate. She just wasn't ready. If they put her into counseling, they would find out she was crazy too. Just like Daddy.

"I can't do this right now."

"I know it's difficult with Dan gone. I know I miss his father when he travels," Beth added, her voice suddenly wavering. "I miss his voice, having him around."

Via wondered why she didn't feel that way about Dan. Shouldn't she feel that way too?

"I'm here, whenever you want to talk," Beth said. "You should go, so you don't miss your ferry."

She should have rushed into Beth's arms and hugged her. Said something special. Instead, she just turned and walked away. She had a meeting at Hotties and didn't want to be late.

\* \* \*

# VIA

**CARLOS HAD CALLED** the day before, just a quick call. He'd said he needed her help with something—very polite, professional. She couldn't think of an excuse, and her curiosity got the better of her. Plus, she hated to tell people no. It was the reason she handled the Bethany Christian auction every year, and the gift-wrap sale, and the bake sales. It was why she was teaching youth group. Why she had helped Matt and Nick with the home tour.

As she walked into Carlos's cave of an office, she couldn't help but feel the wrongness of it all. She wanted to chalk it up to the decor. She hadn't really paid much attention to it the first time she had been there; it reminded her of a video game, like a troll's dwelling. There were no torches or lanterns lining the walls, just a lava lamp on top of the bar. Most everything was black—the bar chairs, the long leather couch, the shiny cement floor. The one glaring exception sat atop the mirrored black-lacquered coffee table in front of them. It was that fancy, white-marbled box with gold trim. Next to it, four lines ready to go.

"You interested in a little skiing?" he asked. "Please join me. Help me sample the product."

She felt an excited flutter in her stomach. "Alright."

"Here, ladies first." He leaned in with the straw, the great deliverer.

She took the straw and felt giddy. Just holding it brought about the pre-high, knowing brilliant happiness was just a few seconds away.

"I've been looking forward to talking to you," he said as she leaned over and made the white powder go bye-bye.

He was still talking when she sat back, pinched her hand over her nose, and sniffed hard. "I hope you don't mind me being so forward, but as manager and owner, I have a good sense of what men find appealing. I have the best girls in town." He was talking super fast. He seemed pretty high already. "I've got three clubs in Portland, too. Gaming too. Did you know that?"

"Like casinos? No, I didn't, but Nick said you were big time."

He laughed. "Nick is the smart one. But watch out, he's a bigger slut than Mattais."

A dull thud smacked into her solar plexus, but the pain was quickly drowned in a flood of cocaine-induced joy. Matt's history was none of her business, she reminded herself. But wait, it was. Had she really had unprotected sex with some guy in a band? She couldn't stop replaying their special day in her head. What if it had all been in her head? Had she really confessed the truth about her parents? Had she really cheated on Dan?

"They've worked for me since they were kids," Carlos was saying. "Like fifteen, sixteen years old. They used to come for open mike at the Rainy City Tavern, that's mine too, you know."

She had never heard of it.

"It's at the Admiral Junction, just down the road from Nick's house. When I first saw them, they were on skateboards. Mattais, on a skateboard with his guitar."

"Guitar?" she asked. "You mean bass guitar, right?"

"Sure, whatever. He looked like a little goober," he laughed at his own burn. "Nick used our drum set. Nick was always the shit. A band is only as good as its drummer, you know, and Nick is on fire. Mattais is decent."

She smiled as she remembered their "Drums are the heartbeat, bass is the spine" explanation.

"When they turned eighteen, they started here." Carlos spewed his words closer. More and more words. "Hotties is my base of operations. Back then, they were cocky as fuck. They were sure they would be famous within the year. I've tried to help them out. They're like brothers to me, really."

His manner was easy, but she saw him roll his eyes. It was just like the way the pastor's bitchy wife Sarah had complimented Beth's banana bread at youth group the week before. "It is delightful," she had said. "Well, considering she can't use walnuts. It must be hard to be creative when you cook for children with allergies. Though I think this must be from a box—which is fine, of course."

"What does Matt do, other than paint girls?"

"He does henna sometimes, and—" He hesitated and started messing with the blow in front of him. "Interested in Mattais, are you." He stated it not as a question, but as an irritating matter of fact. "He runs errands for me," he said. "He also hosts some regular clients too. He makes sure they have a good time. Nick too. Chris, J.R., and Leon do most of the bouncing."

His words faded into the background. She hyper-focused on her next line. He must have noticed.

"Here, baby. Do another. You'll notice I only use straws cut to size. Bills are dirty. I don't need Mattais to tell me that."

She sucked up the next line and couldn't believe how lucky she was to have befriended Carlos. He could keep her very high. Everything was amazing.

"He and Nick like to play it nice, but they aren't any better than the frat boys who come in here—boys playing boy games."

He leaned in, put his hand against the side of her waist, and looked into her eyes.

"But, I'm sure you're too smart for that."

He latched his fingers into the belt loop on the back of her jeans. "Best not to get sidetracked with a guy who can't help you get ahead," he said as he released his grip and sat back again. "I always tell my girls to stay selfish. It's funny, I never, ever have to remind the guys."

She was confused, but felt so good she just wanted to soak in her high. She would just listen, go with it, and then deconstruct the conversation later. People always wanted to talk. She knew they needed to be heard.

"You know, Miss Via-Vixen, you've got a powerful thing going on. Your look is versatile."

"I don't really want be a stripper," she confessed, her heart galloping, her nerves overtaking her. "I don't want to lap dance. I'd be too nervous." Would he toss her out of his office?

He didn't seem fazed. "I'd like to go over my plans for you."

She straightened up and looked at him. "Plans?"

"Here is how this place works," he said. "Most men who come in will have a type in mind already. Some like petite Asian anime types; we have a few of those. Some enjoy blue hair, pierced nipples, ink; we have that, too. Alicia rocks the cougar act. And for clients who want the obvious blonde slut type, we've got several. You've met Kaytlyn."

"And what type am I?"

"You, my dear, are every man's type."

She felt a surge of satisfaction and thought about Matt telling her she was pretty. She smiled at the thought of him, but it faded when she considered what Carlos had just said about his game playing.

"If you don't want to work the floor, that's fine, you can start with stage shows, two an hour. You would be the appetizer, so to speak," he said.

Her stomach burned. Vodka-soaked cocaine was probably not great for her ulcer. She didn't know what to say so she kept her mouth shut.

"Even just a shift a week would help me out. You know, my wife used to be my best stage dancer," he offered. His voice cracked when he said the word wife. "Soon to be ex-wife," he added. "You've probably already heard; she left with my kids. Left me for an associate of mine down in Portland. But, I'm going to get them back," he said.

Something like a projector seemed to click on behind his eyes. She wanted to ask him to continue what he was saying, but the tight, anguished expression that had overtaken his face made her think otherwise.

"She wants full custody. Doesn't want me to see them at all," he continued. "She wants to hurt me. She made some accusations. The worst."

Her eyes grew wide; her heart creaked open.

"I was a good father," he added. "Doesn't matter, I'm guilty until proven innocent."

She wished she could say just the right thing. "Not *was* a good father," she corrected him. "*Are* a good father."

He laughed. "You correcting my grammar?" he asked dramatically.

Her high made her bold. "Seriously, don't make it past tense. You'll see them again."

"I didn't mean to bring the mood down like that," he said, the snag in his voice betraying his emotion. "I'm sorry, I don't know why I just told you that."

"I'm glad that you did." It was true. The holidays were marching toward her, cruel and relentless. Her misery could use the company. The brokenness in her recognized the brokenness in him.

He leaned back and cleared his throat. "The truth will come out, I know it will," he said. "So, Vixen, have you ever been in love?"

"Me?" she asked. "I think so, I'm not sure."

He chuckled. "That's a big no. If you had been, you would know. I hate her," he said. "I hate what she's done to me. She makes me crazy, but I love her anyway." He started messing around with the coke. Skim, skim, skim. Tap. Tap. "Don't ever fall in love," he told her. "You'll never get yourself back."

She wanted to throw her arms around him and comfort him, yet his intensity scared her. "I could help out, just until you find someone else," she said. "Just for a few weeks." The cocaine rushing through her made her fearless. "It could be like a little adventure," she said.

A slow smile spread across his face. "You'll help me?"

She nodded. Yes, of course. How could she refuse?

He passed her the straw again and said, "I'll watch out for you. You'll see. I'll be there for you."

His protectiveness soothed her. He thought she was worth his time and attention. She couldn't shake what he had said about Matt. He hadn't texted after all. He never even gave her his number. Maybe it was for the best. She admired her mother's ring, and wondered.

# CHAPTER 19

## VIA

**"DO I NEED** to handcuff you and drag your ass up here?" Whitney stood on stage with her hands on her hips. Handcuffs hung from the front belt loop of her blue short-shorts and matched the shiny "Officer Friendly" badge on her bikini top.

"I can't get up on stage, Whitney. There are customers over there. They'll see me practicing."

Whitney shook her head. "Never let Carlos hear you say customer," she said. "They're clients, guests, or special friends."

Via didn't care what they were called. She wished she could stumble her way through cowgirl dress rehearsal without them ogling her. She didn't feel sexy, like that first night. The suede top was okay, but the matching skirt itched. The white boots were downright evil. Her crowded little piggies were slicing into their neighbors.

Whitney came down the stairs and looked at her critically. "It's not a great look," she said. "It's too long for you. Kaytlyn usually wears it. She rocks the cowgirl thing."

"She must have crazy-skinny feet," Via said.

"Okay, let's just sit for a bit." Whitney yelled to a curvy black girl who was walking by dressed as a super hero. "Hey, Syndi, can you please go grab her something else?" She looked back at Via. "That's Super Sistah. She can dance circles around anybody in here." Whitney reached back and ran her fingers through her long, dark hair, which now appeared to have dark blue highlights. "I have to be straight up with you. You may not be cut out for this."

Via felt like she was getting fired. Whitney's expression was one of compassion. "Everyone thinks dancing is so easy," she said. "But the shoes never fit, the hours suck balls, and it's super embarrassing going to the bank and depositing hundreds of wrinkled one dollar bills. That's just the R-rated stuff."

She wasn't sure what she was supposed to say, so she waited.

"So, what's your deal?" Whitney asked. "Word is you're getting married. You're wearing a ring. He cool with you working here? You trying to earn money for a big-ass wedding or something?"

She looked down at her left hand. "This was my mother's. I'm going to wear it, whether I get married or not."

"Don't do it—and don't get knocked up either."

"How old are you?"

"I'm twenty-five," she said. "Kaytlyn says I'm a reverse cougar, outside of this place, I act twice my age." She stopped to wave to the incoming deejay. "Sad but true. Now, back to you. You can't dance. Why are you here?"

That was an excellent question. She wasn't really sure anymore.

"You know this place isn't even about dancing, right?" Whitney asked. "It's about the clock. You've got to hustle every minute. Every client is going to try to get as much from you as he can, as cheaply as he can. Our goal is to make them pay, then make them pay some more."

Super Sistah came up with some clothing in her hands.

"Stand up." Whitney leaned over, pulled the Velcro tab, and ripped the cowgirl skirt right off of her.

Super Sistah attached the new skirt, which was teeny, black, and lined with a red satiny material. "I will say, Whit, she's got a black girl's booty," she said, as though Via wasn't even there.

"The guys loved her the other night," Whitney said. "Carlos wants her stage dancing for now. But she's relying on club moves, no pole work, so I don't know what we're going to do with her." She glanced over Via's shoulder. "Hey, Kaytlyn."

Kaytlyn was there. Great.

"Don't you know you can take a pole dancing class anywhere?" Kaytlyn asked. "Think they even offer them at the Y now." Her laugh was harsh, her glare abrasive.

Via groaned. This was not fun anymore. Why *was* she here?

"Syndi," Ben yelled from the hallway. "Backstage, you're up next."

"Good luck, girl," Super Sistah said as she shook her head toward Kaytlyn. "Don't sweat the haters. If you've got the vibe, you'll figure out the rest later."

She appreciated the support, but still felt more confused than ever.

And Whitney seemed to recognize it. "Kaytlyn, give us a minute?" She waited until they were alone. "Don't mind her. She's not that bad, just insecure. Anyway, let's just do this another time. After closing one night this week. I won't come in early. My afternoons are reserved for my daughter."

"Thanks."

"And sorry, don't mean to be bitchy," Whitney added. "I've been cramming for midterms and haven't had a chance to blow off any steam lately." Her face brightened. "Hey, that reminds me. Bella is spending the night at her friend's house on Halloween. It's a better trick-or-treating neighborhood. Want to go see Obliviot?"

Via didn't know what to think. She had been tormented by the flirty texts Matt had sent the past couple of days. She had read them over and over and couldn't bear to erase them. Same with the voice mail; the sound of his voice made her quiver. But, she couldn't help but wonder why he'd taken so long. Why had he left her waiting, wondering? While it killed her not to answer back, the thought of falling in love with him was beyond hopeless. Even if he wasn't a player, he would want her to open up more to him. What would he think of her then? And Dan. She kept forgetting about Dan.

It was cool Whitney wanted to go out, and it would be Halloween at a bar. Matt would be on stage, and probably wouldn't even know she was there. She would be able to see if Obliviot was any good. She was so curious. And Halloween would be Day 51, the gloomy death day halfway point. Going out would be the perfect distraction.

"Alright." Excitement shot throughout her body while she tried to appear casual. "I'll buy the drinks all night. I owe you, for all your help."

Whitney burst out laughing. "You're on, except I never buy drinks," she said. "And baby girl, you shouldn't either."

* * *

# NICK

**NICK STOOD** at the podium, thoroughly frustrated by Matt's persistence. "Fine, fine," he said, peeking over into the main room. Rihanna was playing, or maybe Beyoncé. He had trouble keeping them straight. "She's not even on stage. Whit's putting her into something black; I don't know—a mini goth skirt, maybe. Now, can I get back to work?" He couldn't look at Whitney's ass too long or he'd get distracted. He needed to get back to the stack of Red Bull invoices in his hands.

Matt sat on the couch in the lobby, looking down, probably counting floor tiles. He was hunched over like a guy in a hospital waiting for his wife to have a baby. Not that Matt would be caught in a hospital— dead, sick, or otherwise.

"Why don't you just go back in and watch her? Leon and Ben are. I've got shit to do."

He was stressed. The inflated beverage sales numbers were crucial to their operations. He didn't ask about the details, but it didn't take an accounting degree to see that Hotties was some sort of shell. He had heard the term laundering thrown around, but Carlos said he was just maximizing interstate relationships. The three Portland clubs were bringing in a ton of money; they had gaming and no sales tax. There, with booze on-site, it was much easier to bilk horny men out of their money.

Matt finished mumbling whatever he was mumbling before he answered. "Nah, I should just go." If there were an Olympic event in mumbling, he'd take home the gold.

The Skeeze seemed to have a narcissistic man crush on Matt since they'd started working for him back in the day. He was always saying how Mattais was like a younger version of himself. Nobody else saw the resemblance. The past few years, Obliviot had been getting bigger and better gigs, which seemed to annoy their boss. Neither Matt nor Nick wanted to be groomed to take on more responsibility.

He remembered her first night, amateur night. She hadn't worked the pole or the clients. Instead, she had spent much of her song dancing with her eyes closed, in her own sexy little world of Metallica.

Later, when he'd tucked her into his bed, she had told him about dancing under the pretty lights. She had wanted him to stay and snuggle; her hair had smelled like an orange smoothie. But, she was into his best friend, so he would keep all of that to himself.

"She's blowing me off," Matt offered, out of the blue. "But I asked Whit to bring her to the Halloween show."

"Right on," he said. "Get her there, work your magic. You'll want to get in some extra practice time. You know, rehearsing? That thing you used to do?"

Matt didn't say a word to defend himself. Had he even been listening?

Nick gave his full attention to his pathetic friend. "You botched it, huh. You fumbled already? What, wasn't she any good?" He had to ask.

Without looking up he just replied, "A-fucking-mazing."

"Nice," he managed to say, but his congratulations were halfhearted. "How long did you wait to text?" Nick would have called her right away because she seemed sensitive, a delicate flower in need of reassurance. He knew the type and tried to avoid them—way too much work.

"'Til day five," Matt admitted.

"Ouch, dude," he said. "Flag on the play, half the distance to the goal." Now he felt bad for his no-game friend. "She's gonna make you work to regain that yardage."

"I didn't want to seem whipped," Matt added. "Got nothing back so I called and left a message yesterday. Still, nothing, so it's been a whole week now."

Harsh. Nick shook his head. Ignoring a guy was the worst thing a woman could do. When girls left snarky messages or cryptic texts it at least showed they cared enough to be pissed. No contact was the ultimate head trip.

"I think it's 'cause we shared some heavy shit that day. Maybe too heavy, too fast." He rubbed his temples like he had a headache. "And fuck, she's engaged."

"Really, professor?" He couldn't resist serving his friend a generous helping of I-told-you-so stew. "It's a shame nobody warned you." He felt a disturbance in the force and looked back toward the main room. "Hey, Kandy is on her way over."

"Gotta bolt," Matt said, and was gone.

She walked in from the main room looking like she smelled something funky.

"That girl is such a bitch," she said. "Thinking she can work my look." She tried to lean against the podium, but he shooed her away. "Kandy Cane, I'm trying to do math here."

"So?" she asked.

He obliged her. "Your Nipples the Nurse costume is distracting me and you know it." She lit up, victorious, and strutted over to sit where Matt had been just a moment before.

Kaytlyn was lava hot, but strained his patience. He tolerated her because he worked with her. He had pulled plenty of guys off of her in the past. Guys who didn't understand that the stripper is always right. Nick would throw down for all his girls, anytime. No questions asked.

He was just getting back to his fuzzy math when The Skeeze joined them, crossing his arms over his chest and looking out into the main room. "Damn, I'm liking her," he said.

"Seriously?" Kaytlyn asked, her voice creaking. "Did you say Whit could put her in my cowgirl shit?"

"Don't worry about it," Carlos said.

"And she says she won't couch dance at all. Why did you even hire her?"

"Are you really so stupid?" he asked. "Don't you see how her dancing without working the floor would mean more money for you?"

Nick looked down and shuffled invoices. He wished the podium would gobble him up so he wouldn't have to listen to Carlos berate her. Still, his boss made an excellent point. It's exactly what Sonia used to do. She got the clients rock hard and ready to spend while the other girls swooped into the crowd and mingled. The girls had always complained about having to leave the floor for their scheduled stage dances.

"Now shush and go make me more money," Carlos told her. Nick saw him slap her ass as she went by. She just smiled. Nick had to look away, back into the main room, where Via and Whitney sat talking.

Carlos looked in too, past Kaytlyn. "Yeah, I'm liking the new one. Girl next door, but dirty."

Nick kept his mouth shut, but couldn't be blind to the situation developing. It was good to know Carlos wanted to keep Via top shelf for now, away from the grubby hands of the clients. Matt would love hearing that.

But what if The Skeeze had other plans for her?

# CHAPTER 20

## VIA

**VIA HATED BEING** late, but she had missed the eight-ten p.m. ferry from Vashon and parking in the Capital Hill neighborhood on Halloween was nuts. Whitney texted to let her know she would be waiting outside Chop Suey, so she wouldn't have to walk in alone. She turned the corner and was caught off guard by the costumed crowd waiting to get in.

Whitney waved her over from the front of the line. "Argh!" she bellowed, loud and cocky.

God, she loved Whitney. "Vikings don't say that," she teased. "That's a pirate thing."

She was the tannest, hottest Viking Via had ever seen. Caplet sleeves hung from her tight leather bra, which matched her short suede skirt. Her thigh-high brown high-heeled boots made her legs look like they went all the way up to her neck. She wore a horned Viking helmet with a built-in braided blonde wig. At the moment, the costume was accessorized with an oversized look of disappointment.

"What are you supposed to be?"

"You don't like it?" Via spun around in her Little Red Riding Hood costume. The cape was thin satin and hit her mid-thigh. Underneath, she wore a white top and a fairly short black skirt with five-inch black patent-leather heels. She had just blown out her hair like always because wigs were itchy, and she had the hood. She was hoping the night would involve hours of dancing and she didn't want to get too hot.

"We're getting you into the ladies' room ASAP," Whitney said, while she pulled her by the basket over to the bouncer checking ID.

The podium was much like the one at Hotties, except it was black, grimy and plastered with upcoming event posters. He looked up, saw them, and smiled.

"Hi, handsome," Whitney told him. "Sorry, you have to work tonight. No fun."

"Nice of you to say," he said, leaning in. "I'm Max, off at two." He couldn't seem to keep his eyes off of Whitney's thighs.

"We're on the list. Whitney Hunter and Via—" She looked over. "What's your last name?"

"Sorenson," she said. Not even her driver's license said Rabbotino.

The bouncer scanned his list and read aloud, "Whitney Hunter." He scanned the second page. "No Via Sorenson."

What? Psyche-crushing disappointment toppled her.

"Oh, wait," he chuckled. "Via Yorpretty. You're in."

By the time she realized what he had said, Whitney had pushed her inside where another guy was stamping her wrist. The place was dark, thirty degrees warmer, and packed. It was uncomfortably loud; she hoped her ears would adjust. They made their way through the crowd. Burnt-orange colored lanterns hung above the bar. A long half wall divided the bar from the main room. Whitney pulled her into the belly of the beast. A band was already playing. The singer wasn't so much singing as lecturing. It sounded like a sexy anthem of some kind.

The walls thumped in time to the beat. Wait, she felt a chill of recognition. That was him. Were they already on? She couldn't see over the sea of shoulders in front of her.

"That's Matt," Whitney shouted. "He does 'Rock & Roll Lifestyle' and a few others. Jeremy sings most everything else. They have a guy on horn for some of their Cake stuff."

Overwhelmed by the crush of the crowd, she realized she was one of the few people in the place who didn't know the words.

"If you hang with them, you'll learn to appreciate Cake," Whitney continued to shout as she pulled her back toward the restrooms. "We've got to take care of business first."

"Just one sec?" She had found a pocket in the crowd through which she could see a sliver of the stage. She walked into it and her line of sight opened up. Matt stepped back from the front of the stage. Damn, she had missed it. The song wrapped up and the room filled with the sounds of applause and generalized screaming. Freddy Krueger bumped into her and spilled half his beer at her feet. He didn't seem to notice or care. Everyone started swaying or jumping to a new—fast— beat. She recognized the song as Blink-182's "All the Small Things." Girls were screeching in her ears.

A glowing sphere, like a beach ball, skipped past her, and then another. People were throwing streamers back and forth. Whitney yelled into her ear. "This is why everybody comes to see them." Another ball flew by. "This isn't a Halloween thing. They're always fun as fuck." The women next to them threw flower petals into the air like confetti. Pink and purple lights flashed on and off, on and off. The beat intensified. Matt had described Nick as a hard hitter, and now she knew what he meant. She couldn't see Nick past the heads in front of her, but she could feel him through the beat.

She leaned to the side until she got a better vantage point. The stage was set into the corner, with twelve-foot-high speakers angled out from both sides. People jumped up and down belting out, "Na-na, na's," while strobe lights flashed from the corners of the room. Nick was up high behind his drum set, moving his head in time to his own beat. He looked commanding, even while sporting a rainbow clown wig. But, her heart pulled her attention back toward Matt, who stood to the right. He was standing in an open stance with his head down. He wore a Rasta cap and a Bob Marley t-shirt. Her face grew hot and she couldn't hold down her smile no matter what. He wasn't moving much, just hanging back, bobbing to the beat. He held Envy. She sparkled under the golden stage light. If Via hadn't been in love with him before, this was the clincher. Game over. Whitney yanked her arm, and because she didn't want to come off as star-struck, she followed her back through the field of "na-na-nas." They continued past a long banner that read, "Obliviot: No requests! No regrets!" Another one read, "Obliviot: You get what you get!"

Whitney dragged her into the back corner of the bathroom next to a row of sinks and fumbled with Via's top. "Why did you wear a bra under this? Are you Amish or something?" she asked. "Toss it."

She took it off, just as she was told. Anything to get back out to the main room again. That smile was back, just the thought of him.

Whitney started assisting a mermaid next to them whose shells were lopsided. Mama Whitney to the rescue. The girl thanked her and waddled back into the main room. Unzipping the wallet hanging from her wrist, Whitney pulled out eyeliner and a lipstick. "You just need a little eyeliner," she said. "You have these great almond-shaped eyes."

"Sure, I get it," she said. "It's slut night. But no lipstick. I hate the feel of it."

"Look up."

The crowd was cheering like crazy and Via couldn't hold herself down anymore. Every moment spent in the ladies' room was killing her. She couldn't bear to miss another song. "It's fine, it's fine," she said as she squirmed away from Whitney's forced-beautification. "Let's go already."

"What's the rush?" Whitney wore a wicked grin. "Don't worry, if your ferry turns into a pumpkin at midnight, you can just crash with the prince on bass."

"You know about Matt? How?"

"Bitch, please," she said with Super Sistah style.

"It's that obvious?"

"To me it is. He left the room when you started practicing the other day. He won't watch you dance. It's sweet." She adjusted her Viking helmet. Her cat eyes were playful and full of fun. "Which is a good thing, by the way, because your moves are so weak. Oh, and also because he point-blank asked me to bring you here tonight, Via Yorpretty."

# Chapter 21

## Via

**VIA DIDN'T WANT** to walk into the party alone, but standing on the sidewalk in front of Nick's house, so close and yet still so far, was agony. Whitney seemed to befriend everyone she met and had spent five minutes counseling a broken-hearted girl they'd found crying curbside. Whitney had helped her fix her mascara, which—like the boyfriend in question—had gone astray. "Fuck him, he's a pig," she had advised her. "Men who make you cry aren't worth your tears. You're dressed like Wonder Woman, so act like it."

Via pulled her away and up to the porch, which was free of raccoons but packed with zombies and sluts representing every era of civilization. They walked into the foyer and took it all in. She saw fifty or so people, most in costume, crowding the living and dining rooms.

Whitney looked past the dining room and into the kitchen. "I need to go talk to the keg master," Whitney yelled over the sound of Sublime. "Want a cup while I'm there?"

"There's an actual keg?"

"Boys don't grow up," Whitney said. "They just get better beer."

"Sure," she said and then turned to look around the room. She didn't see Matt anywhere, but then she wasn't sure if he was still in his Rasta garb. She stood next to an angel with a white whip and a belly dancer, only slightly slutty. The house smelled like weed. She leaned against the stairway railing and thought about her romantic stairway adventure with Matt. The house had been theirs that day, and only theirs.

A guy dressed like Zorro came up, wrapped his arms around her waist, and pulled her in for a sloppy beer kiss. She fought him off. It wasn't Matt. The pheromones were all wrong. She pushed him away.

He smiled but didn't let go. "I'm sorry, I thought you were somebody else," he said in a voice that sounded rehearsed. "But hey, let's get to know each other. I'm Zach."

Matt, sans dreadlocks, came up behind the guy, spun him around, and pushed him up against the nearest wall.

"I'm gonna kick your ass."

"Hey, I'm a kissing bandit," he said. "It's my costume. I'm sorry, man."

"Don't tell *me*, assclown." He turned the guy back around so he was facing Via. "Tell *her*."

While she wiped Zorro's spit from her mouth, she glanced around to find that they had the attention of everyone in the room.

"I'm sorry," Zorro said. "My bad."

She tried to manage a forgiving smile. "It's fine, I guess."

"So, Red," the guy added. "What's in your basket?"

Matt scowled, pulled him away from her and pushed him into the kitchen. She heard him say, "Son, we're going to have to talk about your behavior."

She was disappointed. Matt hadn't said anything to her, barely looked at her.

"Oh my God, are you okay?" the angel asked.

Whitney walked up and handed Via a red plastic cup of beer. "What did I miss?"

"Some random guy just started kissing her, but Matt was all over him," the belly dancer explained. She pulled herself into classic gossip stance then whispered, "He looked super pissed. You guys going out?"

"I barely know him," Via said. "I mean, he lives here. He's probably just watching out for everyone."

"Do you know if he has a girlfriend?"

Whitney had a look on her face that was downright evil. "No, actually," she said. "He's a virgin, saving himself for marriage."

"Really? He's religious?" the belly dancer asked.

Whitney leaned into the gossip huddle and lowered her voice. "He's training to be a shaman, like a medicine man."

"That's crazy."

"Yep. He's half Native American. His mother is a warrior princess of some kind." Via couldn't believe the words coming through her friend's glossy lips.

The belly dancer was looking at the angel, doubtful.

"It's true," Whitney said. "He goes out into the woods and smokes peyote, and he's not allowed to shave his pubes."

With that, the two girls turned away and started talking to a couple of corporate vampires.

"Who are you talking about?" It was Kaytlyn, dressed as a beauty pageant contestant. Her sash read, "Miss Rock Yo World." Her hair was vast and wavy and held a diamond tiara. She looked amazing, impossible to cut down. Jealousy screamed inside Via's chest until she noticed Kaytlyn's poor arms covered in goose bumps. She looked away and took comfort in her soft red cloak.

Nick joined them. He looked flustered, downright pissed off. He frowned at Kaytlyn. "Sup, Miss America? You the one telling everyone we were throwing a par-tay?"

"No. No, I did not." Her voice shook with odd formality. "Where's Mattais?"

"Putting out the fires you started," he said, sneering at her. "He's had to boot two guys already. We just wanted to keep it mellow tonight, just friends. I don't even know who brought the keg, and now I have to tell half these people to leave. Now I'm the asshole."

Via listened to him vent, looked around the room, and guessed there were fifty people there. And who knew how many were in the kitchen and backyard.

"Nick, Nick!" Josh yelled from the landing. "There's some girl-on-girl action going on up here, and they're filming!"

Nick's mouth dropped open before turning up into a half smile. "I'll pass."

"I thought you should know," Josh yelled. "Because they are in your grandma's room."

"Hell no," Nick muttered and ran upstairs. Kaytlyn turned and made her way toward the kitchen.

"Hey, Whitney!" some guy was calling over from the couch.

Via turned and saw a big guy with short brown hair wearing a "Portland Sucks" t-shirt who was trying to get Whitney's attention.

"Whitney!" he called again.

"Hey, Jake!" Whitney called over to the guy. "Come on," she said to Via and led her into the living room. Coke, Via realized when she got closer. *They have coke.* She was suddenly much more interested in meeting Whitney's friends.

"Via, this is Jake," she said. "Brittney's boyfriend."

"I wouldn't go that far," he said. "These are my boys, Justin and Trevor. We've got party favors and no hot girls to play with. You ladies down?"

Whitney sat on the edge of the couch. "Are you saying we're not hot?"

Jake's friends started laughing, but he didn't look fazed. He skimmed and chopped the blow against the glass table. "Why you so insecure?" he asked. "You know you're smokin' hot."

Trevor, who was at the other end of the couch, looked Via up and down. She acted like she didn't notice, but she loved the attention. He took a long drink from his cup and said, "Ladies, if a man offers you free drugs: he wants to fuck you—period."

Whitney didn't look impressed. "Then they're not really free drugs, are they?"

"Touché," Trevor said without taking his eyes off the coke.

*Pretty fancy,* she thought while she tried to restrain a blatant eye roll. He reminded her of Carlos, trying too hard to sound intellectual. It was easy to see this guy was a dick, but still. Her eyes followed the path of Jake's credit card as it organized the blow into columns. She felt herself amping up, like her chest was blooming and turning inside out.

Whitney continued to rag on him. "You know I don't do that shit."

"What about her?" Trevor asked. "You want some, Miss Riding Good?"

Via looked over to Whitney for permission. "It's up to you," she answered. "But, watch yourself. That shit will mess you up."

Jake handed her a rolled up bill, but the table was low, and there was nowhere to sit. Was she supposed to bend over and show her ass to half the room or get down on her knees?

"You can sit down right here," Trevor offered. She walked over to his side of the couch, but instead of scooting over, he pulled her on top of his knees. She knew it probably looked bad, but figured she could do a quick line and be up before anyone noticed. She leaned over the table, which brought her ass up into lap dance position. She felt his hands inch down her waist and come to rest on her ass. She snorted up the line, sat back and pinched her nose. Heaven descended upon her.

"Hey, Matt," she heard Whitney say.

Without looking over at Matt, she said, "Thanks," and tried to get up, but Trevor wouldn't let go. "Oh you have to stay for a minute, at least," he said. "No fair, teasing me."

"You're the one who pulled her onto your lap," Whitney said. "Now, let her up." Via was afraid to look over, but she could tell by the way Whitney was defending her honor that Matt wasn't pleased.

"Whatever," Trevor said then let her go.

Matt hadn't jumped in to save her and she wondered what that meant. She finally looked over and met his offended eyes.

"They're all teases, man," he said. "You still have to let them go when they want." She noticed Matt's right hand was pulled in toward his side and wrapped in gauze. He held it up and said, "I'm done for the night."

Whitney gasped. "What, you hit somebody? I can take a look at that for you."

"Nah, I'm good," he insisted, then passed through the living room and headed upstairs. Before Via could decide if she should go after him, Kaytlyn beat her to it.

"Come on," Whitney said. "Let's go." She flicked her head toward the front door so hard her Viking helmet almost fell off.

"Already?" Jake asked. He sounded like a spoiled child.

"Sorry," Via said. "Thanks again."

She got up and followed Whitney to the front door and was surprised when her friend stopped at the bottom of the staircase, turned around and whispered, "Go up and deal with him. You can't let Kaytlyn swoop in like that. I'll be waiting for you in the car. Five minutes. If you don't text or come out, I'll assume you two made up. "

"He's pissed," she said. "I can't go up there right now."

"You can't *not* go up there right now."

She stood up on the first step so she was tall enough to straighten Whitney's Viking helmet. "Thanks, Whit."

"Only my closest friends call me Whit," she said in a stern tone that developed into a southern drawl. "So, yep, you can call me Whit. Now go on, git."

"Are you a cowgirl now? I thought that was Kaytlyn's thing."

Kaytlyn. Duh, she realized. Kaytlyn.

"Gotta go." She turned and raced up the stairs.

* * *

# VIA

**SHE KNOCKED ON** the door twice. "It's Via."

She was relieved when he immediately opened the door looking happy to see her. Kaytlyn, who was sitting on his bed, did not look happy at all. Her disdainful gaze focused on Via. "Really, Mattais?" she asked in a tone Via found hurtful. "Her?"

"That's enough," he said. "I want us to be cool, but you've got to let it go."

Via pulled the riding hood around her body and wished she could slink back downstairs for another line. "I can come back."

"No," he said. With his left hand, he pulled her close and rested his arm against her lower back. She watched the look on Kaytlyn's face grow more emotional. Was she going to cry?

"Don't, Kaytlyn," he said. "Don't make me out to be a dick. We hooked up a few times. That was it. I told you that's all it was ever going to be. I told you that up front."

"Why her? You just met her."

Via was dying to hear his answer. But he didn't say a word, just held his ground. Via tried to step back toward the door, but he grasped her by the arm and whispered, "Don't go."

His plea was enough to make Kaytlyn stand up and storm past them. "Your loss," she said as she stomped out the door.

Neither of them spoke. The room was quiet except for the vibrations of the music coming from downstairs. He turned to face her and pulled her in for a hug. They fit.

"I'm sorry you had to hear that," he said. "I guess it's good that you did."

She tried not to care about Kaytlyn.

"I'm so sorry," she said.

He tensed up. "Oh, you mean the guy downstairs?"

She nodded, afraid to look at him.

His hand came in under her riding hood. "Don't try to make me jealous. That's messed up."

That hadn't been her intention at all. She had only wanted the line. Its effects on her were minimal anyway. It didn't seem to pack the same punch as the stuff Carlos had.

"I'm sorry," she said. He smelled so good.

"You haven't been texting me back, which is even more messed up." He pulled back and looked down into her eyes. "Maybe you do love that guy—the fiancé," he said. "Maybe it's time for me to back off."

"No."

"Okay then, let's do this. Time we had the talk." He stood back and motioned toward the foot of his bed, like he wanted her to sit down. She stood her ground, not wanting to sit where Kaytlyn had just been.

He moved in close again, so they were facing each other again. "So Via, what's up?"

"What?"

"With us. I want to know what's up."

Clueless, she wanted to touch his face. If only he'd just shut up and kiss her. She attempted a smile.

He shook his head at her, but his expression was playful. "I don't think I've ever been the one to bring this up before," he said. "It's such a girl thing."

She didn't want to think about the other girls.

"You make me act like such a pussy," he said.

Her stress smile relaxed into a real one. "Did you really just say that word to me?"

"Sorry," he said. "I'm not exactly romantic. I've never really had to be."

"It's okay," she said. "Neither is Dan. He's super practical."

He brought his head back and twisted up his face. "Please don't ever say his name. You know that bums me out."

"Sorry," she said. It was such a stupid thing to say. Maybe he wasn't going to kiss her at all now.

"You said you didn't love him."

"And I meant it. But..."

"But?" He kept his eyes trained on hers. She felt so out there. Nowhere to hide.

"But, I don't want to hurt him."

"That's not a good reason to marry someone."

She found it hard to hold eye contact with him anymore, so she nuzzled in close to him. He was warm and wonderful. He made her forget her worries. The death day countdown. She wanted to be happy. While part of her was sure she didn't deserve him, the other part—the part that wanted and trusted him—was stronger and more insistent.

"I'm just scared," she confessed.

He sighed against her ear. "We don't have to figure it all out tonight, but you'll have to cut him loose," he said. "I can't get attached if you're not in this with me."

Of course, he was right. "I'm in," she said. He relaxed against her. Had she really just said that? She felt a wave of terror pass over her, but then it was gone. He was still there, holding her. "Can we be done with the talk now?" She felt saturated in the potential of the moment; she didn't want to waste it talking.

"One more thing," he said. "Do you think about that day? What I told you?"

They had said so many things that day, but she knew exactly what he was asking her.

"To remember how we felt that day."

"Yep, that's all we have to do," he said. "And we'll be good."

She wanted to believe him. "Forever is now?" she asked, her cheek still against his chest. She was hopeful, but still found it hard to pull away and look at him.

"Exactly, Isoldey. Exactly."

She lifted her face up toward his to find his lips already waiting for hers. Their conversation had been so thoughtful that she was surprised by the intensity of their kiss. He caught her off guard when he walked her back a few steps and leaned her up against the door. Still kissing her, he reached around her and she heard the lock click. Then he pulled her over to the tablet on his desk.

"Marley?" he asked, breathless. She nodded, and they held off kissing just long enough for him to hit play. He pulled her back to his bed.

"I'll need some help with my jeans," he said, holding up his bandaged hand for her inspection.

Oh, that's right, she realized. She had been so focused on Kaytlyn and the big talk that she had forgotten about his injured hand. Now she was even more impressed with his smooth door-locking move. "Does it hurt?" she asked. "Shouldn't we go have a doctor check it out?"

"I don't do hospitals, they make too many mistakes," he said. " And, I've been waiting—hoping—for this all day."

"You've been thinking about me all day?" She felt blindsided with happiness. "When you were onstage, and all those girls was screaming for you?"

"Enough talk. You're killing me here," he said. "Undress me, woman."

Carefully, she eased his t-shirt off over his head and worked her hands down to his belt.

He pulled away. "Stop. Wait."

She stepped back and watched that familiar smile curl up on his face. She was hooked on that smile. "You're pretty," he said.

She felt pretty, more than pretty. "You going to say that every time?"

"It's lucky, and you do look good in red." He brought his good hand up between her hood and her hair. "You can leave your riding hood on."

She had him naked before the second verse of "Is This Love" was over. The riding hood stayed on well into "Three Little Birds."

# CHAPTER 22

## VIA

**VIA CAME DOWNSTAIRS** and heard Nick and Matt in the kitchen. Matt's Black Flag t-shirt was long enough that she didn't feel overexposed. Her hair was a rat's nest. She wanted a cup of coffee, but they sounded like they might be fighting, so she decided to hang back and listen.

"You're an idiot," she heard Nick say. "Sooner or later you're going to need real medical attention. Someday you'll need to actually *enter* a real hospital."

"Like hell."

"You can't google your way out of every illness."

"Dude, look, it's fine. It's not that swollen anymore," Matt pointed out. "I'll just ice it and rest it a few days."

"Just get your shit straight before you throw a punch," Nick instructed. "Wrist straight. Strike at ninety degrees."

"Okay, okay. I wasn't thinking."

"If Obliviot is important to you, you'll take care of your hands."

"I'm sorry, K?"

"Straight up apology so soon? No arguing?" Nick asked. "You're damn chipper this morning. Short Skirt must have been decent in the sexual healing department."

"Whatever, something like that," she heard Matt reply.

"SHFT soundtrack?"

"Johnny Cash, some blues," he said. "We had KEXP on this morning, Positive Vibrations—perfect since I need to get her into reggae. All she knows is Marley."

She was only slightly offended at the condescension she detected in his voice because it was true.

"No dubstep?"

"Not yet. Maybe next time. She picked."

"You let her pick?"

"Just cause Johnny Cash was a good call," Matt said. "I would have vetoed Taylor Swift or some shit like that."

"Shut up, you like her," Nick said. "You wouldn't have missed SHFT because of lame music."

She wondered what a "shift" was and why missing it was bad.

"It's not like that. I'm no chump."

"Not yet."

"You cool with her, or not?" She hadn't heard Matt sound so offended before. His voice was strained. "You said you were, and now you're giving me shit?"

"Nah, she's alright," Nick said. "Just watch yourself. Just be careful with the engaged chick. When is she marrying that guy?"

"I'm thinking the day after never."

Her heart froze. She had forgotten all about Dan. Again.

Matt grumbled, "So, just drop it—dumbass."

She was surprised to hear Nick laugh, and then Matt joining in. Their heated argument seemed to have vanished without a trace. As if dumbass were a magic word.

"And how'd you do, Grohlly?" Matt was asking the questions now. "You hook up with the Girl Scout or her friend?" It was silent for a moment, and then she heard Matt cracking up. "You joined that situation Josh told me about? In G-Dane's bed?"

"Of course not, sick bastard," Nick said. "We moved it over to my room."

"That video will come back to haunt your ass."

"It's not like I'm running for office."

She smoothed her hair down as best she could and stepped into the kitchen. She knew she should announce herself somehow, but wasn't sure how. Matt was leaning against the stove on the far end of the kitchen and Nick was sitting at the island. Neither had noticed her.

"But wait, there's more," Nick said like a TV commercial announcer. "That slutty witch blew me on that beer run."

"Good morning," she said. They both looked over, surprised. Matt smiled, but Nick did not. She tried not to laugh, and assumed his witchy chick had taken off her hag wig and hat first.

"The witch with warts all over her chin?" she asked. "They looked so realistic. Not sure if they were part of the costume."

Nick looked horrified, like he couldn't believe she had gone there. He bowed his head and shook it a few times. His cheeks developed red splotches.

Matt grinned as though he approved of her insightful observation. "Should we offer up a healing spell for your junk?"

She couldn't help thinking of church. She'd never been involved in a please-don't-let-him-have-genital-warts prayer circle.

"Shut your face," Nick said. "But, that reminds me, it's your turn to refill the SHFT dispenser," he told Matt with an exaggerated wink. "All we've got left are the giveaways, so buy some today—unless you want to get your glow on." She was lost. Nick gave an awkward sort of wave. "I'm off to see G-Dane." She was relieved he didn't look too annoyed with her. She wanted him to like her. "Later, tater," he whispered as he passed.

"Tot," she told him. It was stupid, but she was realizing they were all stupid, so it was cool.

She looked back over to Matt. He was staring back at her with a hungry Wile E. Coyote expression on his face. She waited until she heard the front door close, and then asked, "He's off to see his grandmother again?"

"He goes twice a week. She's super sweet and he's a good boy."

"Not from what I overheard. What's the shift machine?"

"You said you were on the pill, right?"

Embarrassed, she nodded, though she would have to be better about taking them. Now that she was actually having sex.

"So, then, no worries."

"Well, what does missing a 'shift' mean?"

"Damn, woman, how long were you standing there?"

She could tell he wanted her to come to him, but she continued to smile from the doorway waiting for an answer.

"Not a SHIFT, some S-H-F-T," he said. "It's Super Happy Fuck Time. You ready for some more?"

He put his arms out toward her, but she didn't go over because he had a weird look on his face, like he wanted to tickle her.

"Come to me." His tone was playful. "Come to me," he repeated. This time he looked serious. She loved the way he looked at her. She felt like someone new, and special. He made it seem like January wasn't too far away, after all.

He started walking toward her like they were playing tag and he was it. She shrieked and ran back into the living room with him right behind her. She ran up the stairs laughing and screaming as she felt him trying to pinch the backs of her ankles. She ran for his bed. If she could outrun him, it seemed the obvious choice for home base.

# Chapter 23

## Via

**"VIA, SWEETIE,"** Nick called down from behind his drum set. "Will you please grab me a beer? The fridge is next to the washer and dryer."

She hadn't thought to hesitate until she was halfway across the basement and heard Matt scold him.

"What was that?"

"What? I can't ask your girl to fetch me a beer?" Nick asked. "Or I can't call her sweetie?"

She opened the refrigerator and leaned in. "You want light beer, right, Nick?"

"Please, no chick beer!" he yelled over. Of course, she had already grabbed him a bottle of the darker ale she knew the guys liked.

She turned to see that Josh had put his guitar against its rack and jumped down from the stage. He was headed toward the coffee table, eyes cast on the last line of cocaine. "Can I have a beer too, hon?" he asked before snorting up the last of the party favors.

She brought Nick his beer and turned to Josh. "You didn't say the magic word." Matt and Nick both stuck out their tongues at him. She didn't mention the real reason; he was bogarting the last line.

Nick hadn't done any. He rarely did, said it messed with his timing. She was learning that, to Nick, timing was everything. Neither booze nor weed seemed to bother him, a little here, a lot there. He took a swig of his beer and put it down on the wooden rail behind him before he taunted Josh with a rimshot. "Josh, gettin' schooled by the Sunday school teacher."

They had been practicing The Offspring for an hour, "Gotta Get Away" over and over. She thought it sounded good, but the guys seemed to hear things, problems, that her ears didn't recognize.

"And, turn down your amp," Nick was telling Josh. "You sound like shit."

There seemed to be different levels of sounding bad. Sounding like shit wasn't all that bad. Sounding like ass was worse, and sounding terrible was worst of all. The guys also had an entire language devoted to the amps and sound mixing. They were forever adjusting dials, knobs, and sliders. Matt seemed to love the technical stuff. Nick said he was a wizard on a soundboard and a real wolf tone tamer, but she didn't dare to ask what they were talking about for fear they would launch into a twenty-minute explanation. There was this thing called a Neve board they talked about, like the ultimate sound toy.

They also had a fog machine, a bubble machine, and a trunk full of crazy hats. She had only been to three shows so far, but at the last one, at Nectar in Fremont, they had tossed down a My Little Ponies piñata and let the crowd tear it apart. Inside were goodies from Archie McPhee's novelty store—candy, wax lips, x-ray glasses, glow sticks, and an array of freaky-colored condoms.

"Let's do some Radiohead now," Matt said. "'The National Anthem,' just the beginning. I want her to hear the sick bassline."

Josh furrowed his brow and shook his head. "Dude, we don't have horns or the synthesizer or anything." He adjusted his green beanie back against his forehead and sniffed hard. "That would sound rough as hell."

Nick scowled. "Let's do 'Suck You Dry' again," he insisted. "Need to get Mudhoney back into the set, and then maybe some Melvins."

"No, first Radiohead, then Mudhoney, then Beck," Matt said, his eyes locked on hers. His eyes were soft, like he was in love.

"No, man," Nick said. "You know I love that song, but it's not even nineties. Came out in 2000."

"Just bass and drums," Matt persisted. "Come on."

"We've got to run through shit for the show," Nick shot back.

"All she knows is 'Creep,'" Matt said, soft but urgent. "It hurts deep inside; that's the only Radiohead she knows."

Nick gasped and looked down at her like she had smothered a puppy. "Damn." He brought his sticks over his heart. "Okay, maybe we should run through 'Fake Plastic Trees' too."

Matt leaned over, adjusted his amp, and brought his hand up the neck of bass; then he gave her a sweet but serious look. "Close your eyes and listen," he told her. His eyes seemed focused on her lips.

She sank back against the couch and tried to restrain her schoolgirl smile. She closed her eyes as he unleashed a growlish vibration through the speakers. After a couple of false starts, she heard him carve out a heavy bassline, intense and almost wet against her ears. Nick joined in. It felt so good to kick back and take it all in. The groove they were offering was sultry, almost hypnotic. But then Nick just stopped. She opened her eyes to see his face contorted and tense. Something wasn't right.

"Hold up," he yelled down to Matt, who stopped and waited without looking up. Just the way he had the first time he'd kissed her, when she had been on his lap. She had asked him to stop and he had obeyed. He had just paused and waited. The memory made her grateful.

They had only known each other two months. How was that possible? He meant so much to her now.

Nick was fiddling with the hi-hat, the set of twin cymbals on the stand to his left. One was inverted an inch or so above the other and he fussed with it a lot. While he often hit it with his drumsticks like the other cymbals, the hi-hat also had a foot pedal. She watched him work it with his left foot until he seemed satisfied. Whitney called him a syncopation stud. Whit actually talked about Nick a lot. Via tried not to watch him too much because Matt could be sensitive about all the attention tossed Nick's way. Still, it was hard not to be impressed. When Nick got going—each limb with a mind of its own— he frenzied her into a trance.

She returned her attention to her Tristan. His hands remained over the strings of his old brown bass. Envy seemed to be reserved for shows. She hadn't realized there were so many ways to play the bass. On some songs he used a pick, always a Fender Heavy, and on others he just used his fingers. Sometimes he changed the position of his hand and used his thumb to pop the strings. He called that slap bass. He also had a foot pedal he used sometimes, though she had no idea why. She found herself confused by all of the terms he used to describe the sound he was going for: sludgy, grimy, juicy, crunchy. All she knew is that he looked so happy when he was playing, so strong and above it all. Flow, he called it. While he asked her a million questions, trying to unearth every little detail about her, she found all she had to do was watch him play to learn everything she needed to know.

Matt was staring at her. It felt like there was nobody else in the room, in the world. Sometimes when he looked at her, she knew he must have her figured out. He was capable of destroying her, and she hated it. But then, she would tell herself to mellow out. Maybe it was becoming real for him too. She wanted that to be true. But, then what would they do? Her mind hyperventilated with possibilities that she had never considered before.

She leaned back on the couch, and closed her eyes. Matt started playing again and she couldn't believe how intense they sounded. Nick's energy was crisp, and encircled her. Matt vibrated and entranced every cell in her body.

The side basement door flew open and she jumped a foot off the couch. She looked over to see it was just Alicia and Kaytlyn. The guys stopped playing. She sat up and tried to appear casual.

Alicia shot Nick a sexy grin and sat down on the end of the couch. "Hey, Via." She had always been nice, but was usually pretty quiet. When she wasn't at the club she looked pretty normal, like a busty soccer mom with extra long fingernails. Sometimes they had designs painted on them or sported tiny fake diamonds. Tonight they were plain old metallic violet.

Kaytlyn didn't bother to sit down or take off her tight brown leather jacket; she seemed to be more interested in examining the white powder residue on the coffee table. "Hey, Vixen. How's your husband?"

Ouch. Mortified, Via tried to compose herself. Nobody said a word. She couldn't bear to look up at Matt, who still stood on stage. "Fiancé," she finally answered. "And, I have no idea." Her hair was hot and heavy against her scalp. The back of her neck was damp with sweat. "Fine, probably."

Kaytlyn cocked her head to the side, muttered, "So shady," and flopped down on the other couch. She looked up to Matt. "Carlos wants to know if you're coming in tonight."

He leaned over and unplugged from his amp, hard. The cord's end flicked like an aggressive snake. "I've already talked to him today," he said. "Don't worry about it." He set his bass on its stand and jumped down from the stage.

"Aren't we running through the new ones?" Nick asked. "Gotta get on the new shit—you're killing me."

"Later," Matt said as he grabbed Via by the hand and led her toward the stairwell. His hand felt hot and frustrated wrapped around hers. He must be so pissed, she thought. He was going up the stairs two at a time.

"We're going long tomorrow, then," Nick yelled over. "Or you owe me a hundred bucks, *fo sho* —consider it a slacker tax!"

She could tell Nick wasn't too mad because he was using his ironic urbonics. And it sounded like he had already refocused his attention onto Alicia. "Alley Cat, come check out that Macklemore song I told you about."

\* \* \*

# VIA

**UPSTAIRS, HE DIDN'T SAY** a word, just closed and locked his bedroom door, then yanked her into his arms. She didn't want him to feel how sweaty her neck was, so she leaned away. For all this talk of being a germaphobe, he never seemed to mind her cooties.

He came back in for another pass, less Wile E. Coyote this time. "I'm sorry about her," he said. He put his hands on her hips and pulled in her close. She leaned in for a hug. His t-shirt smelled fresh from the dryer. She was going to start associating sex with the little Snuggle fabric softener bear.

"Is that why you pulled me up here? Sex?" she asked. "I was scared that you were going to break up with me."

He didn't answer at first. His lips were investigating the crook of her neck, moving along her jawline. But then, he pulled back and gave her a smug smile. "If you were afraid I'd break up with you, that means you're admitting we're together," he said.

He had her trapped. Right there. She couldn't manage to form any words, but she could tell by his grin that she didn't have to. The cat had torn through the bag.

"Is that okay?" She just had to ask.

"You finally want to know what's up," he said. "You want to know what I'm feeling."

"I just..."

"Why are you so embarrassed?" he whispered in her ear. He planted mini-kisses down the side of her neck. She couldn't just ask for what she wanted. It was a fuzzy foreign concept. She couldn't very well tell him that what she really wanted was for him to drag her into bed so they could sex away the afternoon, snuggle through the night, and forget about tomorrow. She couldn't tell him he brought out something hopeful in her, something real and alive.

He wasn't giving up. His eyes entreated hers. "Then tell me what to say. What should I say?"

"You don't need to say anything," she said. "Just be nice to me."

He pulled back a little, but his hands didn't leave her hips. The smile she was growing to love disappeared. "I'm not being nice to you?"

"No. I mean, yes." She was confusing herself now. "I mean, keep being nice." What was with him? All she wanted to do was get down to it, to feel his warm skin all over her. Talk was scary. It was like the more she shared the more he wanted. Soon she would say too much, or say the wrong thing. Then maybe he wouldn't want her at all anymore. She started to unhook his belt.

He trained his eyes upon her lips and his stubbly cheeks pulled back into a semi-smile. He brought his hands up her back, through her hair and up behind her ears. He backed her toward his bed. "Now we're talking." He pulled her sweater up and over her head and tossed it on the desk. "I love that bra," he whispered. He seemed to say that no matter what style or color lingerie she wore. She helped him out of his sweatshirt.

Her lips meandered a trail of kisses from his neck down his chest to his stomach, but she stopped just short of his boxers. "I don't want to come off like a groupie," she said. His stomach heaved as he laughed, and she stood up tall for an instant before he flung her down onto the bed. "You're never going to forget that, are you? Brat." He straddled her. She laughed until he brought her arms up over her head and pinned her. He came in for a kiss.

"Stop it," she begged. Panic rushed her.

He released her, his face horrified. "What?" he asked, sounding baffled. "Did I hurt you?"

No. He hadn't been the one to hurt her.

"I'm so sorry," she said, sitting up and reaching for his hand. He hesitated before bringing his hand over to join hers. Their fingers intertwined.

"It's just, I just don't like being held down like that." She wanted to backtrack, to tell him it wasn't a big deal, but from the look on his face it was clear he would never believe that.

Her father had pinned her down, more than once. It had never been sexual. He had never touched her. It hadn't been anything weird like that. He had never hit her, though that last time her arms had been bruised. Memories of those last months had been terrorizing her more and more.

*Her father's questions were relentless. His furious face just inches from hers. "Where did she take you?" He sat on her, and held her hands above her head. He was so heavy. He pushed her wrists harder against the hardwood until her knuckles split and stung. "Did she take you to see some man?"*

*She was so scared.*

*Her mother's voice was on top of them. "Please. Leave her alone."*

*His weight was gone. He was stalking after her mother now.*

*Mama's voice was farther away. "We were at the store. Bags are in the kitchen. Bags are in the kitchen. Check the kitchen!"*

*"Why do you lie to me?" he yelled after her. "Why do you make me crazy?"*

Via couldn't stand to be in that old place, so she smiled now and tried to will it all away. She still wanted Matt. More now. She needed him to take her away to some new place in her head. She would focus on him, how sensitive he wanted to be. She moved in closer to him and pushed it all aside. "Pinning *you* would be another story, though," she said. "I would be cool with that."

"Are you sure I didn't hurt you?"

She shook her head and tried to smile. And then she remembered their first time—on the stairs under the orange oval vortex. When he had asked if she was okay. "We can play the gingerbread man game," she said, hopefully. "I can jump upon your stomach and you can carry me across the river."

His laugh was tentative at first, but then he rolled closer. "Hell yeah, I'll carry you across the river." She straddled him and they just sat there awhile. He looked up at her and she couldn't believe how lucky she was.

He rested his hands against the sides of her waist. "I need you, want you." His voice mirrored his expression, soft and sure. "I want to be as close to you as I can possibly be. How can we make that happen?"

His words were as welcome as Seattle sunlight in February. Without a doubt, she finally understood. This was what love felt like.

* * *

# MATT

**MATT'S PHONE BUZZED** atop the bedside table. He reached over and read Nick's text. *SHFT w/AC d-n-d.* Good for him, he thought. Alicia was cool. Then another text popped up, *KC, Josh gone.* Thank God, he thought. Miss Kandy Cane had finally taken the hint. Relieved, he turned off his phone and put it back on the table. He didn't want to be an asshole, but he absolutely would be if pushed hard enough. He figured any man would.

He put his arm back against Via's back and drew her in closer. He felt the most amazing sense of mellowness. They were listening to The Foo Fighters, and he knew "Everlong" would never sound the same again. It would be burned into his brain as "Having Sex with Via" music, like Marley, Johnny Cash, and Billie Holiday. She turned on her side and laid her cheek against his chest. She still wasn't close enough, so he pulled her in and used his feet to lace her ankles over his. He wanted to get tangled up with her.

Why did this girl make him feel like such...a girl? He was the guy. He was supposed to be lazy and aloof after sex. She was supposed to be chatty and try to negotiate labels and commitments.

He wondered if she was sad, missing her parents. Should he ask about them?

"I want to know more, about you," he said. Damn, that sounded smooth, he thought. It hadn't been a line. He had meant it.

She slid over until she was on top of him and leaned her chin against her hands halfway up his chest. "Am I too heavy?" she asked.

Why did girls always ask that? The answer was always no. He let out a little "whatever" groan and started playing with her hair, which spanned the width of his chest and tickled him. "It's really hard to keep my hands out of your hair," he said as he worked his fingers through like a slow comb. He was love drunk. They resonated. He had never been so sure of anything in his life.

"You want to talk about your parents?" He had no idea where his words had come from. They'd just arrived on the scene as awkward as religious freaks at the door.

The moment was toast. He could hear it in the oppressive silence. Still, he needed to know. How could they possibly have anything real if they didn't go there? "I know how it ended." He made a point of not saying he was sorry. "But, were there some good times, before that?" He would get her to think about something positive. There must be something.

"He was mental," she finally said. "They thought bipolar, but it was more than that. They could never get his meds figured out. He would go off sometimes, hit my mother. I don't know, maybe he was just abusive. A lot of people are bipolar and they don't kill people."

Her words made him beyond uncomfortable, but he didn't squirm. He wouldn't do that do her.

"I don't remember a lot," she said. "As the anniversary gets closer, I feel like I'm remembering more, and I hate it." She hugged him hard. God, she was stronger than he had realized.

"Anniversary?" he asked and felt her soft breath tickle into the crook of his neck.

"The shooting was ten years ago, December 21st."

"Just before Christmas?"

"He was an artist, like you. A painter."

"What?" He pulled back far enough that she had to look at him. "Is that bad?" he asked. "I mean, that I paint? Does that scare you?"

"You would think so, but no," she said. "You're nothing like him. Not at all. You seemed balanced."

"Me?" He laughed out loud.

"He was fixated. Sixteen hours a day—every day—for months on end. His world hung on the end of his brush," she said. "But, you've been able to take a break, shift to other outlets. It doesn't own you."

"Nick calls me a renaissance slacker."

"I love that. Slacking isn't the worst thing in the world. My father let his need for perfection tear him up." She paused a moment, then asked, "What about your parents? Why didn't you go to Arizona with them?"

Of course, he realized. I'll share my shit with her. That will make her feel better.

"I was a senior in high school when they moved. Grandma Daney offered, and staying with her and Nick just seemed the thing to do. My parents worked a lot, so I was over at Nick's all the time anyway."

"They're pretty normal?"

"*They* are normal," he said. "Me, not so much." His chest felt tight, heavy. "I was never a normal kid. Learned to read when I was three, blew out the standardized testing, that kind of thing. They wanted me to be a physicist or something. When I was in the fifth grade, they transferred me to the Highly Capable program. It was at a different school and I kind of freaked out."

"Like panic attacks?"

"I'd get worked up, then couldn't settle down. I started repeating things to sooth myself. 'I'm good, I'm good, I'm good.' Pretty much, I just wanted to be left alone. My parents were desperate to fix me. I'm their only kid; they couldn't have more. The more they pushed, the worse I got. It got to the point where I refused to go to the doctor anymore. I didn't even want to leave my room."

"And then you got into music?"

"Yeah, and I was good. It gave me a sense of control, somehow. The more time I spent with Nick and G-Dane, the better I felt. She got me into meditation. She's the one who taught me to paint. She used to paint too, before the Parkinson's got bad."

She nuzzled in closer. "And so you moved in?"

"My junior year my parents spent the winter in Arizona; they grew up there. I just stayed with Nick and G-Dane. My parents sent G-Dane checks—for my art classes, for food, whatever. When they came back and told me they wanted to move down there permanently, I was like, 'Nope.'" He paused to collect his thoughts. Slowly, she brushed her hand across his chest and waited. "Nick and I had been working for Carlos and he'd been paying us cash. Music was where I wanted to be anyway, so I didn't see a need for college. That was really hard for my parents. They still bug me about getting a degree. Still think I have potential."

She turned into him and kissed his neck. A tender little kiss. Her lips lingered there and he closed his eyes until he felt her reposition herself against his chest again. That one little kiss meant the world to him.

"And lucky numbers?" she asked.

"Twos are my favorite," he said. "I don't know why. And repeating numbers are all lucky."

"Repeating numbers?"

"Like 111, 1111, 222, 2222—no matter what number it is, that's lucky. G-Dane calls those angel numbers. She says that when you see them, it's the universe's way of telling you that you are right where you are supposed to be. That day we did Molly you said you hated the number four," he added, "but what about 444 or 4444?"

"It was four p.m., four days before Christmas," she said then rolled away from him before he could stop her.

"Wait," he said. He had gone too far, asked one too many questions. Why couldn't he have left well enough alone?

She was getting out of bed, suddenly in hyper-drive.

"Don't get up," he said, reaching over for her. "More snugs?"

She hung her legs over the edge of the bed. Did she even know? Did she even realize that she held the power now? Hadn't he made that as clear as that Jimmy Cliff song?

Her gaze upon the desk chair was seemingly fixed, scared even. He wondered what he was going to have to say to get back to where they had just been. He held out his arms and tried in vain to coax her back into bed.

"Can we go downstairs and do another line?"

"Now?"

"I'm coming down. I can't deal with it right now."

"Coming down is unavoidable, you know," he said. "That's why it's a terrible high. After the first few lines it's not about being high anymore, it's about not coming down. That's how people get hooked."

She stood up, pulled his t-shirt on over her head, and let it fall over her naked body. "Please? Just a little more?"

He had no clue as to why the sight of her wearing his shirt was such a turn on. It was like she was his somehow. And now that shirt would smell like her. He knew he was in trouble; he was in love with her. He knew her interest in nose candy was a problem, but the larger part of him wanted her too much to say anything about it. That would be another talk for another day. She was just going through a hard time, and he would help her. He had already told her she was pretty, earlier downstairs, but he almost said it again.

# CHAPTER 24

## NICK

**NICK PULLED** the special brownies from the oven and took a whiff. Ah, they smelled like stoner heaven. He left the pan on top of the stove because most of the countertop was occupied with tasty-looking vanilla cupcakes topped with white frosting. He took a seat at the kitchen island where Via sat frosting one of her creations. Her hair was up in a bun. She looked like a librarian, but not in a good way. Matt seemed to like the minimal makeup thing. Nick thought at times she looked like she could still be in high school.

"So, tell me more about this fifty-thousand-dollar donation thing," she said as she spread white frosting, twisting the cupcake as she went.

He wasn't surprised she was curious. He still couldn't believe it. "Well, Obliviot has a no-request policy," he explained. "So, we're headlining the Kidz Rock holiday concert at the Showbox, and somebody sent them a fifty-thousand-dollar donation, but Matt has to sing a chick song—Sheryl Crow."

"Bizarre," she said.

"If he accepts the challenge, that is. He never sings, except on a couple Cake songs. And that's really more like poetic rhythmic talking."

She frowned. "Of course, he'll do it," she said. "Right?"

"He thinks it's a hoax. Fifty grand is more than we expected to raise in the first place. The Kidz Rock guys haven't tried to cash the check yet. I think it's legit. I think it's from Mike McCready and those guys. They're always donating money."

"Who?"

"Think Pearl Jam, you know Eddie Vedder, of course. I met their drummer, Mike Cameron, you know. He came last spring and did a four-hour workshop for the kids. Such a good guy; brought them all drumsticks. He was with Soundgarden too." Nick was captivated by the cupcake in her hand. His sweet tooth was raring to go.

"How long have you two been teaching there?" she asked.

"We started as students in junior high school, weekly lessons, small shows. As we got older we took on mentoring some of the younger kids. It wasn't like one day they were like, 'You're a teacher now, go forth and be awesome.'"

"Oh? You don't get paid?"

"Just in green-room food and praise." He was ready to change the subject. It sucked when women brought up the subject of money.

"Matt still hasn't texted?" she asked. Again. "Shouldn't he be back from Portland by now? Should we be getting worried?"

He looked at the wall clock and did the math in his head. Matt's trips were a quick twelve to fourteen hours. Portland was only three hours away, but Matt picked up then delivered to Carlos's three clubs down there before driving back to Hotties with the bulk of the product.

"It's not even midnight," he told her. "Chill. He'll be back in an hour or two."

"Thanks for letting me take over your kitchen," she said. Again.

"I told Matt I would be a good host." He didn't mind. In fact, he was hoping to use their time alone to figure her out. He wanted to ask her about the fiancé. He wanted to ask her about her sincerity. He wanted to confess that he was worried because he'd never seen his best friend so ape-shit idiotic over a girl before. Instead, he just watched the meticulous way she swirled frosting atop the cupcake in her hand. "So, when can I have one?" he asked.

"Take one of the crappy ones," she said, pointing to the reject tray. "The good ones are for youth group."

He wanted the one in her hand.

"So, when is Alicia coming over?" she asked in an ooh-Nick-likes-Alicia voice.

"Settle down," he told her. Alicia was cool; one of several cool women he spent time with. She was older, independent, and told him exactly what she wanted from him. They had just negotiated a mutually beneficial sexual contract. He wanted enthusiastic blow jobs and the freedom to see other women without guilt or penalty. She wanted passionate kissing and lots of snuggle time. He had also promised to shave before she came over. He didn't mind her terms because he loved to kiss and cuddle, so it was the least he could do.

He licked his lips and watched Via. There must have been sixty cupcakes there. Each batch had gotten progressively better looking. He couldn't stop lusting for the one that she held. She was like Eve in the garden, except she wouldn't give it up. She had been working on it for like five minutes. Her quest for pastry perfection was beyond annoying.

"Damn girl, you know you're crazy too," he said, matter-of-factly. "You and Matt are like two OCD peas in a pod."

She stopped and gave him the strangest look—wide-eyed, like he had called Santa Claus a child molester.

"OCD?" she asked, her voice little more than a hush. "He's never called it that," she said. "I didn't think you ever called it that. You know he hates labels."

He laughed in her face. Was she really schooling him on his best friend? "He's a big boy," he said as he leaned over, snagged her cupcake, and started undressing it. She reached for it, so he licked it.

"You dick!" She gave him a swift smack on the side of the head, but it was so worth it. She punched his shoulder and then his arm while he scarfed it down.

"Hey, watch the arm," he protested, his mouth full of sweet satisfaction.

"That's right, don't want to wreck your epic drumming career." Her tone was playful, but tinged with snark.

He thought she was hot when she embraced her inner bitch; he liked it so much more than when she gave off the Christian-girl vibe. He tried not to think about kissing her. How he wished he hadn't. But at the time, he hadn't known they were going to end up being friends.

"You know it," he said.

"Matt says you are crazy-talented. Like Dave Grohl in training."

Her words seized him and held strong. He felt himself blush. While he knew he should be asking her questions about her life on Vashon and her intentions toward his best friend, he never tired of compliments. And so he waited for her to continue. He wanted more. Praise was his currency. It was time to get paid.

"He says you're way too good for Obliviot, for covers."

It was true, but it didn't feel good to hear it. Her words just reminded him that he and Matt needed to get serious about their own material soon, or else he was going to lose it. Crawl out of his skin and slink down to the snake pit that was LA.

"What else does your man say?"

Now it was her turn to blush. Her hair was pulled too far back to provide any cover, so she had nowhere to hide. Her flushed cheeks were all the evidence he needed. Matt wasn't in this alone. Good to know.

"He says you've been playing since grade school."

"Yep. My grandma bought me a cheap little drum set for my eleventh birthday. I'd only been living with her for a couple of months."

They had set it up in the basement and she'd told him to wail away on it all he wanted. She had bought him a punching bag, too. Damn clever woman, providing outlets for his inevitable emotions long before he admitted to having any.

"Tell me about your mom," she said, hard at work on another cupcake.

He rarely told women too much about his childhood, but it didn't seem like a big deal to tell her. It was probably because she was Matt's, so the possibility of sex with her was off the table anyway. He wasn't running a game, trying to get in her pants, so could let his guard down. Matt had mentioned she had an uncle in New York. Sounded like he was her only family, so there must be a story there. It was quiet for a moment. She just sat there frosting and waiting.

"My mom had me young, and my dad didn't hang around," he said. "She has shitty taste in men. We ended up living with some loser in Tacoma, and after him, some other loser out by the airport."

She looked up at him and nodded. It was subtle, but he found it comforting. As if his story, his "scary tale," wasn't too pitiful.

"And then?"

"And then she met a new loser, some guy from Florida. He promised her this great life in the Keys. She hated the rain, so she bailed."

Via finished a cupcake, put it down, and reached for another. "Have you seen her since?"

"She comes out for a week every summer," he said. "Leaves the loser at home. She says she's happy. She hugs me like every five minutes. She's come to see Obliviot. It's cool." Of course, it was not. Being around her was a feast of awkward. She served up a dozen different flavors of negativity.

"It's cool, really?" she asked drawing him out. "Seems like it would be rough."

"I guess," he confessed. "But my grandma does her best to keep the mood light. It feels kind of fake, but it's easier to just smile and hug than to be honest." Thinking about his grandma's antics made him smile. "You know what my grandma does every year after my mom leaves?"

"What?" She was already smiling, anticipating.

"She clarifies the house with sage. She cranks New Age lute music and walks through the entire house with burning sage. I give her shit for doing it, but I actually kind of appreciate it. It feels symbolic. Like an annual reset."

"Maybe..." she began, but stopped.

He leaned in. "Maybe what?"

She pointed to the jar of sprinkles on the table. "Maybe we don't need sprinkles after all." She admired the cupcake in her hand. "This one's pretty close to perfect."

"Oh."

"And," she looked into his eyes. "Maybe your mom knew you deserved the best. Maybe she didn't trust herself to give you the best and knew you'd be better off here. She loved you too much to raise you herself."

He smiled at her. Maybe she was right and maybe she was wrong. Either way, it was a cool thing to say. He would abandon his qualms about her worthiness. Matt would be lucky to have her. They would be good for each other. Now, if she could just inspire him to write some fucking lyrics.

She stood up, looking quite serious.

"Nick?" she asked as she held out her latest cupcake, the one just shy of perfect. "Will you accept this cupcake?"

"Yes, dork," he said, flattered she remembered their balloon animal exchange. "Yes, I will." He took his time pulling down the paper this time. He decided not to eat this one like a mangy beast.

She went to the sink and started washing her hands. "So, it's midnight. Shouldn't Alicia be here soon?"

Alicia. Shit. He stood up and popped the rest of his cupcake in his mouth. He needed to shave in a hurry.

"Via, let her in when she comes?" he called back on his way through the dining room. "Grab her a drink?"

"Got it," she called back. "And Nick?" He stopped at the bottom of the stairs so he could hear her. "Nick, can we do a little blow tonight? While we're waiting up for Matt?"

He knew Alicia would be up for that. Plus, he had promised to be a good host. "Yeah, but you don't want to stay up all night. Remember you've got your Jesus kids in the morning."

*   *   *

# MATT

**MATT GRABBED A BEER** from the fridge, turned around, and took in the tower of cupcake trays occupying the island. On the counter was a plate of brownies with a note that read, "NOT for Jesus kids." He grabbed one and made his way back to the living room. He was so done with blow for the night. Three lines was three too many. He resumed his position on the couch next to Via. Nick and Alicia had taken up the other end of the sectional. They listened to KISW as they discussed random questions of the day. It was only three a.m., but it had been a long-assed day. His mood was fluctuating between cool and cranky. He had hoped to find Via snuggled up in his bed when he'd gotten back from Portland, not snorting rails with Alicia. His supposed best friend was serving as line-tender, high only on brownies and beer. Matt's whole day had revolved around the shit. He was upsetting himself, so he took a deep breath and tried to center himself.

Nick was describing the television show he had watched the night before about alien sightings throughout history. "And so, what if the dark hooded figure they saw wasn't ghostly at all?"

"I still don't get it, dude," Matt admitted. He looked over to see if Via was getting the gist of Nick's claim. She leaned over the coffee table, situated the straw, and snorted the first half of the fat rail on the end. Some of her hair fell in front of her face and she paused. He reached over to tuck it back behind her ear and watched her expression soften into a smile. It was good to see her smile.

"Nick's saying the Grim Reaper is an alien," she said, then snorted the rest of her line.

"Think about it," Nick went on. "People see the Grim Reaper just before they die, right? This show said medieval villagers saw a dark hooded figure in the fields spreading some sort of mist before the plagues hit. Maybe the Grim Reaper was actually an alien charged with reducing the human population."

Matt didn't bother to laugh. "That's some crazy-assed speculation, even for you."

"Whatever," Nick said. "But, *Ancient Aliens* is a good show. It's on the History Channel. It's not bullshit. It's been fact checked."

Matt rolled his eyes. "How in the hell do you fact check medieval aliens?"

Nick glared at him and they stared each other down. Finally, Nick leaned back and said, "Fair enough," which was his way of saying, "You win." Such a smug bastard.

"Have you heard Nick's worm idea?" Alicia asked Via.

Alicia was getting on Matt's last fucking nerve. What was she talking about now?

"So, if the early bird gets the worm," Nick said. He leaned over the table as though he were imparting sage advice. "Then the smartest worm is the one who sleeps in, am I right?"

Via nodded, but didn't laugh. Instead, she grabbed the eye drops from the coffee table and unscrewed the tiny plastic top while giving him a lame little, "Good one." Then she leaned hear head back and put a few drops in each eye.

Matt watched as a few drops of stray saline made their way down her cheek. Gently, he used his finger to push them aside. His gesture made her stiffen; it seemed to annoy her. There was no warmth in the moment. He hated the disconnect.

She had been a tease all night, first flirty, then distant. No SHFT all night, no snugs, no private time at all. He couldn't even get her up to his room. Couldn't pull her away from the cocaine/coffee table. She was focused on Nick's hand. He had been swiping triple time: skim,

skim, skim, tap, tap, tap. Matt wanted to slap the credit card right out of his hand.

Nick saw him glaring. "Here, Rain Man." He handed over the credit card. His tone was significantly snotty.

Matt swept the coke back and forth over the glass. Skim, skim. Tap, tap. He felt better now, in control. Via began rubbing his back. She mirrored his double-time movements. Rub, rub. Scratch, scratch. Rub, rub.

Her touch felt amazing. He wanted to drag her upstairs and keep her there for a week.

"I'm done with this shit," he vowed as he lined up two long bumps for the girls. "I'm going to bed." He had hoped she would offer to join him. He had hoped she would drop the straw and take his hand, but she didn't.

\* \* \*

# MATT

**HE TENSED UP** when he felt something hard whack him on the side of his neck, just under his ear. Surprise, surprise—she had finally come to bed. Not only that, but she had actually fallen asleep, in spite of the half gram of coke in her head—must have been the weed brownie. He opened his eyes and saw that his bedroom was still dark. He turned toward her and brought her arms in and under his. He couldn't help but notice the insult she had added to his injury. He hated that damned "enragement" ring. It was bad enough he had to see it sparkle in bar light at Hotties or feel it when he reached for her hand while they were driving home. It was messed up that she was now literally hurting him with it too.

She had been spending the night more and more often, so he had come to expect her nightmares. He had learned that the best way to stop her thrashing was to wrap his arms around her and whisper "shh" until she stopped resisting. Once her breathing returned to normal, he inhaled the sweet smell of her hair. She still wouldn't tell him what made it smell so good. He couldn't help but wonder if her fiancé did the same when he was with her. That inconvenient asshole who would be home in a couple of months. The thought turned his stomach sour. Did he love the way her hair smelled too? What was she going to do when he got back into town? Was she really going to leave that guy? How was that even going to work? These were the crazy questions that occupied his mind.

Coming down from coke was hellacious. It was an ocean of evil and he was tired of treading water. He fucking hated coke. He hated himself for building his life around it. The weed brownie hadn't helped soften the landing.

She started thrashing. "Please," she whined, "pretty lights." He braced his calves for the onslaught of her boney little feet. His flannel pajama bottoms did little to protect him. Lately, her dream world had seemed a horrific place. She called out for the pretty lights often, but he couldn't tell if they were good or bad. When they had done Molly, she had explained them in positive terms, but tonight, like so many other nights, they seemed to be tormenting her.

"Shh," he told her. It wasn't like he enjoyed seeing her like this, but it was like their demons connected them somehow. He held her while his mind wandered back fifteen years to that therapist, Tadd, the one with the train set taking up half his office. He had asked a lot of questions about responsibility. "Do you sometimes feel responsible for the others? Like if you don't repeat certain things or do certain things something bad will happen to them?" He had been the one to tell Matt's parents it wasn't their fault. That certain neural pathways in their son's brain were wired differently.

He nuzzled in as he felt her starting up again, shaking her head, mumbling. Sad stories were common at the club; most girls had been either molested or ignored at some fundamental level. And it was obvious there was something not right about Carlos. His dad was in prison. Whitney, however, seemed to like her family. They had been there for her when she'd gotten knocked up at seventeen. They helped her limp through senior year. She still lived with her mother, who thought she was a bartender. Word was, Bella's dad died of a heroine overdose. He had never known the guy. He and Nick had never gotten into that scene.

Via had stopped thrashing. He relaxed his grip on her, but still held her close. He whispered in her ear. Now that he had her in his life, he needed to tell her she was pretty every time he saw her, or else he worried he wouldn't see her again.

\* \* \*

# VIA

SHE SAT BACK against his pillow and closed her eyes again. That had been a bad one, so real. Like the devil himself had been running the projector. She wiped sweat off her forehead. Were her nightmares getting worse or was she just remembering them more? She used to have dreams where Mama would sit next to her and run her fingers through her hair. She would sing to her in Swedish. That dream always felt real, as though her mother was using a portal to reach back into her life and touch her. Why weren't those dreams visiting her anymore? It was almost Thanksgiving. And on its heels was Christmas, ugly goddamned Christmas. And then New Year's. She loved New Year's.

She heard Nick screaming up to her from the bottom of the stairs. "Via, you getting up? You've got to go kick some bible study ass—kids today really need Jesus."

Damn it, of course. She'd need to make a run for the ferry. Would Beth notice she hadn't come home again last night? If so, she would ask about the shelter. Via dreaded the thought of it. Beth praising her for her good works, her compassion for women and children in need. The devil's hands were doing double duty. His knuckles kneaded into her neck and solar plexus. She got up and found her clothes from the night before, folded neatly on top of the dresser. Matt had offered her a drawer of her own, but the implications made her queasy. What was she going to do? Blowing off January was becoming more and more difficult.

"Is Matt here?" she yelled down to Nick as she started stepping into her jeans.

"He's teaching this morning," Nick answered. "He didn't want to wake you."

God, how she wished he had. She was snuggle deficient. They hadn't gotten much connection time because she was all about staying high. It was a losing battle, but somehow a part of her thought she could win it. Be the one person in the history of mankind to snort a line, just one, and stay high forever. Regret was kicking her ass. The holidays were coming. What day was it anyway? Somewhere in the thirties? She wondered. That was great news—she had lost track of her countdown. At least she had that going for her. Her life of deviance had helped her with that. She had been catching glimpses of good lately, here and there. Matt told her to focus on the good, on what she wanted more of. But positive thinking felt so unnatural. It was tiring.

She went to the bathroom and washed her face. She cupped some water into the palm of her hand and sniffed as hard as she could. Water up her nose was far from pleasant, but she needed the last of last night's blow to go as deep into her brain as possible.

She reached for her clothes. If only she could stay high forever. Or at least through the holidays. But then, Dan would be back. What was she going to do then? She checked her phone; there was a message from Carlos. He always called, never texted, which was unfortunate because it was hard to tell him no over the phone.

# CHAPTER 25

## VIA

**WALKING INTO YOUTH GROUP** late was now the norm. She did her best to look innocent, just another rough night at the domestic violence shelter. Hiding behind the big-ass tray of cupcakes helped. Coming to church the day after a coke binge was the worst. Paranoia gripped her and she knew a quick booster line would help, but she had none. She should be done with it. Matt was right. She wanted to get her shit together, but it was hard. Coming down was evil.

Carlos had left two messages. He wanted her to come in early for her shift tonight, so they could hang out. She hadn't called him back for fear of saying yes.

She put the cupcakes down on the back table, retied her big sweater a bit tighter around her waist, and turned to face the room. As she had hoped, most everyone was sitting on the floor listening to Greg begin his lesson. There were two obvious exceptions, however. Beth was sitting with her group in the front but had her curious face turned back and was trying to make eye contact. Via acted as though she didn't notice and nonchalantly walked toward the other exception, Nate, who looked thrilled to see her. He and the rest of her kids—her Jesus kids, as Nick called them—meant the world to her. They weren't always easy— they asked dumb questions and squirmed and required a lot of patience— but they made her feel needed and worthwhile. She sat down between Nate and Taylor and then unzipped her leather bible, but she couldn't remember what verse they were on.

"Let's break up into our small-group time," Greg said. "You can recite your verse of the week and then discuss with your small-group leaders."

She offered what she knew must be a stiff smile and opened her bible, "Okay kids, lets go to this week's verse. Who wants to go first?" They had all opened their study bibles to Luke 18: 13-14. She would only have fifteen minutes to get through everyone and then go over the question of the week.

"The parable of the Pharisee and the tax collector," Nate began.

Without thinking, she sniffed hard and rubbed her nose. "Sorry," she said. "Allergies again. Go ahead, Nate."

"The Pharisee stood by himself and prayed. 'God, I thank you that I am not like the other people—robbers, evildoers, adulterers—or even like this tax collector. I fast twice a week and give a tenth of all I get.'" Nate paused, took a breath and continued. "But the tax collector stood at a distance. He would not even look up to heaven, but beat his breast and said, 'God, have mercy on me, a sinner.' Jesus said, 'I tell you that this man, rather than the other, went home justified before God. For all those who exalt themselves will be humbled, and those who humble themselves will be exalted.'"

"Awesome, Nate," she said, so proud. But his words had latched onto her guilt receptors. She sniffed again. She was worse than any tax collector.

Taylor leaned over and pointed. "Miss Via, what is that? On your bible? Is that blood?" They all looked over toward Via's lap. She slammed it closed before they could see it. She stood up as fast as she could with her hand over her face. Head held high, she went straight into the small bathroom at the end of the hall and locked herself inside.

"No, no," she scolded her reflection. She kept her right hand over her nose, but unrolled a foot or so of toilet paper. It was the worst bloody nose ever. Gruesome and absolutely her fault. She tilted her head back and sat on the floor.

"Via, open the door. Let me in please. Via?"

"I'm fine, Beth," she said through her toilet-paper-laden face. "Just a nose bleed. I'm fine."

"Via, sweetheart, I'm worried about you. Please come out."

Sweetheart? Her mother had called her that. Except Mama had always been the one locked inside the bathroom. Via had always been the one on the outside, begging her mother to come out and talk.

*She gave her mother twenty minutes. It often took that long for the sound of her sobbing to slow down. Then Via knocked again. "Please come out. He's gone now." The door creaked open and her mother came out with her hands over her face. As she passed, Via handed over the washcloth she'd carefully wrapped around some ice cubes. Her mother sniffled and said, "I just need to lay down for a while, sweetheart. Really, it's fine." Via pulled up the blanket from the foot of the bed and cuddled up with her.*

That had been the time he had gone through her mother's purse, on the hunt for proof of God knows what. He'd thrown out her lipstick. It had been too whorish. Was that why the taste and feel of lipstick made her want to gag? So many memories had been coming back lately, too many to deal with.

Beth had stopped knocking.

Via went to the sink and splashed cold water on her face. Blood still seeped from her nostril. She didn't recognize the hollow girl in the mirror. Must be Vixen, which was cool because Vixen didn't give a shit. Vixen would run home and get a quick shower before going back over town. She would go into Hotties a bit early.

\* \* \*

# CARLOS

**"IT'S GOOD TO** see you," Carlos said. He walked behind his desk, opened a side drawer, pulled out his white goody box, and brought it back to the coffee table.

"You sick?" he wondered. Her typical smile was absent.

"No, it's just been a hard day."

He pulled out one of three plastic baggies. It was his private stash—pure, not the lower-grade shit he would have served the average skank. He knew she was used to the good stuff. Word was, she was banging Mattais, which would explain why he had no interest in the club girls anymore. Via looked enough like Sonia to make her appealing anyway, but knowing rock star wanna-be was so sprung on her made her even more attractive as a plaything. Mattais was too busy to hang out after his shift like back in the day. Too many shows. Too many options. He seemed to be growing a bit cocky and needed to be reminded who really ruled the roost.

He stood up and walked over to the bar. "Want a drink?"

"What do you have?"

He looked down at the array of bottles underneath the bar and shook his head. "I don't know, baby. I only have forty-five bottles back here."

"Vodka and tonic, please. With lime, if you can."

He tried to suppress his smile. She was hot and everything, but he wasn't going to cut up a lime for any chick. He needed to check himself. Soon, he would have her fetching the drinks. He gave her a splash of 7UP instead. Girls seemed to like that.

She had wandered over to the side of his desk and admired the picture of Maya's kindergarten graduation. It was uncomfortable, seeing her so close to his gun drawer. She leaned over and examined the coffee cup, the one he used for pens, scissors—the one with the photo of Sam on it. From that sunny day at the aquarium. He missed them so much. It wasn't fair.

"Your son?" she asked.

He motioned for her to come join him on the couch. "Yes, but that's an old picture." He tried to regain his psychological balance while he poured out about a gram onto the middle of the glass-topped table. "I haven't seen them since March."

She came and sat next to him, but not close enough. With her hands clasped together in her lap, she wore a relaxed smile and remained quiet as her eyes searched his. Not launching into a story of her own, she sat so attentively. Just waiting. Waiting for him to talk. He felt like he could tell her his real story, but he fought the urge. He felt an odd connection with this girl, like they were watching the same channel, the same psycho show. She was like a counselor, except he felt safe talking to her. She was not focused on a notepad in her lap. She was not wrinkling up her face into a scowl. Her soft expression was full of acceptance, approval even.

"I don't normally talk about them," he said. "It's been a rough year."

"Please, forget I asked. I didn't mean to—"

He waved her off, casting his best smile. She was embarrassed now, had some color in her cheeks. He imagined it would be fun to get her a little sweaty. The thought of taking her home occurred to him. None of his girls had ever seen the inside of his house, but this one, maybe she would end up being more than a couch girl. He would answer her questions.

His hand fell into the familiar rhythmic motion of arranging the blow. He loved line-tending, the power, the attention it garnered. His heart began to beat faster, anticipating the rush. He had been doing a lot lately, even hitting the pipe from time to time. He used to think doing coke alone was for losers, but he hadn't been bullshitting her; it had been a rough year. The roughest of his life, and that was saying a lot. He sectioned off half of the pile and started moving it into generous bumps. He smiled — the sexier the girl, the fatter the line.

"You come from a big family?" he asked as he handed her a fresh straw.

She brought her hand up to her nose and sniffed hard. He laughed when she had to stop midway. She threw her head back and sucked deeper into her innocent little head.

"Good God," she said, before gasping. She was pleased, he could tell. He was going to rock her world. She was going to be so much fun to unravel.

"You know that I don't fuck around," he promised. "The best shit, always."

He wanted to rub her back while she composed herself, but didn't dare. Not yet. "Now finish, you've only done half of it."

She leaned over to the table, but hadn't changed nostrils.

"Wait." He would help her. "Use the other side. You need to switch it up. Consider it nostril training." She laughed. She was so fucking high already.

"Your family," he reminded her.

She finished her line, sat back, and sniffed hard, twice. "My parents died when I was a kid," she said. "No brothers or sisters, just an uncle back east, but he was more of a legal guardian."

Ah, the glory that is cocaine, he thought. She'll talk about anything now. She would tell him everything he wanted to know.

"I can relate," he said as he snorted up a line. He sniffed hard. The bitterness both pierced and soothed his brain. "I was a foster kid." She looked at him with such earnestness that he decided to go on. He would be straight up with this one. "My old man strangled my mother when I was three. I don't remember her."

"No other family?"

She would understand him. It was evident in the way she held eye contact. She hadn't looked away or shaken her head in pity. Her eyes displayed what seemed like empathy. She hadn't said she was sorry.

"You don't think that's insane?" he asked. "Found out she was cheating. He's doing life in Walla Walla." He was talking too much. He needed to check himself. "What about your parents?" he asked. Her supportive smile faded. She looked down into her lap. He knew he must be onto something good.

"I used to never talk about it. Guess I need to get over that, and..."

"And?"

"And since you shared," she said, eyes still downcast toward her hands. "My father shot my mother, then himself. They died together, just like that, on the living room floor."

He couldn't believe her confession. He didn't feel so alone. He started feeling as though he wanted to tell her everything. "We're the same then," he said. "We know what it's like to grow up alone." He wanted to pull her close, but thought better of it. She wasn't there yet. He would lighten the mood instead. "Like siblings of the same past. Except I want to have sex with you, of course."

She looked away.

"I'm dead serious." He leaned in. He wanted a better look at her eyes. They were nice.

"You know about Matt, don't you?"

"Sure, sure," he said, as he pulled back. He would break them up soon enough. It would be a piece of cake. But he needed to know more about the other one.

"And you're engaged too, right?"

"I don't know. Can we not talk about him? More about you."

"My wife, soon to be ex-wife, is with an old associate of mine down in Portland." He couldn't bear to say the bastard's name. "He can have her, but I want my kids. Maya is almost nine now and Sam is six. We go to court down there in a couple of weeks."

He stopped to take a breath and felt a sense of relief. It did feel good to get this out. He looked over to Via again and she was smiling at him encouragingly. It was starting to unnerve him, the way she was so patient. Why wasn't she trying to talk over him, laugh her way into her own stories?

"I'm sure they can't wait to see you again," she said.

He should take this girl with him to Portland for his court date. Sonia would get one look at Via and realize how replaceable she was. He could introduce her as "New Sonia." He cracked himself up. It was definitely time to snake this little gem away from Mattais. All he had to do was mention his private time with Via to Kaytlyn when he saw her later that week. He realized he should have the rock star go out on the road more often, too.

# Chapter 26

## Nick

**NICK PULLED UP** in front of his house. While he was happy to see the absence of raccoon activity, he was not pleased to see phone books had been left on the porch again. Phone books were a travesty of environmental justice.

This talk with Matt would have to happen right away because he felt like he was digesting a wrench. He had already taken six antacids. He didn't want to believe Kandy Cane. He wanted to blow off her gossip because he wanted to believe Via was the girl Matt needed her to be. No doubt she was a sweetheart, a great listener who never gossiped, she was never critical or catty—so unlike most of the girls they knew. She brought over beer and groceries. She kept trying to give them money for the blow they shared with her. Rare. Girls never did that. But then again, the coke was the problem. Matt seemed so happy with her around, maybe even mellow. Nick knew his best friend liked her, too much. He tried not to wonder what would have happened if he hadn't been such a gentleman that first night.

He came into the foyer. No turning back now, he thought. Time to do this. He leaned his body up toward the top of the stairs and shouted, "Hey, bro! You here?" He heard nothing, but a mellow reggae groove coming from the kitchen. Matt must be cleaning.

Let's get this out of the way, he thought as he came through the kitchen doorway. Or, maybe not. Matt's boxers were down around his calves and he had Via on her back on top of the island. He was giving it to her in time with the reggae backbeat. Super slow. Apparently, they didn't have enough room because Matt had a hand under her head, sort of cradling it over the edge. They were kissing so intently they hadn't heard him walk in.

Nick turned away, but not before noticing two things. First, that kitchen island was steady as hell. There would be no need to worry about standing on it while changing the smoke detector battery. Good to know. Second, it was obvious from the sweet intensity of their display that they were crazy about each other, probably even in love. It shouldn't have surprised him, but it still sucked to see. He had to talk to Matt, pronto.

He averted his eyes up toward the light fixture. Shit, was that dust? Everything was so messed up. What had this girl done to his best friend? He was able to back up into the living room without them noticing. He wished to God he could un-see his friend's naked ass. He was going to lose his breakfast. That island was where he and Via baked cupcakes for Christ's sake. How was he even going to look at her now?

He slid open the cabinet under the flat screen. His favorite bong was still loaded from the night before. He pulled it out, along with a lighter, and sat on the couch. He turned on the television, bowed his head, put his lips into position, then flicked the lighter and sparked up. The room was filled with the sound of Elmo's laughter and the smell of Super Silver Haze. Watching puppets recite the alphabet was about as much as his brain could handle, so he didn't bother changing the channel.

*       *       *

# Matt

**MATT FELT HER SHUDDER** beneath him and finally let himself go. He always tried to hold on for her. It wasn't easy, but he wanted to satisfy her more than anything. He pulled her in even closer and bestowed kisses behind her ear. He nibbled his way down her jawline, back toward her lips. He just couldn't stop kissing her. He loved her. The words welled up inside his throat, but died there. She must know anyway, he told himself. How could she not? It was brightly woven into every "You're pretty."

He realized she must not be comfortable, so he pulled away and looked down. Her dark hair looked wild, spread out against the yellow countertop. Her skin was flushed and peachy. He searched her face for that look of primal satisfaction he wanted to see, a sort of I've-been-well-fucked-thank-you expression. He recognized it and felt a particular kind of high no drug could ever match. He was about to pick her up and take her upstairs for a hot shower and a nap when he heard the TV in the living room switch on, and then what sounded like Sesame Street.

His Isoldey's eyes widened. While she looked alarmed, he only smiled. Nick probably didn't even know they were there—and if so, oh well. While she scrambled to find clothes, he simply pulled up his boxers and walked out to the living room.

"Morning, bro," he said, and sat at the other end of the couch. His cheeks felt like they'd been injected with helium. He hadn't planned it. She had just looked so damned good, standing there next to the kitchen island, drinking her apple juice. He had told her she was pretty and it was on.

She came into the living room, but had her eyes set on the front door. She stopped and gave him a lame little kiss as she handed him his sweatshirt. "You're going to freeze," she whispered. "Hey, Nick," she said, still looking at the door. "Gotta go, going to miss the ferry."

Matt stuck out his lower lip and offered up his saddest little-boy face. "You always say that. You know, we have a ferry schedule now, so you can't bullshit me anymore." He was only half joking. He hadn't gotten enough of her apple juice kisses. He licked his lips.

"See you Thursday," she said. "I'll stay all night, I promise." He could see her face was still flushed and it reinforced his sense of excellence.

"Sweet, like a Thanksgiving Day miracle," he said. "Don't forget, we're leaving for Wesley Gardens at noon. It's the early, early, early-bird dinner."

"Got it."

"And you'll eat," he yelled after her. She was getting too skinny.

He watched her leave, pulled on his sweatshirt, and started replaying this latest sexcapade in his head. It's not like they acted like porn stars—no rodeo moves or toys or spanking. Stunts and props weren't necessary. There was something amazing about the way they moved together. Close and emotional. He knew he should be terrified about her hold on him, but it felt so good. He wanted to write about it, but how could he ever do her justice?

Nick pointedly cleared his throat. "Hey, man. We have to talk."

He looked over, and started trying to explain, "Hey, sorry if you saw anything—"

"Don't worry, it's cool." Nick sat up, looking hella awkward. "But, we have to talk about your girl. She's been doing a lot of blow."

His first reaction was to laugh. "So have I, so what? Dude, we fucking sell it."

He looked over to his friend and was surprised to see he wasn't laughing or even smiling. Instead, he squished up his nose as though he smelled something rank and then came at him again. "Look, she's been partying with Carlos. Did you know that?"

He felt blindsided, like Nick had just coldcocked him in the head. "Who the hell told you that?"

"She's been hanging out with him in his office—alone."

Matt stood up, clenched his fists toward his sides and walked toward the window. "Nah, no way." He was overcome with nausea at the thought of his girl being one of Carlos's back-office coke skanks. Nick was wrong.

"I'm not saying she's done anything, but he's working on her. You know he's working on her. He's getting her high. You know he's talking shit about you."

"Whoa," Matt said, turning back around. "Who? Who told you this?" Nick hesitated. "Kaytlyn."

"Are you fucking kidding me? Kaytlyn?" His throat cinched down tight and burned, like a sudden case of strep throat. He made himself swallow down through the pain.

"I can't believe you are coming at me with this shit," he finally managed to say. He was dragged into a vision of Carlos and Via, naked on the kitchen island. No, no, he thought, but thinking it wasn't enough. "No, no," he mumbled. He tried hard to chase it from his mind.

"I'm sorry," Nick was backpedaling. "I didn't want to freak you out, but—"

Matt had no choice but to undo what was playing out in his mind. He bolted for the kitchen and grabbed a beer from the refrigerator. He slammed the door but the photo of Matt, Via, and Nick held strong, secured by the Space Needle magnet. It was the only printed picture he had of her, from the day she'd helped with the tour of homes.

Nick never lied. He always had his back. It was not like he was accusing her of doing anything except being naïve. He misted the island's countertop with disinfectant. He took a big swig of beer, then he misted it again.

Nick came into the kitchen, turned down the music, cleared his throat, and reengaged. This time, he sounded apologetic. "Maybe you forgot, but we're family," he said. "I've got to tell you what's up. I don't think she's done anything; she's into you—she loves you. That's obvious."

Yes, Matt told himself, though she'd never actually told him so. He agreed that Carlos hadn't touched her because he couldn't bear to think otherwise. Wait, she was taken anyway. He kept forgetting that. It was hopeless. If she really loved him, she would have broken off her engagement by now. No, no, he thought again. It's not hopeless, as long they remember how they had felt that day. When they had pretended everything was going to be okay.

"We'll quit," Nick insisted. "We've got money saved. Not as much as we'd planned, but we'll figure something out. We can't afford to stay any longer. I've been telling all the girls it's time to bail. Kaytlyn says Carlos is riding the crack pipe, hard."

"I'm in," Matt agreed. "And we're taking Via with us." He was reinvigorated by both the smell of disinfectant wafting up from the countertop and the prospect of starting a new life. It wasn't too late. But he was going to have to talk to Via. He needed to man up. If he was going to save her, he was going to have to save himself first.

# CHAPTER 27

## VIA

**VIA GOT OUT** of Matt's car and couldn't believe how cold it was. It was a stunning, blue-skied, Seattle afternoon. He had insisted they stop on the way home from the Wesley Gardens Thanksgiving luncheon. He said he wanted to "blow the stink off." He was in a bizarre mood, like he was nervous about something. She wondered if the combination of pumpkin pie and sparkling apple cider was making him loopy.

"Where are the gloves I got you?" he asked as he zipped up his coat. "You lose those too? Woman, I'm not made of money."

She tossed him a flirty pout as they made their way toward the West Seattle boat launch.

"Seriously, hope you don't have expensive tastes," he said. "If so, I'm not your guy."

"Because you've renounced all possessions on account of Eastern philosophy?"

He and Grandma Daney had been talking about New Agey stuff at "linner," which is what the guys were calling their two p.m. dinner. Apparently, there was some global "Great Awakening" going on.

"Attachment to things brings stress, true," he said. "Like G-Dane's house. I love it, but that's because it's not mine to worry about."

He pulled off his gloves and gave them to her; then he pulled his black beanie down over his ears.

"You look like a bank robber in that."

He looked quite serious. "This is a holdup," he announced so loudly that an old guy walking by did a double take. "I'm here to steal your heart." He pulled her in for a quick kiss.

"I can't decide if you're the corniest guy on earth or the most romantic," she told him.

"Can't I be both? I embrace your inner spaz, and outer."

Truth. She looked over and took in the crisp splendor of the Seattle skyline. In the distance, snowy peaks of the Cascade Mountains popped against the sky. What a gorgeous city, she thought as she scanned the scenery from left to right: the Space Needle, the skyscrapers of downtown, Century Link, Safeco Field, and the Starbucks headquarters in Sodo to the south. The snow of Mount Rainier held a faint blue tint.

"Do you know how many car commercials they've filmed here?" he asked. "From this vantage point? Like fifty."

Her thoughts turned to Grandma Daney, such a wonderful woman. "I've been meaning to ask you something," she said.

"I'm an Aries," he said. His deadpan look was priceless.

She ignored him. "Couldn't you get one of those electric chairs for the staircase? Grandma Daney could come back home then, right?"

"Yeah, we've talked about that," he said. "We could build her a ramp for the stairs outside. The bathrooms would need to be modified. We could do it, but she's not a fan of the idea."

"Why not?"

"She says it's because it's too expensive. She'd have to have a private, live-in nurse, but I think it's because she is getting to like Wesley Gardens."

True, Grandma Daney had seemed happy that day, but then again, she seemed happy every day. Just that day she had pulled Via aside and whispered, "Please yourself first, then everything else will fall into place."

"And Nick? All he ever talks about is playing the drums. What does he want?"

"Other than a day at Disneyland with Dave Grohl?"

"How do I even respond to that?"

"What he really wants is to see the world, but in a nonmilitary kind of way. He wants the band on a West Coast tour next summer. Just six or eight shows, down to LA. From there—the moon."

"You don't sound all that excited by the idea."

"If we tour or get some studio time, cool—I'm there. And I'm also good with just playing acoustic sets in coffee houses, running soundboards. And I like teaching kids," he said. "Maybe I'll go back to school part time. Shoreline Community College has a killer sound engineering program. I've been thinking about doing that."

She leaned into him. "You love that stuff. You should totally get into sound engineering."

"I don't know, though. Probably wouldn't be much money in my future."

She lost herself in her own laughter.

"What?"

"Nothing. It's just...I'm not into materialism either."

He pulled her back over to their side of the walking path, away from the oncoming bicyclist. "Let's go sit." He led her over to a picnic table.

"I thought we were walking." She was cold enough as it was.

"I need to talk to you about something," he said. "We need to be able to look at each other."

She was taken aback, but did as he asked. As she sat down, she couldn't help but wonder. He had been in such a weird mood. He couldn't be breaking up with her, could he? Maybe she had mistaken fun-loving banter for nerves. She examined him again.

"I'm one hundred percent done with cocaine," he said with confidence. "And, I want you to be too."

Of course, she realized. He was absolutely right, but somehow his words made her want to close her eyes. He was illuminating something in her. Something ugly that she didn't want anyone to discover. She looked down, waiting for him to go on. But he didn't. She felt his chilled hand come in slowly under her chin.

"Look at me," he told her.

She peered up into his eyes, dark yet bright. They had been waiting for her.

"We're cutting you off. We're cutting ourselves off."

She knew there was nothing to say. His tone sounded urgent and utterly decisive. This wasn't a negotiation. He wasn't screwing around. He was in love with her, and she with him. How was this ever going to work out?

Could he see how conflicted she was? She wanted to tell him that she had been fiending hard the day after binges, having chills. All she could think about was doing it again—not only because it felt good, and not only because it distracted her from the countdown. But because without it she was a sick, shaky mess. With Thanksgiving out of the way, there would soon be decorations, Christmas trees for sale. Breathe, she reminded herself, but it brought her little comfort. The frigid air she inhaled burned her lungs.

She wanted to confess. Tell him that she was in too deep, that she couldn't quit. Didn't want to quit. But then he would know. He would want to send her off somewhere for treatment, and she just couldn't do that. What was there to say? There had to be a way to defend herself, protect herself, deflect this somewhere else. She couldn't quit yet. Her brain spun through the possibilities.

"I need you to remember how we felt that day," he said. "That day we fell in love."

Bingo. Of course, she would make it his fault.

"That day we were high out of our minds?" She watched his steady expression crumble.

"What are you saying? That it wasn't real? That we can't move past that?"

"I think you're a hypocrite," she told him. "Cutting me off when you're still selling it yourself." She got up and started walking back toward the car. Sick with herself, she couldn't look at him. This would have to be all on him. She couldn't quit yet. He couldn't cut her off yet.

He followed her. "Really?" His sharp voice caught in the wind. "Did you really just say that to me? What do you expect me to do? Be a chump and let you lead the way when you obviously need to check yourself? We need to get away from that whole toxic scene." He caught up to her and spun her around. "Look, Carlos is bad fucking news. I know he's after you." He looked like he had even more to say, but a woman with two dogs was passing by, looking concerned.

She gave the woman an awkward smile, then looked down at Matt's boots. "I think we've been spending too much time together. I need to go home and get some sleep. I need to think."

He stepped toward her and lowered his voice. "Don't be like this."

She managed to look at him, really look at him. He exuded certainty and strength. He wasn't some quirky musician anymore, some guy she partied with, some guy she loved. He stood there with the Seattle skyline perfectly situated behind him, seemingly oblivious to the wind gusting up all around them. He was a man, and he was taking control. Just when she desperately needed him to.

"Look," he held her gaze, "Nick and I were on our way out of this, before I met you. We had a plan, a Hotties exit plan. You've got to bail with us. You've got to see where you're heading if you don't. You see, right?"

She hugged him. She couldn't *not* hug him. He was warm and wonderful—too good for her. It's like he saw something in her, something worthwhile that didn't really exist. He needed her to take the leap with him, to fly across some chasm. God, she wanted to. But she would only weigh him down. She hated herself for being so weak. She could try to quit; she could try. But even as she considered it, she felt her impending failure. Carlos would be just a call away. She was craving coke this very minute, with this amazing man standing right in front of her. It was insane. She was insane. What was she going to do? She needed to think.

"It's freezing." Her voice snapped into the wind. "Can we go?"

"If you want." He walked next to her, but left some distance. He didn't reach for her hand.

"You know, if this hasn't been real for you, if you've just been pretending, this is when it will all fall apart, now that you're cut off."

"What does that mean?"

"If you want to be with me, you have to break up with him," he said. "Before he comes back. I'm not sharing you."

"Over the phone?"

He just looked at her, like he knew there wasn't an easy answer to be found.

She took off his gloves and handed them back. "Here."

He took the gloves. "Does this mean something?"

"They're just gloves."

"Bullshit," he mumbled as they got into the car. He turned on the ignition and cranked the radio. It was The Mighty Mighty Bosstones— inappropriately happy for the situation. She dialed it down and turned toward him.

"I'm sorry, but I'm scared," she said. "I want to quit. I'm going to quit, but maybe we can taper down, quit in January. We'll start fresh in January."

The harsh expression he wore softened a little, but he shook his head. "I know this is hard, but we've got to do it. Our future selves will thank us for it. We'll be happy, you'll see." He took her hands in his.

He leaned in. It was a slow kiss. It still did that thing to her. She still got that jolt. That familiar, fundamental feeling of love that made her want to believe.

"You really have to go back to Vashon tonight?" he asked. His lips still inches from hers.

"Yes, I have a bunch of church stuff tomorrow and Saturday," she lied. She needed time to think. "That SeaKidz holiday party is Sunday afternoon. I'll come after that."

"I'll be on the road Sunday, back Monday afternoon."

"Portland run?"

"You got it, my last drug run ever," he said. "Then I won't be a hypocrite anymore." He looked away.

"I get scared when you go on your runs." It was something she hadn't even admitted to herself.

He turned back toward her and just looked so damned victorious.

"You worry about me?"

"Yes," she said. "I don't know why it makes you smile like that."

"It's cute that you worry, but don't. I won't get arrested. You're lucky. You're my lucky charm." He was still smiling.

"What if I'm not?"

"You are, and you're pretty, too," he said. "Especially when you're mad."

"Stop saying that."

"But you are." He still didn't get it. He was still flirty.

"I'm serious. I've worried about you getting arrested, but it's more, too," she said. "It's so stressful. Think about it; that's got to aggravate your OCD."

Those three letters killed his easy expression. He looked at the steering wheel, pissed.

"I'm sorry, but it's true. If you're going to be honest with me, then let me be honest with you."

He turned up the radio. "We'd better head back. I know you have a ferry to catch."

# Chapter 28

## Via

**WAITING IN LINE** at the dock was just part of living on Vashon Island, but today it seemed everyone on the north side of the island was trying to catch the three o'clock over town ferry. She could tell by how far back on the dock she sat idling that she wasn't going to make it. She would be even later to the holiday party at SeaKidz. She could have driven with Beth, who'd caught an earlier ferry, but being around Beth was becoming next to impossible. There were always so many questions—about her supposed overnight shifts at the women's shelter, about her weight loss, about the wedding.

She turned her car off and thought about calling Matt, but he would be practicing with the guys. Then, he would be off to Portland for the night. She knew she wasn't supposed to call or text him until he got back. They hadn't talked at all since their chilly conversation at the boat launch. He hadn't so much as texted.

She felt her mother's ring edging its way toward her knuckle again. Had she really lost that much weight? Her phone was buzzing from the passenger seat and she saw that it was Dan. She decided to answer this time.

"Hey," she said.

"Via, it's Dan."

Duh.

"I'm heading off to the faith center, wanted to call and check in first. How are you?"

Her throat felt dry. She reached for her tea and took a sip.

"How are you?" he asked again. "Mom says you are helping with the holiday party for the inner-city kids. That's great. You're staying busy—just three more weeks to go."

Day 21, of course; she had forgotten.

"I'm so proud of you," he said. His voice irritated the hell out of her.

It was odd. How could she be so annoyed with the man she had been betraying on a regular basis? She was the cheater, yet somehow he seemed like the bad guy. Distancing herself from him was the only way she could live with herself. There were so many lies and uncertainties weighing her down. They were draining the life right out of her.

"We can talk about it when I get home," he was saying. She had zoned out. "On January 12th. I already told you that, right?"

"An extra two weeks?" she asked. "No, no you didn't tell me that. What about the meeting in New York? I'm going to be alone for that?"

"I left you a message. If you would bother to answer your phone—"

"You told me to stay busy," she said. "I'm staying busy."

"Via, you know we have to communicate. We have to work through this. Remember what Pastor King says, that love is a verb."

"I've got to go," she said, unable to bear the conversation any longer.

"Don't be like this. I miss you, okay? You've just got to hang in there a little longer—be patient."

It was quiet. She knew it would always be like this. This would be her life.

"Are you always going to want to be in Africa?"

"What?"

"Or Asia? Are you always going to want to be as far away from me as you can possibly be?"

"Where is this all coming from? Are you putting in too many hours at that shelter? Mom says you had to work all day on Thanksgiving. She said she's asked you to go with her to a women's bible retreat in Montana, but you won't go. I think you should. It sounds relaxing."

"You're changing the subject."

"You'll travel with me when we're married," he promised. "There is so much good we can do here. The money will do so much good. Everything will be better when we're married."

"No, I can't. I can't do this."

"Honey, I know it's hard, but you know that God will never give you more than you can handle. You're stronger than you realize," he assured her. "I know, let's pray."

This would be her life, she realized. His life would be her life.

"Our Father, please hold Via close in the days ahead —"

"I can't do this," she said. "I can't marry you."

He just kept on praying. Hadn't he heard her?

"Help her as she struggles to follow your plan for her."

She had a call on the other line. Her heart fluttered; maybe it was Matt.

"I've got to go," she told Dan.

"Wait, I love —"

She clicked over. "Hello?"

"We have to talk. Right now," her uncle said. "No more blowing off my calls."

The Chelan was already on its way out, cutting through the grim, glossy waves. She sat and watched it go. "Okay," she said. Another ferry was already approaching.

"I need you to listen to me," he said.

She felt his words on the air, just before he spoke them.

"They found another painting."

She gasped. "What?" She would drive her car off the end of the dock. Give herself over to the icy will of Puget Sound.

"They found it in a police evidence locker in the Bronx," he said. "It was wrapped."

Of course it was. White with a gold bow.

The funerals. The funerals crashed down around her. The horror was shiny and new.

*Two separate funerals, both the day after Christmas. Her mother's was small. Private. A choir sang "Bridge over Troubled Water." Her uncle said she didn't have to go to the reception afterward.*

*Later her uncle escorted her to her father's funeral. Some famous soprano sang "Ave Maria." It was a long service, full of people she didn't know who shook their heads and watched her cry. Photographers waited outside. "Violetta, Violetta," they called out to her, but she didn't have any tears left to share with them.*

"Via," her uncle asked now. "Listen, it's a beautiful work. Real life — such a departure from anything he'd ever done. They're authenticating it now. You have to see it."

His words were nonsense. It was real life and not a portrait? She knew it must be a portrait. That day from the summer before it all came back to her. Such a small thing, but it had made her so happy.

*Daddy took her out onto the balcony and took dozens of pictures of her in her white sundress. She smiled for him. She knew what he was doing. He spent much of the autumn locked inside his studio, working. She couldn't wait to see it. She was so good, so patient. Until that last day.*

"You have to see it," her uncle insisted.

"No!" She hadn't intended to scream at him. "No. Never."

"Please come to New York. Spend Christmas with me. I'll book your flight. When can you come?"

She began to hear musical chatter, the Verdi aria her father used to play as he toiled away in his studio—the one declaring love as the heartbeat of the universe. The sick smell of her father's turpentine tumbled into her awareness.

"I can't," she told him.

Cars were starting up all around her. She looked up to see the Klahowya easing itself against the Vashon dock. In a couple of minutes, it would be time to board, but where would she go? Going to the kids party would be brutal. Impossible. She just couldn't deal with Beth and the church crowd right now. Their goodness would burn. Matt would be off on his Portland run soon. He was too good for her, anyway. She needed some time with someone who understood her. She needed to be high.

# CHAPTER 29

## VIA

**CARLOS'S GAZE WAS SOFT,** his voice smooth. "I'm so happy you came."

"Nobody else could ever understand," she said. He was damaged. She craved his company.

"I want to be here for you," he said as he stood at his desk and cut new straws. "Look, I have a vodka tonic waiting for you."

She hadn't noticed. There it was, right there. This time with a piece of lime. Nervous, she found it hard to hold herself down on the couch. He came and sat down beside her, so close.

"Maybe I should call Whitney first," she said. "Let her know where I am."

"Relax."

He lined up a nice, fat rail and offered it to her with a gentlemanly, m'lady gesture.

She leaned over, inhaled deeply, and welcomed the bitter buzz into her head.

"My custody case is next week in Portland," he said. "You should come with."

"Me?" She was beyond confused. "Why?"

"I would like for you to meet her," he said. "My ex, and if you want, Sam and Maya."

He moved in close and leaned in. "I'm going to get my revenge soon," he said. "I'll clear my name. Everyone will see what a little liar she's been. She's not going to get away with defaming me like that. Making me out to be some pervert."

Uneasy, she focused on another line.

Part of her wanted to get up and leave without another word. But, there was still so much coke.

"I'm sorry," he said. "Forget about Portland for now. I can't wait any longer." He opened his box and pulled out another baggie. It was off-white and didn't look as fine as coke. He poured out a small pile and started chopping it into a chunky powder.

"I have a special treat, Ketamine—Special K."

Special K sounded fun, but she'd never heard of it. Must be a pure kind of cocaine.

"Maybe I should call Matt," she said. "To see how the trip's going."

Without stopping his prep work, he frowned. "We never contact him while he's on the road," he said, his tone sharp. "Never. No need to worry. He's the ideal driver. Never speeds. Always signals—always." His tone was rich in condescension. "In fact, I'd like you to avoid him. You can get your coke from me, you know. I'll take good care of you. Mattais has got his shit fucked up."

"What?"

He looked up at her. "You know he's bat-shit crazy, right?"

She just stared and waited for him to laugh. But he didn't.

"You don't want to get too close to him," he said. "He goes into some very dark places. Sick bastard. Word is, he loves mind games. It's cruel what he did to Kaytlyn, what he's still doing to Kaytlyn."

No, she thought. No. That couldn't be true.

"I should go," she said. "I'm sorry, I shouldn't have called you," she told him. She kept her gaze lower than his. "I can't do what you want me to. I'm sorry."

"Do you think I'm a monster?" His voice held a duality she had never noticed before. Warm and sure, yet harboring a twisted undertone. Had it been there all along? He reached for her chin and lifted it toward him. His deep eyes held a glint of something sinister. It had been a mistake, coming here.

He gave her a soft smile and sat back. "Sure, sure, go if you want. I understand. The truth is hard to hear," he said. "Just have this one drink with me before you go. He handed over her vodka tonic. "Look, I even cut up a lime for you, so be a good girl and drink up. I know you don't want to hurt my feelings."

She looked to the doorway. It seemed a mile away. While she tried to think, she did as she was told. She took a sip, but the glass began to slip from her sweaty grip, so she put it down on the table next to the new powder he was lining up for her.

"Just try this before you go," he said as he handed over the straw. "Your first trip down the K hole."

She hesitated for a moment, overcome with dread. "But—"

Guilt rose to mingle with her fear. He had done so much for her, she told herself. She was the one who had called him. She didn't want to hurt his feelings.

"Ladies first." He seemed so determined.

How could she say no? She told herself it would be fine. Just one line. He was excited for her to try this Special K, so she would try it. She would make him happy and then she would leave. And never come back.

"It's pretty long," she said. "Maybe I'll just do a little."

"No, baby, you've gotta do the whole line. Just snort super hard and get through it fast."

He gave her the straw and nodded as she leaned over the table. She couldn't seem to still her shaky hand. He gently reached out for her wrist, steadied it, and guided her down the length of the line. All she had to do was inhale, so she did. Hard.

She knew immediately this was not blow. It burned her nostrils like hell. She powered through the pain and made the long line disappear into her head. She succumbed to it—a new kind of terrible, torturous magic. She threw back her head, fell back on the couch, and pinched her nose as hard as she could. Acid burned from the inside out. Instant and overwhelming euphoria fell upon her, soaking through her bones and into her highest being. She felt no pain. When she released her hand from her nose, her arm just floated away. She couldn't feel her face. She didn't even feel human anymore. Instead, she felt apart from who she had been before, like an all-knowing version of herself. She was her own God.

Mama's voice was melodic, "Remember who you are." Yes, she realized. I am God, and this is just a life I'm having. She heard a new voice. She knew it must be Jesus, "The kingdom of God is within you." She wanted to scream it loud and strong, but there were no words. Everything became clear. Death was just the remembering of what we knew before we were born. Every single person walking the earth was just God, weighed down by a human body. But just for a short time.

This is how her mother must've felt when she died. Was she even dead? No, because energy doesn't die. God doesn't die. Via's focus evolved into a broad, diffused sense of knowing. She hoped she would be able to remember this feeling, but felt it slipping away and morphing again. How would you describe a rainbow to someone who can only see black and white? All of this time, she had been living in black and white.

And then she started hearing waves of music—whom, whom, whom. She could hear even more music between the beats. Had that music been there all along? It was thrilling. There were ten or twelve songs playing within one song—maybe more—and she could hear them all. She was the heartbeat of the universe. All music played for her.

Unable to move, her arms and legs might as well have belonged to someone else. She didn't want or need them anymore. She was floating and tingling and vibrating at the highest frequency. And Carlos was there, so happy, sitting next to her, telling her how special she was. That she was different. He called her an angel, and she agreed. His lips were kissing hers. She couldn't feel him over the tingling.

She closed her eyes and saw pretty lights in the newest colors. Never-seen-before hues, yet she recognized them all. They wanted her to reminisce in their meaning. They surrounded her with those outer-worldly colors. No white though. No white tunnel. No angels. Then she started laughing. Oh, that's right, she realized. She was the angel.

He was having some trouble taking off her boots, but she was content just floating along. The pretty lights wanted her to laugh and dance with them. Carlos was kissing her and she realized she must love him. He was her, but from a different point of view. Everybody, everywhere was the same being, experiencing life from a different perspective.

He was telling her the most amazing things, but she could barely hear him over the sounds of her pretty colors. *It's not real* they hummed. *Come and play. Let's pretend.* Some were fuzzy and others were smooth, and they all beamed unconditional love. They tasted like cotton candy.

Now he couldn't get her bra off. He pushed it up around her neck somehow. How did he even do that? She just laughed at him. Something was sliding down her thighs and calves, like a silk scarf. His hands were everywhere. He was whispering in her ear, telling her to be safe. He was talking nonsense.

She was called back into the colors. Time seemed to revel in its own power. It jumped and landed where it pleased without limits.

He was kissing her again. She could feel how much he needed her to love him. She felt a new sensation from within. Their skin blended and she couldn't tell where he left off and she began. He needed love. Everybody needed love. The couch was going to break. Then they would fall, fall far away.

Everything changed. Pain. She had forgotten there was pain in the world. Something was tight around her neck. It was hard to breathe. She realized he was taking something from her. He was saying something or moaning something, but she couldn't hear him over the sounds of the pretty lights. They were beginning to pull away now, leaving her alone, again. She had already forgotten what they had told her.

"Please, pretty lights," she said, startled by the sound of her own voice. Sounds were real again. Her inner being was gone and she was naked without it. She had given it away.

Carlos was moaning, "Oh God, oh God." But God was not there. There were no angels. But then suddenly there were, they came to her. Disappointed crystal angels who hung from silver strings, tied to branches. Holding her hands above her head, he kept hurting her, again and again. She tried to scream, but it sounded to her like a whisper.

He was the devil, groaning into her ear, more and more. She felt his weight now. "Yes, baby, yes," he told her as he grunted. No, please, no, she tried to say, but then she realized it was over. He let go of her wrists and settled down on top of her, heavy and wet. His sweat seeped into her.

Oh dear God, get him off of me, she prayed, but God was brutally absent. Carlos leaned his face into hers and gave her a tender kiss and then another, but she couldn't kiss back. She prayed to Jesus, and to Mohammed, and to the Buddha, and to the winged fairies of the universe. Her lungs were stuck. But she couldn't tell him. There was still something hiked up around her neck, her bra. She tried to alarm him with her eyes, but he just smiled.

"Good girl," he whispered in her ear.

She knew better. She prayed death would swoop down upon her. The room waved up and down, but she couldn't move. She willed her eyes to close, but they refused. Then he was up, getting dressed. She couldn't find the rhythm of her breath. He was walking over to the bar, talking, laughing about limes. She called out to him. He needed to come help her breathe, but he couldn't hear or didn't want to hear. The world went black. It wasn't the world anymore. It wasn't a good place. She wanted Mama.

*  *  *

# VIA

*MAMA HELD HER HAND as they waited, sitting backwards across from Daddy, who looked so handsome in his tuxedo. They were outside the MET, but the driver said they couldn't get out yet. It wasn't their turn. Via's mother looked out the limo window. "Look Via, there are only a couple of news crews. Oh, and a few photographers. I told you this would be low-key."*

*Via scratched her neck. Something sharp was biting into her. She hated her high-collared, poofy little-girl dress. "Are they just going to have presents for the little kids like last year?"*

*"Violetta, don't be rude," her father scolded as he straightened the American flag pin on his lapel. "It's a fundraiser," he said. "There's a war on terror going on, you know, so chin up."*

*He was in a good mood, and she knew she shouldn't press him. "I'm sorry, Daddy."*

*Her mother leaned in; her silky voice tickled Via's ear. "You already have more presents than can fit under the tree. We'll have to get a bigger tree next year."*

*Daddy laughed. Thank God, he laughed. He didn't usually put up with whispering. "If you want an even bigger tree, we'll need a crane," he said. "It was hard enough getting this one set up."*

*The car nudged forward, then stopped. An attendant opened the door and helped Mama out first. Via watched in awe as her mother met the crowd outside. She held her head high with her new red-beaded clutch at her side. Her blue dress accented with white trim clung to her perfect figure. Flashes of bright light flickered and voices called out, telling her how beautiful she looked.*

*It was Via's turn, but she couldn't move. She dug her sweaty fingers into the leather seat. Her father got out and shooed the attendant away. "I'll assist my daughter," he said, seemingly proud. He leaned in and reached for her hand. "It's time to smile now Via—my heartbeat." He gazed into her eyes and she felt that connection they shared from time to time. It was as though he really saw her sitting there. Like he understood just how much she needed him. "Smile now, be a good girl, and you'll have presents to open in less than a week." The warmth he conveyed melted her nervousness. Yes, she would make him proud. Smiling, she put her hand into his and stepped out onto the red carpet as flashes of light lit up around them. "And, there is one present in particular I can't wait for you to open," he added. Yes. She'd seen him put it back in the corner. It was huge and flat, white with a big gold bow. Finally, the painting, she hoped. The portrait of her.*

The flashing lights hurt her brain. Her eyes opened and found the room, but the rest of her body was still dead to her. He was talking. He was in a good mood. But, it wasn't her father. It was Carlos, talking to someone on the phone. "I need you to come in, I have a friend who needs a ride home," he said.

Her mind was still hanging around in 2004. That night in the limo. The last happy night before Daddy turned. He was often at his best right before the crash.

She hurt all over. Carlos was still on the phone. "Because you're better than a taxi, that's why. And because I said so. Within the hour. She'll be waiting. Thanks, Nick."

She tried to come to terms with what was happening. Nick was coming for her? No, no, she thought, but she still couldn't find her voice.

Carlos was seated next to her, laughing as he untangled her bra from her neck. "Wow, what did we do here?" he asked, his tone playful. "Guess we were pretty into it, huh?" He reached for the throw blanket on the end of the couch, still talking while he covered her up. "I'm leaving your boots off." The blanket's fibers prickled and poked her sensitive skin. Heat tingled through her limbs. She thought about trying to move again, but she didn't want to encourage him. "I've got to go, babe," he told her as he stood. "But I'm leaving you some blow. Nick will be here for you soon—guess we won't be a secret anymore." He lingered over her with a sort of romantic look on his face. It made her want to cave into herself and die. "They can call you 'New Sonia' now."

He made his way to the door, but he paused and looked back at her. "You'll be coming with me to Portland next week. Can't wait to show you off."

She feared he was going to come back over and kiss her some more, but he just left. She heard the heavy door click closed behind him. She was thankful for that. She couldn't endure any more kisses. She wanted to get to her phone so she could call her Tristan, but then she realized he wouldn't be hers anymore. Her lungs found their place and she gasped for breath.

All at once, she felt a part of herself again, but forever changed, tainted. Nothing will ever be okay again. She loathed the feel of her own skin. She sat up slowly so her brain wouldn't explode. She had to escape herself. This was exactly what she deserved. She looked around. He had left her a fresh drink. Once she was able to coordinate her trembling hands, she grabbed it with both hands and pounded it, but it wasn't enough. She would go to the bar and get the whole bottle, as soon as she was strong enough to walk. No, she realized. It would never be enough. There wasn't enough booze in the world to change what she had just done to Matt.

There were two lines waiting for her as well as his white drug box. He must actually trust her. She looked inside. There were baggies of what looked like blow. There was also a small bag of what looked like the Molly she had done with Matt. Their love potion. She licked her finger and dipped it inside. Perhaps it would reset the spell she'd just broken or even make her fall madly in love with herself. Maybe it would kill her. She brought it to her lips. It was bitter. So bitter.

# CHAPTER 30

## VIA

**THE STAGE FLOOR GLINTED** and glossed. It dipped and curved in time to the music. The beat was fast, yet slow. There was the beat, and then there was her beat. She rose and dropped in slow motion, feeling the warmth of the violet lamps. Pink. Purple. Pink. Purple. Static, like air through violin strings, filled the air around her and lifted her up. Her arms were out to her sides, swaying through the waves coming through the giant speakers. The deejay looked down. He was her God now. Only music could save her now.

"She's too wasted to be any fun and she's gonna fall," Leon was telling Nick. "I tried to get her to stay in the office, but she says she needs the lights. She's freaking the clients out."

Nick reached up and guided her down from the stage. She didn't fight him. She jumped down to meet him.

"You're the girl?" he asked. "I'm supposed to drive one of his bitches home, and it's you?" His anger was scaring the music away; it fled into the background. His coat was open, revealing his white Hotties shirt. It glowed under the bar light. He looked critical, too serious to be filled with such light.

She stepped closer to him and touched his sleeve. "Have you come to rescue me from the dance floor? Are you here on King Arthur's behalf?"

Colors played across his face—bright, dark, bright, dark—but he never blinked. His stare blazed into her as if he, too, knew the secrets of all mankind. If he were Sir Lancelot, that would make her Guinevere. She knew that story. They would be getting naked together soon. But wait. She realized she couldn't be Guinevere because she was already starring in some other man's story. Stories were mingling together, confusing her.

Isolde. Yes, she remembered, but where was her Tristan? Then Dan came crashing down on her shoulders. She couldn't escape the role she had played in his life.

"Let's go," Nick told her as he grabbed her by the wrist. His touch burned. He pulled her through the main room; the few clients who were there looked away when she walked by. She looked back and saw silver beams shooting down upon them. She and Nick were making their escape from the hellish gunfire. The same gunfire had been reverberating through her life for nearly ten years. He led her through the cold, white lobby, past Ben, who looked more than a little concerned. "I've got her," Nick told him. They passed by several men, whose whispers were sharp against her neck. When they got to the door, he stopped, turned, then yanked her elbow. "So, what are you on, 'shrooms? You wasted, or what?"

"Nothing happened," she tried to say, but her own voice didn't believe her.

"Bullshit!" he said. "I can't fucking believe you!"

"You shouldn't swear so much."

"Let's go," he said again as he pulled her out into the frigid rain. It seared into her cheeks and neck and chest. Nick leaned in and put his coat around her shoulders. It seemed a healing cloak, already warm. He reached around her and pulled the hood up over her head.

"I can't even believe this right now." His face was close as he pulled wet strands of her hair and tucked them inside the hood. She turned her face up toward his. His eyes were pale, but passionate.

She heard her mother's voice urge her, "Let's not make Daddy angry." She pressed her eyelids together tight and strained her ears, but her mother was gone, again.

Nick's voice cut through the frigid night air. "Violetta, you make me so angry. Why do you make me so crazy?" She was afraid to open her eyes because this man wasn't Nick anymore.

Guilt-laced droplets landed upon her shoulders. They soaked through the coat, through her skin, and bore into her bones. "I can't remember what the pretty lights told me." She turned from him and started to run away. She didn't care where.

He wasn't prepared. He knew his expression was giving him away. He felt the shift. Everything changed. Really changed. Like the light bulb above her head had finally flicked on. She'd probably known all along, at some level. He would do anything to go back three minutes. Three months would be better. Hell, three years.

She backpedaled. "I didn't mean—"

He held up his hand and dismissed her. "You're wasted." He clicked into bouncer mode. Hopefully, she was so toasted she would black out the whole conversation. Just like she had forgotten that on the night he'd tucked her into his bed they had kissed and cuddled for an hour. She'd tasted so good, and smelled so sweet. He could have had her, but he'd done the right thing. She had worn his favorite Green Day shirt. He hadn't washed it since.

She seemed to sober up, right on the spot. "I didn't know."

"Get over yourself. There's nothing to know," he said. "Somebody's gotta tell him—and it should be you!"

She kept her tears at bay, but her jaw began to quiver. He couldn't let himself care.

She was a dumb bitch. That is what he would tell himself. He had to tell himself something. She was not his, so she was not his problem. Let her go crawl into Matt's bed and sleep it off. He was furious with Matt for ever trusting her.

He turned and made his way for the basement door. He was too full-on-crazy-furious to do anything other than play the shit out of his drums. He would practice Soundgarden's "Jesus Christ Pose" until his arms fell off. Maybe "Song for the Dead." Yes, he realized, Queens of the Stone Age would be better, not so complicated. He needed his life to be uncomplicated. He needed to make it about the music again. He would be all about the beat. His grandma had been right all along—it was time to cut the band loose and go off on his own.

# CHAPTER 31

## MATT

**SHE KEPT CALLING** his name, over and over. He felt her sitting on the edge of the bed, but she stood up before he was able to grab her. He sat up and stretched. "You're pretty."

He reached for her, but she stayed put. Just an arm's length away.

"Hey," he said, disappointed. "Why are you dressed already? Where are you going?" It was barely even light outside. He noticed her hands were shaking. He pulled the comforter back. "You're cold. Come. Get into bed."

She gave him a little smile, but it was weird. He sat up. Something was wrong. "You sad?" he asked. "About your parents? Is that why you texted? Come snuggle."

"I have to go in a few minutes," she said.

"What? Why?" He got up and went to her.

Pulling her into his arms, he went in for a kiss, but stopped. Her breathing was shallow, emotional.

"I never told you about my annual death day countdown," she said.

"Your what?" He rested his hands on her hips.

"There are one hundred days between my birthday—the night you and I met—and my parents' death day." She went over and swiped his tablet.

That first night had been her birthday? How had he not known that? "Death day?" he asked. "You call it that?"

"Today is Day 20. You've been asking for a long time for me to share with you." She had a song queued up. "Please, sit down?"

He was thoroughly lost, but did as she asked and sat down in his desk chair. "Okay." He would pull her onto his lap and hold her as soon as he had the chance.

"I want you to hear the most beautiful, meaningful, music in the world—at least to me," she said. "It's Wagner, from *Die Walküre*. It's opera."

She had his full attention. He kept his hands to himself, but it wasn't easy. He couldn't interrupt her determined pace.

"My parents met at an opera, sat next to each other. I can't remember which one, but they went to like five a year. They played it all the time," she said. "Wagner's *Ring Cycle* is one story, told in four operas. It's fifteen hours long. But this is the part my mother loved most." Her voice quivered. "After my father had—" She stopped.

He didn't dare say a word, just waited. He was so in love with her, he didn't care. Whatever it was. He guided her onto his lap and wrapped his arms around her waist like a belt. She was so skinny. He would have to talk to her about that, later.

"After my father beat her, he would play Wagner for her," she said. "So, when I heard Wagner, I knew it was safe to come out from under my bed. They would be like lovebirds—for weeks, sometimes months. Until it happened again."

The words "I'm so sorry" rose up into his throat, but he swallowed them back down and propped his chin over her shoulder.

She leaned into him. "I know it's sick, but I want you to hear it. I want you to understand why I wanted to marry someone I didn't love, someone safe. Someone the exact opposite of my father. Why I've been so stupid."

Something caught in his chest, an energy shift in his heart. *Wanted.* She had used the past tense—wanted to marry. Past tense.

"It's not long, like four minutes." Her tone was apologetic, though he had no idea why. Didn't she know he would listen to the whole fifteen hours for her?

He had expected it to be soft and lovely, like Mozart maybe, but it began with horns, like hunters issuing a warning.

She sat back against him, but it wasn't close enough. She seemed a million miles away.

With every bar, the music grew into a storm of strings and woodwinds. They weren't easy though; instead, they were urgent.

Even the flutes were foreboding. And then chimes, bells, joined in to create the most haunting melody he had ever heard.

"It's called the 'Magic Fire Music'," she said.

He gave her a small kiss behind her ear. She was his lucky girl, better than magic. "What's happening?" he asked. "In the story—this isn't our story, right? This isn't about Tristan and Isoldey." God, he hoped not. It was disturbing. The horns were barreling back in.

"This is Brünhilde and her father, the Norse God, Wotan," she said. "She was a mighty warrior, but she had disobeyed him. Tried to save Siegmund, a man meant to die. Now Wotan is about to punish her, to turn her into a mortal woman. He's going to leave her out on a rocky ledge, alone in the wilderness."

"But, he's upset about it, isn't he?" he asked. "He doesn't want to leave her there."

"Her father didn't know what to do. He wanted to love her. At least, that's what she told herself—" Her voice faltered.

It was clear she wasn't talking about the music anymore.

"It's okay," he told her while he nestled in against her cheek. Still not close enough. She wasn't letting him all the way in. "Go on, then what?"

"Wotan kissed her eyelids and she fell into an enchanted sleep. Then Loge, the demigod of fire, cast a wall of flames around her, so that only the bravest man could claim her." In the background, the horns mingled with the bells, arching up the scale, higher and higher, until they beat back the beautiful melody, back into submission. "Many years later, that brave man did come for her. He was Siegfried, the son of Siegmund."

Without thinking, he said, "Now *that* sounds like an opera." She stiffened and pulled away. He reached for her, but she was up; she had slipped through his hands. The horns faded and the bells were solemn.

"Playing this music was my father's way of saying he was sorry."

"Wait." He stood, but hesitated. She was like a nervous deer on alert, and he was afraid to spook her.

"I just wanted you to know," she said. "My father left me on a rock, but I'm not worth walking through fire for. I'm not a warrior."

He was clueless. What was she saying?

He wanted to rush over and grab her, say the perfect thing. But he stood still, frozen.

"Wait," he finally managed. "I know this is all hard for you, the holidays and all, but I've been thinking about it. Let's start building new memories."

Her demeanor remained solemn. "You would go ahead and say something amazing like that," she said. "I love you."

He wanted to grab her and hold her tight, but she looked so anguished. He would help her through the next two weeks. She wouldn't be marrying the other guy, next summer or ever, he was sure of it.

"You'll still come see G-Dane tonight, right?" he asked. "We'll talk more about it. You'll stay with me tonight."

She just nodded and turned for the door. But then she turned back around, reaching out for a hug.

He was there, catching her up in his arms. He had been so afraid to tell her, but now he was too afraid not to tell her. "I love you, too," he whispered against her neck.

"I'm such a mess," was all she said as she pulled away and made her way out into the hall. He followed her, but stopped at the top of the staircase.

While he wanted to follow her down to the front door, it was obvious by the way she was taking the stairs two at a time that she didn't want him to. So he just leaned over the banister and watched her go.

When he heard the front door close, he returned to his bedroom and went to the window. Poor baby. His heart ached for hers, for what she was going through. Christmas was coming, and on the heels of her parents' death day. Of course she had issues. How could she not? The sound of Wagner's hunting horns jolted his senses. Wait, was there even more to it? What the hell happened last night? Had she used again? He wished he could shake the feeling that it had everything to do with Carlos. He knew he couldn't ignore the situation anymore. It was time, he told himself. Time to tell his boss what was up.

# CHAPTER 32

## CARLOS

**CARLOS COULDN'T BELIEVE IT.** Not only had the feds busted the Portland crash house, but Mattais had somehow missed it. He had just turned around and driven back home. What the hell? Carlos had been suspicious of some of his guys lately. He smelled a narc.

"Shouldn't you be happy?" Matt asked, standing next to the couch with his hands in his crazy-professor hair. "Your money is safe."

"But it's here and not in Portland," Carlos replied while he ran his index finger along the rim of his near-empty glass of whiskey. "How's that possible?" What was going on? He was coming down and needed to get high again. He couldn't deal with getting sick today. Couldn't deal with the shaking and sweating. Had to go see the lawyer. His wife, he realized—she probably alerted the DEA. Maybe the IRS. Dirty little bitch.

Matt stared him down. "It's luck. I know it sounds insane, but it's true. She's lucky."

"Who's lucky?" What was he talking about?

"Via," Matt said, with an obnoxious little grin. "She texted last night because she needed me. She told me to come back home, so I did."

"From the Oregon border?" he asked. "That's bullshit."

"You don't believe me? You think I'm a narc?"

"You're too stupid for words, that's what you are. Do you have any idea how bad this is for me? How does this make me look? The LA guys would love to bend me over, snake my operations."

"So, you'd rather I'd gotten smacked down? You'd rather I was facing time? Sitting in some dirty cell?"

It was quiet. Matt shook his head. "Unbelievable." Making his way for the door, he turned and said, "I'm done with road trips. Fire me. Please."

"I would have bailed you out. You have no priors, you would have been fine."

"It's not even about that now. I came to tell you to leave her alone. You leave her the hell alone, she's done here."

The moment had arrived. Carlos cleared his throat because he wanted to savor it. "I fucked her." He watched Matt's sense of determination slide from his face and fall to the floor. "Last night. Right here on the couch."

"I don't...don't...believe you," Matt stammered.

"I should probably call for backup," Carlos taunted as he walked back behind his desk. He pressed the intercom. "Ben? I could use a hand."

But Matt hadn't rushed him. He just stood there, aghast. "I don't believe you."

Ben came in, confused at first.

"She didn't tell you that we're Eskimo brothers again?" he asked. "Tight little body, but she's really no better than Kaytlyn—or Sonia."

"What? Sonia? I never—"

"Banged my wife? Sure you did. You think I didn't know that you're the one who told her to go—to bail with my kids. I'm thinking you nailed her too. I saw the way she used to look at you."

"You're high; we were just friends. I never touched her with anything more than a makeup brush. We just talked."

Ben just stood there in an awkward standby stance, listening to Matt's plea.

"Sure, sure. Just like I talked the shit out of your girlfriend last night." Carlos smiled, satisfied.

Matt lunged, but Ben was all over him.

"You won't be quitting. We're not even yet." Carlos reminded him. "You still owe me. Take a week or two off, though. Get your head together. You've got your shit fucked up."

"No, I don't believe you," Matt said again as Ben dragged him out.

"And Ben, no interruptions."

Carlos went to his desk and found his pipe. Just a little rock would make everything all right.

Via wasn't answering her phone. It was maddening and he would punish her for it. He wanted to believe she cared, but she could be a two-faced little liar, just like Sonia.

He put in the rock. Hello little friend.

How had she known about the Portland bust? Who could she be working for? It had probably just been a lucky guess. She'd probably just called Mattais to confess her sins. He would have to do a little online research on her.

His LA contact had told him not to worry too much. Swore the Portland crew was solid. Swore they wouldn't turn. But, of course, nobody could be trusted.

He found his butane lighter and lit the glass. Vapor crept up through the pipe and into his waiting mouth. Oh God. Oh, yes.

# CHAPTER 33

## VIA

**VIA HAD BEEN** looking forward to seeing Grandma Daney again, but her own hands were so shaky now. Someone might think she was the one with Parkinson's. She held them together in her lap as best she could, each hand attempting to hold the other down tight. She was craving coke so much; it felt like demons were licking her brain. Her emotions had been all over the place. Earlier, she was sure she and Matt were hopeless. With each hour they had been apart, just twelve so far, she became more desperate to find a way—some way—to hold on to him. She would beg, confess she needed his help. Maybe Grandma Daney could save her somehow—tell her what to say. What words could she possibly say to make him understand?

She glanced around at Grandma Daney's things, and got choked up looking at an eight by ten photo of Nick and Matt. They were standing by a ramp, confident, holding skateboards in their hands. They couldn't have been more than thirteen.

"Those two," Grandma Daney said as she carefully sat down next to her on the couch. "Always thick as thieves. Please, have a cookie."

Via looked down to the plate of yellow, pink, and brown wafer cookies. While she wanted a pink one, she just shook her head because her stomach felt like it was eating itself from the inside out.

"You look unwell dear, what's wrong?" Nick's grandmother's kind eyes flashed with concern.

Without even trying to restrain herself, Via leaned against Grandma Daney, and let herself collapse into the old woman's soft, periwinkle sweater. She surrendered, lost in the smell of lavender. "It's ru-ined. I cheat-ed," she said in a soft, shameful whisper.

"Oh, sweetheart," Grandma Daney said as she put her arms around her. "All is well. It really is."

"I have to tell him, and he's going to hate me."

"Try not to focus on him right now. Get right with yourself first."

"It's terrible. I've been terrible."

"Nonsense," Grandma Daney insisted. "Why do young women today insist on loading themselves up with so much guilt? That isn't what we wanted for you, back in the sixties and seventies. You know, I was active in the ERA movement."

Via was even more ashamed now. She knew the ERA was a women's lib thing, but didn't understand its significance.

"Dear, your sexuality belongs to you, not any man. Now, if you feel you've let yourself down, that's something you can work through."

"But—"

"You two are so young, still learning who you are. The kindest thing you can do for him now is concentrate on yourself. Accept yourself where you are, and make new choices."

Her words were like honey, sweet, but sticky. They helped, yet they didn't—but her hug was safe and snug, so Via stayed there and soaked in her comfort.

"You'll get through this. The way I see it, young women give mistakes too much power. It's not our mistakes that bring us down, but the guilt about our mistakes. It's that guilt that leads to more mistakes, bigger mistakes."

Grandma Daney's embrace felt so good, like hug therapy. It made honesty almost easy. "I am so stupid," Via admitted.

"Shush now. Don't ever tell yourself that. The words that come after 'I am' carry the weight of the universe."

"What do you mean?"

"The words that follow 'I am' will define you," Grandma Daney said. "When a woman tells herself, 'I am powerful' then she is. Don't ever talk about yourself in negative terms because *you* are listening."

That actually made some sense, she realized. She sat back against the couch and looked at the sweet old woman's determined face. Her wrinkles could not hide her inner youthfulness.

"Imagine yourself like me, seventy-one and happy, for the most part," she said. "Imagine that you don't have to give a rip what people think anymore. So many mistakes, mistakes so huge you could drive a truck through them, but you just don't care anymore. And, you know why?"

"Why?"

"Because when you're my age, most of the people you've hurt have either forgiven you, forgotten you, or are dead."

Via smiled. The heaviness that had loomed over her earlier was breaking up like clouds before a sunbreak.

"Now, imagine feeling that freedom right now. There is no reason to wait until you're my age. Forget trying to please everyone else. Recognize your power now, while you're young enough to enjoy it."

They were quiet for a moment. Via didn't care that this woman didn't know her whole life story. Her words weren't as important as the unconditional love she was sending out.

"Don't stop," she said. "What else?"

Grandma Daney laughed. "I can't dole out all of my pearls of wisdom in one shot. You'll have no reason to come back and visit me."

"Can I?"

"Anytime, whether you come with the boys or not," she said as she paused and looked over toward the open door. She turned her attention back to Via and gave her a billion-dollar smile. "You are such a sweet spirit. Please honor yourself."

"Hi, G-Dane."

It was Matt, hovering in the doorway. Oh Goddess, not yet.

"Hi, handsome. Come sit, I have cookies," Grandma Daney said. Her tone with him was equally kind.

"I'm sorry, but I need Via. We need to talk."

\*   \*   \*

# VIA

HE WALKED THREE STEPS ahead of her, head down, all the way to the main room. He led her to the window, but an old woman was there, working on a jigsaw puzzle, so he pulled her over to the front corner, next to the partially decorated Christmas tree. Nick was over on the other side of the room, talking to one of the nurses.

Matt finally looked into her eyes and the connection—usually full of love and understanding—was full of confusion. She felt the brunt of his words before he even opened his mouth.

"I know where you were last night," he said. "When I was on the road. I know who you were with." She heard something in his voice she had never heard before. Fear. "Please tell me you just got high with him."

She knew she couldn't shut down, couldn't back down. She would lose him forever. Her words felt like mud in her mouth. All she could manage to say was, "Please."

He was staring her down. The eyes she loved were harsh and hurtful. He wouldn't look away.

"I don't want to have to do this right now," he said. "But I can't wait until January. I can't wait another hour."

"Please," was all she could say. He really was breaking up with her. Of course, she had expected it. But, there had been a meager speck of hope that she had been clutching onto. Now, she felt it shrinking itself out of existence. She would do anything to save it.

"I was stupid, I was high," she said. "It didn't mean anything."

"It means everything to me." Her hands came up against her chest, perhaps in an attempt to keep her heart in place. She remembered that day at the boat launch when he'd threatened to steal it. Their faces were a foot apart. He was right there, looking right at her. But it was like he wasn't seeing her anymore.

The lights of the Christmas tree lit up. Of course they would, she thought. But they weren't pretty or special, and neither was she. They didn't have a special message for her. They didn't want to save or protect her. They were just lights. She wanted to jump onto that goddamned tree and rip it apart. She wanted to strangle herself with those lights, but she knew it would land her in the nearest mental ward—her greatest fear realized. Her father's daughter.

She reached for him, but he pulled away. "I can't believe you played me like this," he said, shaking his head. "This fucking kills me."

"Please, remember how we felt that day," she said.

"Don't you dare throw that in my face." He raised his voice; his eyes drew into slits. "I was so busy getting you to trust me, ripping myself wide open for you, that I forgot I was dealing with some fucked up girl, already cheating on someone else. Did you even break up with him?"

People were watching them, but she didn't care. "I love you."

He just looked down at the floor. It was the worst kind of silence. It went on forever.

She leaned in a few inches closer, but he stepped back again. "That's it?" she asked. "That's all you have to say to me?"

"Actually, I do have one more thing to say."

"You do?"

"You make me sick."

"Oh," she heard herself say. "Oh, okay." She knew her tone sounded casual, almost breezy.

She turned and made her way to the door where she met a group of kids coming in. Carolers. She stepped aside as they came into the lobby and began singing "O Holy Night." She looked back, but he still wouldn't look at her. She knew he was gone. He really wasn't her Tristan anymore.

Uneasy on her feet, she went out into the night. Food would be impossible. Her ulcerated stomach was a scorching pit of fire. Where was she going to go? Maybe she needed to find a new sign, one that would lead to a new beginning. But, she couldn't bear a new beginning. A wave of chills crept over her shoulders and down her arms; her fingers shook. Her wicked thoughts were all over the place. Her sick body needed to be high—or dead. Nothing was ever going to be okay. There was only one person wretched enough to deserve her company, and he would have mountains of blow.

# Chapter 34

## Carlos

**CARLOS SHOOK** his gold lighter up and down twice then flicked it with his thumb. He lit the new red candle on top of the bar. He hoped it would enhance the mood he was going for. Ben had just called over the intercom to announce that Via was on her way back. He picked up the vodka tonic he had prepared for her—no lime—and carried it over to the glass coffee table.

He felt conflicted, almost sorry, about what he was about to do. It's just the coke, he told himself. He had been hunkered down in his office smoking most of the day. Except for the Kaytlyn quickie, he'd been alone all day. His thoughts were too random, too fast for his tired brain to decipher.

No doubt she was special, but he couldn't let that be the case. Follow through, he told himself. She was the devil—ignoring his calls, making him wait and wonder. Her childhood wounds complimented his well, but knowing she had already gotten to him only reinforced his need to destroy her. He knew he had shared too much about Maya and Sam with her, but otherwise the story he had given her was tight. She hadn't asked about his business, so she had nothing on him there.

She came in and sat down on the couch. That light he had so often seen in her eyes was gone. Her sweater was stark white with busy black pattern. It did nothing to warm up her complexion. She wore a black skirt and heels. Other than being too long, the skirt pleased him. Jeans would be a hassle. She adjusted her hair so it fell back behind her shoulders, then offered a waxy smile. Her gaze lingered on the glass coffee table, which was laden with coke smudges. Would she lick her finger and swipe up the residue that Kaytlyn had ignored a just few hours ago? That would be perfect.

Of course he knew what she wanted, but instead of going back behind his desk to fetch this princess her nose candy, he went over and sat next to her.

"Did you and Mattais have a fight?" he asked, his cheeks warm and excited. "That's too bad."

"He'll never trust me again," she said, bringing her shaky hands into her lap and holding them together.

He didn't even try to restrain his deep laugh. "Well, should he? You're here with me, right?"

She didn't give him an answer, so he continued his assault.

"Remember when you first came here? What was that, like three months ago?" This was the best part of the hunt for him. He had psychologically pulled her panties down and was prepared to give her psyche a pounding. But first, he wanted to make her squirm a little longer. "You looked so hot. I could tell right away you were special, nothing like the other girls."

As he expected, her face relaxed into an assured smile. "But now you're just a another skinny blow whore. No wonder Mattais doesn't want to fuck you anymore."

He kept his disdainful glare set upon her and waited. Her smile disappeared and her expression fell into a blank stare, an emotional five-second delay. This is where he hoped things would get interesting. Would she start to cry and run from the room or would she throw herself at his feet? He hoped she would stay and beg, try to convince him her body and her soul were worth a gram.

"And now you've come back to me. What *shall* I do with you?" He wondered if she had noticed that the candle he was burning smelled of Christmas spice. He hoped it would give height to the emotional tailspin he planned to witness.

But she just sat there. The tears he had expected to enjoy seemed to be held at bay. Instead, she furrowed her brows, squinted her eyes. Ah, she was surprising him after all. Sparking his attraction to her. She was offended and possibly furious. Her response was deliberate and condescending.

"Using words like 'shall' doesn't make you any smarter, you know."

Direct hit, right to the heart. He felt like a fish being gutted. Fucking whore. Of course, she would call him dumb. He tried to play it off. He would be cool and controlled. "Yes, be a little bitch. I like that."

It had been good before, but this time it would be rough and ruthless, and she was going to love it. He couldn't wait to provide Mattais with the colorful play-by-play. Oops, I did her again.

He went behind his desk. She sat there, strung out and broken hearted, just as he had hoped. He pondered his options for a moment—how to proceed, how to proceed? He could start by making her dance for him while he pointed out her flaws; every woman had flaws. Or, he could have her blow him while he told her what a dirty slut she was. But first, if she wanted cocaine—really wanted the full experience—he would give it to her.

"Come on," he said, sweet as candy. "Let's just forget the drama and have some fun."

He didn't want her to leave. He was getting hot thinking about other ways to put her in her place. He smiled, imagining her on her hands and knees in front of the mirror. He would pull her hair back hard enough to pull her head up—she would have to look at herself. He would need to think of some brutal insults to inflict upon her—something about poor Mattais.

First things first, his hand still on the top desk drawer, he called over to her. "I have something extra special for you, and you're going to love it."

She looked confused for a moment, but didn't respond. He opened the bottom drawer and pulled out his marbled goody box, which made her smile. Then he grabbed his clear glass pipe and butane lighter, which made her mouth fall open.

She didn't say a word; her silence was his answer. She could still bolt, so he eased over and sat next to her. He poured some blow into a pile. His own anticipation made him smile. She would be his again, no doubt. He began chopping it, fanning it out against the glass, fully aware of the rhythm of his hand—back and forth, back and forth. There it was, one fat rail with her name on it. He was starting to feel warm and tingly. He could feel her warm, sweet breath on the side of his neck. She was already leaning in for it. Silly girl, she didn't know she would have to earn it first. He picked up the straw, but instead of handing it to her he placed it next to her treat.

He brought her hands into his lap. She tensed up, but didn't fight him. He felt himself growing harder and knew she could feel it too. "Don't you see what you do to me?" he asked. She pulled her hands back. What a shame. "I know you're sick, that you need this," he said. "I know you want to be in a better mood for me. You want to please me." She still hadn't said anything, so he continued his display of reassurance.

"I didn't mean what I said before, you know that. First, you're trying this," he explained. He dropped a nice rock into the round belly of the pipe. "Then, you can do that line, if you even still want to." He wondered if she would believe that. He wouldn't tell her that he had plenty to smoke. That he would keep her very high—all night long and into the next. "Don't worry, you're ready for this." He was almost there; he didn't want to lose her now. She was a miserable little bitch. He was lonesome, and he would soon secure her company. Just one hit.

Via reached over, picked up her vodka tonic, and sucked down half of it. She was beginning to shake. "I should go," she said. "I'm not going to be any fun tonight."

Like hell, he thought. This little tease wasn't going anywhere. "It's just cocaine, just freebase. We're just smoking it. Better delivery system. Right to the heart, baby."

She took another swig of her drink. He held the pipe toward her, ready to light it.

"I just can't," she said, trying to stand up. The glass in her hand knocked into his arm and he dropped the pipe—his favorite pipe. It shattered against the cement floor.

He felt cool vodka soaking into his pants.

"Shit!" He seized her arm and her empty glass went flying, falling victim to the floor as well. "What's wrong with you?" He pushed her back down on the couch. She struggled, but he had her by one arm, and then both. He had to hold himself back from choking the dumb bitch. He leaned over her, his hands wrapped around her wrists.

"Stop, please," she begged. "I'm sorry."

Damn straight, she should be sorry. Though this was just want he wanted anyway. He couldn't wait to punish her. He would show her. He pulled her up off the couch, but she fought him, so he caught her by her hair. "I've already banged you on the couch. I want you over here. On your stomach."

"It hurts," she whimpered, grabbing at his hands in her hair.

He just pulled harder until he had her on the floor. He dragged her in front of the mirror, but couldn't get her onto her stomach. She was on her back, flailing her arms and kicking. He managed to climb on top of her and straddle her hips. He let go of one of her hands to wipe the sweat from his brow and she reached up, and tried to scratch his face.

He loved her for fighting, but he hated her more. He was so amped up. Only one other woman had ever been able to set him off like this.

He pinned both her arms again, above her head. "Don't you want to watch?" he taunted her. "I want you to see me nailing you in the mirror. I want to see you trying to look dignified."

\* \* \*

# VIA

**WITH HER BACK** against the hard floor, Via fought him with everything she had. His eyes were dark and sick and horrifying. This was so much worse than before because this time she was alert and sober. She tried to scream, but he managed to press his hand over her mouth, still keeping her arm held down with his elbow.

"I like that. Fight me," he threatened. She felt him try to jam his knees between hers. He used his weight to force them open. "If this is how you want it, fine."

An out-of-body sensation seized her. She would pretend it was happening to somebody else. This was happening to Vixen. No matter what, he couldn't touch *her* because *she* was Via. He had pulled open Vixen's sweater and forced down Vixen's bra. He leaned in and began sucking and biting her hard.

Hell no, she realized. Not even Vixen deserved this—nobody did. This was not going to happen. She tried to get a hand free again so that she could claw into his eyes, but he only pushed down harder. How she wanted to feel her fingertips tear into his flesh. She pushed against him so hard she feared the bones in her wrists might break. He rammed his legs against her inner thighs. The harder she fought, the more it hurt.

And then she felt herself go limp. Maybe she was in shock. It seemed automatic. Her body had decided it was time to stop fighting altogether. Her life was over. He might as well take her body now, the body her soul had been dressed in.

She turned her head away from him and closed her eyes tight. Something clicked, and with it came a stunning sense of peace. The epiphany blazed through her—she was worthy. It was so simple. Why couldn't she remember? The pretty lights found her. There they were, in the most stunning shades, breathtaking and pure. They twirled and spun in reflections of their own brilliance. What were they saying? She couldn't hear them over the beating of her heart. She tried to sense their meaning. Through their hums she heard, *It's not real. You're not her.*

She felt him respond to her surrender by loosening his grip on one of her wrists. He leaned in more and used his shoulder to keep her down while his hand moved down to his belt. What felt like his sweat was smearing against her chest and neck.

"Baby, you can stop fighting now," he said into her ear. His voice sounded so gentle, so sincere. "We belong together." He kissed her neck.

He wanted her to be Sonia, but she would deny him that pleasure. She would go for his jugular, exploit his wife's greatest lie. It was time to thrust into his soft spot. She would torture him with Sonia's evil accusation. She leaned into his kisses and gave him a little moan of pleasure.

He pulled his head back and looked down at her, surprised.

"Maya," she said, strained. She relaxed her legs for him. "Maya." He pulled up, seemingly baffled. She found her voice. "I'll stop fighting, Daddy, and I won't tell." His weight against her lessened, and he gaped at her, stricken. The passion in his eyes flickered, sputtered, and died. Victory, she thought.

But then, he sat up, straddled her again, and slammed back down into her left cheek with what felt like a brick. The pain resounded throughout her head, agony. He was yelling at her, but she couldn't make out his words because her brain was sending out an all-encompassing distress call.

And then his voice came back into focus. "Don't fucking talk about my baby!" he yelled. "You sick bitch! I never touched her!" His hand crashed back down—into the same side of her face, but higher. Its force warped the ringing in her head. "I will kill you!" He got up.

Such pain coursed through her. She couldn't open her left eye; it hurt too much to even try. She felt something burning into her cheek. Tears? No, it was blood, or brains.

She brought her hands up against the side of her face. Adrenaline jolted her senses. Her brain screamed for survival. It tried to rouse her, but she was too dumbfounded to save herself. With her right eye she saw him standing over her. Was he taking off his pants? No, she realized. He was taking off his belt.

"You evil bitch," he said as he sat back down on top of her. He reached up and ripped her arms down, pinning them against her sides by straddling her again. "You'll pay for that."

All she could do was turn her head away. She felt his weight shift as he drew back and then whipped the belt down against her. A new, crippling pain seared into the left side of her chest and shoulder. She froze against the sound of her own scream. It hurt too much to beg or struggle anymore. The belt whizzed back down and lashed against the side of her chest and neck, overwhelming her with even more pain, too much to even comprehend.

All sound shorted out, then buzzed back on. His voice came back into focus. "Oh God," he was saying. "God, baby, what am I'm I doing?"

Via felt his weight ease off of her as he rose, then moved somewhere else in the room, maybe over to his desk. She rolled onto her side and curled up tight and small. She writhed in pain and wailed against the comfort of that cold, hard floor. Her hands trembled toward her face and found what felt like an old, soggy peach. It pulsed and grew against her wet fingers. Through her good eye, she tried to look over at him. Did he still have the belt? Was he just taking a break? His labored breathing gave her hope. He was tired, done with her now.

"I'm sorry you made me do that," he said, trying to catch his breath. He leaned against the edge of his desk. Still holding the belt. "Fuck, so now I'm the monster. You think I'm a monster."

She drew in breath, in brief notches, but couldn't remember how to exhale. She kept her right eye on him and prayed he would have mercy on her.

"Goddamn, that was low," he said. "Maybe that worked tonight." He relaxed his grip on the belt until it became limp and then tossed it aside. His voice bordered on a growl. "You'll want to be high again. And I'll be here, you psycho."

Could he truly think she would ever come back? She couldn't even be sure she would make it home alive. Her face, her neck, her chest, all ablaze, yet each pulsated with its own brand of heat. She peeled herself off the floor and tried to crawl to the couch. While she was beyond dizzy, her body insisted on escape. Everything became warbled, surreal, almost calm. Where was her purse? Her car keys were in it. Through her right eye, she saw it on the coffee table—next to that line of blow. She hadn't gotten her blow, her last line; she hadn't gotten it.

"Go ahead," he said as he pulled out his desk chair and sat down.

She turned her right eye toward the table. There it was. The last line. The one she would never do. Never. Never.

"Snort that rail. I know you're sick. I know you need it."

"No," she whimpered over the sounds of her cranial chaos. She winced as she pulled herself up onto the couch. From there she was able to get her stuff. Tentatively, she was able to stand up.

"Don't come back until you're ready to play." He opened his desk drawer and pulled out what looked like another glass pipe. It was shaped like a light bulb. It was hard to see for sure. He was pulling out another plastic baggie.

She limped to the door, utterly convinced that she would never step across this threshold again. He would never hurt her again.

"And Via," he called to her.

The door was so close, just an arm's length away.

"Keep your head down, your face is all fucked up," he said.

She reached for the door, her hand streaked with blood.

"So sad," he added. "You used to be so pretty."

# CHAPTER 35

## VIA

**SHE BLINKED HER EYES**, again and again. Had she fallen asleep in her car, right there in the Hotties back parking lot? It was light outside; at least her blurred field of vision seemed lighter. Her face felt like a screaming block of cement, her neck and chest felt engulfed in flames.

"Here's some ice." The voice she heard was familiar. Beautiful strands of blonde hair hung like a soft curtain. Mama, Via realized. She used to bring ice for her mother's face, but now Mama was bringing her the ice.

"It's going to be okay," her mother said. "God, this is so fucked up."

No, wait, Via realized. Mama would never say that. Who was this angel?

"What, are you stupid?" It was Kaytlyn's voice. "Do you think Carlos is fucking around?"

Something cold, maybe a rag, came down on her face. It changed the pain, made it dull.

"Shit, you're bleeding all over the place."

"Carlos," she heard herself say.

Kaytlyn's husky laugh surprised her. "No doubt who did this," she said. Her voice dropped and became little more than a whisper. "The bouncers would never let a client do this to a girl—only Carlos."

She tried to open her left eye and look toward Kaytlyn, but couldn't see much, just a talking blur. "This is bad," the blur said, while it weaved back and forth. "You need to see a doctor. Why didn't you just fuck him? It's not that bad."

"No," Via managed. "No."

Kaytlyn's face wouldn't stay in one place. As she spoke, her mouth spun—one long rotating pink strip.

"Your mouth looks like a dog chasing its tail," Via told the face.

"Why are you blinking so much?" it asked. "Stop doing that, it's freaky. Put the ice pack back on."

Then Kaytlyn was talking, maybe on the phone. "I don't know how to help her. You're the wannabe nurse," she said. "Just bring Bella in her pajamas. Hurry. If he finds out I helped, he'll go off."

Via felt herself trembling, and she couldn't stop.

"Going to my car. I'll be right back," Kaytlyn said, and was gone, but not for long.

"What's another jacket, right?" Kaytlyn was asking. Her voice was like warm velvet. Then Via felt something soft being draped over her. It felt loving and safe. She wanted to say thank you, but she was so tired. She was probably dying. That would be cool. She didn't deserve to be breathing in air anymore.

Everything around her turned golden and she just wanted to sleep. The side of her head collapsed against the window. Maybe if she kept her eyes closed and prayed hard enough, she would just die. She didn't want to hurt anybody anymore. She didn't want to hurt herself anymore.

Kaytlyn began talking to somebody else. She was moving away. It was foggy. Was she ever coming back? Via hadn't thanked her.

Somebody was there, shining a light in her good eye, then prying open the other.

"Oww!" Via pulled away from the agony.

"Good lord, baby girl," the voice said. It was Mama Whitney. "Can you manage to slide over?" she asked. Via did as she was told, then wiped drool off of her own chin. It felt like drool, but maybe it was blood. Her neck hurt, her chest, her arms, her thighs, her head, her everything. The cloth wasn't cold anymore.

Whit was yelling to somebody outside of the car. "I'll leave my car here. Okay, okay. Put Bella's booster seat in the back, and her backpack, too." Then she was gone. Then she was back. "Sweetie, just go back to sleep now."

"Okay," Via told her. "I will."

"No, no. I was talking to Bella, not you," Whit said. "No more falling asleep. Keep your face covered. I can't take you to my mom's house like this," she said. "So, I'm taking you to Nick's."

"No, I can't ever go back there. Take me to Vashon." The shrill of her own voice hurt her brain.

"Shh," Whitney said. "You'll wake up Bella. She's in the back."

"Please, Vashon, please."

# CHAPTER 36

## VIA

**VIA'S GROGGINESS** was fading back into her miserable reality. She squinted as she tried to make out the time on the microwave, twelve forty-four a.m. I'm such a busted-up Cinderella, she thought—home past midnight, a gory disgrace. The ice cubes Whitney had gotten from the soda dispenser on the ferry had melted into the washcloth, creating a bloody mess. Via couldn't wait to throw it in the kitchen sink. It felt as though her cheek had swollen up into the side of her forehead.

Whitney seemed ready and able to bust out her nursing-school skills and had brought along her first aid kit. "Bella, get in here please." She turned to face Via and gasped. "It's swelling up even more. I still think you need to go to the emergency room."

"No, too many sick people."

Whitney didn't look amused. "You can't use Matt's hospital phobia to get out of going yourself."

"You know they'll ask questions," she said. "Questions we can't answer."

Bella came in, rubbing her eyes. She was wearing pink flannel pajamas with rain boots and had on a little pink princess backpack.

"Via," she said with a cringe. "Did you fall down?"

"Yes, I fell down outside and a rock hit my face. I'm okay though. Hey, want to see your room?"

She took them down the hall and opened the first door on the right. Whitney peeked in and did a double take. Dan's clothes were scattered all over the floor. He was a messy packer. He had forgotten his shaving kit. It sat on the dresser.

"Is this—?" Whitney asked, her eyes darting back to Via. "You two have separate bedrooms?"

Bella came in, jumped on the bed, and started digging through her backpack.

"I can't think about Dan right now," she said. "I really can't." But it was too late. His memory had been summoned. Just when she thought it was impossible to feel any worse, her chest was weighted down with the densest darkness. "He and I have," she began, but then stopped, and looked at Bella. "*Been together*," she said. "But sometimes he got weird about it after."

"Like, guilty?" Whitney asked. A snort escaped her. She covered her mouth with her hand. "I'm sorry."

"He's been gone since June anyway."

"Mommy, Mommy. Are you going to read to me?" Bella had found a storybook.

"One minute, sweetie." Looking back at Via, she was seemingly at a loss for words. "Via, you're not going to marry him, are you?"

"I can't talk about this now." She was sick with herself and just wanted her bathtub. Her body craved cocaine something awful. It was insane how much she needed it. Her body would shut down without it, what was left of her body. Her head and heart were fried. Her arms and legs had been tenderized.

"This isn't about Matt. This is about you," Whitney said as she came closer. "You need some time to get yourself together, figure out who you are. You're barely twenty-one, for Christ's sake."

"Please, just read to Bella, make yourselves at home," she said. "I really need a drink, a hot bath."

She took a step for the door, but Whitney stopped her. "Okay, but you can't try to do this on your own." She gave Via an extra gentle hug. "I'm not going anywhere."

Closing her eyes, Via wished with all of her heart that she was in her mother's arms. But the fingers that stroked the back of her head were not her mother's.

"I'll come check on you in a few minutes." There was warmth in that voice, but it was not her mother's.

"Just get me a vodka tonic?" Via pulled away. "Please." She could barely get the words out. Talking hurt her mutilated face. "In the cabinet above the toaster."

"Okay, but you'll have to take a break from the booze, too. Maybe forever. We'll talk about detox stuff tomorrow."

Gingerly making her way down the hallway, she couldn't get her father out of her head, like he was trying to tell her something. Maybe Carlos's punch had shaken something loose in her head. She paused and leaned back against the wall, careful not to leave any bloody prints.

A new memory popped into her awareness. She remembered the day her father had bought her a purple balloon from a booth at Central Park. She had been little, five or six years old.

*He wanted to tie it around her wrist, but she resisted. She stood her ground. "Fine, Violetta, but hold on tight," he cautioned. Within a minute, it slipped from her hand. It just slipped away. He wasn't even angry. He just shook his head at her. "See?" he said as they watched it break for the high blue sky. "Now, be a good girl." He bought her ice cream, but in a kiddie-cup. He didn't trust her to have a big-kid cone. She didn't even want a cone because she didn't trust herself either.*

Her chest felt so constricted it literally hurt. Maybe cocaine had weakened her heart, or maybe heartache was real and not just some sappy expression. She wanted Matt—so obviously, so thoroughly, like she'd wanted that balloon.

She closed her bedroom door and made her way past her bed and toward the bathroom. She began peeling off her sweater, then her bra. She stepped out of her skirt and panties, leaving a trail of blood-speckled clothing as she went. She knew her striptease was unattractive, possibly the worst in the history of the world. Going straight for the bathtub, she flicked on the light switch and groaned as she leaned over to turn on the water. Carlos may have cracked a rib or two, but she wouldn't mention that to Whitney. She poured in her favorite bubble bath—vanilla orange blossom. She imagined resting against Matt's chest so his energy could envelope her, like the pretty lights. Being in his arms reminded her of the pretty lights. Why had she never realized that before?

As she turned around, she finally saw herself in the mirror. Gone was that sexy girl who had stood in the wings that first night at Hotties. Skinny brown bruises shaped like Carlos's fingers wrapped around her upper arms. Her wrists were laced with blue and violet. The side of her face had swollen purple. As she leaned in and turned her head to the side, she got a closer look at her ruptured cheek. The bleeding had stopped, but the whites of her eye were bloodshot. How could that be? Had he hit her more than once? She just couldn't remember.

Her face was just the cherry on top of her mutilated body. Collarbones and ribs jutted out from her pasty skin. She had never noticed her hipbones sticking out like that before. "Oh God, you *are* a blow whore," she told the unlovable girl in the mirror. All she could think about was running back to Matt, but he wouldn't want her. She was ugly and empty and had nothing to tempt him with. She felt her bottom lip quiver.

"Via?" Whitney was calling from the bedroom. "Via?"

She eased herself into the water, wincing all the way.

After a minute, she felt Whitney standing over her, and gasp. "Oh—my—God."

"Please," Via said without making eye contact. "Just don't. Don't say anything."

Whitney set a blue plastic picnic cup on the edge of the tub.

Via closed her eyes. "I can't talk about Carlos. I can't talk about Dan. Not Matt, not my father." And she punctuated her declaration by raising her cup with a flourish and guzzling down her vodka. It numbed. It was everything she needed in that moment.

"Just close your eyes and enjoy your bath," Whitney told her. "I'm not leaving you, though."

Via sighed as she watched Whitney pull out her phone and lean against the makeup vanity. It was built into the wall, not like the freestanding antique vanity Mama used to have. Via had forgotten about that old vanity. Another memory swept in, caught her up, and crystallized her back into the past.

*She was stretched out on her parents' bed, watching her mother as she sat in front of that old makeup mirror. Snow was falling outside. Her mother looked like a movie star in her dressing room. They liked to talk while her mother got ready to go out. Her parents seemed like they were happy when they were out, or maybe they went out when he was happy.*

*"Are you going to an art show?" She lay on her tummy, the dark red bedspread silky-stiff beneath her arms, her face propped up against her hands. She marveled at her mother's cleavage. When was she ever going to look like that?*

*"No, the opera," her mother said as she dusted powder over her nose. Then she turned toward the open bedroom door. "Joseph, turn up the music, won't you?"*

*Oh, the opera, Via thought, no longer sad about having to stay home. Operas were boring.*

*Via stretched as Verdi filled the whole apartment. "Is it the opera about me?"* she asked. *"The one where Violetta coughs up blood into a hanky? She's stupid."*

*"Shh,"* her mother said into the mirror. *"Don't let your father hear you say that."*

*"I wish you didn't name me after her. I like the one with the Viking girl with the flying horse."* She sat up and imagined what it would feel like to fly, to be brave. *"She jumps into fire at the end, but Violetta just coughs."*

*"Sweetheart,"* her mother said, fluffing out her collarbone-length blonde waves. *"When you're older, you'll realize Violetta is a beautiful name."*

*"I can't wait to get married and get a new name. I hate being called Rabbit. The boys always call me Rabbit. I hate my name."*

Her mother came and sat on the edge of the bed. Hungry for a hug, Via slid over and nestled into her mother's waiting arms. *"I know the life I've chosen for you hasn't been easy—being the daughter of Joseph Antonio Rabbotino."*

Her mother's blue eyes were bright as she pulled back and looked down. Via was distracted by what she saw peeking out through her mother's blush: a bruise along her left cheekbone. Her mother caught her looking and returned to her vanity. She peered into the mirror, critical.

She sighed. *"You are also the daughter of Ingrid Sorenson, so there's some Viking in you too."* She found her blush brush and applied another coat. *"I used to be strong, I think,"* she said. *"I want to be again, but I have forgotten how."* She made eye contact with Via through the mirror and held it. *"That can never happen to you—remember who you are."*

*"It's time to go,"* her father yelled.

*"No,"* Via said as she realized what was happening. *"Stay with me, I need you."*

Her mother looked through the mirror, almost amused. *"You know this all turns out okay, right?"* she asked. *"Don't worry, this is just a life you're having."*

*"No."*

*"Then this must be a dream. That's nice. I like when you dream about me."*

Via turned her attention to her father's shadow in the doorway. *"No,"* she begged. *"Please, she's not ready—I'm not ready for you to take her."*

But then the shadow was gone, and so was her mother. She heard the wall clock chime, though it need not have bothered. She knew it must be four o'clock. Via looked for the wall clock so she could turn its hands back to three fifty-nine and then smash it. But it was gone, too. The wall itself was gone. Everything was gone.

# CHAPTER 37

## VIA

**NOT YET,** don't wake up yet, she begged herself. She had to find that fucking clock. She could still sense her mother. Her presence was still an arm's length away. Via tried to reach out and catch it, and hold it forever. But a whisper of sweet spun air pulled them apart.

"Via, Via. Do you see the pretty lights?"

She tried to open her eyes, but then the pain seized her. It must have been waiting. It consumed her. Overtook everything but that angel's voice. Who was that, Bella?

"I used to see them when I was little," Bella said. "They're fairies. When my daddy went to heaven, he sent them to play with me."

Via turned her head. So much pain. She winced.

"Is she waking up, sweetie?" It was Whitney. "Go back to the dining room and color some more, okay?"

"But, Mommy—"

"Sweetie, go."

Via wanted to tell Bella to stay, but her voice caught in her dry throat. She felt the sting of a straw pressing against her lips. She sucked in the most amazing apple juice she had ever tasted. The price she paid, however, was more pain. "Ow, it hurts." Her cry came out as little more than a whisper.

"I Steri-Striped your face."

"What?" Blinking her eyes a few times, the room came into focus. Whitney was putting a tray of food down on the desk. It smelled amazing, like soup and bread.

"It's surgical tape." Whitney came over, leaned in, and examined the wound critically. Then she sat back and sighed.

"Am I hideous?"

"It looks better today—stopped oozing—and it's crusting over nicely. Must be all the beauty sleep. You've been pretty out of it since Tuesday morning. It was a royal bitch getting you out of the tub."

"What day is it?"

"Thursday." Whitney cocked her head to the side, concerned. "December 4th. Why? God, I knew I should have taken you to the emergency room. Let me get a look at your pupils again." She leaned in again.

Via held up her hands. "No, it's okay." She felt alive. December 4th. Four would be her lucky number now. She still had 17 days to go, but it would be okay. The calendar had somehow lost its power over her.

Dreaming of her mother in front of that old mirror had opened the door to other memories. They began tumbling into her awareness like happy toddlers. There had been other days, hopeful days.

She spied a bright crayon picture on the side table. It looked like a house with a tree and two dogs.

"Bella drew it," Whitney said. "Several actually, but that's her favorite because of the deer. She's never seen deer before coming to visit you. She's been out on your back deck this morning, all bundled up, waiting for the deer to come back so she can draw them some more."

"Has she befriended the neighbor's ponies?"

"Shut up," Whitney said. "Ponies?"

"When I get my butt out of bed, we can take them some apples." Via felt hope percolating up from the soft recesses of her mind. It felt like a new reality, like her life had been given back to her. "Whitney, how long can you two stay? Are you missing school?"

"Finals are next week, then I'm off until January. My mom was going to watch her while I worked, but—" Whitney stood up and went over to the desk, returning with the tray of food. "I'm not going back there now."

"Because of me? I'm sorry." She sat up. Her side hurt. Her face hurt more, but not enough to stop her from trying some tomato soup.

"You were the final kick in the ass," Whitney said with a sly grin. "I just have one more semester, I was going to quit soon anyway. Ben's been telling me to leave for months. Nick too—and Matt."

His name. Whitney might has well have gouged out her heart with an ice cream scoop.

"I'm telling you now, the next two weeks are going to suck for you," Whitney said. "I'm going to be a hard ass. Detox time. Tough love."

"Okay, I get it." She took a bite of her gooey grilled cheese sandwich. Chewing would be tricky. She drank some apple juice. The roof of her mouth had grown scales.

"When the bruising goes down, I want you to go see your doctor," Whitney told her; her expression was so serious. "Tell him you've been using. I've done some online research and there are some medications that help with cocaine cravings."

How could she possibly tell Dr. Gillian? She would have to see him at church. He couldn't tell Dan though, not technically, but he could offer up some cryptic prayer request at men's bible study.

And then Dan came back into her mind. She was going to have to break his heart.

"It's either that or you go into a treatment center," Whitney said. "I'm not a fan of the twelve-step thing, but then I'm not counselor. Staying away from anyone who uses is crucial. I know that much."

Via looked at her friend. Her cat eyes looked so earnest.

"We haven't talked about Bella's dad, but heroin was why we split up. He just couldn't kick." She looked away for a minute. "You should have seen Bella when she was three. Like an angel. He really wanted to get it together for her, but he couldn't. Not even for her. Smack was too much."

Oh God. "I'm so sorry, Whit." She had to say it.

"I know you've got a pride thing going on, but you have to ask yourself what's worse, being embarrassed or being dead."

She hadn't been so sure before, but now she was leaning toward life. She would find a doctor in Seattle. She felt relieved, like something had shifted, like someone had pulled a thorn out of her brain. Maybe she had a concussion.

Whitney looked uncomfortable. "So, you've been talking in your sleep. About your mom. About some other stuff. I don't want to pry though."

She needed a good prying. She needed to get it out. None of it would ever go away until she named it, called it out for what it was. Wrong and twisted and *not her fault*. It seemed the universe had been trying to get her attention for some time, but she had been...too afraid, too insecure, too embarrassed. It was time to step up and into the spotlight. The real spotlight.

"I want to tell you about my past, in New York," she said. "There's some stuff I need to deal with."

Whitney dragged a chair over and sat down. "I've confiscated your phone, you know. I didn't listen to your voice mail messages," she said. "But there is a particular 212 number that calls so often, I practically have memorized—so spill."

Via felt a rush of anxiety, but the expression on her friend's face was so encouraging, she pushed on through. "On December 21st, it will be ten years since—" she stopped. "Wait, let me start it this way." She finished off her apple juice and leaned back against her pillow. She took in a deep breath and slowly let it go. "Whit, have you ever heard the name Rabbotino?"

# Chapter 38

## Matt

**MATT COULDN'T CATCH UP** with Via because his feet were fused to the stage. At first it seemed like a stage, but then he realized it was the side of a jagged mountain. It began rumbling. He reached for her, but his hands grasped away at nothingness. He was stuck there. Clumps of dirt were falling on top of him and into his mouth and lungs. The toxins in the contaminated soil were leaching into his skin. He was melting into himself and he could smell his brains burning. Someone threw roses on him, but they smelled like cigarettes.

"You're just having a dream," she said.

He looked over and saw her dark hair fall into waves against the white pillowcase. She smiled, but then looked confused, and pulled the blanket up over her tanned skin. "What's wrong?" she asked.

He sat straight up. "You have to go," he said. "You have to go!"

He crawled out of bed and found his underwear tangled within his jeans on the floor. An empty shiny black condom wrapper contrasted against the light beige carpet. The sight of it brought him both relief and disgust.

She was sitting up. "But –"

He raced out into the hall and swung open Nick's door to find him sitting at his desk, wearing his Kermit the Frog boxers. He was rolling a joint. Dubstep reverberated throughout the room.

"What the hell?" Nick yelled.

He looked over to see that his best friend had company in his bed as well. A pair of unfamiliar eyes were peeking out from under the covers.

"Get her out of my bed," Matt told him. "You have to get her out!"

"Whoa, whoa, shhh!" Nick said, abandoning his work in progress. He stood up and came closer. "Shut up. She can hear you. Don't be a dick!"

He didn't care. He started rubbing his hands up and down his arms. "Now, Nick!" He had to get into the shower, but he couldn't go back through his bedroom. He rushed into the main bathroom, but couldn't make it to the toilet. He knelt in front of the bathtub and started puking.

He could hear Nick in the hallway just outside the open door, "No, it's not you," he was saying. Matt wiped his mouth, but then hurled again. He averted his eyes as best he could. He had had pizza the night before. It was all coming back to him now, beer and pizza. A river of beer. He couldn't remember the girl, nothing about her, not a thing. He spit then wiped his forehead with the back of his hand.

"You're a sweetheart," Nick was saying. "He's just super hung over. Just went through a bad break up."

Both girls were talking now. He heard one of them say, "He's such a prick." They must have come as a package.

He reached over, turned on the tub's faucet, and started running the water so he could rinse his stubbled face. Using his hand, he encouraged the puke toward the drain. Electrical pulses of pain were bouncing through his head. He didn't know exactly what it felt like to have a brain aneurism, but he was sure he was having one now. His soupy brains should go down the pipes too, into the sewer where they belonged. He heard the front door slam, so he turned off the water, stood up, and made his way to the shower in his own bathroom.

He met Nick in the hallway and yelled, "Get out of my way! I hate you right now!"

Nick looked surprised and then glowered at him. His face was blotchy. "I told you not to bring her up to your room," he said, following Matt down the hall and into his bedroom. "You should have stayed down in the studio. I told you that you weren't ready."

The sight of his disheveled bed made Matt want to puke again. He went over and reached up to unlock the latches at the top of the window. He heaved it open all of the way, stuck his head out, and felt cold rain tap against his face. He noticed Mr. Noble out walking his Labradoodle, Leo, so he knew it was just after seven a.m.

He heard a car starting up and looked down to see the girls leaving. The brunette from his bed rolled down her window long enough to yell up, "Asshole!" He pulled his head back in before she could hurl any more insults. He went over to his bed, pulled off the comforter, bunched it up, and threw it out the window far enough so it cleared the roof edge. He watched it land on the front lawn.

"Dude, it's going to be okay," Nick said from the doorway. "We're going to get through this." His tone had become measured, but his attempt at reassurance was in vain. The smell of cigarettes and rosy perfume seemed to be growing stronger with each passing second.

Matt pulled off the blanket and threw that out. Next, he tossed the top sheet and the fitted sheet. The mattress pad was bulky, so he had to roll it up before it would fit through the window. He picked up both pillows and heaved them as well. Parting with Via's pillow sucked because, up until the night before, it had still smelled like her, fresh and perfect. Now, everything was disgusting and wrong and ruined.

Mr. Noble had stopped walking and was looking up at him with great curiosity. He always had been a nosy bastard.

"What the hell are you looking at?" Matt yelled down. He reached for his jeans and t-shirt on the floor and threw them out the window. Next, he pulled off his underwear like they were full of ants and tossed them out, aiming for their crotchety neighbor, but missing by a long shot. "You want these, old man?" he yelled.

He looked back to his bare mattress. It wouldn't fit out the window. He would start cleaning that after he showered. There was just so much cleaning to do. He would need to go to the store for more disinfectant spray and to rent a steam cleaner. Maybe a bug bomb too. After he showered he would bring the coffee grinder up and overwhelm the room with the scent of a dark Kona roast. Even better, he would have one of G-Dane's hippie friends come over and cleanse the room with sacred sage.

"Dude, you've got to get over her," Nick said, holding his hands in front of his eyes. He had forgotten Nick was there. "We've got the show in less than two weeks. Focus on that. This is big for us. You can't go off the rails. Also, clothes would be good."

Matt turned around and made his way for the shower. "Maybe I don't want to get over her. Maybe I didn't know what I was missing before her." He looked back at Nick. "You think I'm crazy, don't you? The cleaning, the hospital dodging, the things I say—I'm crazy, huh?"

Nick stood there with his one hand still over his eyes and didn't say a word. He didn't have to.

"Maybe she made me feel like, I don't know, maybe I could be normal. And maybe..."

"Maybe what?"

"Maybe I don't care about the music anymore—not like you do," he said. "Maybe you should do what you want to do. With or without me." He had never been so serious in his life.

Nick leaned against the doorframe and folded his hands in front of his chest. He looked up to the ceiling. "You're just hurting right now, but it's for the best."

"I mean it, bro. Whatever happens. I'm cool with it, really."

"You two were bringing each other down." Nick seemed to be having an entirely different conversation. "The club, the coke, Carlos—"

"Fuck the coke, fuck the club—and fuck him too!" Infuriated, he couldn't even bear to say his boss's name. "And don't you dare say it. If you remind me she's engaged, I'll toss *you* out the window too."

Nick's cheeks were past splotchy now, almost purple. "Don't forget how she screwed you over." He shook his head. "And you can't blame The Skeeze for being The Skeeze." He paused to look Matt in the eye. "And, she *is* engaged."

Matt rushed him, but Nick was ready. He thrust his arms out and kept Matt at a distance. "You're butt-ass naked. Don't come at me like that. What the fuck is wrong with you?"

Neither spoke for a minute. They just faced each other, Nick's outstretched arms holding Matt away; his pissed off expression already replaced by one of concern. Their fights never lasted long. Matt knew he should be embarrassed, but he just didn't give a shit. Nothing mattered anymore. Finally, he turned away from his friend's classic bouncer block and headed toward the bathroom.

Nick was still talking, but his tone was less hostile, more practical. "He'll be in Portland for his custody case for a few days. We'll quit when he gets back. We'll figure something out. You can get back to teaching. You can run the soundboard for that event company."

Matt stopped in his tracks and let out something between a laugh and a snort. "Can you seriously see me interviewing for jobs or teaching kids right now?"

"Well." Nick offered a weak smile. "Again, clothes would be good."

Throwing up his hands, Matt went into the bathroom and slammed the door. Once inside, he kept his eyes low so he wouldn't have to look at himself in the mirror.

# CHAPTER 39

## NICK

**NICK LEANED AGAINST** the weathered rail and watched the outgoing twelve-fifty ferry. He couldn't remember the last time he had gone over to Vashon—probably that field trip to the Strawberry Festival back in the sixth grade.

The sharp breeze nipped against his cheeks. His hands were freezing. His favorite weather girl, a slinky smooth talker with slick, red lipstick and beauty-contestant hair, had predicted a chance of sun breaks, but so far the sun was a no-show. She was such a heartbreaker.

Lincoln Park's rocky shoreline seemed stark and empty except for sloppy rows of beach logs and an old guy with a yellow Lab. The swings were still. Three seagulls shrieked and soared overhead. He thought of that eighties band, which made him think about his own. They had spent most of the week working out the new set, which still sounded pretty rough. It should have made him happy, finally getting Matt back to the music. But he felt selfish. His grandma often encouraged him to be more selfish, but it wasn't sitting well with him. Thinking about Matt's freak-out the day before, Nick knew he had to at least try to get her to come to the show.

He had tried calling Via that morning, but couldn't get past Whitney. It took his very best groveling before she'd let it slip that Via had a doctor's appointment in the city and wouldn't be back until early afternoon. He had been hanging out, creeping on ferry commuters, since noon. Eight cars were already waiting for the next ferry, which was well on its way. He squinted and saw it atop the water, inching its way closer, its shape growing more defined every minute. The ninth car was pulling through the ticket booth. A silver Civic. His chest tightened as he recognized her. She pulled into line, parked behind the eighth car—not fifteen feet away—and looked over. Her jaw dropped in surprise. Another car pulled up behind her. She wasn't going anywhere. And neither was he. No climbing the rail and jumping the dock, he told himself. No going back now.

As he walked over to the passenger side of her car, he went over what he was going to say. "I'm sorry I called you a whore," he mumbled. No, he scolded himself. Idiot, don't say that word again.

He had hoped she would ask him to get in, but she just rolled the window down. He leaned in while trying to convey a casual, I'm-not-a-stalker vibe. Wait. Her sunglasses were not only inappropriate for such a dim day, but were also huge, like she was channeling Roy Orbison.

"What's up with the glasses?"

"I just had my eyes dilated—at the doctor," she said. Her voice was pitchy. It snagged and skipped.

He had come to apologize. He had to get her to come to their concert. But as he looked at his reflection in her sunglasses, his list of objectives dissolved. He got in and reached for her sunglasses. She let him ease them off without a struggle.

"Oh, sweetie."

She stared at the steering wheel. Son of a bitch, he realized. He wanted to grab the nearest seagull and shove it down his boss's loser throat. It looked like he had hit her more than once. And her neck— had he thrown her down a flight of stairs?

"When?" He found it hard to keep his cool. He didn't own a gun. Such a good thing.

"Please don't tell Matt," she begged without taking her gaze from the steering wheel.

Oh shit, he hadn't even thought about Matt. When he found out, he would gut Carlos like a fish. He'd spend the rest of his life locked up in the state pen.

"When?" he asked again as he leaned in for a better look. "It's god-awful, but looks like it's healing up."

She shook her head and looked at the ferry attendant walking by. When she reached for her sunglasses, he held them tight. "Tell me."

She sat still and focused once again on the steering wheel.

He raised his voice. "Tell me or I'll keep asking. I'll scream out the window like I don't give a fuck."

She offered up a desperate look. "This is hard—humiliating. But, it was that night when Matt—"

Her voice caught and she looked at him. God, she had been clocked so hard the whites of her eye were bloodshot. Don't go off, he told himself. Stay calm.

"I needed coke," Via continued. "I thought I needed it, so I went back to the club." She leaned over and put her head on his chest. "Please don't hate me." He let her lean in, but not too much. He was afraid to hurt her face. "I went there. Please don't tell Matt. He'll be so disgusted with me."

"He's dying without you," he said. "It's bad, that's why I've been trying to reach you." He handed her back her sunglasses and watched her sit up, put them back on, and fluff her hair over her cheeks. He couldn't comprehend how she could be so hard on herself. Why wasn't she furious?

Leaning toward her, he wanted to get a better look at her neck, but was distracted by the crunch of paper. She reached for the white bag on the console between them, snatched it up, and tossed it in the backseat.

"What was that?" He had to ask.

"Um," she said. What he could see of her face began to flush. "Okay, I guess I can tell you my news. I'm on my way back from the pharmacy."

Girl with white pharmacy bag—with news. He put his hand over his mouth and sat back. Fucking hell.

# CHAPTER 40

## NICK

**HE CAME UP** the stairs and heard Matt in his bedroom. He was singing a song Nick had never heard before. It was a welcome change from the intricately depressing Tool basslines that had been pervading the house the past few days. The sharp smell of cleaning solution wafted out through the open door. He leaned in and saw Matt standing on the second highest rung of their eight-foot aluminum ladder. He was scrubbing the textured ceiling with rag. "She's worse than hiccups, more like cancer."

Nick leaned against the doorframe and surveyed Matt's bedroom deconstruction project. Since the incident with the Bambi in his bed, his need to clean had rocketed into a whole new level of absurdity. He had taken down his drip-drop painting from above his bed; it leaned against the far wall. He had scrubbed all of the walls, twice. He had given the same absurd level of attention to the light fixtures and window shades. After steam cleaning the carpet, he'd ripped it all up and washed the hardwoods underneath. This morning, he had gone off to rent a machine to refinish the hardwoods.

Nick assumed that would be next on his list, after scrubbing the ceiling.

"In my brain, in my bones, don't want to shake her, but she's killing me."

"Hey," Nick said. "That's darker than it was before, downright bleak actually, but it works. Taking a break from Sheryl Crow, huh?"

He walked over to the window and looked down. He wished Matt would feel compelled to take two trips to the dump because it looked like a Bed Bath & Beyond bomb had gone off in the front yard.

He moved back over toward the door and just blurted it out. "I just saw her."

Matt stopped. He dipped his rag into the bucket sitting on the ladder stand and rung it out. Nick could see his hands were red and cracked.

"Matt."

"I don't want to hear it. Just, don't."

"I have to."

"She probably looked super good, super happy," he said. "Spare me." He tossed the rag back in the bucket and made his way down the ladder. He ran his hand over the side of his new breakup beard.

Nick knew this conversation wasn't going to end well, but seeing Via had made him realize that secrets were the devil. "He hit her."

"Her fiancé?"

"No, I think he's still gone," he said. "Carlos."

"When?" Matt squinted his eyes into slits. "Is she okay?"

"Yes, she's getting clean," he said. "She's got a prescription, to help with cocaine cravings. She's serious, fessed up to her doctor and everything. Has an appointment to see a counselor—" He stopped when he saw Matt's expression seize into a crazed sort of fury. He had hoped Matt would focus on the fact she wasn't using. "Whitney is staying with her."

"How bad?" He drew his hands up, just under his ears, like he didn't really want to hear the answer.

"She's going to be okay."

"How bad?"

Nick couldn't lie. "She's got a black eye and her cheek is split open."

"He punched her? Like, full-on punched her?"

Before he could answer, Matt grabbed the ladder, gripped it with both hands, and coiled it back like a baseball bat. The bucket of cleaner was the first to fall. Nick could only jump out of the way and watch as Matt swung it back around taking aim at his drip-drop painting against the closet door. Nick turned and heard metal hit canvas and plaster and sheet rock. Before he could look up, he felt Matt rush past him toward the door, toward the stairs.

"No! No way," he yelled after him. "Man, stop! He's not even there. He's still in Portland."

He was relieved to see him stop at the landing. He sat down and looked up at the orange painting on the wall. The eye in the sky.

"I have to kill him."

Nick took a few tentative steps, because he didn't want to spook him, and then settled against the banister. "He's back in town tomorrow afternoon," he said, his words slow and steady. "We'll go together and quit then. Getting yourself arrested for assault—or murder—won't solve anything. Tomorrow afternoon. Okay?"

"This will never be okay," he replied. "I can never make this okay."

Nick felt his own chest constrict into itself, but he couldn't think too much about it. He had to refocus his friend. Stay positive. "Tomorrow afternoon. And we go together."

But Matt didn't answer. He was off somewhere else in his head.

"Okay, Matty?"

"Nick?" he asked, and then was quiet again. He brought his hands together like he was about to pray, resting his chin against his fingertips. "Was it that night? When I cut her loose?"

He didn't know what to say.

Matt put his face into his hands. "I didn't tell her she was pretty."

# CHAPTER 41

## VIA

**VIA HAD TO ADMIT,** Whitney had been right; getting some fresh air was making her feel better. She had been clean just under two weeks, and while some of the emotional symptoms were subsiding, namely the desire to kill every living creature around her, she had been alternating between having chills and sweating like an NBA player after a game. Frequent waves of nausea seized her and her face hurt like hell when she chewed.

She and Bella had brought some green apples over to the ponies next door. Her energetic little houseguest couldn't stop clapping her hands together and jumping up and down. It should have been precious, but Via could have done without the dolphin-pitched squealing.

"That's my pony!" Bella shrieked. She stretched her arm out and tempted the chestnut pony with an apple slice. "That's my Sparkles!"

The pony was actually named Nutmeg, but she kept that to herself, not wanting to minimize a little girl's imagination. The other two ponies didn't seem as social as they hung back to nibble grass.

She adjusted her sunglasses, then took off her coat and set it down at her feet. Puget Sound wasn't visible from this side of the house, but she could smell it. She took in a healthy dose of fresh sea air. The gash in her cheek looked much better, and the bruising had evolved from black and purple to bluish green and yellow. She hadn't bothered trying to hide it with makeup because she doubted the ponies would care. Her tank top was damp against her skin; there wasn't enough antiperspirant in the world. She turned and stretched. Her arms were still tender. Her back was still stiff.

"Matt said I could have a unicorn named Sparkles." Bella giggled as her new friend extended his moist pony lips in her direction.

The sound of his name made her stop in mid-stretch. "Matt told you he would get you a unicorn?" Sweat was building up on her forehead, along her hairline.

Bella looked up and shook her head. She was adorable in her striped purple hat. Via was quickly learning that if it wasn't pink or purple, Bella wasn't wearing it. "No. He made up a story. I was a princess and my unicorn was Sparkles."

Bella's sugar-and-spice energy was so bright that it must have been some story. Via's heart flipped itself inside out. She was tempted to call him and ask about it—an excuse to hear his voice—but Whitney still had her phone on lockdown. And besides, Matt hated her. There were other things she ought to be thinking about.

It sounded as though the garage door was opening. Via reached for her coat, but then stopped. Bella looked so little-girl happy that she decided to give her another minute or so before telling her it was time to go in. Sparkles was already munching down the last of the apple slices. They would bring more tomorrow. She looked over at Bella, so adorable, so innocent and expectant of good things. A spunky little girl lucky enough to be born to a confident woman with a plan and a support network. But what about those kids who weren't so lucky?

She thought about that volunteer gig at the domestic violence shelter—the non-existent one. An ugly sense of regret pervaded her chest. Beth would be home from that women's retreat soon. Via hadn't seen her since the day before Thanksgiving. It seemed so long ago. She didn't even feel like the same person anymore. The realization brought her a tinge of peace. A smile crept up her face.

"Okay, let's go inside and wash our hands," she said. "Sounds like your mom is back, and she said she would get hot cocoa."

"And marshmallows," Bella said, holding out her hand, moist with pony saliva. Via took her slimy little hand in return for a smile. On their way back to the house Bella stopped. "Come on," she said, pulling Via by the hand. "Let's skip."

She tried to keep up but she knew her drug-starved, heartbroken half-skip was pathetic. So she stopped.

Bella stopped too and looked puzzled. "Are we playing a game?" she asked with a smile. Her rosy cheeks matched her coat.

"I just remembered something, Bella. Wait." Via closed her eyes and breathed in the bitter-cold air. The memory fell upon her, toasty warm, and tucked itself in around her. "My mother used to skip with me. When I was your age. We used to sing a little Swedish song."

"Ooh, I want to learn. Sing it, sing it."

"Okay, love." Via began skipping again. Her grin was irrepressible. "Rida, rida ranka; hästen heter Blanka."

"You're silly," Bella laughed. "You're making that up."

"Okay, English it is," she agreed. "Ride, ride on my knee; The horse is named Blanka."

"Ride on your knee?"

"No way, that's for little kids," Via said. "Bigger kids skip."

They heard the garage door close, so they skipped even faster, giggling all the way.

\* \* \*

# MATT

**MATT COULDN'T BELIEVE** this quiet wooded haven was her neighborhood. This was the life she had been hiding from all along? Walking up the driveway, he passed a little wishing well with a "Jesus Loves You" sign on it. Funny, he had always thought of Vashon as a hippie haven. He hadn't realized there were pockets of conservatives, too.

The day was clear and crisp. He zipped up his black coat, but left the hood down. His beard was keeping his face warm. If she liked it, he would keep it for the rest of the winter. The house wasn't anything special, one story with eaves on both sides. But as he got closer, he realized it was built on a bluff overlooking Puget Sound. He passed into the side garden and stopped in his tracks. He saw the white and red radio tower down on the beach a couple hundred yards away. Across the water, he saw the over town bluffs and greenery. Via always called it "over town." In the distance stood Mount Rainier, snow capped and beautifully situated. So, this was KVI Beach. She had said the fiancé's parents owned the place.

He felt his heart beating hard and fast, though he hadn't done blow in weeks. He couldn't just turn around, drive back to the ferry, and go home like a kid. He had to man up, had to see her. Even if she hated him.

He noticed something bright pink out of the corner of his eye. He turned and looked through the wooden split-rail fence separating her yard from the lot next door. On the other side, past a row of bushy trees, was a little girl in a pink coat and a purple striped beanie. He knew that hat. It was Bella.

And there she was, too.

They were with a brown pony with a white patch between its eyes. It nodded its head up and down and flicked its brown tail.

He snuck up to the fence, leaned against it, and put his foot up on the bottom rail. The top rail ran across his chest; he folded his arms over it. He peered through a gap in the bushes. They were about twenty or so yards away. Close, but not close enough. He wished he could hear what they were saying. At first he just took in the satisfaction of seeing her. Her hair was pulled back in a ponytail. She wore a dark green jacket, jeans, and boots. She looked so good that he melted against the fence.

She turned to the side to say something to Bella and he saw what The Skeeze had done to her. She was wearing big sunglasses, but her cheek was bruised; he could see that even from a distance. He had to look away, down to the frosty grass at his feet. His breathing was uneven. He had to pull it together. It shouldn't have surprised him, he had expected it, but seeing her like that had jolted his senses anyway. She took off her coat, revealing a white tank top. Wasn't she freezing?

He saw her upper arms were marked up with what looked like black tribal armband tats. She stretched her arms up high and held them there a moment. The undersides of her wrists were bruised too. He imagined what position Carlos had had her in when he had done that. With all of his weight on top of her, he'd pinned her arms above her head.

He looked away and up toward the scattered clouds. "He's fucking toast," he told himself. "Toast, toast."

She turned to say something to Bella and revealed the side of her neck. He steadied himself against the fence, closed his eyes, and breathed in the damp country air until he couldn't take it anymore. He wanted to pull down that fence with his bare hands—one fucking rail at a time. But it wasn't his fence. It wasn't his to destroy.

He heard an approaching car and looked back over his shoulder, surprised to see Via's car turning into the driveway. It was Whitney. He needed to confront her and find out why she hadn't told him about this. But first, he took one more look at Via. She seemed so happy. After everything that had gone down between them, her smile still managed to do something to him. He figured that had to mean something. Forever was still now.

He turned around and made his way toward the garage door, which was rolling itself up. Whitney frowned when she recognized him. As she pulled into the garage, he hung back just outside the door. She got out, walked past him, opened the trunk, and started to unload two bags full of groceries.

"Can I help with those?"

At first, he thought she was going to ignore him and go into the house, but she stopped, put the bags back into the open trunk, and turned around. Looking perturbed, she said, "Via's not here."

"I know, she's next door with Bella," he said. "I've called and texted her fifty times since last night."

Whitney smiled as she zipped up the black jacket she wore. "I know. I have her cell phone," she said. "Church people call on the landline and she doesn't need to be talking to anyone else for a while."

"Does that include *him*?"

She put her hands on her hips like she meant business. She kept looking into the garage like she was in a hurry. "How did you even find us? This isn't even her house."

He pointed down to the KVI radio tower. She had told him once that she could see it from the deck. She had also mentioned the wishing well in the front yard. He remembered.

"How come I had to find out about this from Nick?" he asked.

"You're the last person she ever wanted to know."

"Nick and I are getting out. We haven't been doing blow for a while anyway, but now we're quitting Carlos too. Finally." He stepped closer to Whitney and dialed down his volume from five to three. He needed her to believe him. "I'm so, so happy she quit, you know." He leaned in and turned his voice down another notch. "I'm not Carlos."

Whitney's expression was hard to read, sort of a stressed assurance. "You want another shot, but it can't be right now. She has so much to work through; you have no idea. And, I know you do, too."

"Will you at least tell her I came? And tell her to come see us play the Showbox Sunday night? I'm leaving her a ticket at will call." He knew he had moved past pathetic and decided to just own it and even advance to all out groveling. "I've written songs for her, just like I told her I would. I'm even singing one of them on Sunday."

She looked at the ground and shook her head. "Sunday. That barely gives her a week. Is it going to be a scene?"

"No, not at all, it's for charity," he said. "The Kidz Rock kids are opening for us. And we never get loaded before shows. Besides, we're not using at all, I just told you that. And somebody donated fifty thousand dollars to Kidz Rock. I'll be singing a Sheryl Crow song. So I'll be singing two songs, that one and the one I wrote for Via. She's got to come."

She raised an eyebrow, but he just kept talking, explaining, hoping to sway her. "There's a band coming to check out Nick. Bigfoot Nasty. They need a drummer. And—"

She put up her hand. "It's a bad idea. Via needs to focus on her recovery first."

He looked back at the radio tower. It was mocking him now. So close yet still denied.

"You have a pen?"

She looked confused but opened her purse, pulled out a black felt-tip pen, and handed it to him.

He leaned over and started writing on one of the bags, which wasn't easy. It was reusable, probably made of hemp. She looked down at his message and gave him a stern eye roll. "How can you two be so cute? Seriously, you two are such a train wreck—have been from the very beginning."

"We're like an opera," he said. "About love potion."

She scrunched up her nose. "You do know that operas never end well, right?" she asked. "So, you need to scram."

"I'm going," he said, reaching for the trunk and closing it for her. "You'll make sure she helps you put the groceries away?"

She tilted her head to the side. Was she wavering?

He would beg. "Whit, please."

She grabbed the two bags from inside the trunk. He held out his hands, but she shook her head, turned, and walked into the garage. "Save it for your songs, Romeo."

He stood there in the driveway, wanting so much to follow her inside. "Not Romeo, it's Tristan actually," he corrected her as the garage door came down between them.

# Chapter 42

## Matt

**MATT CRUISED THROUGH** the lobby, past Ben, as fast as he could without looking suspicious. He had just seen Nick's truck pulling into the parking lot. He only had a minute. Wrist straight, he reminded himself. He couldn't wait to fuck him up. He needed to feel his boss's brains against his knuckles. Between his fingers.

The Skeeze was sitting behind his desk on the phone, unaware. He just waved him in and pointed to the couch. "Look, I'm not paying you two hundred and eighty bucks an hour to lose!" he yelled into the phone. "Her cunt lawyer is making you look like a fucking joke!"

Matt bypassed the couch and came at him—seething. He could smell Carlos's nasty scotch breath from across the desk, mixed with the sick smell of incense. The image of Via's injuries came back to him. He felt a Big Bang of adrenaline bursting out through his pores.

"I'm here to kick your sorry ass!" He would launch his skull through the wall.

Carlos's scowl turned to surprise, before shifting into understanding. He stood and reached for the buzzer. In one fluid motion, Matt came around the desk, hiked him up by his shirt, and heaved him up against the wall.

The door swung open and Nick came in, yelling, but Matt was too amped up to decipher his friend's words. He was hyper-focused on the dread on Carlos's face. He saw Via's fear there too. He imagined how scared she must have been. No girl should ever have to be that scared. No girl. Ever. Nick was coming up behind him, but there was enough time for one quick shot. He would make The Skeeze feel her pain, and so much more. He brought up his fists, full of potential, and pivoted his body back. Nick grabbed him as he pulled back around, but he powered through and still got a solid piece of his boss. His knuckles crushed through, past skin and muscle, against bone. He watched Carlos's head bash against the wall with a heavy thud then rebound from the cracked plaster.

Nick's voice came into focus. "Enough."

But it wasn't enough. So he brought his hands up and clutched his boss's throat. He would ring him out like the slime rag he was. But Nick pulled him back. "Matty, that's enough."

"No, no, it's not." He had him now. He was taking his air away. What was he without air? He watched Carlos's eyes squint and flutter with primal desperation. "It'll never be enough." The Skeeze had stopped struggling and seemed captivated by some far off place in the distance. His sweat burned into Matt's raw, cracked hands.

"Don't kill him." Nick was pleading, pulling harder.

Ben and Leon leapt in, soon joined by two of the bouncers from the Portland club. They all began tugging on Nick. It felt like rugby. Nick had always been awesome at rugby, so he managed to keep his balance. "Back off," he told them. "I've got him. Back off."

They all fell into a heap on the floor. Matt was up, going back for more, but Leon got up, grabbed him by the back of his shirt, and pushed him onto the couch.

"We're not done!" Matt yelled, straining against his handlers. "I'm going to fuck your shit up! I'll be back!"

Nick got up and put his hands out like a referee. "Chill. Everyone chill." He went over and sat next to Matt, buffering him from the room.

Now it felt like basketball, two on four, not including Carlos, who was on the floor on his hands and knees, gasping for air. Ben brought him up into the desk chair and began checking his neck and head, but Carlos slapped him away. Everyone was breathing heavy. Leon went to the mini-fridge behind the bar and underhanded a bottle of water to Ben, who opened it and gave it to his boss. Carlos sat there, looking stoned out of his mind, staring down at the bottle of water in his hand. His right eye was already swelling up, but it brought Matt little satisfaction. This wasn't over for him. He would finish the job another day.

Nick got up, reached into his inside coat pocket, and walked over to the desk. "We're done with this shit. We should have quit years ago." He threw a thick wad of cash and an one-ounce bag of blow down on the desk.

Matt wanted to ram it all down The Skeeze's throat, first the baggie, then one filthy bill at a time. He would let Via have the honors.

"You don't own us anymore," Matt said. "But don't worry. Your secrets, your operations, are safe. We'll never talk. We can't wait to forget that we ever worked for you."

"Ungrateful," was all he said. He touched his throat, took another drink, then let the plastic bottle fall to the floor. He pointed to his glass of scotch at the edge of his desk and Ben got it for him.

"This is the last of it," Nick said. It was their last ounce of unsold product; twenty-eight grams—a bundle of eight balls, ready to go. "No more Portland runs, no more hosting horny, out-of-town businessmen, no more bachelor parties."

"Keep it." His voice was hoarse, just above a whisper. "And I'm supposed—" He had to stop and take a drink of scotch. "I'm supposed to just let you leave here, and trust you, after you've betrayed me like this."

"We don't want any part of this," Nick told him, clear and confident.

"We were just kids when you lured us into this nasty pit," Matt added. "We didn't know you were such a waste of skin, but now we do."

"Is that so?" He tried to laugh, but it came out wheezy. "Going to be big rock stars now? Leaving your slum life behind?" He looked up for the first time, seemingly indignant and unashamed. "You always thought you were better than me," he said, his voice regaining its power. "But you're not. You think you're too good to speak Spanish, but your old man is just a Mexican, same as mine." He pushed the money to the side of his desk, and swigged some more scotch. "You're the one who's pathetic—you actually fell in love with her?" He finished off the rest of his scotch, leaned past Nick, and threw the glass at Matt. But it was a pathetic attempt, way to the left. Not even close. Matt didn't flinch, though Leon had to lean out of the way.

"You should be thanking me," Carlos said. "You dodged a bullet. Did she tell you her old man was a nut job? That he killed her mother, just like mine did? Except mine had the decency to wait until March. What kind of asshole kills his wife just before Christmas?"

"What are you talking about?" Nick asked. "What have you been smoking?"

Of course, he's been on the pipe. Matt took a whiff of the sweet air—free-based coke. That's what the room smelled like, not incense. Then he asked the question; he had to. "Is that how you—? How you got her to—?" He couldn't say the words "have sex with you."

The Skeeze just shrugged. "No, Mattais. She's more of a Ketamine girl."

Nick fired back first. "Special K? You piece of shit! You might as well have roofied her."

Carlos gave Nick a sick semi-smile. "Why should you care, Nick? Ah, you must be banging her too. Bitches always drop their panties for drummers."

Matt jumped up while the Portland guys tried their best to sit him back down. "Shut your fucking face, you maggot!" he yelled, trying to rush Carlos. He only made it a few feet before he was pushed back to the couch. "I'll come back later and we'll finish this, just you and me. You're going to hell. Maybe real soon, too!"

He would kill him. It would be an early Christmas present to the world.

Nick was pacing back and forth, swearing like he'd come down with Tourette's.

Sick with himself, Matt sat back down, but kept his death glare on The Skeeze. He didn't know who to hate more, Carlos or himself. How could he have failed her so horribly?

"I should have known you'd do something like this," Matt yelled. "I knew what you did to Sonia. I was the one who painted over those bruises you gave her. That's how Gallery Night started in the first place, right? So, you could hide what you were doing to your wife. This is all my fault, for being so good at keeping secrets."

"Yes, secrets," Carlos said, his eyes still glossy. "Via's got some good ones. Stay, we'll talk. Did you know she's got more money than God? She's a Rabbotino." He began looking under the papers on his desk. "Did some research—have a copy of the article here somewhere. Such a sad story."

"Let's go," Nick said. "You are better than this. You know you are."

Carlos stopped searching. "It's here somewhere, but fuck it. I'll just tell you."

Rabbotino? Why did he know that name? He knew he should listen to Nick, but that name was so familiar.

"Do you know where she was hiding?" Carlos asked, his voice excited. "When her old man shot her mother?"

Nick was more insistent now. "He's fucking with your head. Let's go."

Matt stood up and assured the Portland guys, "I'm not going to touch him. I'm leaving." He turned for the door. "See? I'm leaving."

"You don't want to know?" Carlos asked. "It just explains so much. Why she's such a head case."

Matt had so many questions, but couldn't stand to hear any more of The Skeeze's truth. So he kept walking. He was just a foot from the door when it hit him—Rabbotino, the painter he'd learned about in art class, the one who had killed his wife, the Broadway actress. It had been all over the news. Good God. He remembered that story. Via was *that* little girl?

Carlos yelled out, "Spoiler alert: she was behind the Christmas tree!"

# CHAPTER 43

## VIA

**DECEMBER 20TH,** she reminded herself. She was so close—just one more day now. Via reached out and ran her fingers along the edge of the nursery room counter, wondering where Beth could be. It wasn't like her to be late. The service had started ten minutes ago, but nobody had come in. No babies today? If so, the timing couldn't be better. Maybe it was a holiday gift from Jesus.

Beth should be back from her women's retreat and Via hoped the thick layer of foundation she had slicked across her face would be enough to hide the fading bruises. While she hated the filmy feel against her skin, being a less-is-more girl wasn't really an option these days.

She sighed, homesick for Nick's house. It was as though that staircase was calling to her somehow. She knew it was absurd, but she wanted to go there and sit under Matt's painting. She wanted to go there, sit on the landing, put her head in her hands, and cry. She imagined looking up to find him there, at the foot of the stairs, looking at her like he used to.

She felt her body screaming for her to go to his show. It seemed that, somehow, he still loved her, but she was terrified to find out for sure. Either way, she would save that grocery bag forever. His handwriting was strong and sure. She wanted to go to him, but she was scared. Not only because she had betrayed him, but because she would have to tell him about the money, about her crazy father. How would he react, knowing who she really was? That messed up little girl from the news. Would he go to New York with her?

She hadn't had blow in almost three weeks. She thought she had been feeling better, but this morning she had been so emotional. Like the drugs had been a plug in a dam of dysfunction. Whitney had been her Florence Nightingale of at-home detox, and she knew she should be thankful. Whit predicted it would get worse before it got better. And Via hated her for being right. So many problems and nowhere to bury them. She couldn't go back to her secret life, but couldn't go back to being Sister Christian either. She had nowhere to go.

The nightmares had been torturous, and now she woke up alone with nobody whispering "shh."

The bell above the door jingled. She looked up to see Beth coming through the door, then Sarah and Nate's father, Ben Kester. They all wore strong smiles, but nobody said a thing. They just walked past the counter and pulled up a few chairs next to the rocking chairs.

Beth came over for a big hug, but still didn't say a word. Just offered an odd sort of smile.

Mr. Kester, still smiling, nodded to Via. "Please, sit with us."

As she did, she realized they all looked nervous. She was clueless as to why at first, and then it hit her.

"Is it Dan?" She hadn't talked to him since that day waiting for the ferry. The day she went to see Carlos. The day she ruined her life. "Has there been an accident? Is he dead?"

"Gosh no, Via," Beth said. "No."

Via should have felt better, but she didn't.

"Via," Mr. Kester said. "You may not know this, but I am a chemical dependency counselor."

She was confused. He had helped Dan with his taxes. He coached football. He was a counselor too?

They all stared at her like she was an injured bird and they were going to coax her into a shoebox. Sweet Jesus, she realized. This was an intervention. Her internal organs lurched like they were trying to escape through her throat.

"I'm fine," she said. "Please, I'm not using drugs."

"Denial is the norm with drug addicts and alcoholics," he said.

"But, I'm not denying anything," she assured them. "I've already quit."

"A couple of days ago, I got a call in Montana, about you," Beth began. "Sarah was worried that you'd been absent from youth group

and ladies' bible study and services. I know you've wanted your
privacy, but—"

"We have been concerned, so we've been praying for you," Sarah
interrupted, seemingly too excited to wait her turn. "But then, it was
recently brought to my attention that you've had liquor on your
breath while working here."

Alcohol? How could she possibly argue the fact that alcohol
hadn't even been her drug of choice? She couldn't say, "No worries.
The vodka just helped me come down off the cocaine—really it was
nothing. The Ketamine, that was a real bitch though." She kept her
observations to herself.

"You're right," she said, just needing this conversation to die. "I
was wrong. I won't work in the nursery anymore."

"Via, please," Beth said. "We aren't trying to offend you. We
understand the past few months have been difficult for you and Dan."

Via put her hands over her face. She didn't have an inch of
emotional slack left. No faith to grasp onto. Fine, she thought. If they
wanted an honest conversation, so be it.

"Dan can help you," Beth added.

"How?" she asked. "He's not here. And since he's been out doing
God's work, I've been alone and vulnerable to the wiles of the devil."

Sarah maintained her composure. "You'll learn, being a wife isn't
easy," she said. "But we need to remain faithful to the guidance of
our husbands, just as Jesus was faithful to the church."

Oh, it's so on now, Via thought. "You forget that Jesus hung out
with prostitutes and freaks and not the rulers or Pharisees."

"Via, can we get this back to you?" Mr. Nester asked. "Your addiction
issue?"

She ignored him and kept her focus on Sarah. "Jesus loved. The
church corrupted," Via said. "You see, while you have been gossiping
and offering up condescending prayer requests, I have been teaching
your children the word of God. I know my fucking bible, lady."

Sarah stared back, aghast. Via knew she was projecting her anger at
the wrong person, but she just didn't care. Sarah somehow represented
years of passive-aggressive, self-righteous teachers who spoke so
often of Jesus and his all-encompassing love, but who led judgmental,
petty lives.

Beth stepped between Via and the pastor's wife and delivered the classic bouncer block. "Please stop."

"Now, Beth is a real Christian," Via added. "She and so many others, they treat people like Jesus did. They're the quiet ones. If only people understood how many decent Christians there are—but bitches like you are too loud."

"That's enough," Sarah said walking past the counter and to the door. "I'll keep her in my prayers."

"Fuck you—and your prayers," Via shouted after her. "Me and Jesus are cool. Thank you very much." She watched Sarah walk out and make her way down the path to the church office/gossip mill.

"Won't you please sit down?" Mr. Kester was asking. "You obviously have a lot of stuff going on. Addiction is a complicated issue."

Beth started to offer up a smile, but then nervously rescinded it. "We love you, Via," she said. "We are your family."

"Beth," she said. "I have no family, don't you see? I have no family!"

The bell on the door jingled and she looked over to see him walk in. Her brain couldn't make sense of what her eyes were seeing.

Could that really be him?

\* \* \*

# VIA

**THIS IS NOT HAPPENING,** she told herself. Not yet. I can't do this. I'm not ready. Her stomach twitched and churned. Dan reached her in four long strides. Before she could reconcile what was happening, he was holding her in his arms. He was so thin. His grip on her was so tight.

"I'm home," he said and gave her a kiss on her forehead. "Back early. I'm here." He lifted her a few inches off the ground and swished her back and forth as he spoke. Other than nauseated, she didn't know what to feel. His breath was cold and smelled of peppermint. It had been three years since their first kiss. That windy day in front of the fountain in Red Square. That kiss had been sweet and full of promise, but now she hated him.

"I'm sorry if I'm late. I had to stop at the house and—"

"It's fine," Mr. Kester said, smiling. "Come and sit with your fiancée. Let her see you are here to support her recovery."

Dan took off his coat and hung it over the back of a folding chair. Via sat down next to him in a rocking chair. She felt him watching her, but she could only offer him brief sideways glances.

"Mom, she looks sick," he said to Beth as though it was her fault. Via stifled a laugh. He should have seen her three weeks ago. "She's so skinny," he added.

I'm working on it, she thought. Whit had found a little smoothie shop in town that made thirty-gram protein kale smoothies, and they weren't half bad. Dan's weight comment made her think of Matt, who had been bugging her about her weight loss for at least a month. She knew she must love him. Why else would she be thinking of him now?

Dan lurched forward in his chair, reached over, and grabbed her hand. "You're wearing a wedding ring?"

"It was my mother's," she said. "Uncle Erik gave it to me. On my birthday. When I was alone. When I started to realize."

"Realize what?"

The shame of the situation filled her awareness, but the truth was more intense. "That I don't want to live your life with you."

Had she really just said that? She couldn't take it back now. She didn't want to. Something was loose inside her, jamming up her gears. It was like a penny thrown into the machinery of her very being.

"How could you say that?" he asked, his voice little more than a whisper. He let go of her hand and sat back in his chair. "This is nothing to be talking about now."

She full-on screamed and everyone jumped. She stood up and dug her fingernails into her palms. Words erupted from her mouth, too explosive to keep inside any longer.

"You made my grief—*my* grief—everyone's business. I told you again, and again, that I couldn't bear that. Still, you did it anyway."

"What are you talking about?"

"You told the elders to pray about me. You told them my Christmas story."

"I knew it would be best if people knew, so they could help." He stood and looked over at Beth.

"Don't look at your mother that way, like she dropped the ball," Via scolded. Each word she spewed at him brought her greater relief. "She was wonderful—is wonderful. I love her. But I'm not marrying her," she said. "And I'm not marrying you, either."

"I'm not going anywhere," he said as he stood up and took a step toward her. "I won't let you run away from your problems." She saw the way he was looking at the side of her face and took a few steps back, but it was too late.

"Have you been in a fight? Let me see your face." He reached for her.

"Don't touch me," she screamed.

He pulled back, but kept looking critically at her bruise.

"It's my life. I get to decide what to do with it," she insisted.

Dan put his hands up in front of his face and just shook his head while Mr. Kester shouted, "That's enough!"

Beth let out a faint gasp and started to cry.

"This is part of the recovery process," Mr. Kester affirmed, seemingly to himself. "I'd like to discuss an inpatient recovery center outside of Fall City, out in the country, it's—"

"Yes, of course," Dan said. "Do I need to sign something? She'll have to go, right? She's in no position to refuse."

"No, that is not happening," Via said as she tried to downshift her voice into something close to normal. "I told you, I am not using. I already have a treatment program in place at home. I've already talked to my doctor. I've found a counselor on my own, a hypnotherapist."

"Hypnosis? You can't be serious," Dan said.

"Yes Dan, and I'll use acupuncture and healing crystals and voodoo dolls if I want to."

"No, that's crazy. I'm home now and I'm going to help you get through Christmas."

"It's not about getting through Christmas," she said. "For a long time, I thought it was, but it's so much more than that. I don't want to just *get through* anything. I want to live."

"Honey, please be reasonable," Dan said, just above a whisper. "This isn't you."

His tenderness, his stricken expression, reminded her of the Dan she'd first met. The one who had wanted to take care of her. She was the one who had changed the rules of the game. He wasn't the bad guy. He was just the wrong guy.

"I know this is hard for you," she said. "But it just has to happen this way. I have to please myself now. I can't live your life—"

Dan was talking over her. "Should they do some sort of psychological evaluation, too? You know her father had mental health issues."

"No," she tried to say, but it came out like a whisper. Everything slowed way down. She knew this moment. She had lived it a thousand times in nightmares. It was the moment she had feared her whole life.

"This is for your own good," Dan said. "Just a few days in the country, so you can rest. You need to rest."

"No!" She tried to make a break for the door, but he was there.

"We should pray over her," Dan told the others as he held her tight. "The enemy is at work here."

She heard Grandma Daney in her head, "You know who you are. Listen."

"No, Dan!" she screamed. "Namaste, Dan! Namaste!"

# CHAPTER 44

## MATT

**MATT PULLED BACK** the heavy red curtain, and peered past both bars and all the way back toward the chandeliers fanning the back wall. He knew the chances of actually spotting her were next to nothing, but he was compelled to try. Had they still been together he would have had her backstage. He scanned the faces of the girls lining the back right and back left railings but could barely make out their faces at all.

Headlining the Showbox had been their dream for years. It was right in the middle of everything, just across the street from The Market. It was the ideal party venue—there was plenty of room, and two thirds of the way back, a half-flight of stairs led up to another level with seating that wrapped around each side of the theater. There were bars lining the side walls and another in the very back.

The place was packed, but when he looked out at the eleven hundred or so people milling around, he felt so alone. The first two bands had played strong sets, so expectations were high. He looked over at the stage and saw the stage crew hard at work changing out gear and checking amps.

Nick was beside him. "You got that Sheryl Crow down tight?"

As if he didn't have enough pressure deflating his will to live. He sighed. "I don't know if I can do it."

"It's a good song," Nick said, taking a quick peek through the curtain himself. "Could have been so much more humiliating—'What a Good Man' or 'I'm Too Sexy' or some shit like that."

"I just can't." His head felt dense and tingly. The back of his t-shirt clung to his sweaty back.

"You've got to sing the request," Nick said. "Kidz Rock has already cashed that fifty-thousand-dollar mystery check," Nick said. "They're setting up a scholarship fund. Getting the kids new gear too."

Matt realized he should embrace the force of the universe, like Luke Skywalker. He remembered that day on the porch, when Nick had issued his warning about Via.

"Dude, you've been practicing all week—you are so ready for this," Nick said.

There was no way out of this. He had to go out there and sing the song he had written for her, whether or not she was there to hear it. After that, he would stumble through the Sheryl Crow song. The lyrics had been haunting him all week. Was he strong enough? Was he a man? Would he ever be?

"Just breathe," Nick reminded him. "Think of this as just another show. No biggie."

They both knew otherwise. It was a huge show for Nick, who had met with the manager of Bigfoot Nasty the week before. Their drummer was going to rehab and they needed a sub for the West Coast leg of their spring tour. It would mean national exposure. Matt knew Nick would nail it tonight. No doubt, they would love him.

Nick put a hand on Matt's shoulder and said, "You going to be alright?"

"I have to be alright." He inhaled slowly in spite of the urge to hyperventilate. He thought of Via again. He had left a VIP pass for her at will call. Hopefully, she'd remember to tell them to look on the list under Y.

Nick leaned over and took another peek through the crack between the curtains. "We're headlining the Showbox. Crazy, right?"

"Truth, Grohly," Matt said. Taking another deep breath, he was starting to feel a bit better. "Hey, man, I'm sorry."

"For which part?" Nick asked, turning away from the curtain. "For falling in love when you were supposed to be my bass monkey? Or for going OCD-ape-shit crazy on my grandma's house?" He gave a half-assed smile and nudged Matt with his arm.

"Just for being a dumbass in general," Matt told him, pulling Nick in for a solid, man hug. They rarely ever hugged, not even when they were drunk, but whether Via showed up or not, it was a huge night. They walked back to the green room where he would choke down his own issues. He would man up and remember what this night could mean for Nick.

\* \* \*

# NICK

**NICK SAT HIGH** atop his drum stool and took it all in. There were four rows of VIP seating on the far right and far left, but the majority of space was open for standers, dancers, and moshers. The stage was lined with people who were already clapping and cheering. The stage lights lit the faces of those in the first few rows, and per his usual custom, he found a pretty Bambi to use as his muse. She had long black hair and was offering up a flirty smile. She was wearing a white sweater — and she was wearing it very well.

His hands were crazy-sweaty; he rubbed them against his old cargo shorts. They were ancient, but cool and comfortable as sin. He wanted to puke, but in the best possible way. Reaching down for a fairly fresh pair of Vic Firth sticks, he had to smile. Their smooth feel excited him; they had no idea what he was about to do to them. His left foot was poised by the hi-hat pedal. His right foot set to bring life to the base drum. The red and yellow stage lights were hot against his face, while the white floor lights seemed to make his drumheads glow from within. He looked down and saw Matt and Josh plugging in. Jeremy seemed to be having trouble adjusting his mic.

He heard Matt yell up from his mark at stage center left. "Break a leg!"

He heard his grandmother's soothing voice in his head, "They will love you, Nickolaus."

He raised his sticks high in front of his face and waited for the guys to look up for the count off. Breathe, he reminded himself, as he brought his sticks together: one-two-three-four.

They were starting off with Blur's "Song 2" — always a crowd pleaser. Keeping time with his trusty hi-hat, he summoned the almighty beat.

All of the toms and cymbals would be getting his attention tonight. The Bigfoot Nasty guys had been cool. No need to try too hard. Matt was in good form and sounded smooth and relaxed. Josh wasn't too drunk and his amp wasn't too loud. Jeremy's voice was a tad screechy, but that was typical. Nick threw himself into his drum kit and figured that if they sounded half as good through the house speakers as they did on his monitor, they were golden. He held his sticks lightly and let them rebound on their own against the snare. He looked out at the rolling motion of the crowd. Their movement—the reflection of his own groove—was mesmerizing. He got lost in the moment. And then, just like that, it was over.

He pulled his arms up and closed his eyes as they were enveloped by the sounds of applause. It felt orgasmic. The crowd was kind. He took in the sweet sounds of approval. Pretty Bambi was still screaming for him. He figured she would be in love with him now, at least as long as he was onstage. All was well; he wished he could freeze time. But he knew they wouldn't clap forever. They would be expecting him to lay down a new beat, one that would lead Matt into another groove. There was always another groove; he hoped there would always be another groove.

Matt's eyes were asking, "We good?"

Nick gave his friend a fuck-yeah smile. Damn, it was hotter than balls. He was sweating through his black Sound Garden t-shirt but he didn't have time to take it off. He needed to set up "Welcome to Paradise." They had been playing Green Day since high school and he loved getting into Tré Cool mode; it felt like home. It was one of those songs that gave the bassist a chance to show off a little. Nick peered back into the VIP section, where he picked out Via, standing in the second row behind his Bambi, but at the very end. God, Matt was going to be so happy.

After walking up to the front of the stage for his solo, Matt stopped between Jeremy's wedge monitor and a house speaker. Girls screamed for him to come closer to the edge and he did. The stage was plenty high. They would never be able to leave their fingerprints on his perfect bass. And besides, his friend had grown up so much since the summer. Maybe because he'd had bigger things to worry about.

Nick jumped back in on the snare—soft at first, letting the beat build. Next, Josh came back in, then Jeremy. Going by the reaction of the crowd, they were killing it. He issued the final strikes against his crash symbol and bowed his head in thanks. More applause and cheering—so loud that just to reward them he added in an extra drum fill with a snare roll, and then around the toms, crash, crash! What an awesome crowd.

It was time for one of Matt's new songs, the one he had been playing the hell out of all week. It started with a Tool-inspired bassline. He tried not to be nervous. This was exactly what he had asked Matt to do, come up with something different. Something original. But original was scary. And would the crowd dig it?

He sat ready, sticks above the snare, waiting. It wasn't a unison start, so he hadn't counted in. This one would open with Matt, but he was just standing there with his head bowed like he was praying. He was taking his time—too much time. One silent second, then another. A hoot came from the back of the room, which led to more from the drunks at the side bar. Matt looked back over his shoulder, seemingly unsure.

He gave Matt a firm you-got-this nod and was relieved to see him smile and turn to face the now rumbling crowd. Envy answered back with a deep grumble, which crawled through the house speakers, sludgy and full of soul. Relieved, Nick came in on the snare, easy at first. He would build tension. He had promised Matt that he would keep it simple, no extra fills. After two bars, Josh joined in with a mellow guitar riff—nice and easy, just like Matt wanted. It was complex, but subdued. Nick kept the beat and waited for Matt's opening line.

"Playing pretend, stuck in your dream world, at first that was enough for me."

Nick looked down and saw Via. She was wearing dark clothing, so he could only see her face and neck. She wasn't returning his attention, seeming smitten with the awkward Romeo singing at center stage. Had Matt even noticed her yet?

"Building a place, to get away, where nobody else could be."

Matt looked back again, so Nick grinned like an idiot, squinted hard, and flicked his face toward the right, giving his best Via's-here look.

Matt turned back toward her and then took a few steps toward center stage before he stopped. Via's expression brightened even more. Nick could only imagine the look Matt was flashing down at her based on the one she was beaming back.

Matt sounded even better than he had in rehearsal. The song was heavy, but tinged with silk. Josh and Jeremy backed him up, both sounding decent, thank God for that.

"But you've closed your eyes, so now it's dust, you know that it's killing me."

The crowd seemed to be into it, but still, the first-time material was making Nick mega nervous. He increased the tempo for the angst-y chorus.

"I can't shake you, and it's killing me."

The room was theirs, Nick realized. It was working. Matt's words were like chocolate cake and the crowd was all over it. More, more. They wanted more. Of course, he knew the song was intended for an audience of one.

"Nothing matters, unless you wake up." Matt's voice softened and trailed off. "Cause maybe then you'll see."

Applause, applause—and then they were on to the next song. Thank God. They'd loved it. Something all new, something all their own, and it had worked. There were two more new songs later in the set. Then Matt would wrap things up with Sheryl Crow. They would announce how much they raised. They would bring the kids back on stage for an encore. It would be fucking sweet. First, the crowd would need "Santa Monica." Jeremy started with that haunting Everclear riff the crowd always loved. Matt backed him and bolstered the vibe even more.

He looked again for his crowd cutie but noticed something wasn't right. Behind her, two bouncers were talking to Via and she was shaking her head. He recognized one of them as Charlie from one of Carlos's Portland clubs. Whoa—what?

Matt was still looking down at his fretboard, so Nick trained his eyes on the back of his head, hoping he would feel the weight of his stare. He squinted, laser-focusing his eyes on Matt until he finally turned around. Nick flicked his head toward Via's distress. One of the bouncers had her by the arm. She was resisting, but together they must have outweighed her by four hundred pounds.

Matt pulled his head out through his bass strap, turned around, and offered up an I'm-so-sorry look. Without hesitation Nick nodded his head and threw down a duh-go-get-your-girl head flick.

He watched Matt drop Envy, turn around, and fall back into the crowd. "Santa Monica" was way too slow to be moshable, but the crowd caught him anyway. They weren't putting him down though. They surfed him back around to the right and then he disappeared. Oh, shit, did they drop him? Nick looked down toward Jeremy and Josh, who had stopped playing. Both were just staring at the stage manager, standing in the wings looking frantic. What? Nick couldn't believe those two. He couldn't see where the bouncers had taken Via, maybe out a side door. He just kept the beat, and added a few fills. Just a little improv, a little vamping. Obliviot was spineless for the time being, but it still had its heartbeat. Josh and Jeremy seemed to be waiting for a another bassist to come bridge the great divide, so Nick decided to freestyle an extended drum solo indefinitely. If they could drag Greg from Bigfoot Nasty onstage the crowd might even think Matt's whole stage-dive departure had been planned.

He retreated back into his drum set, went at it hard, and felt the crowd's energy coursing through his veins. He worked his pedals, his snare, his toms, his cymbals. He thought back to all of those hours he had played in his grandma's basement. How many hours had he fallen asleep at night looking at that poster of Michael Shrieve from Santana? Tonight, he would make the Showbox his own little Woodstock. He went on and on: around the toms, ride, ride, back down the toms, crash, crash. He rolled the snare and looked out, at his tight-sweatered sweetie. She looked like she wanted another drum fill, so he gave it to her. She was screaming for more, so he gave her that too—crash, crash! Her love swept in and over the stage.

He looked right at her. All the girls around her thought he was looking at them, but he was all about her. "C'mon, Bambi, check me out," he said and then hit the crash cymbal. "You like it. You want me. You know you do." Snare roll, down the toms, crash, crash!

\* \* \*

# MATT

**"AH, HELL NO,"** Matt said, though it wasn't loud enough for his mic to pick up. He had just seen her; she was there and everything was going to be okay. She had said so in the way she had smiled up at him just a moment before. But now he was losing her again. Were those The Skeeze's guys? That bald guy from Portland had her by the arm. Who was the other one?

"Get your fucking hands off her!" he yelled. This time, he heard his words kick back through the house speakers, over Jeremy's voice, over Josh's guitar, and in place of his bassline, which had died. His hands were pulling his bass strap off. The beat was still strong. He turned around to see Nick beaming his high-bright glare down into him. With his eyes he was screaming, "It's cool. I've got it. Go, get your girl!"

The beat *is*, he thought as he let Envy go. That's all these people need. He went to the edge, turned around, spread out his arms and fell back into the arms of the crowd. Cheers went up around him as he crashed back down into a mass of shoulders and hands and what felt like somebody's head. Afraid he would kick someone, he tried to keep his feet high. He turned his head to the side. "Back! To the back!" he screamed to them. "I've gotta get her!" But they didn't seem to hear him as they surfed him and curved him back around toward one of the side bars. The bar rail was so close—he reached out. All he managed to get ahold of was a beer glass, which slipped from his grasp and fell to the floor. They were moving him back to the middle again. "Put me down!" he yelled, but they just cheered.

The shouting in his face was punctuated by the beat, still steady, though the rest of the band was now silent. The crowd didn't seem to care. It really was just about the beat, he thought. Nothing else matters. "Put me down!" he screamed again, but they kept rolling him over, hand by hand. Hot beer breath spewed against the side of his face. His stomach lurched.

And then, under his right armpit, he felt nothing where a hand or shoulder should have been. He latched onto somebody's arm as he slid sideways and slammed onto the concrete floor. His face smacked into what felt like a boot. He brought his hands together over his face. Pain shot up his right shoulder and neck. People were yanking him up to his feet by his right arm. His shoulder must have landed in lava. He wanted to yell at them to stop hurting him but he couldn't focus.

"Via!" he screamed. "Via!" He was too amped up to think straight. She would never hear him.

And then someone else had him by the back of the shirt. "Come on, man," he heard from behind him. "Step back, step back! He's hurt!"

the guy yelled out in front of them as he pushed them both on through the crowd.

"This is supposed to be a holiday show," the bouncer bitched. "This is supposed to be an easy night, a charity thing." Then he looked at Matt and grimaced. "Dude, are you okay?"

He ignored him and stumbled for the door. "Via!"

"Wait, you can't leave, you just landed on your head," the bouncer told him when they reached the door. "Do you know what day it is? Do you know where you are?"

Matt looked up and tried to look coherent. "They've got my girlfriend!" He was going to run to his car, but realized his keys were in his gig bag backstage. "Please man, get me a cab. I've got to get to Hotties, they've got my girlfriend."

"You need to chill," the bouncer said in the same tone Nick had used during the underwear-out-the-window incident. "You'll get a cab, but straight to the ER. You need your head checked. And I'm no doctor, but I know for a fact that your arm isn't supposed to hang like that."

# CHAPTER 45

## CARLOS

**SHE STOOD THERE** looking as pained as a rabbit in a trap. A Rabbotino. Ben had been MIA an hour so nobody was covering the door, but she didn't know that. She didn't know her escorts were already on their way back to Portland. His high had fallen out from under him, but there was no more. He'd been high three days, the bender to end all benders. He checked his goody box again. He licked his finger and ran it inside the silky interior. Maybe there was a stray rock. Just one more hit. Nothing. He went to his desk to check one more time. The three envelopes were there. Ready. One for Sonia, the others for his babies.

"I've had enough," he told himself as he rummaged through his goody drawer, his gateway to despair. "I'll never freebase again." He found his favorite crack pipe and threw it hard against the wall behind the bar. She startled and stepped over to the couch but didn't sit down. Didn't say a word.

"There are two fat lines left," he said pointing to his final offering on the coffee table. "The big one has your name written all over it: Violetta Rabbotino."

"I don't want it," she said. "I want to go."

Her voice was strong, like she was trying to act tough. Silly rabbit. Her good-girl attitude was pissing him off. The cocaine called to him and he obeyed. He sat on the couch, leaned over, and quickly inhaled the line on the left—the smaller of the two. He would be a gentleman to the end. He turned, happy to see she hadn't tried to bolt. She really was such a sweetheart. He loved her, more than he had ever loved Sonia.

He held the straw out for her. She stood her ground, clueless as to the futility of her abstinence.

She cocked her head to the side and took a couple of steps closer. "Your eye. You got into a fight?" she asked, looking more curious than concerned.

She didn't know. Interesting. "Yeah, you should see the other guy." He gave her a wink with his good eye.

"I can't believe you didn't tell me your real name," he said, taking a drink of his scotch. He'd opened the good shit. The bottle he'd been saving for his big court win, the vindication day that was never coming. He picked up the article and held it up for her. "Found this," he said. "Such a sad story. Read it to me."

"No."

"Your parents died ten years ago today; isn't that a coincidence?"

She just stood there and trembled. He'd never seen her look so pale, like she was dead already.

"You can sit down," he said.

She ignored his advice. "Do you want money, is that it?"

Offended, he looked her up and down. "Money means nothing to me now." He held the article out for her and enjoyed the way she leaned back in repulsion. "Look at this picture of your parents. Your mother was stunning. I would have enjoyed knowing her. I can see now why you're so fucking insecure. Trying to live up to this? Impossible."

"I hate you."

Yes, he thought. Hate is good. Hate means she loves me. If I can hurt her, then she loves me. Something wet smudged against the paper in his hands. Sweat. He needed another hit. Goddamn it. Where was Ben? He set the article on the coffee table, bent over, and sucked up the last line. It would be his last. The soul splintering was over. Cocaine couldn't hurt him anymore.

"Why am I here?" she asked.

"The media won't cover suicides," he said. "But they will cover murder-suicides, especially if the poor victim is a Rabbotino."

She looked at the door. Ah, he thought. She's starting to get it. It would be for the best. He was doing her a favor. He loved her too much to leave her behind.

"You know," he began. "Your father loved you."

She just looked at him. Worry lines crossed her forehead. Her jaw quivered ever so slightly. It was obvious that she needed a man to hold her.

"He wanted to kill you because he didn't want you to have to pick up all of his pieces. He wanted to protect you."

"Carlos—"

"It's my turn to talk," he continued. "I saw Maya and Sam yesterday." He felt his voice waver, but he forced himself through. "I had to meet them at a fucking McDonald's with a court-appointed chaperone." He reached down, found Kaytlyn's vodka tonic, and finished it off, not bothering to wipe his chin. "They want nothing to do with me," he said. "Their mother and her boyfriend have brainwashed them."

His brain synapses were firing messages his convoluted mind couldn't comprehend. He was a stupid man. Nobody ever told him so, but he'd always felt it. The way teachers ignored him. The way girls talked down to him. It wasn't his fault, he told himself. His life wasn't his fault. There were too many fucking foster families—eleven placements in fourteen years. There were too many visiting days at the state pen. Too many awkward hours spent with his old man. He would do better for his babies. He wasn't a monster.

"You had it easy, you know that?" he asked. "You have no idea what a rough childhood is like." She just stood there, listening. He wished to God he could believe she cared for him. He needed somebody to care. But what were the odds? Still, she was such a good little actress that it was hard to tell. No matter. Shit was about to go down.

"You father was badass, taking your mother out the way he did," he said. "But then, he had access to his cheating wife. I don't. All I have is you." He looked over at the stripper pole in the corner. "And I have her too, I guess."

\* \* \*

# VIA

**SHE TURNED AND SAW** her—a blonde, crumpled up next to the stripper pole in the corner.

"Is that?"

"Kaytlyn, yes it is," he said.

"Oh my God. Is she?"

"Dead? I would think so," he said. "She's been like that for half an hour. I just wanted her to dance for me one more time, but she wouldn't shut up. I just couldn't listen to her another minute."

"You strangled her?"

"I'm not sure," he said. "I used my hands. Technically, I think that's choking." He laughed in a way that made the hair on the back of her neck stand up. "She always said she was up for trying erotic asphyxiation." His speech was faster now. His voice more excited. "Mattais is the one who gave me the idea actually. Oh, and that's how my old man offed my mother. I guess it's a classic."

His words just passed over Via as she stepped toward Kaytlyn, who was lying on her back with her arms and legs sprawled out. She was wearing the cowgirl outfit. The suede bra clung against her ghostly glittered chest. The skirt hugged her pale thighs, and she wore one white cowboy boot. Her cool-blue eyes were open, but not looking at Via, not attempting a connection with the world.

She remembered that her mother's body had been in much the same position. An image no child should ever see played again inside her head. Mama's hair had been shorter than Kaytlyn's, and a richer shade of blonde, but her blue eyes had also been open. It was all so vivid again. Mama's chest, blown apart, flesh and intestines exposed. Her blood, speckled across the wall, or maybe it had been Daddy's blood. Most of his face was gone. It must have been a big gun, though she hadn't seen it. How she wished she hadn't seen any of it. Why hadn't she listened to the pretty lights? They had told her not to look, that it wasn't real. What if this wasn't real? What if her entire life up to this point had just been a dream? Maybe she would wake up and start over in some other realm. Better luck next time.

"Is this a deal breaker?" Carlos asked. She turned to see him with a black handgun in hand. He wasn't pointing it at her. He held it at his side. "You won't love me now?"

She felt the pressure of the room imploding, squeezing her into a speck of dust. Matt and Nick were probably still on stage. There would be mingling after the show. Ben hadn't been at his station and hadn't seen her come in. Nobody knew where she was. Carlos was going to kill her. It had been what she had thought she wanted. What she had thought she deserved. That was then. The death day countdown was over, but now that it was happening, she needed to live. What would he do with her body? She didn't want to spend the rest of the winter in a shallow grave in the forest behind some tree.

"What are you going to do with her?" she asked. "And with me?"

"Vixen, baby, we don't need to worry about her," he said. "No escape, no trial. I'm never, ever going to prison. You get it? You must not have been listening before. You and I are going out like your parents did."

He held the power. He held the gun. Maybe she was mental like her father, insecure like her mother, but this was her life. She wanted it now. Just because they hadn't realized their power didn't mean she couldn't. Her life had to mean something. It didn't mean anything yet, so she couldn't die.

"You should start begging," he suggested. "Your body. Use that. That's what women do. They complain, act like victims, but everybody knows bitches run the fucking world."

She had no idea what he wanted her to say.

"You look good tonight," he told her. "I want to see your body. On my desk."

"Wait." She had to stall, but her brain was betraying her, simmering into a sludgy stew. "You say you want to hear my story," she said. "If you put that down, I'll tell you."

A grin spread across his face. He turned around and put the gun on the desk, then stretched his arms out wide. She walked over and put her arms around his waist, leaning her head against his chest. He spun her around and backed her toward his desk. His breath was hot and nasty.

"So sad you wanted to confide in me now," he said. "It's too late for us." He leaned over and slid the gun further out of her reach, and then pressed her up against the desk. "Still, tell me."

What did he want to hear? She would figure this out. She was going to get out of this alive. "My father had gone through highs and lows before. When he was high, he worked in his studio for days on end. They went out all the time. They loved each other. I know they did."

"Sure, sure," he said. "Then what?" He kissed the side of her forehead and then her cheek, along the now faint bruise from the beating he had given her. She wanted to pull away, but instead she brought her arms back down to her sides and held them there. Her stomach churned and tormented her.

"His doctor had checked him into some psychiatric hospital a few days before. I don't remember that part. I have big gaps between my memories."

He had his hands under her dress. "Why are you wearing tights? You should be wearing stockings with garters."

What was he talking about? He was becoming erratic. "It's freezing out," she said. "I wasn't planning on impressing you."

"Or your big rock star? Cause I'm sure he prefers garters too. All men do. You weren't planning on banging him tonight?"

She couldn't answer.

His expression crept up into a smug grin. "He doesn't want you anymore, does he? Now that I've had you." He laughed. "So, I win."

No. Maybe she was a loser, but there was no way Carlos was going to come out of this a winner. She had to keep him talking until Matt came. He had to come for her. He had to notice she was gone. She called for him with her heart, as hard as she could, but she knew she couldn't wait for him. She had to rescue herself.

Carlos pulled back, putting some space between them, but stared her down. "Take off the boots, and the tights. And keep talking."

She leaned down and unzipped her left boot. He pulled it off and tossed it over his shoulder. She unzipped her right boot. Ready with an arrogant smile, he tossed that one as well. It reminded her of a wedding reception somehow—like a depraved garter toss.

"Now the tights, but not the panties," he said. "I want to take those off myself. And keep talking." She complied as he watched.

"I shouldn't have been hiding behind the tree in the first place, but there was this present."

His sweaty face lit up, excited. "Present?"

"Yes, a portrait of me that my father painted, and you can't kill me tonight, because they've just found it. It's in New York. I've never seen it. I have to see it before I die."

"How do you know it's of you?" He held her by her waist. She shivered. He was pulling her in.

"Because it's the one thing that I ever asked for, and because he promised. He had hinted about it for months," she said as she felt bitter acid gurgle up the back of her throat. She coughed.

He chuckled. "You're just like every other stripper then," he said. "Daddy didn't give you enough attention."

She stiffened against him. Ouch. The old sting of her father's rejection raced through her like it was brand new.

He inched his hand up her arm over her shoulder to her neck. His gentle touch sickened her. He brought his fingers up just under her chin. "Fucking look at me," he said, forcing her chin up.

She looked in his eyes to find that his expression, so brutal just a moment ago, was now hollow and hopeless. It terrified her even more.

"He would have killed you too, you know," he said in a way she found almost tender. "Do you wish he had?"

"I used to."

"It will be best this way, dying tonight, with me. I won't leave you behind. You're just a bit late, but you'll be with them again, very soon."

She didn't dare speak. Her next words would make all the difference. Whether she would ever see Matt again. Ever see anyone again. She wanted so much to skip with Bella again.

"The dress," he told her. He stressed the s's like a snake. "The neck's so high. Get it off. I want to see the bruises. I want to see what I've done to you." His eyes became crazed, like he was desperate to get through to her. "I didn't want to do that, you know, but you love it when I hurt you."

She acted like she was finding the zipper at the back of her dress. She took her time. She had to stall longer. It couldn't end here like this. They couldn't find her body here, naked.

He was slick with sweat, even his hair. His eyes were wild. God, he was the picture of delusion.

"Sonia did this. She did this to me," he insisted. "I never touched my daughter. I swear to fucking God. She knows that. Sonia will have to live with this. She did this to me."

Via closed her eyes while his words, "She did this to me," hung in the air. She didn't need the pretty lights to tell her what was happening. It was as though her own father was gripping her tight. She was caught up in Carlos's sick embrace, but also her father's. His desperation reactivated. His thoughts whirled her into the darkest night.

In the silence, she relaxed back into the loop of time. She was reunited with herself and the place she had once belonged. She would tell him the words she hadn't said before. The words her father had needed to hear. The words that could have saved her mother.

"It's not real," she said, her voice calm as she held him and pulled him in even closer. Leaning in, she whispered in his ear, "It's not real. None of it is real. It's the drugs. It's just your mind playing tricks on you." It was quiet. She felt him waiting for more. He needed more. "You're not alone. You are loved. I love you," she told him. "It's all going to be okay." She pressed her eyes closed and lay the side her head against his chest. His breathing felt wet and ragged.

She let herself hope. She listened for it, but it never came. Mama's feathery voice never came. This was the part when she should have felt Mama hugging her too, saying, "Via's right. Listen to her. It's all going to be okay. We'll call the doctor. We'll get you help." Via could smell her, sweet and safe and wonderful. But then, where was the smell of gingersnaps? Nowhere.

Via's eyes flicked open. Her heart ramped up. The moment was gone, but she could still sense her mother. There were no burning cookies because this was not that reality. Her mother was never coming back. And this was not her father.

"Carlos?"

He was pressing himself into her, hiking up her dress, grabbing her ass. "It's too late," he said. "There's no going back. But, as long as you love me—you know how I get when I'm high—I need you one more time. You owe me that."

He clutched a fistful of her hair, and pulled her head back and lunged into her neck. His kisses felt rough and desperate. She was able to look back over her right shoulder, but the gun was too far away. What else was there?

"I knew you would love this," he hissed in her ear. "You love the way I hurt you."

Think, Via, think. What else could she say? How far was the door?

He let go of her hair and went for his pants, while he pressed her harder against the edge of the desk. It cut into her lower back.

*Now.* She heard the word—crisp and clear—but wasn't sure where it had come from. There were no lights, it wasn't her mother's voice.

Could it be the instincts she'd been deaf to for so long? *Now* sprang up from somewhere deep within her inner being.

*Forever is now!* Her fingers prickled against the static crisping through the air. Maybe with my left hand, she thought. She leaned back, frantically grabbing for anything. Her fingers grazed the scissors in the cup. She stretched until they were hers, pulled back, and launched them into his back as hard as she could.

"Arghh, bitch!"

He released his grip on her, just for a second. She freed herself and made a break for the door—past the couch, past the coke on the table. Hoping to hear him hit the floor screaming in agony, she heard only groaning and furious profanity. If only she could have used her right hand. If only she had something sharper than a pair of scissors. But she had given it everything she had.

The door was so close. She reached out her hand, but buckled when the ten-year-old crush of resounding gunfire finally found her.

\* \* \*

# MATT

**"SHE'S NOT IN THERE,"** Ben said. "He was in there with Kaytlyn when I left. I wasn't gone that long. And you should get out of here. It's not safe for you—"

But Matt knew she must be in there. He felt her. Nobody could stop him. Ben lunged into his path and tried to block him. But Matt reached around, opened the door, and was rattled by the sound of gunfire.

Via was there, eyes wide, reaching out for him.

Ben screamed, "Down!"

Matt pulled her to the floor and covered her with his body. He looked up as Carlos put a handgun to the side of his head and pulled the trigger. The side of his head flew apart in an eruption of blood and brain.

Ben was yelling, "Call 9-1-1!" It echoed throughout the building. "Call 9-1-1! Call 9-1-1!"

He felt Carlos's warm blood on the side of his face and Via trembling beneath him. Girls were screaming in the other room.

Ben got up. "You good? You good?"

Matt nodded as he pulled up off of Via. He knelt next to her and pulled her in for a hug. She looked okay—thank God. She wasn't crying. But she wasn't hugging him back. His hands were warm and wet. Where was the blood coming from? No. No!

Ben was there, shouting, "She's been hit! Put her down. Put her down!"

He loosened his grip on her, but couldn't let go. He turned her and pulled her onto his lap. She was looking up at him like she was just waking up from a nap, but the color was draining away from her face, neck, and chest. Ben eased her onto her side and began ripping the back of her dress from the neck down. What was he doing? How was he even moving so fast?

Matt's hands were shaking. "Here," someone said, handing him a blanket from the end of the couch. He pushed it away. "Don't you dare touch her with that."

"Somebody, clean towels!" Ben yelled. "And, a first aid kit, or gauze—find something."

As he felt his coordination returning, Matt took her hand in his. She was trying to tell him something. He leaned over. It sounded like she was asking for her mother. Oh God, she was talking to her dead mother—and probably the lights too. Girls were still screaming. His ears were buzzing. He leaned in closer to her face, but he still couldn't hear her. He wished he could turn her up like an amp. He wished he wasn't so slow and worthless. She closed her eyes and he couldn't tell her not to because he couldn't say a word.

"Here, Matt, it's clean," Whitney said and handed him a white robe. He wrapped it around Via and tucked it under her chin. Her face was almost as white. He thought of Snow White and his chest ached because he wasn't a prince. His kisses weren't magical. The ringing in his ears had morphed into the sound of sirens, right on top of them.

A voice shouted, "Medic One on scene!"

He looked up to see two cops coming through the doorway with their guns drawn. They looked right past him, and then back again. One walked past him and toward Carlos's desk. "Shooter down," the cop said into his radio. "Repeat, shooter down."

"Another one here," the other cop said from the corner of the room. "That's two, plus the shooter."

"It's good—scene secure!" Ben screamed toward the doorway. "Scene secure! Get them in!"

One of the cops ran back outside yelling, "Bring them in!"

Via was looking up at him. "Mama." The look in her eyes was desperate. Those lips he loved were turning blue.

Two EMT techs came rushing in with big, black plastic boxes. "Give us room!" one yelled, pulling him away from her. "Get back."

He gave her up and crawled a few feet out of the way. Whitney pulled him onto the couch. "Your arm," she gasped. "Were you shot?" She tried to get a look at it, but he pulled way. "Did you break it?" He marveled at her composure. He couldn't answer. He couldn't think. He sat, not knowing what to do. Whitney turned her attention to the back corner of the room and cried, "Kaytlyn? No!"

Matt turned and saw Kaytlyn on the floor next to the stripper pole. There were cops milling around her. Her body was contorted. Her hair veiled the side of her face. He turned away. It was too much.

The EMTs were buzzing over Via, talking in code a thousand miles a minute. Ben was telling them he'd found two entry wounds, but no exits. A guy in a dark suit was there. He patted Ben on the back and said, "Good work, Agent Stern."

But Ben just yelled at the guy. "I told them we couldn't wait, that it was time to move. I told you!" He shot Matt an awkward glance, and then stormed out of the room. What the fuck? Matt wondered.

The EMTs had Via sitting up; one was shining a thin flashlight into her eyes while asking her questions as a pale blue sheet was eased under her. It looked clean. Another EMT was cutting off the rest of her dress with a pair of scissors, snipping her lacy black bra in half. Matt loved that bra. Damn, he loved her. They covered her with a blue blanket. The cop standing over them said he wanted her clothes.

Her eyes closed again and her head fell limp against their hands. "She's first! No C-spine, GCS was eight, but now unresponsive, sixty over forty—hypotensive!" a paramedic yelled over to the guys bringing in a gurney. "Out of the way!" he was yelling to the cops by the door. Everyone was yelling over each other.

"I'm calling Nick. I'm calling Nick," Whitney kept saying. "Where are you taking her?" she asked a paramedic.

"Harborview."

Whitney leaned in and whispered, "Matt, you have to go."

His brain was shutting down. His limbs were like stumps. He just looked at Whitney, aghast.

"Matt, listen to me. This is Via they're taking away. You can't *not* go," she insisted. "You're in shock. Do I need to slap you?" Her words sprang him back into his urgent reality. They were taking Via away.

"One, two—three," they expanded the gurney. The wheels clicked into place and they rolled her toward the door. He could see her eyes were still closed. He felt himself unfreeze. He jumped up and followed them outside. There were two-dozen people at the door, waiting for them like paparazzi. The Medic One driver was waiting and the lights were going; the back door was wide open. Two paramedics slid the gurney in like a pizza into an oven.

He hadn't told her yet. She would die if he didn't.

"I'm her husband," Matt yelled after them. "That means, I can come, right? I can come?"

One looked back at him. "Let's go!"

# Chapter 46

## Matt

**THE SIREN SOUNDED** muffled from the inside of the ambulance. Matt was crunched into a corner—cramped, but grateful to be there. He held his arm against his side. Nothing had ever hurt so much, but it didn't matter. It was just an arm. He watched as they started hooking her up to wires and tubes.

Via was wearing a mask that covered the bottom half of her face. They had placed another blue blanket on top of the other, but only up to her waist. They kept pulling plastic packages out of drawers. Everything was brand new, just for her. It couldn't have been cleaner.

They were calm, efficient. Each seemed to know what the other needed. Just like the nods and glances he and Nick shared on stage. One was bald and sat on a foldout chair next to Via's head. He kept looking at her and furrowing his eyebrows. The other was skinny with brown hair. He was busy messing with an IV full of clear liquid while looking at a computer screen.

Matt heard the driver on the radio, "Incoming Medic twenty-six: female, early twenties, multiple penetrating GSW, lower left anterior— four minutes out."

The bald one looked over at Matt. "You can help, answer some questions," he said, looking at her bruising.

"I didn't do that to her," Matt told him. "I'd never, ever hurt her." But then he wondered. Had he done this to her? He wasn't innocent in all this.

"No, that's not what I was going to ask you. We need to know what's in her system. She on anything? Meth? Heroin?"

"No." He was insulted. "She's not some hooker. She teaches Sunday school." He had no idea what he was saying or why.

"Sir, every single patient is important," the paramedic replied. Then he began prodding Via's side and abdomen. She winced and recoiled from his touch, but still didn't open her eyes. "PT reactive to pain," he said.

"Could she be pregnant?"

Matt heard the question reverberate in his head like an unchecked speaker. His chest constricted and knotted up. "No. I don't think so. No."

"Three minutes out," the driver yelled.

"We're going to intubate," the skinny guy said. "To help her breathe."

The bald guy opened one of the white drawers and started fishing around. "Here's a fourteen gauge."

Matt remembered that he knew her blood type. She had told him, that one time, that she'd earned an A+ in blood. "Her blood type is A positive," he told them.

"Good to know, thanks," the bald one said and then told his partner, "She's hypotensive."

Matt realized they hadn't been pumping her full of blood. "Aren't you giving her blood?" he asked.

"We don't carry blood on board," the skinny one replied.

"Why the hell not?" He leaned forward, jostled his arm, winced, then sat back.

"Sir, calm down. Sit back. You have to stay seated," the skinny one said without taking his eyes away from the screen.

The other guy lifted the blanket. "I don't like how she's reacting to the IV."

"She ever have issues with penicillin?"

"What?"

"Allergies?" the skinny one asked, now looking back at him. "Betadine, penicillin, anything like that?" Without waiting for an answer, he reached into a drawer and pulled out some kind of syringe. The blanket was in the way, so Matt couldn't see, but he seemed to jab it into her thigh and hold it there. The other guy was putting a shot of something into the IV.

Her cheeks were bright red. He saw hives on her arms and neck. Her breathing seemed to be labored, high pitched.

"Can she hear me?" Matt asked. "I have to tell her something."

The bald one looked over. "You can hold her hand if you can reach it from where you are. But you have to stay seated." He looked at the monitor. "Still hypotensive."

The ring, he realized. It was cursed somehow. It had to come off. "It's bad luck," he told them when they noticed him taking it off. He would find a priest to bless it. He winced again as he put it in his pocket. He pulled his white-hot arm against his chest.

"Can she hear me?" he asked. "I need to tell her something. If I don't, she'll die."

They looked at each other as though they were resisting the urge to smack him. The bald one held up his hand. "Sir, wait." He yelled up to the driver. "Alert them to anaphylaxis, likely from the IV."

"Hypotensive!" the other one interrupted. "Pulse, pulse!"

And then an alarm went off. Beeeeeep. It wasn't loud, but sharp and persistent. They crouched over her and crowded him back into the corner. The bald one reached over to a small black box mounted on the wall. He flipped a switch and pulled off two small paddles. He placed them toward Via's chest and announced, "Clear!" Then he pressed them against her and her body jerked.

It was just like on TV, but he couldn't change the channel. He closed his eyes and yelled over the noise. "You're pretty!"

Over the beeping sound he heard a buzz and a bump, and then "Clear!" Then another buzz and a bump.

"You're pretty!" he screamed over the backs of the paramedics, over the sound of the alarm, and the radio, and the siren. "You're pretty! You're pretty!" His words weren't working. He began to panic. He didn't know what to do. He just wanted her to know. "I love you!" he screamed. He needed her to hear him. "I love you!"

Then the beeping stopped.

"Got her," one of them said. "That a girl!"

The paramedics were so focused on Via, they seemed oblivious to their idiot ride-along. He kept yelling until the ambulance came to a stop, the door opened, and someone pulled him out. He took a breath. His attempts weren't working. She wasn't opening her eyes.

They jumped out and two guys in green came to help.

"We had to defib," the bald guy told them. "Intubated, hypotensive."

They pulled out the gurney and its silver frame sprang into place. He couldn't see much of her face, just some of her hair. It looked wet.

"Two entry lower left, no exit per exposure," the skinny guy added. "She had been responsive on scene, Glaslow was eight. Reactive to pain. She didn't like the IV."

The words they tossed back and forth over her body seemed cold and were meaningless to him. They didn't understand how special she was. He hurried to keep up with them as they went through clear double doors.

They had started down a long hallway when a man stepped in his way. "This is as far as you can go."

Someone else tried to pull him back and toward an open room. Fierce fire shot up his arm. He kept forgetting about his arm. He had forgotten about everything except her.

"Sir," he heard a voice say. "We need to get her admitted, get some insurance information. You're her husband?"

"Isoldey!" he called after her. He knew people probably thought he was crazy, but if he couldn't get through to her right now, nothing else would matter anyway.

"He'll need to be seen, too," another voice said. "His arm."

He was being held back. He could only watch them take her away. They were pushing her through a set of double doors. What if she was seeing those lights? What if she followed them off somewhere?

"Isoldey!" he pleaded at the top of his lungs. "Don't go with the lights. Come *back* to me!"

# CHAPTER 47

## VIA

**SHE HEARD MEN TALKING** about her allergies. Her allergies were killing her? That was weird; she could have sworn she had been shot. She heard what sounded like Metallica playing in a cave. She was shaking. She was on her side. Someone pulled her hair back and away.

"She lucid?" a woman's voice was asking. She sounded irritated, impatient.

What was happening? She squinted. It was bright. There were fuzzy-looking blue people huddled over her.

"Do you know where you are?" Someone was shining a piercing light into her eyes. "Do you know what day it is?"

Yes, December 21st. Her mother's death day, and her father's. And hers. She hurt all over.

She was starting to remember. Had he been yelling, "Come back to me," or had she imagined that? Was she imagining this? Everything rolled and woozed around her. She was shivering so much. A blue hand came down and rested against her hip. It made her think of Matt. She wanted Matt.

She tasted blood. She needed to cough, but something was in her mouth. It hurt.

"We have blood, oral. Not much." She remembered she was Violetta. She remembered *La Traviata* and that coughing up blood meant she was going to die. She tried to speak, but it was too hard, and she didn't know what to say. What's killing me? she tried to ask. She closed her eyes and retreated into the cave with Metallica. "Come back to me." She felt something on her face change to a heavier something. It smelled like plastic. She wanted Mama.

"She in position?" the woman's voice was asking. "Yes, I'll check when we're in. Isn't she under? Let's go, let's go. Okay. Turn up the music."

\* \* \*

# VIA

**THERE WAS BUZZING** in her brain. Breezy vibrations began rippling through her and she relaxed into them. She was numb and an eternity went by. There was no need to care. She was being hidden away from her senses and into still nothingness.

"Come back to me," the deep voice said. She knew that voice. Then she heard another voice. It seemed like her father's, but it couldn't be, because she wasn't afraid.

"Come, come out now," he said. She was aware of him, yet she was not with him. They were together in some way, but time was not time. It was a living thing—not intruding, just watching them. Space was pivoting back and forth. His voice blurred within her; they were the same, yet she was not with him. A cascade of glorious lights kept them apart. The branches felt prickly against her face. She knew this dream. She had had this dream a thousand times, except this time she wasn't afraid.

*"Violetta, it's time to come out," he said. "I promise you're not in trouble. It's your present. I know you've been so curious."*

*"I don't deserve it," she confessed.*

*A memory flitted around her. It waited. It wanted to be remembered. She had never asked about her presents, the ones the police had taken away. She knew they were the devil's toys. Those wrapped boxes had been more important than helping her mother. She shouldn't have been peeking. She should have been in the kitchen.*

*Mama was there. She was there all along, in the kitchen making cookies. "I told you everything would be okay," she said.*

*And the box was there, too. White with a gold bow.*

*"It's time,"* Daddy told her. *He seemed even more excited than she could ever be. Like, he had been waiting so long for this moment. The moment that never came was finally here. She could sense he had been worried about her. He wouldn't have to worry anymore.*

*She brought her hands up and pulled the bow tight against the corner, then down. She tore back the wrapping paper. Power surged through her. Her father helped her with the last of the paper, like he couldn't wait another second. Her mother came to help. It took all three of them to pick it up and set it on an easel next to the tree. The pretty lights were humming,* It's real! It's real!

*"This is how you saw me?"* she asked him.

*Metallica stormed through her, dense and wild. The beat is. It just is,* she realized.

The pretty lights—which had led her to this point—flickered and were gone.

She couldn't feel her parents anymore. She felt them drift away. Maybe if she could stretch her soul enough, she could reclaim them. She tried to reach out with everything she was.

"Daddy, did you love me?"

Plastic overwhelmed her—the taste, the smell, the feel of plastic. She was somewhere new. She was distracted by unfamiliar sounds. Where had she been before? She had no idea. And, where was she now? She heard *wom, wom, wom,* and then, *buzz, buzz, buzz.*

She was drenched in human pain. "Come back to me." She needed that voice. A breath came to her. Such pain. And the breath was gone. Another breath came into her and left again. With each breath came a beep, a new beat. Space expanded out around her and faded into calm.

"Ma-," she tried. "Ma-Ma," she tried in vain. She remembered. It would all be so easy now. But, she would have to remember.

There were garbled voices in the distance. New voices. Proof that the old voices were gone. Misery came in from all sides and overtook her. She could not let reality come and rip her from her mother's arms— vanish away all memory and destroy all meaning. She had to slip away, back to the place she had been before, but she was stuck. This was her now. There was nowhere else to go.

\* \* \*

# VIA

"MA."

"How long is she just going to be asking for her mother?" she heard Dan ask. He sounded tired. Why was he here? "It's like she doesn't even see me, Dr. Lou," he said. "How long until the anesthesia, all the drugs, wear off?"

"Please be patient, she's been here less than, let me see, less than sixty hours," the doctor said. "She's been through a significant surgery." It was the same voice she had heard before. She was the one who had been taking care of her, who listened to Metallica. She sounded too young to be a doctor.

Via didn't see either of them, and she saw no reason to. They had set her up against a pillow. She just stared at beige, and that was fine. It was a wall, she realized. Peaceful. But she could still hear them. She wanted both of them to go away. They had been talking so long that the beige wall was brightening, changing to a color more like the inside of a cantaloupe.

"Is this because she saw her father murder her mother? She would never talk about it. I told her she should go to therapy. She found the whole thing embarrassing. He was violent, bipolar. Maybe she is too?"

"That is a question for the staff psychologist," her doctor said. "But, I must say, bipolar doesn't necessarily mean violent or abusive. It's often misunderstood. In fact, many people living with such conditions are highly intelligent and creative. When addressed it's manageable, and nothing to be afraid of."

Carlos flashed into Via's awareness. She had been with Carlos. Backed against his desk. He had tried to kill her. But that isn't how her story was meant to end. Her heart ached for him. He would go to prison. Just like his father.

"When can she come home with me?"

Never, Via thought.

"Let's talk about that later, when she can take part in the discussion."

"None of these people know her," he said. "They're the ones who are responsible for all of this. She is such a good person. None of this makes any sense. I mean, look at her, so zoned out? Is that the drugs? Is she going to snap out of this?"

"I understand you are anxious to speak with her," Dr. Lou said. Via loved the confident strength in her doctor's voice. "You're not the only one. The police are all over me, asking when they can question her. Please, be patient. She has been through so much, and sometimes patients need time to emotionally recharge after such trauma."

"Dr. Lou, I don't mean to seem unappreciative but my fiancée was in a strip club, doing God knows what. This is a lot for me to take in."

"I also wanted to inform you her tox screen came back clean."

"She wasn't on drugs?"

"No, and also, let me check..."

"What?" Dan was asking. "Also what?"

"Also, the pregnancy test was negative," she said.

"Of course, she's not pregnant," he said. "Why would you even check that?"

"It's routine," she said.

"Of course, I'm sorry," he said.

"I need to go check on my other post-op patients." The doctor's voice was soft again.

"I do love her," he said. "I feel like you don't think I do. Like I'm a bad person because I left her when she needed me. "

"Oh, please, no," she said. "Don't think that. That's just the lack of sleep talking. I have no doubt you care about her very much."

"Not care," he said. "Love. I left her, but I love her."

"Well, the staff psychologist will be in to see you sometime today. You can discuss your concerns with him. Why don't you go get some breakfast? I think some quiet time would do her some good."

"Okay," he said. "I'll take a walk. Clear my head."

Via heard the door open and then whoosh closed. She could feel that her doctor was still there, could hear the sound of fabric rubbing against the bed rail. Maybe the long white coat Via imagined she would be wearing. She felt Dr. Lou lean in close.

"I'm very pleased with your progress. I will see you this evening, unless you decide to rejoin us before then. I can see why you'd like a little time to yourself."

Via felt her hand being squeezed and she smiled at the wall, now a mix of copper and gold.

Her doctor's breath smelled like a latte and was warm against her ear. "You hang in there, girl," she whispered.

"Ma-Matt," she tried to say, then closed her eyes and fell asleep.

# CHAPTER 48

## MATT

**IT WAS A SUNNY** Christmas Eve morning. She had survived the dreaded countdown and was going to make it. Matt hadn't been home yet, but Nick had brought in some clean clothes for him and there was a shower in the men's room.

When he came in, she was sort of lying on her side; one half of her lower back was covered with what looked like a giant blue Band-Aid. Many of the tubes and wires that had held her down in the ambulance were gone, replaced by different ones. He went over to the far side of her bed and was thrilled to see that the color had returned to her cheeks. The lips he loved were pink again.

Dan's voice was stern. "I'm allowing this because my mom insists it's the right thing to do. Say you're sorry, or whatever, and that's it. She's coming home with me." He gave Matt one last glare before he left the room.

He knew he should feel guilty, but he told himself that Dan couldn't possibly love her the way he did. It wasn't possible.

Her hair could use a wash, but she looked well rested. Her eyes were heavy, half open. She looked baked. "Guess these hospital drugs are even better than the ones we did together, huh?"

He wanted to take her hand and hold it, but he didn't want to disturb the IV needle taped there. "I only have a couple of minutes, thanks to your fi-an-cé." Fiancé, damn he hated that word.

He paused, hoping she would talk back. But she didn't move at all.

"Dan and the church people are saying the past few months were just a big mistake for you—a mental breakdown. And they said you bailed from their intervention." He laughed a little. What a little firecracker she was.

He saw she had some hair caught behind her shoulder. It was an excuse to touch her hair and he seized it. It reminded him of those first five minutes, when he'd first painted her.

"When I first met you, it was the same," he told her. "You wouldn't look at me then. And you were having a bad hair day." He felt his throat close tight. "I painted that shield of protection—I'm so sorry it didn't work." He leaned in closer, but couldn't touch her. He couldn't wrap his arms around her. He wasn't going to hurt her anymore. "I'm so sorry."

He had to stand up and take a step back. He couldn't cry.

"Hey, guess who's not freaked out by hospitals anymore?" he asked her. "This guy." He hoped if he were corny enough, she would snap out of her funk, roll her eyes, and smack him.

Why did he get so stupid when he was nervous? He paused for a clarifying breath. In, out.

"I called your uncle; Whitney knew his number. I think he's going to strangle me, but at least he's on his way."

No, had he really just used that word? Did she even know about Kaytlyn? So brutally sad. He kept thinking about all the times he could have been nicer, more supportive. He should have gotten her away from Carlos. He still couldn't believe she was dead. Via could have just as easily died, too.

He leaned in over her ear and whispered, "I love you." He caught himself off guard. It just kind of came out. He would tell her that every day for forever if she would let him. Not because he was compelled to, but because it was his truth. He gave her a kiss just behind her ear.

He heard Dan from the hallway. "That's enough. You've done enough," he said.

"Goddamn, that guy really is a prick, isn't he?" he whispered. "They want me to back off, give you some time," he said. "And I thought about it. About stepping back, giving him his time with you."

She was still the most beautiful girl he had ever seen. He got close enough to see her honey-colored irises. Even though she didn't seem affected, he just knew he was getting through to her somehow. He had to believe he was or he would lose it. The doctor said her brain scans were clear and that they had every reason to be optimistic.

What would he do if she didn't want him, if she snapped out of it and wanted Dan? No, he told himself. Not after everything they'd been through. He had to hold it together and expect the best.

"I'm not going anywhere until you tell me to go yourself. So, that's what's up."

"I said that's enough," Dan said again, now in the doorway.

Matt straightened up, pulled the bedside curtain closed, turned, and stood toe-to-toe with the fiancé. Dan was a good three inches shorter and skinny, but he looked unafraid, like he wanted to throw down, right there in her room. Matt didn't blame him, but he wasn't stepping back.

*  *  *

# VIA

**THE PRIVACY CURTAIN** was a joke. She could still hear them.

"Look, you may—or may not—be engaged to her, but I love her," Matt said, his voice low but strong and steady, so much like his bass. "When she's feeling up to it, we'll let her decide."

"People always talk about love," Dan said. "But love isn't always easy. It takes effort. It's about compromise and sacrifice."

"Well, maybe she needs more than that," Matt said. "She deserves a man who understands her, loves her for who she is."

"How long have you known her? Tell me, how did you meet her?"

"Trust me, dude, you don't want to know," Matt shot back.

She heard a scuffle, like shoes against the floor.

Matt spoke again, but slowly. His words reverberated like a growl, "You'd *better* step off."

It was quiet. Were they done? Via wondered. She needed Matt.

"You know about her money, don't you?" Dan asked.

"Keep it. I just want her."

Her mind filled with bright orange—the painting above the staircase. The image pulled her heart away from the beige wall.

"But you found out it's not just a few million, didn't you?" Dan asked, his voice full of concern. "You know it's like forty million."

"Don't know, don't care," Matt said. "Do you see my old boots? My clothes? Do you think I'm in the market for a yacht? Do you really think I give a fuck?"

"Please stop." Beth's voice sounded frazzled. Via hadn't even heard her come in the room.

Dan didn't stop. He sounded wounded. Betrayed. "I've loved her a long time. Maybe I haven't told her enough. But I never gave her drugs. I never took her to dangerous places."

"Stop it! *Stop it!*" Beth screeched.

"But, Mom, he took advantage of her weakness."

"Listen to yourself! This isn't who you are!" Beth was actually screaming. It struck Via as so thoroughly wrong. It sounded like kittens being burned alive. It jolted her need to check back into her life. It was time. She tried to turn toward the curtain.

"Ma-Matt."

"Please, can't you see?" Beth went on. Her voice was reigning itself in, normalizing more with every word. "They're here now, and that takes courage. Can't you see they care a lot about her?"

It was quiet for the longest time. Via imagined Beth was between them. Killing them with her special brand of spiritual kindness. So much like Grandma Daney.

"Maybe we should get a cup of coffee," Beth said. "Give him a few more minutes with her."

There were dual male grunts. It sounded like agreement. Dan's mother was a miracle worker. Yes, Via thought, reaching out for the curtain. Take your son away so I can talk to Matt. Her mouth was so dry it hurt.

After a moment, the door whooshed closed.

Via was finally able to will herself away from the wall. She blinked and tried to bring her vision into focus.

"Matt."

She heard him turn. He was coming to her.

\* \* \*

# Via

"MATT." SHE REACHED OUT her hand for the blurry white hospital curtain hanging between them. And his hand came around the edge to yank the curtain out of the way. Anticipation buzzed through her body; urgent, like that first day he'd kissed her so well she'd seen spots. She was desperate to see him.

He leaned in. She smelled peppermint. God no, it wasn't Matt at all. It was Dan.

She blinked again and met his gaze. It was terrible. It was one thing to blame him from afar. Now they were face to face. Maybe he did love her; she just hadn't felt it.

"I'm—sorry," she told him.

He sat on the bed and grabbed her hand. The IV needle pinched in deep, it burned. But she felt too guilty to mention it.

"We're not giving up," he said. "I forgive you, and I'm sorry too. This is all my fault. I won't ever leave you alone again. We'll travel together."

The full weight of their failure crushed down upon her chest. She started to cough. Jesus, it hurt so much. What had he done wrong, really? He had done so many things right. He went and got a cup of water: a tiny paper cup. She was so thirsty; it would never be enough.

"No," she told him.

"Shh. Don't talk, drink this," he told her.

"No," she repeated as she took a drink.

He pulled back and looked at her, really looked at her.

"God has someone else," she said and coughed again, "in mind for you."

"But—"

"I love... him," she said. It was a terrible thing to say, but they would be the most important words of her life.

"How?" he asked. His voice caught. He was crying. "How can that be love?"

"It is," she told him. "It just is." She just couldn't keep her eyes open anymore. "Namaste."

"What?" His voice was sharp, desperate. "You said that before. What does that even mean?"

"I'm so sorry, but...Namaste means go away."

# Chapter 49

## Via

THE LIGHT in the room was different. Had she fallen asleep again? Had she missed Matt? When would he come back to her?

Two nurses were there, messing with the equipment at her feet.

"Wakey-wakey, eggs and bakey," one of them said. "Dr. Lou is on her way in."

The other one leaned in and offered a supportive smile. "Hi, honey, I'm Sheila. It's so nice to see you looking so alert."

"I'm really sorry about the yelling earlier," Matt told them from the chair in the corner. Had he been there the whole time? She reached out. And he came to her. She couldn't believe he was really there, holding her hand. Like everything was going to be okay.

"Whatever works," Sheila said. "You managed to rile her up. Too bad the other one left in such a huff. His mother is still out there. I told her she could come in after the doctor's visit. And how's that arm?"

He wore a cast, in a sling. "It's nothing, it's fine," Matt said. "When can she come home?"

"Whoa, easy, fella," Sheila told him with a deep laugh. "At least a few days, more likely a week, but then, I'm not Dr. Lou."

"Your uncle just called, he's on his way here from the airport," Matt told her. He looked down at her. She loved him. He had no idea how much. "Nick and Whitney are dying to see you, Bella too. She's been drawing you pony pics."

She gave his sleeve an urgent tug. He leaned in close. She wanted to ask him what had happened to Carlos. She wondered if he was in the hospital too, or jail. What about poor Kaytlyn? Had there been a funeral? Had she missed it? She wanted to ask him how the rest of the concert was, too. But, for the moment, she was overcome with gratitude. She couldn't hide her tears from him.

"No crying on me now, Isoldey," he insisted. He leaned down and used his bright white t-shirt to wipe away her tears. "Let's remember how lucky we are, how we feel."

He was right. She nodded. She wanted to thank the nurses; couldn't wait to thank her doctor. But then she noticed something in the chair next to Matt.

"Is that your acoustic?" she asked, though she already knew the answer.

He wiped her cheek again before kissing it. "Yes, woman, yes it is." He leaned over and picked it up, then pulled the chair closer to the bed. "I figured I would play you that Sheryl Crow song you requested."

# Epilogue

## New York City, Six Months Later

## Via

"NO WAY," Matt said. "This is unreal." Whispering rose up all around them.

Via couldn't believe it either, even the experts looked surprised. The auctioneer slammed down his gavel three times and repeated himself for the crowd. "Lot number one-thirty-one, *Heartbeat of the Universe*, sold for 3.1 million." He slammed his gavel into the podium again. "This concludes today's sale."

She glanced over at her uncle who was standing at the back of the room. He had been too nervous to sit down. He gave her a huge smile and it felt good. Getting to know him hadn't been easy at first, but as the months went by, they were beginning to feel more and more like family. He gave her a little wave as he made his way out to the reception. Via watched him stop and hug Denise, the woman they'd hired to direct their foundation. They had decided to name it Ingrid's Wish in honor of her mother. Via had done a lot of research and learned there were thousands of children's non-profits throughout the country in need of financial support. So, instead of offering its own programs, Ingrid's Wish would provide grants to community-based services for children and teens affected by domestic violence. She had decided to keep the Rabbotino collection for the time being. There were plans for an Ingrid's Wish international gallery tour the following year. Initially, both Matt and her uncle had been against her selling *Heartbeat of the*

*Universe,* but Via had insisted. It wasn't easy, but somehow it was symbolic. Knowing that it existed—that her father had painted it after all—was all that mattered to her.

Two men came up onto the stage and took the painting away—her father's last work, now owned by some anonymous phone-in buyer.

"Miss Rabbotino, Miss Rabbotino," a photographer called to her. "May we get a few photos of you with the painting before they take it?"

"Of course," she said as she stood up, though she felt conflicted about seeing it up close. Matt rested his hand against the small of her back and gave her a gentle prompt toward the front of the room. At first, the scars from her bullet wounds were hard for her to accept. But Matt insisted those two scars—so close to her spine—were miraculous reminders that she was, indeed, a very lucky girl.

There were two other photographers now—smiling as they waited for her. She hoped that she would eventually get used to speaking engagements and media attention. Her mother's charity needed a compelling ambassador to bring attention to the plight of children of domestic abuse. Her therapist, Dr. Landers, had encouraged her to accept the part. Via would do her best to grow into the role.

She posed with the painting and offered up a soft smile. Then she turned to face it. What a rush. It was vibrant, glorious. She stood two just feet away, taking it in. Here it was. The reason she was alive. It had been wrapped in white paper with a gold bow. It had called her back behind that Christmas tree for a little peek. Her father had unwittingly saved his curious young daughter from himself.

It was rich in muted red and caramel, such a departure from the ten others he was known for, all cool-toned, methodical abstracts. This one was different. *Heartbeat of the Universe* wasn't abstract at all. It wasn't even a portrait, but a genre painting. It was awash in sentimental warmth. Her mother was in the foreground, sitting at her makeup table, tousling her hair. Her dress was black with caplet sleeves that hugged her shoulders. Her smile was graceful—relaxed and radiant. This must have been how her father had seen her, how she had looked in his reality. Via knew he must have really loved her, even in his erratic mind. He had captured something hopeful in his wife's eyes. Via had remembered her afraid and hollow. Her father's version was comforting. He had ensured that she would be young forever.

In the upper two thirds of the canvas lay Via, stretched out on her parents' bed. She was beautiful, her face angelic. Her eyes were set upon her mother in a vague but pleasant expression and her hair was twisted over her shoulder, hanging in a loose braid. Until seeing it like that in the painting, she'd forgotten that her mother had often braided it that way.

So many details, happy details, had come back to her. Dr. Landers had had a great deal of success with adult children of abuse. Via saw him weekly and meditated daily. She still found it challenging, keeping her mind quiet, but she was getting better. She rarely had nightmares anymore. Dr. Landers told her it was a process.

Matt's warm lips were flirting with her right ear. She hadn't noticed him leaning in. "You good?" he asked.

She nodded and felt him step back, but he didn't go far. He was doing well with his therapy too, though he wouldn't let her pay for it. They were keeping their finances separate. Matt was making decent money as a sound engineer. He had also sold a few songs to an up-and-coming musician; one of which was being used in a movie. While the bulk of her own money was going into Ingrid's Wish, she had given Dan a few million to help build schools in Africa. Her friendship with Beth wasn't always easy, but they both wanted to stick with it. Beth said she wanted to stay close to Via, no matter what, and that felt amazing.

"It's almost time," Matt said from behind her. "We can't keep the epic rock star waiting." It was already time for them to go meet Nick for dinner. She still couldn't believe the year he and his new band, Bigfoot Nasty, had been having. She and Matt were lucky to steal him away for a full two hours before he went on the road for a U.S. summer festival tour. She knew Nick would be asking Matt to join them again, wanting him to stand in for their bass player who was too drunk to play half the time. He'd been bugging him for weeks, but Matt kept turning him down. She loved him for it, for wanting to accompany her on her speaking tour, but she wondered if she should encourage him to go. A few months apart wouldn't hurt them. They were simply too close.

"Thank you, I think that's enough," she heard Jennifer say to the photographers. "Please join us in the reception hall for light refreshments."

Before turning, Via took one last look at her mother. It still hurt. It always would. She had a thousand what-ifs, but she would do her best to leave them in New York. Via had come to accept that her mother had desperately wanted her to survive. Via knew her own happiness would be the best tribute—and with that attitude, the donations and public speaking didn't feel like burdens. There could be no shame and only occasional embarrassment—like when the podium at the Met toppled over or when she'd spilled orange soda all over her gown at the governor's ball.

"Remember, Dr. Landers said it would be a process," Matt was saying.

Via knew he was right. Life was so good it felt uncomfortable sometimes. Dr. Landers told her that, with time, she would get better at feeling good. She was struck with a profound sense of her place in the world. She was learning so much about manic depression and domestic violence. There were so many misguided stereotypes about both. Labels that were keeping people from getting help.

She knew now that her father had not only been violent, but also intensely sick. What he did was evil, but *he* wasn't evil. That was a powerful distinction for her because it provided a place where his love for her could live. She could forgive him, and herself, because she understood it wasn't anybody's fault. It wasn't fate. It wasn't ironic. It was just something senseless that had happened. Just like what had happened to Kaytlyn. Via hadn't been able to go to the funeral, but she thought about Kaytlyn every day. Of all the regrets she had about her one-hundred-day suicide attempt, Kaytlyn's death was by far the worst.

Those last minutes with Carlos had been a blessing in disguise. She had seen with her own eyes that in his state of mind he had been intent on death and despair; the same had probably been true of her father. If so, there would have been no chance of saving her mother.

The time she had spent with Bella had been particularly rewarding. Thoroughly into fairies, Bella went through art pad after art pad, drawing delicately winged fairy friends. She made up stories about strong, feisty fairy sisters who went on mystical adventures. In Bella, Via could imagine her own young self. She could see herself growing up through Mama's eyes.

Whitney loved being a nurse and had taken a job at Harborview. She and Bella were spending the summer holding down Fort Daney while Nick toured and Via and Matt were traveling. Bella and G-Dane were becoming thick as thieves.

She sensed Matt watching her and turned to see him paused, waiting. His eyes were entreating her to come to him. Just one more look, she promised with her eyes. There were photos, of course. But she knew she would never get so close to it again. She didn't dare touch it, but mentally hugged it. Her father's last work was full of love and life; the sound of Verdi celebrated throughout her heart.

She turned around and made her way down the aisle toward Matt. He was blushing, though she had no idea why. She thought about the countless little Violettas out there—the kids she hadn't wanted to think about before.

"Nick will be waiting to tell us all about his new life," he said, coming in for a hug. "You ready now?"

It was finally all clicking together. Her life had a purpose after all. Every life had a purpose and she promised herself that she would remember that. She felt more valuable than any painting, more hopeful than any high, and prettier than any lights.

She rested her cheek against his chest and said, "Forever is now."

"Exactly, Isoldey. Exactly."

# PLEASE, PRETTY LIGHTS SETLIST (IN ORDER OF APPEARANCE):

"Comfort Eagle" Cake
"Breed" Nirvana
"Enter Sandman" Metallica
"Nice Guys Finish Last" Green Day
"Skills to Pay the Bills" Beastie Boys
"Stir it Up" Bob Marley
"I Can See Clearly Now" Jimmy Cliff
"Island in the Sun" Weezer
"Rock-and-Roll Lifestyle" Cake
"All the Small Things" Blink 182
"Bad Fish" Sublime
"Suck You Dry" Mudhoney
"Gotta Get Away" The Offspring
"The National Anthem" Radiohead
"Everlong" Foo Fighters
"Royal Oil" Mighty Mighty Bosstones
"Songs for the Dead" Queens of the Stone Age
"Magic Fire Music" Richard Wagner/*The Ring Without Words*
"When the Angels Sing" Social Distortion
"Corduroy" Pearl Jam
"Song 2" Blur
"Welcome to Paradise" Green Day
"Santa Monica" Everclear
"Strong Enough" Sheryl Crow
*Un De Felice* Giuseppe Verdi/La Traviata

For more information about Ina Zajac including upcoming releases, book club visits and author events go to:

www.inazajac.com

Twitter: @InaZajac

# MORE GREAT READS
# FROM BOOKTROPE

·

*The Dark Light of Day* by **T.M. Frazier** (Dark Fiction) Abby survived the most brutal childhood imaginable-barely. Homeless, she meets Jake, a blue eyed biker with secrets that rival her own. If they can accept the darkness within one another, they might be able to learn that love isn't always found in the light.

*Memoirs Aren't Fairytales* by **Marni Mann** (Contemporary Fiction) Leaving her old life behind, Nicole finds herself falling deeper and deeper into heroin addiction. Can she ever find her way back to a life free of track marks? Does she even want to?

*A Medical Affair* by **Anne Strauss** (Fiction) A woman has an affair with her doctor. Flattered, she has no idea his behavior violates medical ethics and state law. The novel is based on solid research of which most patients are unaware.

*Flipka* by **JT Twissel** (Fiction) Part detective story, part psychological journey – Fiona Butters deals with incarcerated teen girls, cave bats and assorted desert eccentrics. Hard to say which is scarier.

*Dismantle the Sun* by **Jim Snowden** (General Fiction) A novel of love and loss, betrayal and second chances. Diagnosed with cancer, Jodie struggles to help her husband Hal learn to live without her. As Hal prepares to say goodbye to his wife, he discovers the possibility of happiness—in the arms of one of his students.

Discover more books and learn about our
new approach to publishing at **booktrope.com**.

CPSIA information can be obtained at www.ICGtesting.com
Printed in the USA
LVOW05s2248220714

395593LV00004B/307/P